Scars Could Love

Book 2 in the *scars* series

I0565038

Scars Could Love

Scars, Volume 2

Philip J Bradbury

Published by Philip J Bradbury, 2025.

SCARS COULD LOVE

First edition. August 9, 2025.

ISBN: 978-0645314595

Written by Philip J Bradbury.

Philip J Bradbury

Published by: Philip J Bradbury, Brisbane, Australia

ISBN- 978-0-6453145-6-4

Website: http://philipjbradbury.com

I lived in Ipswich, Queensland, from 2014 to 2018, and was well acquainted with the dubious practices of many Ipswich dignitaries. The mayor was eventually gaoled for his part in many illegal activities, along with several of his councillors and business associates.

Philip J Bradbury

Who was involved?

Text designed and setup with quiet brilliance by Philip J Bradbury

Cover designed with modest greatness by Philip J Bradbury

And thank you to my beta readers – Anathoula Photinos, Leonie Mulqueny and Monica Zwolsman – and to the members of the Carindale Writers Group, Brisbane, who critiqued many sections of the book.

Website: https://carindalewritersgroup.com.au/

Readers' Comments

I loved it, by the way. You are a very clever writer!! I loved the main characters. They were interesting and 'real'. I liked that Janice was quite an intelligent woman and she had a lot to offer the other characters and the reader. Kassey is developed well and her youthful innocence and typical young teenager attitudes and behaviours are realistic. All the characters were well drawn. Loved the slang and style of the minor characters. Every character had a purpose and the conversations between them were authentic. Excellent characterisation!

Anthoula Photinos, primary teacher and writer, Brisbane

I was definitely invested in some of the characters – James, Karen, Kassey and Janice. Oh, and the owners of the cafe. Actually, loved the entire Maureen story - and George. I loved all the neighbourhood chat, all the philosophising and the chats between the women, and the kitchen chit-chats.

Your writing in a woman's voice was authentic and it did not feel jarring or contrived in the slightest - I felt you captured how women communicate—especially via the dialogue and topics of interest discussed.

Monica Zwolsman, English teacher and writer, Gold Coast

I didn't mean to start reading it right away but got into bed, skimmed the opening lines and was hooked. Still reading at 4.00 am and had to work in the morning. I finished it two nights later. An amazing story, Philip.

Colleen Dyer, business teacher, Gold Coast

Captivating and informative. 'Scars Could Love' is a must-have for anyone seeking an unforgettable reading experience fused with valuable life lessons.

Leonie Mulqueeny, building design trainer and artist, Gold Coast

You have used a simple comparative story to illustrate the age-old themes of racial prejudice and hypocrisy, Philip. For me these was very appealing – no waffle, just hard-hitting contrast.

Judy Rostedt, writer, Brisbane

Whispers and Bricks

1981

My beginning may not be the real beginning but it's mine so that's where I'll start.

See, I was the school secretary, the humble, behind-the-scenes, passer-on-of-information: from pupils to teachers, parents to teachers, teachers to principal, principal to staff, teachers to pupils, principal to parents and so on. I was the hollow, invisible reed that everyone else blew through to play their tunes. I had no music, no tune, no presence, almost. I certainly wasn't allowed an opinion or an opportunity to give a different perspective. I didn't exist in my own right; I only had substance by virtue of everyone else's. The quiet one they never noticed ... well, until the moment I couldn't stay quiet any more.

So, I would pass on messages as best I could, numbing myself to the inanity of many and pretending ignorance to the immorality of others. I can't speak specifics - not just yet - but I can say there was talk of money changing hands to enable dim students to receive accolades and awards they could never deserve. And not only money. Eventually, holidays, gifts of cars and other substantial inducements. I also started to read messages I couldn't understand - messages with references to pizzas that didn't compute. My 13-year-old daughter told me pizzas had something to do with stealing children or homosexuals or something. She wasn't quite sure and I didn't want to know any more. Not till later when I did want to know more. Perhaps the expensive gifts were for other reasons as well. I dared not imagine what those reasons might be.

As a solo mother with no other financial support and little chance of other employment in those job-tight times in Queensland's Ipswich, I needed to cling to the job at St Bede's as tightly as I clung to my daughter. She was the only right and true thing in my shaky world.

So, I said nothing. I even avoided raising my eyebrows and my impassive face, perhaps, encouraged them to become bolder, over time. For that, I feel some guilt ... but I digress, for my feelings are not what concern you, I suspect.

I didn't notice it at the time but, looking back, I see there was a moment - a day, a week, I'm not sure - that things took a turn down a path I couldn't follow. However, it took me some time to realise it. The same as you don't notice your hair growing each day, and, a month later a friend says, "My, your hair has grown," and you realise it has. Yes, like that, except I had no friend. There was just me in my little office, and it gradually dawned on me that the slowly grinding geological plates had drifted so far apart that I couldn't straddle the moral distance between my sense of rightness and the communiques before me.

I could hear my grandmother's gently persistent voice in my head, telling me there was a right and a wrong and nothing in between, that no one could sit on the fence for very long for it hurt your bum. I deliberated long and hard - did I risk my job, throw my daughter and myself back on the state, return to the caravan park and live in dusty poverty again, or did I continue to receive the benefits of this corruption?

You don't need to know how long I stewed on it - it seemed forever - before I finally spoke up. But I spoke to the wrong person.

Sergeant Thomlinson appeared indulgent as his chins wobbled and he listened and took copious notes. Two nights later, a brick was thrown through my window and my hand found wet dog poo in the mailbox the next morning. I was shaken, and every fibre of my body knew it was related to my disclosures to the sergeant. What could I do if the authorities weren't there for me? I knew few people in the town and none to confide in. My mother would be going up or down on yet another drug trip, and my daughter's father, my ex-partner, was still serving time for extortion and attempted rape.

I was afraid to go to work but knew my absence would raise more questions than my presence ... or so I thought.

The principal called me into his office as soon as my foot eased through the front door, two mornings later. A warm Queensland morning, he had his clanking fan spinning from the ceiling, moving little but dust. His greased comb-over could never disguise his pink, shiny pate and, today, it didn't disguise the beads of sweat there, glistening in the weak sunshine coming through the only window in the room, high and wide on the outside wall. The fug of cigarettes added to the feeling of a police cell out of which nothing could escape, not even air. Yes, I've been in police cells, thanks to the two previous men in my life.

He demanded to know why I'd gone to the police before talking to him. But what do you say to the perpetrator? That I was going to the police about his crime? Or, before that, should I have walked in, slapped his hand and said he'd been a naughty boy and not to do it ever again?

Silence is golden, I decided, and I shrugged and smiled apologetically.

"This is no laughing matter," he said through clenched teeth. My expression wasn't conveyed well, obviously.

"I know," I said gravely but, having started with a smile, found it hard to erase it from my face. It's strange how we react to stress in our own ways. My way was with a smile and it didn't help. I waited for smoke and flames to erupt from his nose and mouth, going by his fiery glare and whitening knuckles as he strangled a pen.

"I am sorry, what should I have done?" I asked, lobbing the ball back to him.

"About what?" he demanded, slamming the ball back.

"Well ... about ... you know ..." The ball collapsed over the net.

"No I don't." A flick of his wrist and the ball was in my back corner.

"What did the police talk about?" Another pathetic lob which he immediately pounced on.

"What do you think? The weather? The cricket score? Bribery, fraud and corruption? Trafficking ..."

"Trafficking?" I hadn't mentioned that to Thomlinson. Something had told me not to disclose all I knew.

"Well, maybe." His shots were weakening.

"Trafficking? Of what?" A great backhand, I thought.

"Children ... uh." He grunted and the ball dribbled under the net as he sat up and looked around and then down at something interesting on his immaculately clean and empty desk.

"Children?" I was alarmed to have my suspicions confirmed. I served confidently. "Who's trafficking children, whatever that means?" I'd heard of trafficking but thought it only applied to drugs.

"Uh, no one. No one." The speck on his desk seemed to be endlessly fascinating.

"So why did the police tell you about it?" I was feeling bolder but shouldn't have been. A cornered viper can strike from any angle at any time.

"Enough! Cut the bullshit!" he yelled, leaping up, hands flat on the spotless desk. "You know exactly ..."

"Yes, Brian? Did you call me?" came a timid voice behind me. The vice principal must have been listening at the door. Or was it a coincidence?

"Oh, aah, nothing, Margaret." He looked around the room as if searching for an answer but seemed to find nothing. He shook his head and sat back down. I looked behind me to see the vice principal - I was never allowed to call her by her name - standing there, equally uncertain.

"Shall I ...?" she asked, backing out slowly.

"Yes, yes, please," he said, nodding, smiling and unable to hide his embarrassment. The door closed and he and I waited for the other to speak. I waited but still he didn't speak.

"Shall I go, sir?" I asked, bending to pick up my bag.

"Yes, yes ... aah, no. No you shan't." I sat up again and he seemed to be regaining some composure, staring daggers at me. "We won't talk of this again."

"Of what?"

"This."

"This what? The police or this conversation or the bribery, fraud and corruption ... or the ..."

"All of it. Every all of it."

"Every all ..." I really, really tried not to smile.

"You know what I mean, madam, and it's not funny. You are a dangerous woman."

"More dangerous than the bribers and traffic ..." I was feeling bold and relieved in equal parts till he interrupted me.

"Enough! Enough of that. We will not mention any of it, huh?"

I stood there staring at him, sorely tempted to say something sarcastic. Then I realised I was about to lose my job and thought of Kassey. I couldn't do that to her. "Mmm," I said and turned to go.

"As long as we understand each other."

I nodded, not understanding what I was supposed to understand and left. Then I returned to his office, sheepishly, to retrieve my bag. I was surprised at how quickly my bold and relieved could dissolve into timid confusion.

I didn't see him for the rest of the day and wondered if he had a secret door, or if he was sitting in there, stewing. Or plotting. His door remained locked and all I could do was shrug each time someone asked to see him, saying I'd call them when he came back. I had to lie and I hate doing that.

I felt there were invisible eyes watching me all day and there was an eerie lack of suspicious messages, the usual boring administration memos about health and safety, student absences and a playground injury that was no more than grass stains, in the end.

Back home I should have started dinner but instead sat there on our old couch and stared at the slightly askew print of a Spanish dancer in red. Kassey, my daughter, absorbed my silence and joined my sitting and staring.

"What's wrong, Mum?" she eventually asked.

I jumped, surprised at the unexpected intrusion into my empty world. "Oh dear, sorry love. I've had a tough day. Give me a moment." I patted her denim-clad leg to reassure her. Her frown did not display reassurance. I realised this was a pivotal moment in our relationship. She was growing up and I believed that honesty was always the best. Besides, I really, really had to tell someone. Call me irresponsible, I don't care. I thought seriously about both options - fobbing her off or telling her everything - and I knew I was doing the right thing. I still do. I told her everything, starting from all those months before when it had started for me.

She listened in rapt attention.

"Oh, Mum," she said at the end, sliding over to my side and taking my hand in hers.

"Yeah." I faltered but had to ask her. "Do you know what trafficking is? Child trafficking?"

She explained enough for me to stop her before she was done.

"How do you know?" I knew the answer but needed to know from her lips.

It still makes me shudder to think about it, but I'm going to press on and tell you anyway. Kassey said she had been approached in the schoolyard by a man she thought could be a teacher but whom she'd never seen before. Nicely dressed and all that. Ours is a large town, not yet a city, and most people knew many people. Anyway, there he was, in the shadow of the big elm, calling in girls as they ran past. Kassey stopped, not recognising him. Her inner voice told her not to stop.

"He asked if I'd like to make some money as I was so pretty. He would just take some photos of me." Thankfully, I'd warned her off strange men so often that she had run off. Maybe I'd warned her off all men, I thought, and needed to check on the messages I was giving her. Perhaps I could be more balanced. The man I had trusted had tried to rape my daughter but not all men were rapists. As I was saying, she ran off and had an icky feeling in her tummy all afternoon. She was too frightened to tell anyone, even me, at the time.

Over the next week, she noticed three of her classmates weren't in class. Weren't in school. She asked her teacher, Mrs Knowles, who shrugged it off. "You can't trust these caravan people to stick to anything."

Kassey was numbed to silence. She and I had been 'caravan park people' for two years after Morris, my ex-partner, was led off in handcuffs. It was only after I got the job that we could move out of the caravan park and into this skanky old house down the bottom of Moores Pocket Road, on the northern skirts of the town.

It was a terrible thing to contemplate, especially as my daughter had nearly been lost to me.. By being honest with each other, we had each found a firmer friend in the other, and I now had someone I could talk to.

It must have been a terrible realisation for her to know that those who were meant to protect us - police and teachers - weren't there for her. I felt vulnerable and I'm sure she did.

On Saturday morning, over breakfast, she broke the silence.

"There has to be someone we can go to, Mum," she said, her big blue eyes searching mine.

"No one in this town that I know of, right now," I said. Tough news but true news, nevertheless.

"Tessa's father is a policeman."

"Your friend? The Aboriginal man?"

"Yes, him. Can you talk to him?"

"But what if he's like Sergeant Thomlinson? I don't know who to trust any more, love."

I was stopped mid-sentence by a knock on the door. A loud, insistent knock. I leapt up, rushed to the door and grabbed the door handle to open it, such was my instinct to obey others. Then I stopped and dread coursed through me. I knew this wasn't going to go well. I stepped back as the knocking became louder. I looked back at a wide-eyed Kassey.

"Please, love, go and hide somewhere," I said.

"Why?"

"I don't know. It's a feeling. I can't explain it."

"Right," she said uncertainly. "Where?"

"I don't know. Just out of sight. Outside ... in your tree house, perhaps."

"Yeah, cool," she said, smiling, as if a switch had suddenly clicked on in her head.

I walked back to the door and heard someone ordering me to open up or they'd knock the door down. I opened it, cautiously, standing behind it all the time.

"Uph!" came a grunt as the door swung open and Thomlinson stumbled in. "You being clever?"

"No, frightened."

"Of what? You got something to hide?" He leered at me as he straightened his uniform that had ridden up his tummy in the unexpected rush into my kitchen. I hoped the straining buttons of his jacket didn't give way, as they threatened to.

I shook my head, determined to use as few words as possible. They always say, 'Anything you say can be used against you,' never, 'Anything you say can be used for you.'

I peered around the door and outside was Tessa's father, looking very out of place, staring at the ground, scuffing his boots on my gravel driveway.

"We have a report of drugs," said Thomlinson, behind me.

"Drugs?" I spun around in confusion, looking down on his grinning, florid face.

"Yes ma'am, and this is no laughing matter."

"Sorry," I said, trying to get the smile of incredulity off my face. "I don't smoke, I don't drink and the strongest thing you'll find here is ginger tea. This is the last place you'll find any drugs, I assure you, sir."

"That's what they all say." He grumbled and turned towards the kitchen.

"Just a moment, Sergeant, don't you have to show me a search warrant? Aren't you trespassing now?" I knew my rights but felt he had no regard for them. Or for me.

"A search warrant, huh? Trying to be clever?"

"I'm just asking ..."

"Yeah, sure you are."

"So, do you need one? Do you have one?"

"Yeah, yeah, it's on its way."

"Right." I knew my rights were going to be trampled on by his big, black, scuffed boots and I needed to give Kassey time to hide.

"So, you want to be a pain and hold us up?"

"No, go ahead. There's nothing to find."

He stood there and looked at me as if weighing up whether the pointless search was worth it.

"Okay lady, since you're frightened and stuff ... you know ... I might have upset you a bit. Maybe we come back when the warrant's signed. Okay?"

"Uh, yes, okay." I was dumbfounded by his about-face and I followed him out the door.

Constable Markham was right by the door when I went out and his swarthy hand shot out just after Thomlinson passed us. There was a piece of paper in his open palm and I looked at it. He looked at it and he nodded to me. Finally, I gathered my wits, grabbed it and stuffed it in my back pocket. He smiled shyly and followed his boss down the two steps and into the patrol car. They drove off without a goodbye or a wave from either.

A little giddy from the sudden intrusion and the quick back-down, I leaned against the door jamb. Nothing seemed real. I stared out at the two goats and the horse, quietly nibbling away on the sparse, dry grass, over the rusty, two-wire fence that was my boundary. God, what I'd give for a boring life, I thought. Then I went inside to brew up the strongest cup of tea and I sat, staring at the fly spots on the ceiling.

"Are you okay, Mum?" asked Kassey, suddenly beside me, and I jumped into next week. "Sorry ..." I pulled her down onto my knee before she could say any more. She was the only real and sane thing in my life.

Then a strange thought occurred to me and I said, more to myself than to Kassey, "I don't think Sergeant Thomlinson wanted to do that."

"What? Barge in here? But he did."

"You're right, but I have this really weird feeling that it was a show. I don't know ... that he had to make it look like he was harassing us and he didn't want to. Maybe someone else made him do it."

"Maybe it was Mr Cummings."

"The school principal?"

"Yes."

"Why him? Why do you say that?"

"When I ran out the back to the tree hut, he was in his car, in the empty driveway next door." That house had been empty since we'd moved in, a year before.

"Just like ... sitting in his car?"

"Just sitting there. Grinning. Then he saw me and he drove off quickly."

"Mmm," was all I could say. My mind was about to race off in a hundred directions, none of them happy ones. I had to move my body, think of something else. "Do you want fish and chips for early lunch?"

"Like, bought food?" Kassey looked both excited and confused.

"Yes, why not?"

"You always say we can't afford it, Mum."

I felt slightly admonished by my daughter. "Do you want it?"

Her huge smile told me everything. "Really, Mum?"

"Really. Let's go." And so we did. I know I should have feared going out ... actually, I did fear going out and into town but I was determined to drive and talk myself through it. I couldn't be driven by fear all my life so I kept up a busy conversation about school, friends, food, boys and other topics to keep my brain from frying itself on the obvious topic; the one I wouldn't talk about in this precious, magical moment with my daughter.

The Flight South

I felt trapped but couldn't think of anything to do about it. We sat at home with our fish and chips and stewed on it, tried to console each other, but no ideas came to mind. The more I told myself and Kassey that we'd be alright, the less I believed it. The fear grew, an acidic, molten lava in my stomach, and I soon felt I was going to vomit. I walked to the toilet, nonchalantly so as not to alarm Kassey, but nothing came up. I turned, had a pee, pulled my jeans up and checked myself for vomit inclinations. They'd dissolved, thankfully. I opened the door and Kassey was there, waiting to go in.

"What's that, Mum?" She was looking at the floor, behind me.

"Oh." I picked up the piece of paper that must have fallen from my pocket. Gosh, of all the events that had to happen - if I hadn't felt nauseous, if I hadn't gone to the toilet, if I hadn't had a pee, if Kassey had not gone to the toilet at that moment - that piece of paper could have sat there, in my pocket, for hours. I went hot and cold thinking about the possibilities and knew I couldn't overlook it. "It's the piece of paper Constable Markham gave me."

Ring and ask for Damon Edwards, the note said, with a phone number. Not a local one. I showed it to Kassey and she shook her head and shut herself in the toilet. "Just ring the number. Stop delaying. First things first," she said, quoting back at me two of my favourite phrases I'd learned at a Zen meditation class many years before.

"Good morning, Coolangatta Police Station," was the answer on the phone.

"Can I please speak to Damon Edwards?"

"Can I have your name, please?"

"A police constable told me to phone him." I remembered to divulge as little as possible so I was keeping my name to myself for as long as possible.

"Can you not say at the moment?"

"No."

The phone went dead and I thought I'd been cut off.

"Edwards here."

"Damon Edwards?"

"The same."

"I've been told to phone you by a constable as we've just been broken into ... I think that's the phrase ... by a police sergeant and had a brick through our window and our mailbox ..."

"I'm sorry, ma'am, but we don't deal with police misconduct or assault."

"Oh, right."

"Was there another matter?"

I needed to take a deep breath before I could utter the next words.

"Are you still there, ma'am?"

"Aah, yes, child trafficking."

"Yes, this is the right department. Are you in immediate danger? Right now?"

"No, I don't think so."

"Can you drive out of your town? Out of Ipswich?"

"How did you know we're here?" A shiver of fear slid down my spine and I looked around to see if someone or something was watching.

"We traced your call. For your safety. I'm going to suggest that you pack a small bag for, say, three days away, and come to the back of the Youth Centre in Coolangatta."

"That's over an hour away," I said, uttering the least informative thing I could say as my mind set off at a 100 kilometres an hour. Why three day's clothes? Why Coolangatta? A youth centre? Both of us? I realised Kassey was at my elbow.

"Yes, an hour and a half."

"Right. And my daughter's here."

"Of course, she must come with you."

"But my job ..." Another inane, random thought.

"We will take care of that. Are you okay, ma'am? Are you able to drive?"

"Yes, yes, just so many questions." Then a moment of clarity. "We do have a good map book."

"I understand. Now, please bring any evidence of what you are alleging."

"Alleging?" This suddenly sounded harshly, starkly legal.

"Yes, anything that will help us with our case."

"Our case?" His our sounded reassuring. I was no longer alone.

"Yes. When you get to the back door, knock and ask for Constable Perkins. Constable Trudy Perkins. And please call me if you have any further questions. There's a service station next door and you can phone me from there. Tony is the manager there." He asked me my employer and their phone number and then gave me his direct number which I quickly wrote down.

"Constable Trudy Perkins." I said the name aloud to help me remember. And to tell Kassey so at least one of us would remember.

"Let's go, Mum," she said, and wrote something on the piece of paper she took from my hand. Probably Trudy Perkins' name.

"Yes, we will see you soon," he said and his we sounded reassuring.

I tried to treat it as an adventure and Kassey didn't even have to try. We were soon on the road with our bags, fear, excitement and a full tank of petrol, with Kassey scanning the map book for our route and destination.

We planned to be in Coolangatta by 3 pm, but the map didn't know that we'd be followed for a time. Nor did we, till a large black car flashed its headlights at us from behind. I checked the indicators, my speed, the lights, but nothing was wrong. Kassey had noticed the flashing lights too, and we shrugged at each other and carried on. They flashed again and I wondered if my boot was open.

I pulled over and the black car parked behind me. For some reason, in the confusion, I wrote down the registration number in the little notebook that went everywhere with me.

"Can you photograph that car for me, please?" I asked Kassey, and she grabbed my new Yashika camera from the back seat. This was part of the adventure, I told myself, but it felt off, somehow. Creepy. Suddenly, a man was tapping on my window. Unshaven - was it the current fashion to look wild, windswept and lazy? Towering over my car, he bent and demanded I open the window. His demand convinced me to leave it tightly shut with the doors locked.

"Yes?" I yelled through the glass.

"Open up."

"What's the problem?" I yelled and then, quietly to Kassey, "Can that camera take a movie?

"I don't think so but it can take photos really fast - the flutter shutter function, I think, Mum," she said, fiddling with the camera. "Like that," she said, turning it towards him.

"Open up, lady, or I get to use this." He flashed an iron bar - do they call them crowbars? - with the glee of a viper cornering a rabbit. "An' put that bloody thing away."

I fumbled with the seatbelt for as long as I could, and tried to commit all his features to mind. "A chipped front tooth. An anchor tattoo on his right arm," I said to Kassey. She smiled and nodded, still pointing the camera at him.

There was a loud crack and glass flew into the car. He grabbed my shoulder but the door was still locked and my seatbelt still done up.

"Okay, okay, let me ... ugh."

He kept pulling and my attempt at calm vanished. He was raving mad, and desperation had shaken the logic out of him. The last thing I would do was get out with that crazy oaf.

"Mum, just go!" whispered Kassey hoarsely.

"What?" I asked her, stunned to confusion.

"Start the car. Go!"

I needed no more urging. I'd never done a squealy - or whatever they call them - and his face looked like a slapped arse as he ran beside us, determined not to let go. My top ripped, his hand fell away and we lurched onto the motorway amid beeping horns and flashing lights as vehicles swerved to avoid this mad woman driver.

I kept my foot to the floor and could see him standing there, dumb as a Coke bottle, until he suddenly turned and ran to his car. Kassey kept herself busy brushing broken glass off my skirt and her seat.

"I'd better slow down," I said as the speedo passed the 120 kph mark.

"No, Mum, if the police stop us he'll stay away."

"My God, what great thinking, Kassey. Brilliant." I was terrified and enthralled, in equal measure, for I'd never driven at this speed before. I'd never been physically attacked before either, except at home, and the shots of adrenalin had me flying high. She looked at me with a crooked smile but then her eyes blew up like hubcaps.

"Oh, hell, sorry," I said, swerving around the flat deck of a truck. Thankfully, there was no one in the next lane and I grabbed the wheel more tightly with both hands and continued forward, determined to focus on one thing at a time. The road at this moment.

"One thing at a time, Mum." She smiled at me as she repeated another Zen phrase back at me, one I'd said to her often.

A siren screamed and I saw its flashing lights going the other way on the motorway. My heart leapt and then settled as I remembered it could be our saviour. I pressed back down on the accelerator, pulled in front of the truck, passed a van and got into the middle lane again to pass a car dawdling at the regulation speed.

That was when I thought I saw the big, black car behind me. A long way behind me but he was probably closing in. It disappeared as it changed lanes and I remembered to stay focused on one thing at a time - going forward as fast and safely as I could.

Kassey looked at me and then crouched a little to see out her passenger mirror.

"The black car is chasing us," she said.

"Is he still gaining on us?"

"I don't know. He pulled out and in."

I couldn't make myself focus on one thing anymore and saw he was only four car-lengths behind us. What's he going to do if he catches us? I thought.

"Push us off the road," she said. I realised I'd been talking aloud.

"Oh, Kassey, I'm so sorry I've dragged you into all of this. I really am." I patted her knee.

"Mum! Hands on the wheel!"

I stole a look at her and she looked terrified; nothing like the calm voice she had been using.

"Uh, sorry."

"What if we stay in the middle lane, Mum?"

"What?"

"Well, he can't push us off, then."

"Yes, yes, good idea." I swerved back into the middle lane and was blasted by horns and flashing lights. "Oh hell." I kept my foot down and soon left the anger and surprise behind. It was a lucky strike, for three utes had suddenly sped up as he tried to pass them all. They wouldn't like being beaten by a woman driver. The black nose of his car continued to peek in and out of his lane, like a quivering mouse sizing up a distant piece of cheese.

Then another siren and I saw the flashing lights behind me. My heart leapt and then settled with relief. Our saviour at last. I hoped.

Focusing on the road ahead, I glimpsed the unfolding scene behind me as cars parted like the Red Sea at Moses' command, and then the police car was right behind me. I sighed and smiled at Kassey as I changed lanes, nearly clipping a van, and then onto the shoulder, a large gravelled area. The police car stopped behind me, its siren off but its lights still strobing. I knew one was supposed to stay in one's car and I watched him approaching, the slow saunter of one in charge, the crewcut and pot belly of every police caricature we'd ever seen.

"Mum." I looked at her and she was pointing ahead. The black car had pulled onto the shoulder as well, about 20 metres ahead. The viper lying in wait for the rabbit.

"Ma'am, do you know what speed you were going?"

"Yes," I said distractedly, looking ahead, my thoughts spinning in endless, useless circles.

"Ma'am," he said louder.

"Yes," I said, also louder, wondering if it would be better to take off again. The police would follow and Mr Black Car would have to stay away.

"Why were you speeding?"

"We're being chased by that car. He broke my window."

"Yes, I am sure you were." He didn't believe me. "Can I see your licence, ma'am. Your driving is a serious breach."

"And so is someone driving me off the road and smashing my window." I pointed at the black car sitting innocently ahead of us. "Where do you think this glass came from?"

"Ma'am, you were exceeding the limit by 40 kilometres per hour."

"You asked me why. Surely escaping that black car that assaulted me is something you need to focus on."

"I am focusing on you." He stared intently at me as if his neck was welded on, unable to swivel around to the right, towards the black car. "I asked you for your licence." He was puffing up and I thought he might explode. "Are you photographing me?"

"Yes sir," said Kassey, the camera pointed at him.

"That is illegal. I insist that you put it down."

"Kassey," I said.

"It's not illegal, Mum."

"It's not?" These young people knew way too much, sometimes.

"Put that camera down or I'll be forced to charge you." He was becoming louder with every word and stepped back. Then up to the car again as if uncertain what to do with these two illegal females.

"He's not allowed to put his body inside the car without our permission, Mum," she said, loud enough for him to hear. He stepped back half a step, the dance of the uncertain cop.

"Gosh, is that right?" There seemed to be an alarming increase in the number of things I knew nothing about. She nodded seriously.

"Ma'am, I have asked for your licence three times and you have refused, so I'll need to arrest you and detain you."

"You have asked twice and I haven't refused at all." I felt empowered by Kassey's apparent knowledge of the law.

"If you refuse I will have to arrest you and take you into the station." He pulled at the door handle, which was still locked.

"Look, okay, we were speeding and for a very good reason, Sergeant."

"Constable!"

"Whatever. We were being chased by the man in the black car, there, and he broke this window with his crowbar and ripped my top. See?"

"That might or might not be true but you were speeding."

"To save our lives, Sergeant ... aah, Constable."

"You were speeding, ma'am, and you are resisting arrest ..."

"Hey, arrest for what?"

"Refusing to provide your licence ..."

"I said I haven't refused. It's all on camera." Despite the frustration and fear from this authority figure, I was really starting to enjoy myself. Even if he did end up arresting us and taking us to the station, we'd be safe. Besides, there was an adrenalin rush in saying NO to a pushy cop.

He straightened up, pulled his radio thing from one of his dozens of bulging pockets and called for back-up.

"You're in for it now. The team is on its way." He leered through the broken window and then stood back, smirking like a bear who had just found a beehive. As he stepped back, a police car screeched in front of our car and he looked more surprised than I did. Two men leapt out.

"Thank you, constable, we can take it from here," said a man in plain clothes as another man, in uniform, went forward to the black car. "Please help my sergeant to arrest the man in that car."

"But she's speeding ..."

"With good reason. I'm giving you an order, constable." The plain-clothes cop flashed his badge to us all. It meant nothing to me but the fat cop's eyes bulged, his heels snapped together and he straightened from his slouch.

"Yes sir. Yes." And off he lumbered, scratching his cropped head.

That Magnet Thing

He never thought much about it. Actually, he didn't think about it at all. It was just the way he was and he thought everyone else was the same.

See, he had ... mmm, how do I explain it? As if there was some invisible thing around him. Let's see ... it was a glow. No, you can see a glow. An energy? No, that tells you nothing. Perhaps a magnetism explains it best.

See, Geoffrey's magnetism was gently, subtly unobtrusive. Not compelling or demanding - just sweetly inviting, shall we say.

When you met him, you couldn't stop smiling, no matter what sort of day you were having. He sort-of glowed a smile into you that slid down to your heart, warmly chuckling.

He was the sort of guy you'd first think of if you had a good or a bad moment, the first person you'd want to share your latest stuff with.

There was nothing physical you could pin on his magnetism. Not especially good looking - a mop of black clumpy hair, skinny as a rake, a limp he got from slipping on fat in the kitchen and a happy cough from too many cigarettes, drugs and slugs of liquor; all now forgone for a healthier life. He wasn't well brought up or well educated either.

The story is that baby Geoffrey - no name at that stage - was found on a Brisbane doorstep and he was taken home by a kind and misguided woman who couldn't get herself off drugs or prostitution. Somehow, the authorities found an abandoned Geoffrey in the squalor of an old Beenleigh Queenslander, the smell of vomit, urine and blood stifling the nostrils of his rescuers. Then, from about two years old he was bounced from institution to foster home to institution to foster home till he ran away, at 14, deciding he could bring himself up better than anyone else could.

He trod the well-trodden path of those left in the cracks of life, uncared for and anonymous. He needed food, so he stole. He needed hope, so he drank. He needed escape, so he took drugs. He needed alcohol and drugs, so he stole more. He stole bigger and more often till he was noticed.

He was noticed by two groups.

Firstly, the local drug runners noticed him and he became a street bunny, as they called those at the bottom of the ladder who pedalled the drugs to the desperate and were most likely to be noticed by the police.

Then the police noticed him and he was slapped about and bribed. Free drugs to the cops or behind bars. They'd then overlook his clandestine activities.

To survive on his drug sales, he had to deal harder and steal harder to pay for the drugs he was giving away to the cops as their inducement to stay silent. His drug bosses noticed this, didn't like it, suspected him of split loyalty and cut his supply. He had nothing to give the pigs, the cops, but they didn't believe him. Who would? A homeless, penniless, scruffy 20-year-old with no education or roots. These outer things prompted mistrust, and he was a dried-up leaf in a storm, blown whatever way it was.

The mob disowned him and sent their scouts out for their pound of skin - the last two instalments that he owed or his two index fingers.

Then his angel turned up. An unlikely angel.

On the run from his vicious stalkers, starving and shoeless, there was only one place he knew to run, the other evil he knew.

He quietly tracked down Sergeant Sean Murphy, the large-gutted, six-foot-three block of sneering temper. He snipped open a locked Mercedes and leapt in, knowing that Big Thommo, as everyone called him, was watching. He was a surly pack of Irish tempers.

"I know ye got stash, holdin' oot on me," whispered Surly Sean as he hauled Geoffrey from the car. "A few days in the slammer'll cure yer memory, help you remember ye have me shit. Okay?"

It wasn't a question and Geoffrey was relieved to be behind bars, as long as none of his pursuers ended up there as well. He sat on the thin mattress next to a skinny runt of a man who sweated and vomited his alcohol-induced torrent into the bucket. His other companion was bigger than Sean, a black man with tattoos, missing teeth and a constant, angry rant with somebody not in the cell.

All is perception and, from Geoffrey's point of view, this was heaven.

The next morning he was hungry and sweating from withdrawal. Surly Sean towed him out of the cell and into an interrogation room.

"Me shift ends and so do yer options!" said Sergeant Murphy. Silence. Geoffrey's bottom lip quivered and he wondered if he should say something.

"Jeez, can't stand bloody crying!" said the red-headed hulk of anger. "I'm going and you're coming too! To yer stash."

Geoffrey's chair flipped up and he landed on his back, his head hitting the concrete floor. It took him several moments to realise the sergeant's foot was to blame. He lay there without options, rubbing his sore head and realising his back and left shoulder were now pounding in pain. All he could do was shake his head to indicate, I don't have anything to give you. I'm sorry. A boot went into his kidney and he yelled silently, his voice absent for want of water. And food.

"Ya useless lump. Okay, one more day in here and that's yer last chance!"

The policeman grabbed Geoffrey's dirty, grey t-shirt and towed him back to his cell, his legs scuttling after his propelled body. He was tossed on the filthy plastic mattress - the cell now empty of the others though the stink remained - and the sergeant stood there, shaking his head. Geoffrey noticed his pale, freckled hands were shaking too, now. The sergeant really needed his hit, as badly as Geoffrey needed water and food.

"You're a bloody loser, aren't you!"

Geoffrey nodded. Nobody could argue with that.

"Remember, Geoffrey, ya git, if ya don't obey da rules, ya don't live da life." Surly Sean, his angel, left.

All is perception and Geoffrey's confused mind translated it differently from Murphy's meaning. It was as if a light shone in his brain, from somewhere. From inside, somehow. If you don't obey the rules, you don't live your life. It stuck with him.

The 'rules', his brain told him, were not the sergeant's rules but the rules of the light inside him - the light he'd never seen before. He didn't know he had rules and lights inside him but he immediately knew the life he wanted and, weirdly, knew the rules inside him would take him there - out of this stink and grime and to something beyond his current experiences and imagination.

He'd never prayed before but he tried it, lying there in that hot, fetid cell with commands, thumps and yells echoing around the wooden building. He left the savage, outside world behind and went in ... into the light that welcomed him with an exquisite peace.

Unaware of time, he was woken by the bars being rattled. The smell of cigarettes closed in and he realised he was being spoken to.

"I'm Constable Markham. What are you doing here?" He was the first Aboriginal cop Geoffrey had ever seen.

He tried to speak and indicated his need for water. The constable frowned, turned, disappeared and returned with two cups of water. Geoffrey downed them and found a small voice returning.

"There's no charge sheet for you, sir, so what are you doing here?"

"Not sure," he said timidly.

"Right, to save me paperwork and you more pain, how about you go home."

Geoffrey managed a smile and pushed himself up painfully.

"When's the last time you ate?"

"Two or three days," mumbled Geoffrey uncertainly. It might have been more.

The constable helped him up, pressed $10 into his hand and said, "Go get some food then find a bigger life than this one, hey! Go! Go on, don't stand there staring at me. Get the hell out of here and get a new direction."

Geoffrey was filled with gratitude and wanted to thank the man from the bottom of his faltering heart. All he could do was shake the man's kind hand, step out into the sunlight and head to the nearest tea shop, the precious life-giving $10 clutched desperately in his fist.

There are moments that fall together, as if God has won Lotto and wants to play. This was one of those moments.

He sat in the Lucky Café, looking out of the window, reluctant to leave this cool and friendly place. Ravenous though he was, after downing five free glasses of water, he lingered over the plate of fried food, delaying his departure. It was a hot, cruel world out there and he was reluctant to return to it. Also, he couldn't decide where he should go, in that hot, cruel world. Every huddle-spot of the homeless was known by the drug demons and nowhere was safe.

As he pondered the exquisite safety of this moment and the opposite of his future, there was an almighty crash, then yelling, in the kitchen. The yelling continued for a few minutes, rising in intensity then, suddenly, a kitchen hand was being man-handled out the door by two men, likely the owner and a cook, Geoffrey surmised.

"Look, boss, it's good to have him gone but who's going to do the dishes now?" asked the younger man in his chef's uniform, as they walked back. Then something happened. The only way he could explain it was that the Hand of God grabbed him by the collar, hauled him up and made his mouth work, the most words he'd said to anyone for a long time.

"I can help out, sir," he said, then wondered who had crawled into his mouth and said that. He'd never washed a plate in his life.

The two men stopped, turned and stared at the most unkempt, shoeless man they'd ever seen. A silence stretched across Ipswich and beyond as they looked at each other and back to Geoffrey.

The voice inside him opened his mouth again. "I really need the work and you can trust me. I have nothing to give but my two willing hands and a fistful of trust."

The two men looked at each other and back to him, as if waiting for the silence to unroll from across the town. The older man gave the smallest shrug then handed Geoffrey a towel and told him to wash up as best he could at the basin in the men's toilet. Then he was set to work. Desperate to impress, he learned quickly and, despite a criminal record they didn't ask about, was allowed to sleep there the night - secure for Geoffrey and security for Luca, the owner.

A year later Luca admitted he couldn't understand why he had employed and trusted Geoffrey in the first place. All logic was against this homeless, penniless man with no references. But something inside had told him to trust. So he had.

That was when he told Geoffrey he'd just been diagnosed with cancer, might live another year, and would Geoffrey like to take over the business.

By then, Geoffrey had his own little apartment and the possibility of a girlfriend. He'd met a sweet woman, Sarah, twice and hoped for more. He thought life was as good as it could possibly get. Then this proposal ... homeless druggie to business owner in a year.

His answer to Luca was to break down in tears. His gratitude to Luca, and to life, was bigger than his little heart could hold and it spilled out, all over his face and onto the floor.

Luca, a patient man, waited till the tears slowed down and said, "I take it that's a yes!" He hugged Geoffrey.

After that, Luca popped into the Lucky Café on most days, on the pretext of helping Geoffrey become acquainted with all the details of running a busy café. The truth was that Luca needed to keep in touch with the heartbeat of his life - the café he had started all those years back, the first café in Ipswich and a change from the tearooms that abounded back then. Of course, Geoffrey was grateful for the daily help of Luca, the father he never had, in a way.

Sarah kept her administration job at the local car wrecking yard and was able to look after the accounts for Geoffrey as well, while he smiled and more and more customers came in every day.

Being near the police station in Roderick Street, his Lucky Café was frequented by many down-and-outers -

others like he used to be. He always took the time to sit and listen and, when needed, give extra food for free.

Now, there was one mystery he couldn't unravel. Why didn't Sergeant Murphy ever to there? It was the nearest café to the sergeant's station but, weirdly, the two never met. It was as if each had an opposite charge, like a magnet, and Geoffrey's trusting goodness somehow repelled Big Sean's callous anger. Of course, others came from the nearby hospital, police station and library; a mix of the great and the grovelling of the town.

In the same way, perhaps, Constable Bouddi Markham became a frequent visitor. Like Geoffrey, he spent time talking to those who had lost hope and trust in a life that threatened their every move. Geoffrey put tables and chairs on the street - the first al fresco in Ipswich - so Marky, as everyone called him, could have a smoke with his daily coffee. Fittingly, his Christian name meant 'heart'.

The Lucky Café became lucky for so many, being in the centre of a growing web of information - ex-cons finding work, homeless people finding accommodation, the beleaguered finding legal help and the loose and lonely finding direction. However, the visitors weren't always on the lower side of life and there'd typically be a new BMW or Mercedes parked up the road a bit.

This magnet thing, as Geoffrey called it, seemed to work in fascinating and unexpected ways.

Because Geoffrey and Marky spent time listening to people, the café became the go-to place for those wanting answers to the questions of life.

Eventually, Geoffrey was asked to give talks where halls had been booked and the advertising was done by others. All he had to do was turn up and speak from his expanding heart. He often took Marky on stage with him, to share the talks, and they frequently stood in for each other. The Tandem Talks, they were called, even when only one of them was there.

Geoffrey was asked to go on tours of the country - big money, hotels, limousines, fame and all that - but he was quietly content to stay at home with Sarah and their son, Marcus Luca, or to be at work with his growing number of staff and customers.

He had to expand the premises into the vacant building next door. Luca witnessed the steady growth while he proved the doctors wrong about his impending death. That magnetic thing seemed to work in other ways. As Geoffrey's business grew, so did the community. Other businesses started up in the vacant, run-down buildings nearby and trust and connection grew from the cracked concrete around him.

Of course, no one lives forever and Luca was happy to cruise to a new café in the sky, three years after he sold the business. The day after the funeral a new customer turned up and Geoffrey was at a loss. How to react? It was a sad remnant of Sergeant Murphy, in a worn, holey tracksuit and a body as slumped as the bags under his eyes. Still a large man, his skin now sagged off his thinner face as if his bones were knives.

"I've come to apologise," he said quietly, as he stared out the window, unable to look Geoffrey in the eye.

Geoffrey sat next to him. "All this and more is because of you, Sean," he said, waving his hand around the café.

Sean turned his head, frowned and stared as Geoffrey explained how Sean's last words had changed his world. "You told me 'if you don't obey the rules, you don't live the life' and I decided I didn't want to live my life - not the one I'd been living - and chose to break my own rules of being anonymous and running from everything. I spoke up for myself, for the first time ever, and here I am."

Unable to exhibit anything but gratitude and forgiveness, Geoffrey induced Sean to return day after day. Sean, you see, had been fired from the force for drug and violence offences and had hit the bottom, just as Geoffrey had. And, like Geoffrey, he had called out for help from that bottom place. The magnetic thing had brought him to his angel, Geoffrey, who he had been an unwitting angel to three years before.

Meeting Geoffrey

And that's how I met Geoffrey ... well, there were a few steps in between.

I asked the plain-clothes policeman, on the side of the road with me, why he was there.

"I'm Detective Inspector Miles, from the Child Trauma and Sexual Crime Unit."

"A call from Damon Edwards?"

"Yes, DI Edwards gave us your car registration. We kept a lookout for you."

"Gosh." I was overwhelmed that so many were doing so much for us two, something I'd craved for so long. "But how could you find us among all these cars on the motorway? It's lucky you found us."

"You call it luck, ma'am," he said, smiling. "But we call it good planning and diligence. We had a good idea where you'd be, estimating your time from Ipswich."

"Cool aye!" said Kassey, echoing my sentiment, though in teenage words.

"But hang on, Inspector Edwards said to drive to Coolangatta and I'd meet him there. How did you get pulled into this?"

"DI Edwards, ma'am, called me after you phoned. He had a strange gut feeling something needed following up and I agreed."

"Gut feeling?"

"Yes, we are trained to act on logical evidence but, sometimes, we allow ourselves to listen to our intuition. It's seldom wrong."

"Well, it's working well today." I smiled.

"So, ma'am, would you mind coming with me - you and your daughter - while my sergeant follows with your car?"

"Hey, cool Mum. In a police car!"

The inspector and I chuckled at Kassey's enthusiasm and we did what he asked.

I hadn't realised, but while we'd been talking, another police car must have turned up and three new police had the chipped-tooth driver sprawled against his black car, staring daggers at me. I tried hard not to smile at his predicament ... I really did try but couldn't keep the smirk off my face.

DI Miles dropped us off at the door of the Coolangatta Youth Centre where DI Edwards took us into an office with a tape recorder. Over a cup of tea, he interviewed Kassey and me, individually, with Constable Trudy Perkins beside us each time.

Then Trudy drove us to an apartment overlooking the beach and asked us not to leave for three days. We spent those two days mainly on the balcony, being plied with food and a daily visit from Constable Trudy, who checked whether we could remember anything more than our initial statements in the case against Mr Cummings, the school principal and my boss. He was a large part of Kassey's and my conversations over that time, and we remembered many extra details over those two days.

Kassey and I felt so safe during our little holiday by the beach. It would have been nice to walk along the sand, in the water, but it was a hundred times better than our little, rented house at the bottom of Moores Pocket Road, even while we were confined. We were reluctant to go back, but then Trudy asked for the house keys and said they had found a house for us in Bundara Street, closer to town, closer to the police station and harder for others to find us.

We were delighted to hear that my boss had been replaced by a Miss Malcolm and that other 'reappointments' had been made at the St Bede's. That seemed extremely quick action, especially for the trudging bureaucracy of a school. However, DI Edwards assured us this his team had had Cummings under surveillance for some time. Cummings had been exited from the school the same day we exited Ipswich.

We found out that the apartment we stayed in was used for the witness protection program and was well set up with surveillance equipment secreted about the place. Constable Trudy told us at the end of our stay.

Back To Ipswich

Though we were confined indoors in Coolangatta, our three-day holiday at the beach was over too soon. DI Edwards' instructions seemed too simple - go to our new home, go back to work and school and be sure we popped into the Lucky Café as soon as we could.

It sounded too peaceful and easy, given the fear and privacy-invading we'd escaped from. I expected a list of dos and don'ts and restrictions. I wondered how someone living 120 kilometres away, in Coolangatta, could ensure our safety at home. The puppet masters of those who had abused us were still back where we were headed - Ipswich. I'd never been involved with anything illegal, apart from my ex-partner's incursions on my daughter. I assumed that those at the top of the trafficking pyramid would never be known and they'd simply recruit others to replace Cummings, gap-tooth and anyone else who was taken out of the action.

But DI Edwards assured us we were in safe hands with his team and that there was nothing to fear. But I did fear and I couldn't let the anxiety go while there was no obvious police protection around us. I really did try to look calm for Kassey's sake but the anxiety stayed.

Kassey and I had never eaten out in Ipswich, so we didn't know any cafés, teashops or restaurants, unlike the days before my ex was led off in handcuffs in shame. He'd seemed to have an unlimited flow of money for restaurants, holidays and fast cars. However, for necessities like food, rent and school resources for Kassey? No, the money for those things was always in short supply. I later realised I'd only experienced a small corner of his life, with most of it folded under and out of view.

No black cars followed us to our new home and Constable Tracy was true to her word: they'd moved everything and set the furniture up almost as I'd have done it myself. We just had to unpack boxes of crockery, cutlery, clothes, books, board games, stuffed toys and ornaments, a fun diversion for a day.

However, I still felt a persistent unease. Kassey acted as unconcerned as I pretended to be but, that first night, asked if she could sleep with me, something she hadn't done since her stepfather attacked her three years before. Then, she'd slept with me for a month, and she hadn't changed from the squirmy, disruptive creature she'd been as a baby, keeping me awake most of those nights. However, it was nice to know I could help her sleep through the night, within comfort and safety.

Though DI Edwards had told me to go to the Lucky Café, the thought of it was crowded out by other concerns. It was Wednesday and I wasn't due to start back at work till the following Monday. I wondered what distractions I could dream up to get us through the next few days.

"What's the Lucky Café, Mum?" Kassey asked as she ate the last of her Weet Bix, while my mind was floating around activities for children.

"The what?"

"The Lucky Café. You know, what the policeman said."

"Oh, that. I'm not sure."

"Can we go?" Her big eyes implored me and I knew she wouldn't let it drop.

"I don't really know ..."

"But the policeman said, Mum."

"Yes, but what's a café got to do with us? Or him?"

"Mum, why don't we, like, try it."

I smiled at her enthusiasm and her unassailable logic. I preferred to weigh things up - the plusses, minuses and the logic - while she was always quicker to take a risk, a trait she shared with both her father and her stepfather. I don't know how I attracted rash risk-takers and it seemed I'd never be free of them with her around.

So, we drove around and found the Lucky Café in Roderick Street and I hoped the nearby police station would give the protection it purported to. I was surprised to see Constable Markham sitting outside, enjoying a smoke and coffee while chatting to someone who hadn't washed their clothes since Pontius was a pilot ... well, that's what he looked like. I smiled nervously to Constable Markham, not sure if our last furtive exchange meant he'd want me to keep my distance. He smiled openly back, his teeth glistening white against his dark skin.

"Get a coffee and join us," he said, and the homeless man smiled at us warmly through his tangled beard.

"Are you sure?"

"Of course," the constable said, moving his chair sideways and bringing two others over. How could I refuse? Soon, Kassey and I were sitting with them, cradling our lemonade and coffee.

The Handshake

So, you've been walkabout, we hear," said Constable Markham, smiling as we sat down.

"Aah, yes ... but should we be discussing this here ... you know ..." I said tentatively, trying desperately not to look at the homeless man beside him.

"You can call me Marky, if you like, and this illusion of a tramp is part of our ... shall we say, our extended police force."

"Samuel at your service, ma'am," he said, rising from his seat a little, nodding his head, his behaviour as gentlemanly as his beautifully spoken English. He extended his hand and I faltered. Then shook it. "Yes, yes, I washed my hands this morning." He chuckled as he sat back down.

"No, no, I just wasn't expecting ... well, you know ..."

"A gentleman in such a state of decrepitude? A man of the street and educated?"

"Well, yes, I suppose so ..."

"The element of surprise is a great leveller of the social hierarchy, don't you think, ma'am?" The sparkling glint in his eyes matched his soft chuckle. "I didn't catch your name."

"Janice," I said, my embarrassment deepening.

"And this young lady is?" He stood again and extended his hand to Kassey. She looked at his hand and then at me.

"Shake his hand, love."

She shrugged and put her hand out gingerly.

"I won't break your arm, m'dear," he said, squeezing her hand. She smiled uncertainly. "And now, a quick lesson in safety. Do you know what this means?" He still hadn't sat down and he held up his hand to her. She looked at me and shrugged. I shrugged back as I couldn't see what he was doing.

"If you feel unsafe, do this, see? Now, do it to your mum."

She held her palm up with her thumb tucked in. Then she curled her four fingers over her thumb.

"That's it - your thumb is trapped just like you could be. You're a quick learner, Kassey."

"This is cool, Mum," she said with a huge smile, all uncertainty gone. It seemed like she suddenly felt safe with this simple technique. Or this man.

"If anyone, particularly a child, does that, it's a call for help," said Constable Markham. "Whether someone's being abducted or abused, it's a cry for help."

"Right," I said. "What a simple idea, Constable." I still couldn't get used to giving a policeman a nickname.

"Yes, and it has probably saved hundreds of lives."

"But what would I do?" I asked. "If a child was with, you know ..."

"A paedophile?"

"Yes, one of them. I couldn't defend myself against them, so what would I do?"

"Engage the child in conversation," said Samuel, sitting down. "You could pretend you know them and ask about school or their parents or something. Just keep talking and the paedophile will likely walk away."

"You could call other adults over, wave to a policeman," said Markham. "Keep it social and normal. Casual and friendly. They'll most likely want to avoid a scene and move away."

"This is so cool, Mum," said Kassey, smiling with tears in her eyes. She grasped my hand tightly.

"Kassey was approached by a man at her school, two weeks ago, and told him to go away," I said.

"You were scared?" asked Samuel.

"Bit scared. And annoyed," said Kassey.

"And alone?"

"Yeah, suppose so. Yes, alone. I couldn't tell anyone."

"Not even me, at the time," I said.

"They hate a fuss so, if it happens again, yell and scream and cause a scene. Right?"

"Really?"

"It's better to be embarrassed than abused," said Markham. "Sorry to say it like that but that's the choice, sometimes. Now, are you able to describe this man, Kassey?" He took out a notebook and pen and Kassey told him all she remembered, which was a lot, actually.

"Gee, mmm ..." said Kassey, smiling and staring at the clear blue sky as if digesting this new information.

"Are you feeling a bit safer?" I asked, my hand on her shoulder.

"Yeah, of course. I'm going to tell my friends. Everyone should know this."

"You could do a morning talk, love."

"Hey, yeah, I will!" Her slouch had gone and she was sitting up, leaning forward, smiling at the two men.

"Do you do talks about this in the schools?" I asked.

"I do when I can but most of them don't want to know," said Markham.

"What?" I shook my head in astonishment.

"Some allow me in but some think it's too scary to tell the pupils about ..."

"And some are involved in the paedophilia?" I asked, butting in.

Both men nodded grimly.

"It sounds like the staff at St Bede's has changed, so I hope they're more open now," I said, hope rising in my chest.

"If the parents and pupils apply gentle, respectful pressure, that always helps," said Samuel.

"Mmm, I'm not their favourite employee at the moment."

"You might be surprised," said Markham. "You might be very surprised. Here, let me get you another coffee; yours is cold." I looked down to see I hadn't touched mine and then back up to stop him, but he'd already disappeared into the café.

"So, who are you, Samuel?" I asked, daring to ask the question that had squatted in my mind since we'd sat down.

"I am a mere citizen, accommodated on these sordid streets ..."

"Why don't I believe you?"

"Mum! You can't ask that!" Kassey's hand landed on my arm.

"Look, love, I want to know ..."

"There's only danger in secrets," he said.

"Exactly. So?"

"So, let me tell you a tale," he said, leaning back. It seemed we were to be treated to a long and interesting story. We weren't disappointed.

Markham returned with another lemonade for Kassey and two Anzac biscuits for us both.

"Your coffee will be here soon," he said, "and so will yours, you rascal."

"I should think so. Stories need coffee to oil the vocal chords," said Samuel, punching Markham playfully on the shoulder. "Mmm, where do I start, esteemed listeners?" Samuel had a huge smile, a chasm in his tangle of whiskers, and he was obviously enjoying himself.

"The same place you always start," said Markham, sitting back with a smile, and nodding his head while rolling a smoke.

"Oh dear, have I told this tantalising tale before?"

"Only a hundred times! Now, get on with it, you old drama queen."

"You dashed man, expunging the beauty of my opening lines," said Samuel, sitting back as if to luxuriate in the upcoming story.

"Hurry up, the day's nearly over," I said, venturing to join in the cajoling.

"Mum!" Kassey slapped my arm gently, looking embarrassed.

"Yes, it is extremely rude, young lady," said Samuel. "But in this rough land it seems the better you are acquainted with someone, the ruder you are. It's proof of your friendship, somehow."

"Come on, you old sot, get on with it." Markham kept smiling and shaking his head.

"Yes, well, I certainly was a sot, a drunk, an alcoholic before this day. I was a wealthy businessman. The finest of suits, houses, cars and girlfriends. I believed myself flameproof, impervious to the slings and arrows of the cruel world. My several companies traded in everything from real estate to liquor to children's toys. My portfolio was so diverse I knew my business could never fail."

"But it did?" I suggested.

"No, not the business, but my heart. The stress, alcohol, hotel food and arrogance were too much for this poor old ticker ..."

"Heart attack?" I asked.

"Three, m'dear. Three heart attacks and I learned nothing from the first two, pretending they were anomalies that would correct themselves. But the third floored me. I didn't leave the hospital for nigh on three months and, after that, I leant on a cane, a paid carer and a batch of health professionals - psychologist, physiotherapist, naturopath and Alcoholics Anonymous, mainly. It was only after I was well into recovery that I realised how close to the brink I'd come, how close to cancelling out of the wondrous life I'd been in. It scared the bejesus out of me and a long process - a very long process I resisted for a long time - found me delegating and then divesting."

"You gave up everything?" I asked.

"Everything except my health, sanity and self-respect."

"What about your money?"

"Mum! That's rude," said Kassey, while Samuel and Markham chuckled in unison. I felt the red of embarrassment rising in my cheeks.

"Yes, your mother is very rude and nosey, Kassey," said Samuel. "However, it is the mark of an intelligent being to be asking questions about that which they do not know. If we don't ask, we stay in ignorance. So, she can ask me anything, m'dear, and no question is rude or insulting. I can simply choose to answer or not."

My embarrassment faded to relief.

"Oh," said Kassey, looking at me as if she felt as relieved as I did.

"Much of my money went into healing my body, mind and soul with therapists in England, where I lived, back then. After that, there was travel to many spiritual sites and gurus around the world, particularly Buddhist ones that I mainly resonated with. After focusing on me, filling my soul's bucket, I started looking for others in my previous position - others I could help out ..."

Thomlinson and Bullying Men

Constable, why aren't you at work?" came a bellow from the footpath. Our heads spun to see a florid, fat Sergeant Thomlinson standing over us.

"Where did you come from?" I demanded, my shock inducing more stridency than I intended.

"Oh, God, you again." His head spun towards me, his eyes glaring. "I am addressing the constable, madam ..."

"And you need to deal with police business in private and not out on the street," I said, and realised my fingers in the cup handle were shaking. So was the cup.

"Mum!" said Kassey.

"I'm sorry, love. I ... I've just had enough of this man's bully tactics and I've had enough of men, full stop." I noticed the two men across the table looking alarmed and sitting very erect. Samuel had his hands up, palms out. "Sorry, constable. And Samuel. I mean bullying men. Abusive men. The headmaster, the sods who smashed my window and put poo in my mailbox, that irk who smashed my car window."

"And Dad?"

"Yes, him too, love. We don't need this kind of behaviour and I'm not having it."

"Right," said Thomlinson, muttering incoherently. I'd forgotten he was there.

"So, Sergeant, start again and this time, with respect for everyone." I could see that Marky was trying to suppress a snigger as he buried his face in his empty coffee mug.

"Constable Markham, when does your shift end?" asked a mollified Thomlinson, shifting uneasily from one foot to the other.

"I'm on duty now, Sergeant, as the Community Liaison Officer."

"This is what you do? And these people ..."

"Are part of the community. We are undergoing a post-trauma counselling session, Sergeant. Is there anything else you needed?"

"Yes ... no, right. Good, carry on." Thomlinson straightened up, looked around as if searching for his self-respect, gave up and stalked off.

"I am so sorry, Constable," I said, as the shock faded away to reveal a very embarrassed woman. "Have I made trouble for you? Will there be repercussions?"

"Possibly." Markham cocked his head and shrugged with a sad smile. "However, you are absolutely right to have spoken up, Janice."

"I concur," said Samuel, his teeth flashing a smile through the tangled undergrowth of his beard. "I know you can't say this, my friend Marky, but we may be continually disappointed but never surprised at the capriciousness of bullies. You never know what they'll do next."

"No, I can't say that." Markham smiled and nodded to Samuel.

"But you might possibly think it." Both men looked at each other and smiled.

"But what about Mum?" asked Kassey.

"Yes. You have already been a target at your school and then he demanded that I attend him at your place for that drug ..."

"Charade?" I smiled, having saved him saying the word.

"Mmm, yes." Markham smiled shyly. "I was led to believe you had drugs and I questioned why the drugs squad weren't called. He refused to answer and that was when I wrote the name and number on the paper to give you."

"You suspected something fishy?" I asked.

"Let's just say I went to your place with an open mind."

"And an open palm," said Samuel, sitting forward.

"Pardon?"

"You were ready to help Janice, if need be."

"Well, yes ..."

"But is Mum in trouble? And me?" asked Kassey, her hand gripping my arm.

"I do not know, aah ..."

"Kassey," said Kassey, smiling at Markham who looked a mite embarrassed.

"Yes, Kassey. Things are volatile. They have arrested the headmaster and three of his staff, so school should be safer. But I won't pretend that it's all over. No one can guarantee this. Here is my card and on the back is my private number. You must ring me, directly, if you have any problems, suspicions or insights into any of this." Constable Markham handed a card to each of us. I flipped mine over and there was a hand-written number.

"And you can always come here," said Samuel. "If we're not here, talk to Geoffrey or any of his staff."

"Geoffrey?" I asked.

"The chap who owns this café, along with his wife, Sarah."

"Right," I said, scrunching my eyes up. It was feeling like some kind of ASIO operation, James Bond-like. A strange feeling rose in my chest and it felt like something dangerous, like when my ex-husband attacked me. That will-I-survive-this feeling of being totally out of control with no support anywhere. But, this time, it was tinged with a pall of excitement, knowing that support was here, for the first time ever. I wiped my eyes, not realising they were leaking.

"Are you okay, Kassey?" I asked.

"S'pose so, Mum." She leant her head into my shoulder as I put my arm around her.

"This is confusing," I said, trying to pinpoint my odd feelings. "We were less safe before but we didn't know it was dangerous. Now we know the danger and it's safer but it feels worse."

"That sounds silly, Mum. But sort of right."

"Is it like after an accident?" asked Samuel. "You survive it and do what you need to do in the moment but, afterwards, you go all weak in the knees?"

"Maybe I'd rather not know what's out there."

"Yes, most people turn off their brains to any bad news they can't deal with. They act as if it never happened. Then they insult those who provide the facts they don't want to know about," said Markham.

"Yes, denial is a dangerous comforter," said Samuel. "And now I must go if you would all excuse an exhausted an old man. I will continue with my fascinating saga next time we chance upon each other. For now, a siesta awaits, mesdames."

I realised how tired I felt, like being smothered in a warm, wet blanket.

"Yes, stress is very fatiguing," said Markham, and the three of us got up and left him rolling another cigarette and scribbling away in his notepad.

Maybe it was the extra support around us. Maybe it was knowing what we didn't before - there was more evil than we'd imagined - but I felt the stirring of a need to get out of myself, to stand up, to stop cringing.

I know I had cringed before the abuse and violence of my ex-husband and ex-boyfriend, Deryk and Morris. I'd heard on a radio interview with one of those motivational speakers that we attract more abuse by buying into it, by cringing and by, as he called it, giving our abusers permission to abuse us. That's all very well when you're a man sitting safely behind a microphone. But when you're a woman with her lover's hand around her throat, pinned against the fridge, him screaming abuse at you with a kitchen knife waving about in his other hand ... well, what do you do? You have no choices in that moment.

I know I had agreed with Deryk and Morris a hundred times to avoid the yelling and the threats. Maybe I should have stood my ground, stated my truths and preferences. Maybe I should have ended the relationships at the first sign of intimidation or the first time I felt unsafe. There's a hundred maybes and I can't go back to test any of them out.

What I do know is that I am here with a 13-year-old daughter and both of my exes are gone - one dead, thanks to drugs, and the other in prison. I can only go from this moment and move forward.

We have support from some of the police in Coolangatta and here we have Markham, Samuel and Geoffrey, whom I haven't met yet. They say my job at the school is safer but looking in is very different from being in. Despite the new support, bricks can still go through our windows, my car may be damaged, Kassey might be injured ... God, anything could happen to us and the support will only be there after the event, whatever it is. I get prickly shivers up my spine and in my gut as I try not to think of the awful things that could occur. Anyway, whatever support we have, it'll be too damned late - it'll be over before anyone can get here.

"You know, Kassey," I said as I unlocked the door and let her in, "I think I'll take up boxing."

"What?" demanded Kassey, stopping right in front of me so I bumped into her, nearly knocking her over.

"Come on, keep moving."

She didn't move and stared at me. "You? Boxing?"

"Yes, why not? Come on, go into the lounge room, love."

"But that's for big muscly men ... ooh, okay." She finally moved as I pushed her and she stood in the middle of the room, staring at me.

"Look, I need to be able to defend myself and you ..."

"But people punch you." She winced as if she'd been punched and I felt it too.

"Well, maybe I can learn how to punch bags and how to stand properly and get fit. I don't know, do you have any ideas?"

"Not really. I suppose you're right, Mum." She sat next to me on the lounger in the way young girls do, kneeling with her feet splayed out each side of her bottom. I can't kneel without intense pain and realised how unfit and inflexible I'd become, sitting at a desk all day. She looked at me, smiled shyly, looked down and then back at me, her eyes brighter.

"They teach Tae Kwon Do after school. Tamara does it."

"That's like Kung Fu or something, isn't it?"

"I think so."

"And she likes it?"

"Yeah, she loves it. Actually, I was going to ask if I could do it when she started but I know it costs money."

"Oh, love, and you spared me the embarrassment?" I put my arm around her and she leant her head into my shoulder.

Maureen the Gossip

Who's that?" I asked when a knock sounded at the front door.

"You'll find out if you open it, Mum," said Kassey with a big smile as she parroted another of my favourite phrases to me.

"Okay, cheeky sod." I punched her knee lightly. "I just wondered if we could see them before we opened up."

"Mum, you're making me worried."

"Sorry, love, I'm a bit jittery. I thought I'd got better after Morris was taken away."

"We don't have to open it."

"They know we're here. Our car's outside."

The knock was longer and louder this time.

"I'll check through the laundry window." She leapt up, perhaps relieved to be moving, to be doing something.

"Thanks, love." I stood up and my feet were screwed to the floor. I didn't know which way to move them. Open the door and risk another invasion or something worse? Sit and hope they'd bugger off? Call Constable Markham ... no, that would be too extreme.

"Looks like an old lady."

"On her own?"

"I think so. I could only see the back of her head. Grey hair."

I shrugged and my feet unscrewed themselves. I opened the door, standing well back from the entrance, but no one was there. I stepped forward and nearly put my big hoof in a huge pie dish, covered in a tea-towel. It smelled like bacon and egg pie.

"Ouch!" The black metal dish burnt my hands. Very hot. I stepped out into the porch and saw a grey-haired woman leaving through our paint-peeling gate. She must have sensed me behind her and turned.

"Oh, dear, love, I didn't know if you were home. I don't want to disturb you if you're busy."

"What's this?" I asked, pointing at the pie and then realising how ungracious I sounded.

"Just a welcome, dear. I didn't mean to bother you."

"No, no, no bother at all. Very generous. It's lovely, actually," I said, trying to haul myself out of my graceless hole.

"It's what we do round here for new neighbours." She looked like she didn't know which way to turn, as if I'd changed the script without due notice.

"Look, would you like a cup of tea?"

She suddenly seemed sure of herself as if I'd returned to the standard script.

"That would be lovely, dear." She was at my door before I could count to ... well, before I could say the word count. She whipped oven mitts out of her beige handbag that matched her beige twinset and beige shoes, which contrasted with her string of pearls and blue-grey hair. I felt positively bogan in my t-shirt, jeans and bare feet.

"Oh, hello, dear, what lovely dark hair," she said when Kassey eased around the kitchen doorway, looking as shy as I'd ever seen her.

"I'm Janice and this is Kassey," I said, while my neighbour slid the pie dish into my oven.

"I'm Maureen, love," she said, turning to smile at us and then back towards the cupboards. "Shall I get the teacups out?" She started opening and shutting doors till she found the mugs. "Do you have cups and saucers?"

"No, we don't bother with saucers. The tea tastes the same without them." I reached for the electric jug but she blocked my path with her flitting back and forwards.

"Oh dear," Her voice dropped at the end of the sentence the way disapproving people do. "Where is your teapot?"

"We use teabags, Maureen."

She stopped for one of those short, awkward silences that seemed to stretch into next year, looking as uncertain as she had before, at my gate.

"Maybe it's time for an adventure, try something new," I said, pretending a breeziness I definitely didn't feel. I reached across, grabbed the jug, filled it and plugged it back in while she stood there shifting, ooing and aahing. "We've just moved in and haven't got round to getting biscuits yet."

"Oh ... no biscuits." She brushed at her skirt as if the filth of my lower-class ways were falling like ash.

"Kassey, would you like to take Maureen through to the lounge room?"

"Only if it's no trouble, dear." Maureen looked as if I'd passed her a handful of worms and she backed out of the kitchen. I was sure she would have escaped if I'd given her a chance but I was damned if I would be bullied by this strange mixture of kindness and judgement. Kassey stood there awkwardly, rubbing her hands between her knees, going very red. I nodded and waved her into the lounge room and she shrugged and disappeared. Maureen toddled off, swinging her bag, and I made two teas and a hot chocolate.

"Yes, I'm in class seven," Kassey was saying in a stilted, awkward way.

"Oh, yes, they call them classes now, don't they. Why they can't call them standards like we used to, I don't know."

"Yes, change is awkward," I said, setting mugs down.

"And unnecessary. So unnecessary. Thank you, dear. And do you work?"

"Yes ..."

"Mmm, all these mothers working when they should be home with their children. It's such ..."

"It is necessary as there's no one else to provide for us. I refuse to go on the dole."

"I didn't mean ... you know ... admirable you aren't taking from the state ..."

"So what do you do, Maureen. Do you have a career?"

"Yes, my George was an inspector at the Ipswich Council. Twenty-eight years, dear George."

"Oh, sorry, is he ... gone?"

"No, no, dear. Golfing today. So what do you do?"

"Look, I haven't thanked you properly for the pie. That's so generous. Thank you so, so, so much, Maureen."

"Oh, that's just what we do around here. Welcome folk to the street. A lovely group of people here, apart from that ... black family, two doors down."

"Are they a problem?"

"Well, they're black ..." She looked flushed, smiled without truth and picked up her cup with shaking hands. "So, what do you do for work, love?"

"I work at Kassey's school, at St Bede's."

"A teacher, such an important job for our young people."

"Well, not a teacher ..."

"And such a shame about Mr Cummings, that secretary of his reporting him to the police. Dirtying his name, such a nice man ..."

"Pardon?" My colour and hackles rose and I grabbed my mug tighter, nearly breaking it as anger threatened to rise up my throat and into my mouth. Okay, Janice, breathe. Just breathe. In, two, three, four. Out, two three, four.

"Yes, that vindictive woman who worked for him. Wanted to rub his name in the mud."

"Okay, hold it there, Maureen," I said, looking at Kassey, shrugging. She'd retreated to the back of the lounger, the expression on her face that of someone about to be beaten. My shrug was supposed to assure her but that didn't work. She looked terrified. But I had to go on and not let truth be buried. "I am that scarlet woman, and the police were investigating him and his gang well before I spoke up ..."

"Gang?" It came out of Maureen as more of a screech than a word.

"Of course. You don't think he was working on his own, do you?"

"Well ... well ... I ... I never thought. And you ..."

"Yes, it took a lot of courage to speak up for all those young girls."

"Young girls? He'd never do anything like that. Such a good man in our community. I can't believe it." She stood quickly, as if she'd sat on a needle. "Gosh, look at the time. I ... I really must go." She brushed her beige skirt again, grabbed her bag and toddled to the door. Kassey and I looked at each other in mute confusion. With my confusion was rage. And a fear of the possible consequences. We lived near a gossip, wherever her house was, and her husband had been a part of the council for 28 years, a man of obvious influence. And we were two women alone.

It sounds cowardly but I needed to get away, to leave the house. The only place I could think of was the safety of the Lucky Café.

"She's awful, isn't she, Mum."

"She's certainly frightened of something, love. And frightened people do ugly things."

"Aren't you frightened?" Her expression, as she stared up at me, told me she was as shocked as I was frightened.

"Actually, love, I am a bit frightened. And I'm mainly worried about the future, about what could happen. Then I have to remind myself that over 90 percent of the things I ever worried about didn't even happen."

"Riiiiight," she said.

"You can be frightened, but that doesn't have to be how you make decisions."

"What? That's weird ..."

"Maybe, maybe not. So, let's try this. If you were really frightened that Maureen was going to bring some bad people here to hurt us, what would you want to do?"

"I'd run, Mum. Get out. We should go ..."

"So that's the fear deciding for you."

"Mmm, maybe."

"So then, if you focus on this little moment right now, not thinking about past or future, just about right here and now, in this lounge room on the lounger with me and your cup of hot chocolate, how do you feel?"

"Mmm, well, better. Safe?"

"And peaceful?"

"I suppose so."

"See, we can be frightened about the future or what might happen, but we can always bring ourselves back to this little moment, right where and when we are, to make the next decision with peace in our heart."

"That's cool, Mum, sort of ... but, if I'm peaceful, I still want to go out."

"Where to?"

"To that café."

"Lucky Café?"

"Yeah, that one."

"So, if we're going there from fear, we're running away from something bad. But, if we're doing it from peace, we're going towards something good. It's a more constructive action, not a destructive one."

"Yeah, maybe." She was shaking her head slightly, as if to shake the doubts out. I didn't think it was working as her twisted smile suggested more doubt.

"Both fear and peace say go to the Lucky Café so let's go."

"That's what I said in the first place, Mum."

"I know, but we're going for a different reason - we're going to find something good and not to escape something bad, right?"

"Mmm, if you say so."

Rosie Visits

On our way to the Lucky Café, we got as far as the roadside where our car was parked when a lady pulled up behind ours. She leapt out, her curly tangle of black hair and huge smile impossible to be afraid of.

"Hi, I was just passing and had meant to call in to welcome you to the street," she said, looking around before coming up to us. "I'm a neighbour, two away." I grabbed her outstretched hand gladly, feeling somehow she was a kindred spirit. "I'm Rosie."

"Janice and this is Kassey."

"Hello, Kassey, and what beautiful, straight hair you've got. Not like my tangle of barbed wire."

"Hello. Are you ..." said Kassey, at once animated and shy.

"Is she what, love?" I asked, trying to encourage her out of the shell she usually hid in with strangers. She looked at me and I smiled and nodded my tacit permission.

"Are you, like, Tim's mum?"

"Yes. Are you in his class?"

"No. I think he's in 12B. I'm in 12A. But we're in phys. ed. together."

"Of course. He inherited his father's sporting body and not so much my brains. He also finds some teachers ... well ..."

"Challenging?" I suggested.

"Oops, I might have said too much and we've just met," she said, wiping back an errant tangle of curls, which immediately returned across her right eye. "And we're already on that subject."

"Sorry." I suddenly remembered my manners as this flurry of joy lifted my spirits, despite her stumbling over words in obvious embarrassment. "Look, would you like a cup of tea?" I looked at Kassey, hoping she'd be okay with changing our plans and inviting a stranger into our house. She smiled and shrugged and I think that meant it was okay with her.

"That'd be sweet but I'd better move my car."

"That's okay. We're not going anywhere."

"You don't mind the neighbours seeing my car outside your place?"

"No, why?"

"Well, okay, some think I'm the worst thing since unsliced bread because of my skin." She held her hands out as if not understanding such an attitude.

"Look, you can't help having brown skin any more than I can help having blue eyes. Bugger the neighbours ... oops, I'd better be quiet!"

"Mum!" chided Kassey but she quickly joined our giggling as we went inside.

"Actually, do you have coffee?" asked Rosie, once inside the kitchen.

"Yes." I showed her the jar.

"Oh, instant. I've bought one of those new plungers and I love that coffee. I think I'm a caddict."

"What?" asked Kassey, and I smiled as I got mugs out of the cupboard.

"A coffee addict. A caddict. But instant coffee is fine, Janice. So, Kassey, let's get out of your mum's way so you can tell me about your latest project at school." She steered Kassey into the lounge and I was surprised Kassey went along so willingly.

"We're studying the boring Incas."

"Aha, Machu Picchu and Hiram Bingham and all that?"

"Gosh, you know all about that?"

"I read, dear. I love research, and the Incas are a fascinating race of people. Not boring at all."

"Gosh ..." And off they went, swapping what they knew about the Incas. It was the most animated I'd seen Kassey in a long time. I took longer than I needed to as my heart filled with gratitude and my eyes filled with tears, hearing their happy exchange. Then I wiped my eyes and took the coffees in.

"Sorry, we don't have biscuits yet."

"No worries. Here, Kassey, go fish in the white bag in my back seat. You'll find Tim Tams there."

"But you ..."

"Na, love, they're probably melting anyway. Better in here, right?"

Kassey leapt up with a huge smile on her face and was gone.

"So, you seemed to be implying that your son isn't doing very well, academically ... do you mind me asking?"

"Not a problem, Janice. And I blurt it all out and we've just met. I feel comfortable with you, somehow." She looked away as if considering her next words or if she should say anything at all. She looked back at me. "See, that phys. ed. guy ..."

"Glynn?"

"Yeah, him. He's great with the kids. Treats them all the same, pushes them hard but makes it so enjoyable for them. But Tim's form teacher and English teacher ..."

"Sonia?"

"Oh, right, you know them." She looked embarrassed again, as if she'd said too much. She quickly sat back, her hand over her mouth, looking worried.

"I work in the office and it's okay. I know what they're all like. You're not telling me anything new."

She put her hand down and smiled, leaning forward again. "Yeah, well, her form teacher ..."

"Sonia. Look, I really shouldn't say this but we seem to be in the same ... I don't know ... same thinking. We call her Snooty Sonia."

Her head went back and the most raucous laugh came out as Kassey returned. I couldn't help but join in and Kassey, who had no idea of the joke, joined in too. The room rang with our laughter.

"So, you worked at the school, under Cummings?" she asked as our laughter died down.

"Yes I did, and I was the one who pimped on him." After Maureen's reaction, I was sick of caring what people thought. The idea of stirring people up gave me a tingle of naughtiness.

"You weren't the person, actually. You were last in a long line."

"What? Really?" Not the response I was expecting from Rosie.

"Lots in the community and a few at the school had reported him to the police and the Health Department. I reported him when one of my patients came in with injuries from resisting his and Tommo's advances."

"Tommo?" I had so many questions.

"Sergeant Thomlinson."

"Oh no, not him! We saw him today again, at the Lucky Café."

"He's yukky," said Kassey, shuddering.

"You're right, Kassey and I were surprised he was there. He hates the place."

"He tried telling Constable Markham off."

"Yes, Marky's a good fella. He's one of our mob."

"You're in the same Aboriginal tribe?"

"We're all Jagera round here."

"Right. So, you said a patient. Are you a nurse?"

"No, I'm a cleaner at the hospital."

"No you're not." She didn't look like a cleaner at all, somehow. "I don't believe you."

"You're one of the first not to. You'd be surprised at how many white people expect me to be a cleaner."

"Why?" asked Kassey.

"Because I'm black, love."

"But that's stupid."

"Maybe, but people only know what they know. I mean, people sincerely believed they could drink asbestos sodas and fluoride till we found out how carcinogenic they are."

"Carcino-what?"

"Carcinogenic. They cause cancer. If you've never met an Aboriginal doctor, if you've only seen us as cleaners and labourers ..."

"You're a doctor?" I asked, interrupting, realising what she'd said.

"Yes, a paediatrician."

"God," I said, and immediately regretted it.

"God what?" Rosie asked, looking me in the eye.

God, alright. How do I dig my way out of this one, I wondered I blushed scarlet and looked awkward, despite my desperate attempts to look cool and calm.

"Oh, God, this is so embarrassing," I said, realising I'd been rumbled. Get it out and over with, girl. "I didn't imagine that you were a doctor."

"Why not?" Her eyes kept challenging me.

"I suppose I don't know any female doctors. Nurses yes, doctors no."

"Aw, hell!" yelled Rosie and then she burst out laughing and then coughing on the Tim Tam she'd been chewing. Kassey and I couldn't help but laugh along with her though I didn't get the joke. Her joy was infectious. Finally, we all calmed down.

"Sorry guys, I thought it was my black skin."

"Well, it might have been a bit, I admit, but you're the only woman doctor I've met."

"The first female paediatrician in Queensland and the first black paediatrician in Australia."

"Wow, that's impressive ..."

"Not as impressive as putting up with all the abuse and put-downs from the white doctors and neighbours."

"I bet."

"And thanks for not backing away from my black skin."

"Huh?"

"Well, you admitted it might be a factor. That's the most honest anyone's been with me."

"Thanks." I realised tears were forming in her eyes and I was embarrassed for her. And confused. "You mean no one mentions you've got brown skin?"

"Only to insult me. Never to talk about, like it's ordinary. Not good or bad ... I don't know ... they just never have."

"And now they have." I forced a smile through my confusion.

"God, you're pretty bloody special, aren't you."

"Aw, come on ..."

"You think so, don't you, Kassey? Your mum's pretty special, huh?"

Kassey smiled shyly and leant into me while I looked everywhere but at them, the scarlet of embarrassment pouring up my neck and over my face. I could feel the expanding heat as my lip quivered and I swiped at my wet eyelids.

"So, how about you get up off your big, white bum."

"Big?" we both giggled through our tears.

"Yeah, huge! And give us a hug. Then I've got to go as my next shift starts at two o'clock."

As Rosie strode out to her car, I said to Kassey, "Well, she's a tornado and a half, isn't she?"

"Sure is, Mum," said Kassey, laughing. "She's funny."

Back to Lucky

Ten minutes later, we drove to the Lucky Café because it still seemed the right thing to do.

"They're probably closed by now," I said as we drove out of Bundara Street.

"But they might not be." Kassey had the biggest, cheesiest smile plastered on her face and I glowered back in mock-annoyance. I was amused she remembered so many of the things I'd said to her over the years.

"Smarty pants," I said and we both giggled. My giggle was partly in relief to be out of that house. Yes, Rosie was a neighbour, but so was Maureen and I felt the silence on the street, as if everyone was hiding behind their curtains, peering out. I was becoming paranoid but I couldn't shake the feeling that the bottom of Moores Pocket Road, backing onto farmland and more remote, was safer than Bundara Street, only five minutes from the police station and the centre of town.

"I don't like our new street, Mum." I twisted my head to look at her and then looked back at the road, spinning the wheel right to avoid the curb I was careening towards.

Note to self, I thought, focus on one thing at a time. I breathed out heavily and went all hot and cold, thinking of the near miss. And wondering how Kassey read my thoughts so often.

"They're not there," said Kassey, skipping ahead. My heart lifted to see a bounce in her step.

"Yes. Samuel and Marky have gone," said a tall, slim man with a mane of black hair, some of it flopping in his eyes. He flicked it away and waved us to a table by the window. "The best view in Ipswich for people-watching and, if you want to just sit and relax, no need to buy anything."

"Thank you, but do you have tea?"

"What, tea in a café? What blasphemy!" He looked genuinely shocked, his hand going to his chest. Then he burst out laughing. "Sorry, ma'am, but you'll get used to me ..."

"No you won't," said a woman who appeared from nowhere, smacking him a backhander on the shoulder. She must have been the same age as him, mid-fifties, and as stout as he was thin. "I've known this mad fish for eight years and I'm still not used to him. Now, I'm Sarah and this is my husband, Geoffrey."

"Thank you, dear."

"I'm Janice and this is Kassey," I said.

"Pleased to make your acquaintance," said Geoffrey, bending towards Kassey and extending his hand. Then he pulled it back as she was about to grab it. He chortled and extended it to her again. Kassey giggled and shook his hand. I was pleased she hadn't been put off all men and this one exuded so much fun and caring, he was hard to resist. "So, I shall toil, set the kettle to boil and you ladies can chat a whoil."

"It's okay if you're busy, Sarah," I said. "We needed to get away from our house for a while."

"It's icky and creepy," said Kassey.

"Well, one of our neighbours, Rosie, is lovely ..."

"You're in Bundara Street?" Sarah's eyebrows shot up and she smiled. "And you've met our favourite nosey parker? No need to mention names."

I nodded. "Mmm, she wasn't thrilled that I'd reported the headmaster ... I presume that's who you mean."

"Oh hell, you're the one!"

My heart sank like a brick and I got ready to run. I couldn't deal with more criticism.

"Thank God for courageous people." She patted me on the shoulder, and my shoulders and jaw relaxed again.

"I didn't do any more than Rosie did."

"But you did something."

"Well, yes, but at the same time the police investigation was rounding up suspects. It was just timing."

"But you didn't know about the police operation at the time?"

"No."

"And you did it. The straw on the camel's back, Janice."

"Well ..."

"Don't go well with me, Janice. It took a lot of courage, I'll bet."

"Yes, I suppose so. I thought about it for weeks. Then it got too much and I didn't have a choice."

"We always have a choice and that vice-principal didn't do it. I'm not judging her as we don't know what's in her past but you both had a choice and you made the brave one."

"I don't feel very brave."

"None of us do, Janice, but we've just got to wake up and get up, every day. Look, are you hungry?"

"Mum?" asked Kassey, looking at me and nodding.

"Actually, I think we've only had biscuits and tea today. It's been a topsy-turvy day. A bit unexpected."

"Do you like pizza?" asked Sarah.

"Uh, I've never had it. Kassey?"

"No, I mean yes, can we have it, Mum?"

"I didn't bring much money ..."

"It's our shout as a thank you. Young lass ..." said Sarah, frowning.

"Kassey," I said.

"That's right, Kassey. A milkshake? Vanilla?"

Kassey bounced up and down on her chair and she stared at Sarah, imploring. Perhaps I've been too careful with our meagre finances sometimes, I thought.

"I don't think I've ever bought you a milkshake have I, love?"

"Right! That's decided." Sarah wiped her hands on her blue and white checked apron and bounced off as if she'd won Lotto.

"This is a lucky café, isn't it, Mum." Kassey's huge smile wasn't going anywhere.

"Looks like it, today." I still felt awkward accepting charity but I couldn't dampen Kassey's joy, especially after the last week or so.

"One pot of tea here and a milkshake is coming up, young lady," said Geoffrey.

"Kassey," said Kassey, obviously feeling safer given that she was speaking up again.

"Of course, Kassey. It shall be Kassey from now on." Then Geoffrey was gone and I looked around and noticed that none of the tables matched - all colourful and all

different. Same with the chairs. Same with the patrons -
some colourful, some not. Several smiled while I scanned
and I smiled back, feeling a mite embarrassed. I hoped they
didn't think I was snooping. I noticed Sarah talking to a
couple of people at different tables and them looking at me.
It was slightly disorientating and I didn't know what they
were thinking of me. Probably something bad.

"Mum, you used to tell me stories," said Kassey, breaking
my reverie.

"What? Oh, yes, I did," I said, wondering where that had
come from. "Why?"

"To make me feel better, I think." Her eyes held mine
with that particular look of hers, as if there was something I
should know and she wasn't telling me what it was.

"Gosh, I haven't told you any for ages."

"No." Still that look and I wondered what I was missing.
Then the penny dropped.

"Are you feeling scared, love?" I put my hand on hers as
her milkshake arrived. "Thank you, sir."

"Sir? Oh aye, don't get called that much," said the waiter
with a lovely Irish lilt with a rasp, like sandpaper rubbing
a dog. He was dressed respectfully in black trousers and a
black polo shirt but he looked like he'd just come from a
boxing ring - six foot two, built solid as an ox, red hair, ruddy
face with a bent, possibly broken, nose and several scars on
his face and fists. "I'm Sean."

"I'm going to guess you have a few stories to tell," I said,
wondering where my timidity had gone.

About to turn away, he stopped, looked at me and smiled. "Oh aye, me fists did me tinking and, now, dey obey me mind. Happy to tell you, lass, but I better go now."

"I'd love to hear them. Now, Kassey?"

"What?"

"Kassey, say thank you."

"Thank you," said Kassey without her beautiful smile.

"Dat's okay, lass," said Sean. The pizza will be here soon."

"What's going on, Kassey?" I asked as Sean strode back to the kitchen.

"Mum. Duh."

"Just tell me, love."

After a scowling sigh she said, "I'm scared, Mum."

"You're really scared?"

"Mum, like, we've had bricks in the window, icky men in the playground, poo in the mailbox, classmates not coming back, that horrible lady up the road, that fat policeman ..."

"And a story will help?"

"Mum! I don't know ... I just ..."

I realised she was close to tears and leant over to hug her with all my might.

"I'm sorry. I thought being here with friends ..." I started to say.

"They're not friends. We're alone."

"We're not. We have people on our side now."

"How do you know, Mum?"

"Know what?"

"That they'll be friends? That they won't desert us?"

"Oh, honey, like your father? And Morris?"

"And Nana and your father."

"Oh, Kassey, you've had too many people leaving you," I said, finally realising where her fears were arising from. "Did you think I'd leave you?"

"No." Still she didn't smile but I breathed out, not realising I'd been holding my breath while I asked the hardest question.

"And there's no way of knowing if these new people will stay friends or leave us. That what you're thinking?" I felt it was best to get the worst out on the table right then and there.

"Mmm." The minimal response of a shut-down mind, a mind afraid to open and risk too much.

"Well, I'm sorry, love, but there's no way we can ever tell if a new friend will always be there ..."

"Happy pizza to you, happy pizza to you, happy pizza dear Janice and Kassey, happy pizza to you," said several voices behind us as a huge round thing was plonked on our table, hot and delicious smelling. I looked up and we were surrounded by Geoffrey, Sarah and some of their motley assortment of customers. I looked between them and realised I was wrong - it was all of their customers. The rest of the café was now empty. Kassey looked startled, looking at me and the various revellers around our table. Her uncertain smile turned into a real one, a full one, and then it seemed she didn't know where to look - at the pizza, at me, at each of these strangers who could be long-term friends but who we didn't know yet.

Many pats on my back and shoulders and I knew I was going to cry. Damn it! In front of all these strangers? I thought.

"This is a ritual, Janice, that you must hug everyone around your table," said Sarah, which was exactly what I wanted to do. I leapt up and grabbed her buxom body and cried into her wide shoulder. "And you've got to cry on all of us so nobody feels left out. You'd better get moving - all of us." She and others chuckled. I was happy to obey and so I did. The first was Sean - the cheeky bugger must have rushed out and then back with the pizza. The next was a man in a tatty array of clothes, possibly homeless. Then a man nearly as tall as Sean but wearing a checked shirt hanging out and with an unkempt hair and beard. The next two women were in nice, casual clothes, possibly mums or teachers. One woman was wearing a clinical uniform. One man was in a suit. They seemed quite unsuited to one another and, in any other place, would have been sitting apart, or even socialising in different cafés. They must, I reasoned, have something in common, something bigger than their occupations and statuses. Then I noticed Kassey following me around the circle, looking as happy as I'd ever seen her, hugging everyone.

"Okay, 'nough hugging," said Geoffrey. "Tuck into your pizza before it freezes to death."

Kassey and I sat, still looking around at everyone, still abuzz with the unexpected displays of kindness.

"Do you have knives and forks?" I asked.

"Knife and fork? Does your mother know nothing?" asked Geoffrey, sitting next to Kassey. They both chuckled. "Rip a section out and devour it with a happy sigh."

So we did. Between mouthfuls of this delicious new food, I had a thought. "There must be lots of others you've celebrated with, who've done good things, so how long has this ritual been going?"

"About five minutes," said Sarah, smiling and wiping her eyes.

"What?"

"You're the first."

"Mmm," I said, chomping into a delicious section of pizza. "I had a niggling suspicion, you cheeky buggers. You should do this for Rosie."

"Maybe we should, but today is your moment, Janice." Sarah sat in the fourth chair.

"You deserve it, mate," said a woman behind me, patting my shoulder.

"You might have saved lots of children," said the scruffy-haired man.

"And heartache for their parents," said the suit man.

"Hey, hey, stop this, please," I said, feeling choked up and a bit ambushed and claustrophobic with them clamouring around me. And their comments, nice as they were. "Yes, I did tell the cops - the wrong cop - and that's all I did. I didn't save the world and any saving that was done was by the police who had been investigating for months."

"Years," said Geoffrey, across the table.

"Pardon?"

"The police ... some police ... have been on this for years."

"Years?"

"When they catch one cell of this organisation, another pops up in another place and another guise."

"Geoffrey!" I said, staring at him and nodding towards Kassey. I realised where this conversation was going and knew that Kassey had had quite enough to scare her without him embroidering the negative, true as it might have been.

"Yeah, sorry." He looked embarrassed and sat back, his palm over his mouth.

"Let's think about some solutions." I looked around and it was suit man talking. James, I think his name was, if I remembered correctly from our introductory hug. Quite a nice hug, actually.

"So, you have the grapevine number?"

"The what?" I asked.

"You don't, obviously," he said kindly, his deep, resonant voice somehow carrying authority with it. He handed me a business card with nothing on it but a phone number. "Ring this number if you ever need help."

"Whose is it?"

"It's everyone's."

"Huh?" Everyone smiled at my confusion.

"You tell her, Phil."

"Yeah, well, I fixed up a bit of wiring so that one phone call gets us all. Simple stuff," said this Phil, in the tatty array of clothes. It had to have been a week since he'd shaved.

"Phil worked for Telecom and is actually a bit of a genius with technology."

"Oh, well," said Phil, nodding shyly.

"You are and you can't deny it, mate. It seems Telecom omitted to take a few keys and access codes back when Phil left. So he subcontracts his telephonic skills," said James, doing the two-finger thing when he said subcontracts.

"It's okay, Kassey," I said when she frowned at me, clearly confused by all the banter. "I'll explain it all later. Now, this pizza is delicious but I can't finish it. Do you want any more, Kassey?"

"It's nice, Mum," she said, grabbing up another segment to fill her hollow legs.

"We can put the rest in a doggy bag," said Sarah.

"Doggy bag?" Kassey frowned at her, looking confused.

"The health inspectors say we're not allowed to let humans take food from the premises as it might immediately transform into something toxic or lethal when it goes out the door. However, we're allowed to give customers the same food if it's for their pets."

"We don't have any pets," said Kassey, screwing up her nose in confusion, or in delight at the pizza she was demolishing. Or both.

"But we don't know that," said Geoffrey, chuckling and tapping his nose with his finger.

"I'll explain when we get home," I said to Kassey's continued nose screwing-up. She shook her head, shrugged and kept eating.

"So, we do need to clean up," said Geoffrey and everyone rushed our table, and the other tables, to take crockery and cutlery to the kitchen for washing. In 10 minutes the washing was done, the tables were wiped clean and the outside tables, chairs and sign were stashed inside. This was an operation they'd obviously done before.

"They're a bit weird but a bit nice," said Kassey as we got to our car, holding the doggie bag of remaining pizza.

"I'll follow you home, if you like," said James over the roof of his BMW.

"It's only minutes away," I said, unsure why I needed his help.

His offer reminded me of a promise I had made myself three years before - no more men. Why was I thinking about that now? I soon found out why it was a good idea to have him there that night.

Reminisce One - Unwanted

Hey stop, ya little bugger!" yelled a cop behind me as I fled up the wide, concrete incline out of the Ipswich Railway Station. I dodged between the legs of evening commuters, some cursing and others trying to grab me as I bumped their briefcases or handbags. Just as neural pathways and the body's other defences will activate whether we are sick or are imagining we are, so my face and actions always betrayed guilt whether I had done something wrong or not. Usually I had. Persistent guilt does that. So, looking guilty, I was always presumed to be so.

Out of the station, I headed for the Bridge Gang who accepted me, and not home to Mum, Dad and my older sister who grudgingly tolerated me.

Mum and Dad constantly blamed each other for their own particular deficiencies. When Bronwyn arrived - I think they had her to free them from their confined, critical world - she showered clear blue skies, sunshine and eternal happiness on them, just by being there. By being her. She lived up to the promise they thought she had made to them - don't we all? - and was always the perfect child. Her perfect nails and hairdo and, later, perfect heels, handbags, twinset and pearls guaranteed her place in our parents' Hall of Fame.

I arrived nearly three years after Bronwyn and it seemed that I was born - my fault, not theirs - to cast a cold shadow over every ray of sunlight that Bronwyn ever shone. She could do nothing wrong and I could do nothing right and, like her, I lived up to the promise they think I made them. Where Bronwyn was in their Hall of Fame, I was in their Hall of Shame.

It was lucky that school records didn't enumerate kindness, happiness and friends, for Bronwyn would have had an imperfect school record. Anyway, I'm being bitchy because her 'perfect' school record led her to perfecting the looks of others. She eventually had her own salon where she mainly attended to perms, blue rinses and those whose unchanging fashions were rooted in the year of their birth.

Bronwyn then married Gregory, Mr Perfect, with the perfect job of accountant. They bought a nice house in the swanky suburb of Paddington, close to Brisbane's centre and to Gregory's office. They produced a perfect boy and girl, Graham and Deborah, who were the apple of their grandparents' eyes. The last I heard, though, was that they'd turned perfect upside down and become right little shits by skipping school and doing drugs, alcohol and all those things their mother never dreamed of doing. I don't know whether this is true, however, as I haven't seen any of them for a few years.

Bronwyn could never bring herself to approve of or accept my husband, Deryk, whose attire never improved beyond t-shirts and his occupation as a drainlayer. Then his death from the drugs he'd fallen in love with was the final straw. Mind you, if she hadn't turned away, I would have. The embarrassment was too much for me. I retreated from pretty much everyone I knew at the time.

Without a safe place to fall at home, I sought parent substitutes from my peer group, a group that was far from perfect but at least it was a group, something that Bronwyn never had. We were all around 12 years old, and we became known as the Bridge Gang because we usually camped under the Ipswich railway bridge or in the cavernous, concrete carpark nearby. Our territory was wide enough that we could usually stay out of reach of police and parents who seemed to be constantly after at least one of us.

From about my fourteenth birthday, I realised my expanding breasts were a great way to lure in the attention I craved. I allowed way too many boys to fumble with them while they heaved up and down above me. I always imagined sex would be a real gas but it consistently left me high and dry, wanting more and feeling unwanted and useless ... the same way I felt with my parents.

Wanted kids always get jobs they want and unwanted kids always get jobs they don't want. Accordingly, I started in a bakery, from 4:30 am till school started. I hated the early starts and the heat but I loved that it got me out of the house when the daily breakfast sermon on how-to-be-good-like-your-sister was always the imperfect start to my day.

I left school as soon as I could, at 15, and worked in a tearooms during the day. But it didn't take long to feel my brain drying up and I knew I had to do something with it. So, after a year of procrastination, and my parents saying I couldn't, I enrolled in a secretarial course at TAFE. I worked as a hotel cleaner at nights to pay my way, and surprised everyone - me more than anyone - by topping the class. Maybe it was the amazing teacher, Miss Massey, who saw more in me than I ever did and pushed and shoved and had me in tears many a time. But she didn't give up on me and the tears were always followed by stupid, big grins as I passed yet another test. She was the first person to ever believe in me and I gave her name to my daughter in gratitude. Karen Massey came to Kassey's birth and to every single birthday. Thinking about her now, I don't know why I didn't ask for her help more often. Maybe I didn't want her to see me fail, only wanting to show her my happy side. She did come to our rusty caravan when we lived there, our lowest point. So, really, there wasn't much I could hide from her. She probably knew more than I let on but respected me not to butt in when I didn't ask her.

Shocked, amazed, stunned and astounded that I did so well in secretarial study - that I even finished, let alone topped the class - I was eager to continue with something else while my neurons were still firing and my enthusiasm was up. I then enrolled in a creative writing class at TAFE, for there was always a part of me wanting to be a writer - author of books, journalist for a newspaper, contributor to magazines or whatever. I wanted to write and Karen's encouragement and my success where I never thought I'd have it - academically - sent me off with higher ambitions.

I did the writing course, loved it but took it nowhere as Deryk turned up - the love of my life. He thought all artists were a waste of space as they did nothing useful. I went along with him while a small part of my soul fell away. Teenage love, huh?

I remembered that it was Karen who encouraged me to go to that Zen meditation weekend. God, that was so good. I don't know why I kept dropping it and then returning to it. I should have stuck with it right through as I made much better decisions when I was centred and empty. When I was feeling happy, I would give it up. Yes, it was on one of those giving up periods that I met Deryk in the pub I was cleaning.

They say that the location of your first meeting sets the pattern for your future relationship. Meeting Deryk at the pub was an accurate precursor to our embattled marriage, as he was constantly unfaithful. He paid much more attention to beer glasses and the lines of white sniffing powder.

Like so many young marrieds, I suppose, I saw it as my mission to change him, to improve him, but just like all other hopefuls, I failed miserably. Miserable is the best single word to describe the experience.

The one shaft of light in that six-year tunnel of gloom was Kassey, who arrived about the time I realised Project Deryk was a lost cause. Kassey was one person I could imprint perfection on, to prove my own perfection. Two years later, in a drugged-out stupor, Deryk walked off the platform of the Beenleigh station and a commuter train sent him to the big drug den in the sky.

The Housing Commission felt sorry for me and found me a nice house in Loganholme in Brisbane's poorer south, between a motorbike gang boss and a young couple who had all their arguments with fists.

From that first night there I was terrified and, all too soon, I moved into Morris's place. He didn't drink or smoke and I clung to him like a drowning cat. I clung for too long, I see now, for his apparent cleanliness and sobriety hid a worse addiction - Kassey. She was only seven when I first saw him tickling her in bed in an unsavoury way. I excused it, telling myself I wasn't seeing straight and/or I was making up stories that didn't exist. But they did. Eventually, I had to admit I'd made a dreadful mistake. I couldn't leave him alone with her and I daily shudder to imagine his grease- and oil-ingrained hands anywhere near her.

He'd wanted to take her to his work to show her off to his mechanic mates, but I couldn't allow it. The first time I said NO was the first time he hit me and, like his 'tickling', I pretended the slap was an anomaly. But it wasn't and the slaps, kicks and punches became more frequent, regular and painful. The last time, he left me unconscious and a neighbour, Marci, saw me on the floor through the window when Kassey's screams increased enough in volume for her to visit. Morris was taken off in handcuffs, but I didn't know about it for the 27 hours it took me to regain consciousness.

I took Kassey and the little we had to the nearest camping ground and, a year later, the Housing Commission found me another house 50 kilometres away in Moores Pocket Road, Ipswich, back to where I'd started my life.

I made a promise to myself that I wouldn't have another man in my house, in my bed or in my life. Ever.

The Inspector Visits

They're sort of not normal, Mum," said Kassey as we pulled out of the carpark, she in her usual curled up mode on the passenger seat. James followed in his BMW.

"Kassey ..." I wasn't sure where this conversation was going.

"No, I mean ... you know, not, like, bad or anything."

"Different?"

"Mmm, different, I suppose. But, like, they're all different."

"From one another?"

"Yeah, I don't know. But they're nice and friendly."

"And you feel safe with them?"

"Safe? Yeah, I suppose so."

"And honest?"

"Oh, Mum, I just wanted to say, I dunno ..."

"Sorry, I was trying to work out what you meant."

"It's okay." She sat up from her slouch. "But most adults always have, like, sunglasses on."

"Not sure what you mean, love."

"I don't know how to say it ... like, you don't really know what they're thinking, and what they say isn't what they mean. Like, when they're just saying things to make you happy or so that you like them."

"Right. And the sunglasses?" I asked as we turned into Bundara Street.

"I don't know how to explain it."

"I think you're doing really well, love."

"Really?" Her eyes went wide and happy. "But these lucky people we met today, they're wearing clear glasses and you can see right through them. They don't have to hide."

"You know, Kassey, that's one of the most intelligent and insightful things I've ever heard." I turned into our driveway and James followed.

"Looks like everything's fine," I said as he caught up to us at the front door.

"Do you want us to check inside?"

"What?" I snapped, suddenly angry for no reason. His comment made me more scared than I already was and I didn't like being contradicted. "Do you know something I don't?"

"No I don't, Janice. Just being careful." He didn't try to pat me like a pet dog, like my ex used to do when he thought I was a mere woman needing the protection of his manliness.

"Sorry, I'm ... don't know. Jumpy." I was conflicted; nervous about what could be inside and thinking it'd be nice if he came in, until I remembered my promise - no men.

"Right. Shall I wait here while you look?" He didn't even try to tell me what I was thinking or why I reacted like I did. The thermometer of his approval rating was inching up.

"Look, I'm sure it's okay but thanks."

"Okay, if you're sure." He turned to go and I breathed out in relief that I hadn't had to defend myself in any way. Mr Nopressure hadn't tried to talk me into something, or made me doubt myself. Then he turned at the bottom of the steps. "And you've got the number?"

"Yes, I've memorised it."

Kassey then reeled off the number and he gave us a wide-eyed smile.

"I always remember numbers," I said, and nearly added, "and kind men." But I bit my lip on that one.

"Wow, that's impressive. Both of you."

We all waved goodbye and Kassey and I looked at each other before we crossed the threshold. Then we shrugged and entered a perfectly ordinary, two-bedroom, Australian house, exactly as we'd left it.

"God, it's 4 o'clock and I won't need any dinner. I'm full as a bull. How about you, love?"

"I'm full, too. Can I watch TV?"

"Yes, let's blob out and be grateful we've met some nice people without sunglasses, huh."

She smiled, turned on the TV and then threw herself into a corner of the leather lounger, her usual curled-up pose when she wasn't snuggling up to me.

"Hey, Kassey!"

"What, Mum?" Kassey looked appropriately startled at my untimely outburst.

"Sorry love," I said, patting her knee. "I just remembered Karen Massey."

"That old lady?"

"She's not that old. Maybe 50 or so"

"That's really old, Mum."

"If you say so. I thought I had no friends but I just thought of her and how good she's been to me."

"Old people can be cool, Mum."

"Sorry," I said, pretending to be admonished. Karen Massey had always come to me, often turning up when I was going through bad times. She'd always come to me; I'd never reached out to her. When I thought about it, I'd never been there for her. Never really asked how she was, because she seemed to sail through life as if nothing bad ever happened to her. Maybe it was the meditation that gave her the serenity.

"Do you want to go and see her?" I asked.

"What? Now?"

"Well, probably not. I'll see if she's free."

"We've never been to her place, Mum."

"I know. She's always come to us. But we have five days before work and school start." Kassey shrugged and her eyes swung back to the TV. It wasn't a 'no' from her so I rang and got no answer, only the ring, ring, ring.

"I'll call her later."

"What about ringing her at work?" asked Kassey, her eyes still riveted to the TV. Her neurons were firing quicker than mine, despite the diversion of TV. I don't know how young people do the multitasking thing.

"She used to finish at 4 o'clock. I'll ring the office anyway."

"Miss Massey? Are you a relative?" answered the TAFE receptionist.

"Oh." I was taken aback by the question that sounded like it had been marinated in bad news.

"Are you still there?"

"Yes, yes, I am. Look, I'm not a relative but an ex-student and she's visited me many times since 1969. We're good friends."

"Are you Janice Brown?"

"Yes." A shaft of hope pierced my gathering gloom.

"She specifically mentioned you."

"In relation to what?" My heart had come loose and was trying to choke me.

"She's in hospital ..."

"What? She's had an accident?"

"No, it's more long term than that, shall we say."

"Oh, hell."

"Yes, we're all devastated, Janice. But she said we could tell you where she is. She's such a private person."

"Which hospital?"

"Ipswich."

"Ipswich? But that's where I live!"

"Yes, she's lived there a long time."

"Hell ... aah, thanks so much. So much. I'll visit her now."

"I'm sure she'd love that."

How the hell didn't I know she lived here? Had I really been so absorbed in my own dramas that I'd never inquired? I leaned against the wall by the phone and stared out the lounge room window, then dragged myself over to the lounger and sat, staring at the busy TV, not seeing any of it and feeling empty and angry with myself, if both feelings could coexist. Hell, I must be the worst friend out. It's a wonder she ever wanted to see me. God!

"God what, Mum?" Oops, I must have been thinking aloud. "Mum?"

"Sorry, love, I feel so awful right now. Karen Massey is in Ipswich Hospital with something serious and she's lived here for years. I never knew."

"You do now."

Practical child.

"Am I such a bad friend? I never asked about her. Or, if I did, I don't remember." My mind kept going round and round about the awful person I'd been to Miss Massey over the past 14 years. Fourteen years? And I never knew. I never asked. Not once. God!

"Mum, go and see her."

"Yes, yes, of course." Kassey's logic broke the circular ravings of my mind. "I wonder if we can go in now."

"One way to find out." She was finally looking at me, not at the TV, her cheeky smile beaming.

So I rang and visiting hours were till 6 o'clock, an hour away.

◇ ◇

I opened the door and turned to hurry Kassey up.

"Mum," she said, standing there as if she'd seen a ghost. I looked around the door and was face to face with a pufferfish, all blown up and spiky. He didn't have the wobbling fat of Sergeant Thomlinson but rather, the tight roundness of a blown-up soccer ball on legs. There had been a neck there, originally, but it was now absorbed by a large, florid head and a pink mouth that was stammering.

"Pardon, sir?"

"You, you ..."

"Yes?" Perhaps he had trouble with bigger words.

"You insulted my wife."

"Yes, one of my favourite defects," I said, trying to fit the jigsaw of him and his wife (whoever she was) into my life. Nothing fitted. Then it did. His green and black tartan trousers, white shoes, bright-yellow polo shirt and maroon, sleeveless cardigan could only be worn by clowns and golfers. "Aah, you're Maureen's husband, right?"

"No, she's my wife and I don't appreciate you taking her to task ..."

"Hey, hey, climb out of your tree and let's talk some facts, okay?"

"There is no need for ..."

"Facts, Mr. Facts."

"You insulted her!"

"I did not but, for the sake of clarity, you tell me exactly what I said to her. Exactly."

"You kicked her out of your house."

"Incorrect, George."

"Hey, how'd you know my name?" The pufferfish struck a petulant pose and, if he'd had a chin, it would have been sticking out.

"Maureen told me when we were having tea together in my lounge room."

"She had a conversation with you? In there?"

"Yes, after she rearranged my kitchen, she proceeded to insult me for informing the police about suspicious activities against children."

"She didn't tell me that." He deflated by at least 20 pounds per square inch, looked around, back at me and then turned to the street. "Maureen!" he shouted. "Ya silly bitch!"

A front door opened across the street and there was Maureen, taking a tentative step out, nervously scrunching the floral apron she had on over her beige ensemble.

"Yes, George?" Her voice barely made it across the street, a faint memory of the strident one in my house.

"Did this lady insult you?"

"No, George."

"Why the hell did you say she did?"

"I didn't, George." Her voice trailed off as if trying to escape the scene.

"You bloody did, woman!"

"I said ..."

"Shut up and go inside!"

Maureen meekly obeyed and he turned back to me. "So, why are you interfering in our community?"

"I reported my valid concerns to the police and later found they were investigating the situation, well before I spoke up. As you know, George, the only people not wanting to deal with abuse are the abused and the abusers. Where do you and Maureen stand on that?"

"Are you implying ..."

"Come on, Kassey, we're done here," I said, taking her hand, locking the door and walking past him.

"Hey, woman, I haven't finished!" He puffed back up to full pressure.

"Well, talk to the mailbox then. We've got important business to attend to." I dragged a reluctant Kassey, who was tittering, having picked up my own reaction to stress.

"An you fraternating ..."

"Fraternising."

"Don't interrupt me, woman! Muckin' about with blacks." His little arm pointed at Gloria's place.

"That neighbour of ours who can't help having brown skin any more than you can help having pink skin?"

"You, you, you ..." he muttered. "I have considerable influence in this town and on the council."

"Thirty-eight years, huh?"

"Yeah ... how'd you know?"

"Maureen told me a lot about you, George," I said, stepping right up to him. "You've spent your life poking your nose in others' business. Maybe it's time someone looked into your business, George Inspector."

"That a threat?" Arms akimbo, legs apart, he looked a bit like my alarm clock.

"Get off my property or I'll have you charged with trespass. Now!" I shouted the last word and he jumped, looked around, looked back, waggled a fat, pink finger at me and waddled off wordlessly. As I went round to my driver's door, my eyes followed him and saw, for the first time, a BMW parked across the road, outside George and Maureen's house. James stepped out as George waddled in front of his car. George stopped momentarily and then waddled much faster into his house.

"Are you okay?" asked James as he walked up to me.

"Not really," I said with my hand on the door handle, shaking like Elvis' pelvis. "What are you doing here? And why?"

"You mentioned your chat with Maureen and I knew George would be after you."

"Have you been watching? I mean, how long?" I didn't know whether to feel grateful or spooked but I put my swirling emotions away for the moment and tried thinking practically. Logically. "Look, James, I'm in a hurry to get to the hospital and I'm really grateful but can we talk later?"

"Yes, of course." He stepped back off my driveway so I could back out. "Would you like me to pop back at, say, 6.30?"

"Yes, okay." I smiled and slid into my car, agreement being the path of least resistance. The path of least thinking, as I switched my mind back to Karen Massey.

"Are you okay, Mum?" asked Kassey a minute later as we approached Warwick Road.

"Not really, love." My hands were still shaking, my heart was doing flip-flops and my eyes kept frantically scanning behind and in front of me.

"You were awesome." She stared right at me and I looked furtively at her and then back to the road.

"Really? Are you okay?"

"Yeah, awesome." She patted my knee as I'd done to her a thousand times.

"Thanks, love." I looked at her as we stopped at the give way sign, my heart quieted and my quivering hands stilled. She had that effect on me when all the world had gone mad. My Peace Ambassador.

It turns out you're supposed to know the patient's illness and which ward they're in and their full name. And what colour their undies are as well, no doubt. I didn't know all of this about Karen. However, I eventually convinced the stern-faced, moustachioed madam at the reception counter I wasn't the Ipswich Chainsaw Murderer and she told us which direction to go. Once past this Nazi, the nursing staff were lovely. They couldn't have been more helpful, and a Nurse Hanlon went out of her way to take us down several pale green corridors, her and others' white shoes squeaking on the mottled green linoleum floor. The happy chatter at the nurses' station surprised me, given the gravity of the patients' situations. It almost seemed insolent in the face of the pain around them. But I'm not a doctor and could never be - I hate the sight of blood, injections and anything inside us being on the outside. I don't know how they do it without gagging or passing out every time they see vomit, blood or inside bits. So I stilled my instant judgement and soon discovered that the nurses' happy demeanours were exactly what those in pain, uncertainty and away from home needed.

We were handed over to Nicola, Nurse Brydon, who took us to Karen's four-bed room, the curtains the only privacy. Two beds were empty and perfectly made while thin curtains separated the other two. We waited while Nicola peered between curtains and asked the patient if she would like two visitors.

Karen's clear, English diction took me right back to so many times I'd doubted myself and her precise voice had returned me to certainty. I sniffed and blinked at the memory while my heart went soft and sweet.

"Are you Janice and Kassey?" asked Nicola, stepping back to us. I nodded. Nicola whispered to us, "She's very private and has turned some visitors away."

"Yes, I understand." I wasn't sure if that meant we could go in.

"Of course they must come in, Nurse Brydon," said Karen, adopting her schoolmistress voice, the one that couldn't be ignored. Nicola smiled and shrugged and so did I.

"Thank you, nurse," I said, as I stepped quickly between the curtains and just as quickly jumped back, banging into Kassey. "Sorry, love. I ..."

"You weren't expecting the wiring I've now adopted?" Karen said.

"No, no, I wasn't. I mean, what's ..."

"Going on? Take a seat, Kassey, my namesake. There's two chairs, so plant your bottoms thereon and I shall tell you a story." Kassey tittered and it might have been the reference to bottoms.

"God, I'm sorry, I'm not very good with medical things," I said, affronted by the various machines she was wired up to and the needles in her body, keeping her alive.

"Nor me, dear." Karen pushed herself up while Nicola adjusted the many pillows. "Thank you, nurse," said Karen, puffing from the exertion.

"Visiting time finishes in 10 minutes, Karen, but we might just be too busy to send your visitors away immediately," said Nicola, winking at Karen as she left, her shoes squeaking away from us.

"It'll be a very fast story, then," said Karen.

"No it won't, as we'll be back till you get sick of us," I said, patting her hand, which was much thinner and with more protruding veins than I remembered. Her black hair had gone quite grey and she was a little thinner since I'd last seen her in July when she'd popped in for my last birthday. "So what's happened to you? An accident?"

"An accident of God, you might say." She waved her hand around her space with a questioning look as if wondering what she was doing there. "The label they have given me is cancer. Most likely in the stomach, but the jury is still out on specifics. Now, how are you two?"

"Karen, you're in here with cancer and you're asking about us? This must have been going on for some time and you never told me."

"Oh, dear, am I being scolded?" Karen looked at Kassey and they smiled at each other. I wasn't able to join in as my stomach had rolled itself into a knot.

"Karen, you've helped patch me up for every emotional turmoil I've had and you hid yours from me."

"Oh, I am being admonished."

"Yes, you are. Friendships go both ways, you know." I was upset she hadn't called me, as if we weren't close. But I was also upset at myself for never calling on her.

"Look, Janice," she said, grasping my hand. "I've been graced with this set-back and I'm now in the beautiful embrace of God, in the form of these wonderful nurses, doctors and their equipment."

"And your own strong body and spirit."

"Aah, yes, we can't forget that. But there's nothing else anyone can do."

"How about someone just being here, sharing the experience in some way."

"Oh, Janice, do I mean that much to you?" She wiped her eyes with her spare hand and then grabbed Kassey's.

"Yes you bloody do!"

"Mum!" said Kassey, glaring at me, her first words since we'd entered the hospital half an hour before.

"It's okay, Kassey. Bloody is quite appropriate," said Karen. "I should have told you, but I'm not particularly good at that. I'm much more used to keeping things to myself."

"Sorry to tell you off, my friend, and part of it's my own guilt at not contacting you." Okay, enough of emotions. Time to get my practical on, I thought. "And is there anything we can do?"

"My neighbour, Reg, has my cat and is checking the mailbox. But the house hasn't seen a duster for over two weeks, now." She sat a little straighter, perhaps because we'd moved on to practical matters.

"You've been in here that long? God."

"Yes, days are very much longer when there's so little to do."

"Can I bring you anything? Knitting, magazines ..."

"Okay, you pushy beast." She smiled with a huge release of breath. "I really would love to have my crosswords and some books to read."

"Of course, give me a list and we can go to the library tomorrow. We've got the next few days free."

"Actually, I have three unfinished books on my bedside cabinet and two crossword books on my coffee table."

"Of course ..."

"Are you really sure?"

"Look, you stubborn woman, you've always been there for me so the ripples of kindness you've sent out are returning to you."

"Karma," said Kassey, so quietly I nearly missed it.

"Exactly, Kassey," I said, smiling at her.

"Look, if it's too much trouble ..."

"Just give us your keys and address and the mission's done."

"Only if you are sure."

"We are, so hand them over."

"Your mum's a scary person when her dander is up, isn't she, Kassey." The two giggled, looking at me.

"Come on, keys and address or I'll unplug you from one of these machines. We'll have to go soon."

As Karen was fishing in her side cabinet, Nicola popped her head in. "We can only give you a few more minutes."

"Yes, we're leaving," I said, "and then we'll be back to find out exactly what's been going on for this amazing woman. So, work out your speech before we get back tomorrow, Karen."

Karen saluted and then wiped her eyes with a white, lacy handkerchief she must have had under her pillow. She gave Kassey and me the most beautiful smile I'd ever seen. The smile of gratitude.

Nicola told us we could visit between 10 o'clock and midday the next day and we left, only getting lost twice on the way out. Thank God for helpful and smiling nurses.

"I don't know about you, love, but I'm exhausted," I said, plopping down in the driver's seat. "I think I'll go straight to bed when I get home."

"But that man, Mum?"

"Man?"

"You know, the one with the big silver car."

"Hell, he said he'd come back at 6.30." My heart sank as Kassey nodded sadly. She looked as tired as I felt. "I don't have the energy." I dropped my forearms onto the steering wheel and my head onto my arms, looking sideways at her, trying to smile through my fatigue.

"I think he wants to help you, Mum."

"Mmm," the only coherent word I could summon.

"I think that fat man was scared of him."

"Mmm, I thought so too. God give me strength."

"I'll tell him you're too tired and can he come back in the morning."

"Thanks, Kassey, and that's a lovely idea but it's not up to you to have to do adults' work." Besides, I thought, I don't want my daughter dealing with an adult male, at night, all on her own. Perhaps I'd become too suspicious but I wasn't about to analyse myself out of that one just now. I sat up, drove home and thankfully, he wasn't there ... well he wasn't till we got just inside the front door.

"Go off to bed if you like, Kassey, and I'll deal with him." She gave me a long hug, nodded and went to her room. I think she was too tired to say anything.

"Look, James, I'm not sure why you're here but I am absolutely whacked."

As I said it, I found myself swaying over to lean against the door frame and realised just how true my words were. "I'll need a car jack to keep my eyes open soon." I was too fatigued to be annoyed at him but this really wasn't the time for deep discussions, no matter how attractive he was. There, I've said it to myself, I thought, he is attractive and not at all like the truck driver and mechanic I'd been with before -

his BMW, suit, trimmed haircut, clean shoes ... okay, enough of the ogling! He won't be interested in me and I've got my mantra: no more bloody men. Then again ...

"Yes, yes, of course," he said hesitantly, taking a step back as if he had been expecting a huge open-arm welcome which wasn't forthcoming. "I just wanted to ensure you're safe."

"We're safe, thanks. Two innocuous neighbours who don't have a life and need some drama to spice up their day."

"They're not innocuous. Well, he isn't, Janice." It sounded nice to hear my name in his mouth.

"What, that little wombat?"

"Yes, he's comical looking."

I chuckled, but he with the stony face didn't join me.

"But don't let that fool you. He's been here a long time and has many connections."

"He's only a council worker ..."

"Only? Do you know the mayor here?"

"I don't bother with politics."

"It's Bruno Sparelli," he said, his voice lowering considerably.

"Look, come inside. Sounds like there is something I need to know."

He wiped his immaculate shoes on the doormat and I waved him past the kitchen and into the lounge room. "I'm actually feeling a bit more awake now. Cup of tea?"

"Yes, unless you have coffee."

"Just instant. None of that modern plunger stuff."

"A cup of tea then, thanks."

"You and Rosie ... does no one round here like my wonderful coffee?" Nope, still the serious, unlined face, despite my rapier wit. "Tea and no biscuits, I'm afraid. Milk and sugar?"

"Neither thanks. As long as I can see the bottom of the cup."

"You might as well just have hot water." I smiled but he didn't. I hoped I hadn't invited a robot in.

"So, what do you want to tell me about the funny little man across the road?" I asked as I put the cups of tea on the faded, slightly cracked coffee table. The black iron legs had been bent by anger and straightened by remorse, several times. They were never as they originally were, a bit like a human bent out of shape by abuse ... a bit like me, maybe. And Kassey?

"Okay, Janice, I'm going to tell you some things you'll probably find hard to believe."

"Right." I was intrigued right away.

"I can verify most of what I say so I only ask that you listen ..."

"Okay, okay, I won't say a word," I said, although I wanted to say a lot of words, like cut the preamble and tell me the story!

"It might seem a bit far-fetched and I don't want to worry you ..."

"Come on, cut the drama, James. Just give me the facts. I'm starting to wilt again."

"Yes, yes, of course." He patted his perfectly combed, Brylcreemed hair. "So, George Barbieri ..."

"The barber."

"Pardon?"

"Barberi is Italian for barber and I can't stop thinking about those old barbers with their cut-throat razors."

"Oh, right. Well, he worked for the council ..."

"Yes, 28 years. Tell me new stuff, please." I gave him my best fake smile, hoping my frustration didn't show through.

"Right, well he still works for the company, as we call it."

"Company? It's a council."

"Bear with me."

"Right. But do I need to hear this now?"

"Okay, I'll cut to the quick."

"Do it quick." I smiled at my joke but he didn't.

"There's a group of rich and powerful - but not famous - in Ipswich and they stick together like glue."

"And George the Globe is in this group?"

Yes. The mayor, Bruno Sparelli, heads a drug operation. There's possibly others above him but he's all we know about to date."

"And George?"

"We don't know his full function but he goes away regularly and he continues to associate with known drug dealers."

"Drug dealers? Who?"

"I'll tell you in a minute. Now, this group has moved into human trafficking ... well, so we think. There's too many coincidences and possible sightings to ignore the possibility."

"Are you tracking them or something?"

"In a way. We're keeping tabs and passing along information to your DI Damon Edwards in Coolangatta."

"You know him?"

"Yes. Our cooperation led to four people at your school, as well as three business people, being apprehended last week. One was the manager of the Jets League Club, two were city councillors and one a council contractor ..."

"Hell, four? Cummings and three others?"

"True. I'm not at liberty to give you their names but you'll notice some gone when you go back to work on Monday."

"Hell, you know all about me?" I suddenly felt cold and vulnerable.

"Only what the police shared with me."

"God, that's an intrusion. I feel really uncomfortable now, James. Really uncomfortable."

"The police asked me to keep an eye on you so it's for your safety."

"And no one thought to tell me this? So you're a cop?"

"Not officially. I'm a lawyer."

"And you're a pimp for them?" My growing sense of vulnerability wasn't speaking with any finesse.

"I've never been called that." He chuckled for the first time and I thought his stolid face would crack. "Coolangatta is a long way away so we supplement their eyes, so to speak."

"I suppose I'm meant to feel comforted, but I'm more afraid and confused than before you arrived. And a hell of a lot more scared than I was when I woke up this morning. What else do I need to know?"

"Drat!" he exclaimed and sprang up and rushed outside. I followed tentatively, hearing him and someone yelling. Should I stick my head out or not? I wondered. I saw a figure sprawled on the concrete driveway in front of my car, with someone else - I thought it might be James - kneeling on top of whoever it was. Then I noticed a car parked in the street, in front of my driveway. It was dark green and it was quietly idling. Hang on, someone in the driver's seat. Do I warn James? What to do? A fragile fear kicked in momentarily, and then its opposite rose up - an indignant fury, totally sick of being got at, invaded and shoved around. I dashed out and James grabbed me as I went to run past him.

"Kneel on the prick and hold this knife in his kidneys."

"Oh, right." His quiet surety impelled me to obey and in that moment, the idea of stabbing someone appealed.

He leapt up and at the quietly puttering car that was, I guessed, the getaway car - which would be unlikely to get away, going by James' crouching speed - the driver yelled in surprise as James dived across the bonnet, grabbed the windscreen wiper and pivoted around to stand at the driver's door, yanking on the handle.

I chanced to look up and saw George standing on his front porch.

"This your doing, George?" I yelled, pointing the knife - quite a big knife, actually - at him. He dissolved into the shadows and I heard his front door slam. The body below me started to buck. I'd taken the knife and my mind off the job and quickly jabbed him in the bum. He stopped struggling and I realised he had a handkerchief stuffed in his mouth as he grunted a muffled oof.

"Oh, Mum," I heard behind me.

"Kassey, you shouldn't be here!" God, do I take my daughter inside or keep this man at knife-point? I didn't need to wonder for long, as a stumbling, grunting man lurched towards me with an immaculately attired James holding the man's arm up his back. With just two fingers, James had the man's hand bent at an awful angle, and he looked to be in a lot of pain, which pleased me, I'm now embarrassed to say.

"Hey, Kassey," said James, passing her a notebook and pen from inside his jacket, "can you please write down the number plate of the car and then go inside and ring the police. Triple zero. You can do that?"

I saw her huge, confused smile. She loved the unexpected and the adventurous. She might have been thinking either that all her dreams had come at once or that they'd turned into a nightmare ... or both. She grabbed the pen and pad, wrote down the number and rushed inside while James forced the driver to the ground.

"She shouldn't see this," he said, as he smacked the man's head onto the concrete driveway and gave his wrist a further twist. The man screamed in agony. "So what's your name, mate?" Silence. James jumped on the back of the man's thigh.

"Uh, shit, okay, Danny."

"Danny who?" He twisted the wrist to the accompaniment of more groans.

"Wilber."

"If that's different from your licence, you're in for a broken arm." James plunged his fist into the man's jeans pocket and brought out a wallet. He flipped it open. "You're lucky. So who's your accomplice?"

"Ask him."

"He can't talk with a handkerchief in his mouth." I then realised that might be why he was breathing so hard and fast.

"Oh fuck, it's me brother."

"Name?"

"Garth."

"Any lies and you get broken bones. Okay, Danny?"

"Yeah, yeah, it's Garth."

"Are you okay, madam?" James looked up at me.

"Bit terrified. Bit having fun."

"Good. Don't use our names, right?" He actually smiled at me.

"Okay." He seemed to think of everything.

"You guys okay?" asked another man who seemed to have appeared out of nowhere. Sneaking Bloody Jesus, quiet as a cloud.

"Yes thanks," said James, answering for me but I didn't mind. Not this time.

"You met my wife ..."

"No names, please." James was panting a little but much less than he should have been. Must be fitter than he looks, I thought.

"Yeah, right. Can I help?"

"Do you need relieving, madam?"

"No, I'm fine. This guy's not moving. I hope he's alive." I was joking.

"Prick him," said James and I did. The guy, Garth, jumped and grunted.

"He's petrified," said James. "Bullies are usually the first to crumble. But sir, if you could stay with us and keep a lookout for the neighbour across the road. Let me know if he leaves his house."

◇◇

Two police arrived and Constable Natalie Gallo introduced herself. Her straight black hair was tied back so tightly, I swear that if she'd bent down, it would have made her eyebrows rise. She didn't smile much, possibly on account of her taut face, but she was efficient and caring, more concerned about how I was than what had happened. Constable Markham and James exchanged surreptitious looks of recognition, but the constable was more formal with me than Gallo was, perhaps not wanting to show he knew me socially. I respected that.

"God, you two again," said Gallo as she handcuffed the men and shunted them into the paddy wagon.

"You know them?" I asked.

"Yes, they'd burgle anything for a buck."

"Someone paid them to do this?" I knew the answer but wanted to hear it from someone else, as the panic and uncertainty had shot holes in my self-confidence. I'd been feeling safe and secure, cynical about James' story saying I was in danger, then he went and proved he was right.

"I can't say in this instance, ma'am."

"Janice."

"Uh, Janice. Sorry. But they do have a record of jobbing work, so to speak." I followed her gaze over the road and saw George, briefly, before he slunk into the shadows of his porch columns. "So, we can take your statements now or you can come down to the station tomorrow, if you like. You're looking a bit shaky."

I looked at my hands and they were, indeed, shaking.

"And think about if you want to press charges. James can advise you on that. We'd prefer that you did."

"Look, I really need to sit down." My legs were beginning to dissolve.

"Yes, you're quite white, even under this dimming light, and your pupils are enlarged." She held my hand, perhaps fearing I'd collapse. I feared collapse as well. "We'll go now and let you sit down. Drink lots of water, okay?" I nodded. "We'll see you tomorrow morning?" I nodded again, feeling my lips quivering. I wasn't sure if I could have said anything coherent as my mouth control had gone AWOL. Her hand released mine and someone else took it. A man's hand. James spoke to me quietly and I followed him inside where I flopped on the couch. I felt my legs being swished around and then I was lying down as he adjusted the cushions under my head. Strangely, I didn't feel like giggling or crying, my favoured responses to stress and uncertainty.

A shadow crossed my eyelids and I opened them to see Kassey staring down at me, her bottom lip quivering. I put my arm out and she collapsed onto me and burst into tears. I held her as her sobbing racked her body and her tears soaked my t-shirt. I tried to talk, to comfort her, but it was an effort.

"You were amazing, love," I said, a deep breath between every word. Her sobbing died down but when I said, "Amazing," away she went again, her young body shuddering with the release of emotion.

"Are you okay, Mum?" she finally asked, and I realised I was her biggest concern.

"Yes, love, just overawed by it all."

"But ... but you are okay? You looked so white and still with your eyes shut."

"Yes, I'm okay."

"I thought you were dead."

"Really, love, I'm so sorry. I think I was in shock. James helped me on to here. Sorry." I hugged her strongly as strength returned to my body and she squeezed me back. I didn't complain although it was a bit painful. Then it became too much.

"You can ease off, love. You'll make me wee."

"What?" She pushed herself up a little and looked at me, confused.

"You're squeezing me like a lemon and I might leak." I couldn't keep a straight face anymore and smiled.

"Mum! You're rude." She hit my arm gently and I winced, feigning great pain. "Enough!" Thankfully, she was finally smiling.

"Hey, you two, enough with the violence," said James as he pulled the coffee table closer and put a glass of water and a cup of tea on it. "They're both for you, Janice." He stood there clasping and unclasping his hands as if he'd just discovered them and didn't know what to do with these new appendages.

"Take a seat. You're making the place look untidy."

"Mum! Don't be rude." Kassey sat up, shaking her head. At least she was still smiling.

"Thanks, James." I sat up and the world didn't spin as I expected it to. "Thanks so much. For everything." I took a gulp of water and felt much better, so had another and spilled half of it down my already-wet t-shirt. Okay, girl, be patient with the body while it slowly wakes up.

"That's okay," he said, smiling awkwardly at me.

"Look, put your hands in your pockets or something. They're flailing around like a chaff cutter." I tried a smile and a giggle but that didn't raise a smile from him. "Sorry. Just joking."

"Yes, yes, I know. I'm not very good with ... well, with emotions and things."

"A man of action?"

"Yes, I suppose so."

"And where'd you learn all that Kung Fu stuff?"

"Oh, that? A long story."

"I'm not doing much right now." I leaned forward and patted the embarrassed man's hand.

"Mmm, right ..."

"Come on, out with it." I needed to focus on someone else, have my mind step away from my stupid situation. And from Kassey's plight.

"Right, where to start." He sat straighter as if straightening his mind.

"At the front."

"Front?"

"Start from the front and end at the back."

"Start at the start." He smiled for the first time and shook his head. "Well, okay, my sister was abducted and raped. We found her two days later." He looked a bit choked up and wiped his eyes.

"Oh, shit ..."

"Mum!" Kassey stared at me.

"Sorry. Oh hell, James."

"Yes, still chokes me up. So I went hunting for the bastards ... sorry, for the perpetrators, and it's why I became a lawyer and then quickly tired of sitting behind a desk. I took self-defence lessons, Tae Kwon Do, still do, and somehow became more active in helping the police while still using my lawyer skills. I contract to them in certain cases, let's say."

"Mum was going to learn Tae Kwon Do."

"Were you?" he asked.

"Well, Kassey and I talked about it after all this stuff happened. And you're just the man we need, James." We looked at each other for the longest time, our silent gaze stretching across aeons, as if I'd seen those kind, blue eyes before in some ancient time.

"Mum?" I tore my eyes away from his and looked at Kassey. She looked as awkward as he'd looked moments before. "You shouldn't stare." And now I felt awkward. And he looked awkward.

"Right, right," he said, his hands on the chair arms, ready to launch himself. "Perhaps it's time to go."

"Yes," I said uncertainly, and then realised I didn't want him to go. It was as if an eerie desire had crept in from the dark and suddenly I saw it. "Look, before you do, I have to go in and make a statement tomorrow ..."

"So do I."

"Right. They want me to press charges. I don't know. Do you think I should?"

"Absolutely."

"But they're repeat offenders. They'll do it again and again."

"However, if you press charges, it opens the possibility of taking the investigation further than your complaint. The police, if we strike the right ones, could pursue it to whoever paid these two men and even beyond that. Even if you lose."

"If I lose?"

"They might get off, but if you press charges, the case would remain on their records."

"What would that cost me?"

"I can represent you pro bono."

"Bono?" asked Kassey. "He's cool."

"No, pro bono is Latin and it means for free."

"Oh," she said, and the fire in her face died. "Why would you be free?" My question, exactly.

"Well, you can ask for legal aid and I could be on the list."

"How do I get legal aid. Do I have to prove how poor I am?" I asked.

"Well, yes ..."

"Sorry, just pushing your buttons. I don't care who thinks I'm poor. If I can get you for free ... I mean, your services for free, that's great."

"And I get paid by the court."

"But not as much as a normal case for you?"

"Well, no, but ... but I'm happy to help." His pale face went scarlet and I wondered if his interest in me was more than legal and criminal, so to speak. Perhaps he has dishonourable intentions, I wondered, smiling at the thought.

"You're happy, Mum."

"Well, a free lawyer ..."

"But you like him?"

"Kassey! That's ..."

"Look, can I pick you up at, say, 9 o'clock tomorrow morning?" He leapt up without waiting for my answer.

"Yes, that'd be good," I mumbled as he disappeared out the door. "Kassey, you don't say things like that." I glowered at her, resisting the smile that was about to erupt all over my face.

"But it's true, Mum."

"'tis not."

"'tis." I let my smile out and it matched hers.

"Do you like him?" I asked her.

"Umph," she said.

"Yes?"

"Maybe."

"You confounding brat!" I hugged her. "Now, off to bed. We both deserve a huge sleep."

Beach Ball at the Door

Do you ever have those early-morning dreams that slide into reality? Like the one where you're caught in a traffic jam because there's an accident ahead and the siren approaches ... and then you crawl out of sleep and the siren is the sound of your alarm?

Or you dream you're showering with some handsome hunk, all sexy and fun ... then something drags you from sleep and, sadly, the hunk disappears and the shower is the sound of the rain on your roof?

My dream-awakening was alarming but not sexy at all. Kassey and I were holidaying at some beach, all sunny and cruisy, when a huge - I mean, really huge - beach ball rolled up the street full of its own importance and started bouncing against my front door. I was immediately concerned for Kassey. The beach ball was getting angry as I wouldn't let it in and in my panic, I suddenly awoke, sat up, my hair a mess, eyeballs leaping about in their sockets, checking every tiny object in the room and that nothing was amiss. That damned beach ball was still banging on the door. I leapt up, ran down the hallway to the door, then remembered I was in my nightie. I dashed back to the bedroom, slipped on my jeans and t-shirt, finger-combed my hair in the mirror, shrugged dismissively at my image and trotted back to the door.

"Okay, okay. I'm coming. No need to break it down!" I yelled as I approached, hoping to quell the anger on the other side before I met it.

"Open this door!" A familiar voice.

"I will when you stop knocking and step back."

"Now!"

"Stop knocking and step back."

"Bloody woman!" The knocking stopped.

"If you're still on my porch when I open the door, I'm shutting the door again."

Incoherent muttering.

"You're still too close. Stand back and say, 'Good morning, Janice.'"

"Bloody woman," he muttered. Then louder: "I'm not playing this stupid game." Still too close.

"Then nor am I. I'm ringing the cops and my lawyer." Silence, apart from the muttering.

"Okay, okay. Good morning, Janice."

That sounded further away so I opened the door and there was the angry beach ball ... angry George.

"You step forward one inch and I shut the door and call my people," I said evenly, impressed at the my people thing that had slipped out from somewhere. "And no pointing." He dropped his pointing hand, looking like a naughty boy caught stealing sweets.

"We need to talk," he said, almost sulkily.

"No, you need to talk. I need to sleep."

"Hey, you come here causing trouble and you think you can get away with it."

I waited for him to say more but he didn't. Silence. "And no waggling."

He stopped waggling his finger and looked at his fist as if it was a foreign object, aghast that it had turned up without his permission. "I am George Barbieri ..."

"Yes, we met yesterday."

"I have influence in this town."

"That's nice."

"Look, woman ..."

"Janice."

"What?" He looked at me as if I'd turned from a dog turd into a woman and wondered how that had happened.

"Janice. That's my name. Not woman."

"Yeah, whatever."

"No whatever, George. It's Janice and you will call me that or I will shut the door and press charges for trespassing. Right?"

He looked around as if surprised to find himself on my property. Or surprised that a mere woman was giving him orders. Or both.

"Look ..." It was like his brain had shut down and wouldn't let any further words out.

"Janice."

"What?"

"Was Janice the next word in your sentence?"

"Jeez, bitch."

I stepped back and grabbed the door as if to shut it.

"Okay, okay." He stepped back an inch and I let the door go. "But no woman tells me what to do."

"Till now."

His right foot stepped forward, but I waggled by finger and he reminded it to step back.

"You are making me bloody angry." Again, his brain seemed to shut out any more words and he swayed, trying to entice them out. "You can't just ... just ... I've never been so insulted."

I looked up to see Maureen peering around their front door, a look of terror on her face. Was she frightened for me or for herself, with George in this mood? I wondered.

"Look, George, have you tried anger management? My ex tried it and broke the facilitator's jaw. But it might work for you."

"Look ... look, I did not come here to talk about my anger ..."

"You mentioned it."

"Fuck! Shut up! I'm talking to you!" His voice was becoming louder with each syllable.

I shut up and grabbed the door again. I preferred to win my fights by a hundred yards. His mouth opened and shut with no words coming out.

"George," I said quietly, "do you want to go home, have a think about what you want to say and come back? Perhaps with some notes so you don't forget."

"You can't ... you ... I'm George Barbieri and no one turns me away. I got influence and I got friends ..."

"You already said that. What do you want me to do?"

"You need to bloody ..." I looked back at the clock in the kitchen. Seven thirty. An hour and a half till James gets here. Should I ring him now? "Damn it, woman, you're not listening."

"Janice."

"Huh?"

"Damn it, Janice."

"Shut the hell up!" His voice had gone up another 20 decibels and was cracking. I could see two other men at their mailboxes, taking a long time to open and peer inside them, while looking furtively our way.

"You're causing a scene, George." I pointed to the two neighbours who quickly turned and went into their homes.

"I have never been abused by a woman ..."

"You're lucky."

"... like I've been abused by you."

"I haven't abused you, George, and we can check by replaying the tape recorder." I reached behind the door post and grabbed at thin air.

"What? You've been recording this?" He was still beach-ball red but looked as if he'd just got a puncture. A crumpling beach ball. I nodded, trying not to smile. "You can't ... you can't record private conversations. That's illegal. You bloody ... that's just ..." His volume was decidedly lower after mention of the tape recorder.

"No waggling, George."

He dropped his waggling finger. "You watch yourself, woman."

"That a threat?"

"Yeah ... no, just watch yourself, right!" He stood there as if he'd forgotten his next lines. Then he looked around and back at me, sort of humphed and spun and stalked off down my drive and across the street. A car horn blared and he scampered off the road as the car swooshed by. At his mailbox, he stopped, turned to say something, shook his head and headed to his front door.

"Get inside, woman!" he yelled. I realised Maureen's petrified face was still there as if stuck to the door. She disappeared, he followed her and slammed the door behind him.

I shut my door, turned my back to it and slid down to crouch against it. Then I burst into silent tears. I might look assured to the outer world, but I was still that fragile little girl inside, the one petrified of her father's rages, her ex-husband's beatings and her ex-partner's sordid secrets. I hugged my knees, dropped my head onto them and softly sobbed, determined to hold in the wailing and screaming that was pushing to come out of my throat.

I couldn't stop the tears but I could save Kassey from the worst of it.

I looked up every now and then, expecting to see Kassey staring at me. Surprisingly, she hadn't been woken by George's tantrums. The Master of Dreaming, Hypnos, had her in his tender embrace, the wondrous healing of sleep that she so dearly needed.

In a way, it might have been nice to see her face, to divert me from my own fragile cage of aloneness. It would have been so good to have another human there to listen and to share. But, really, it shouldn't be my daughter doing that very adult of jobs. To hell with a hunk in the shower, I'd happily settle for a bloke with two ears and a smile ... and a yacht a million miles from here. The simple dreams of a simple girl. I do like the quiet things in life, like the folding of a $100 note ... God, where my mind wanders when I want to escape.

I had to acknowledge that my script with George was a direct result of the Living Without Violence workshop on assertiveness I took - keep your voice even, don't react to insults, change the subject, don't answer their questions directly, set appropriate and realistic boundaries. I did it well, despite the constant quivering inside.

Kassey snuck out like a cringing infant.

"How are you, love?"

"Mmm, has that man gone?"

"God, did you hear all that racket?"

"A little bit. I was really tired and I woke up in the middle of it, I think."

"Well, that's the end of it. He's gone. Some breakfast?"

"Pizza?"

"Pizza? Really?"

"Yeah." Her face brightened. Who was I to deny some unhealthy joy?

"Okay, have a shower and get dressed while I heat it in the oven. It'll be ready when you are." And off she rushed, leaving me to wonder how little it took to divert us from the miseries we wished to deny. Thank God for addictions like food, football, friends and fun fairs! And then the phone rang.

Ricky the Neighbour

Hey, it's Ricky here, are you okay?"

"Ricky?"

"Yeah, your neighbour. You okay?"

"Am I okay? Yes, I suppose so." I didn't know the man, so what was I going to say? Tell him all my deepest, darkest secrets right then and there?

"Sorry, you don't know me but I'm just checking. Rosie gave me your number. So, last night I turned up, got roped in and then the police arrived."

"Sorry to sort of brush you off ..."

"Nah, no worries. You okay?"

"Look, sorry, I'm okay thanks and I'm a bit busy at the moment. Can we talk later?" But the persistent bloody man wasn't taking no for an answer.

"No problem. I'll pop around to show you something and you can carry on doing your thing." I could just see his cherry smile and happy brown eyes, quite unfazed by my rebuttal. Damn! I tossed Kassey's pizza in the oven and put the jug on to make her a cup of hot chocolate, along with two cups of tea when I didn't feel like making tea, conversation or anything else. I had to take care of Kassey before I went to the police and she and I went to sort Karen's things out.

God, I'd spent years on my own, just Kassey and me, and now the whole world and his wife wanted to visit. Either a drought or a flood.

Kassey came out of her room, wearing jeans and a t-shirt like me, her long, black hair wet and combed. I suspected she would have been happy to have a quiet breakfast because her face fell with the knock on the door. I was grateful that her look was more of frustration than terror. I opened the door.

"I've put these here for you," said Ricky, proudly pointing at a pair of workmen's boots on the porch that had likely gone past their use-by date back when God was born.

"For me or my rubbish bin?"

"They make it look like a bloke lives here. Deter burglars."

"You think I can't look after myself?" I asked sourly, trying to dampen his enthusiasm. I wasn't sure why, but I felt put-upon, a man telling me what I needed.

"'course you can but it's another deterrent. Cheap insurance." He looked like he was built of springs and sort of bounced before me like a puppy - a 35-year-old puppy. He obviously had so much to do he hadn't had time to brush his haystack of black hair, do up his boot laces or match the buttons on his shirt with the buttonholes. Bossy little fart but, beneath the nervous weaving, I realised he was trying to help. I still resented him.

"Right, what rubbish bin did you steal these from?"

"No worries. They're mine. Old ones ..."

"Yes, I can see that."

"I work in the mines, fortnight on, fortnight off, FIFO ..."

"FIFO?" God, where's this conversation going? "First In, First Out?"

"Fly in, fly out. We're at Emerald right now."

"Mining for emeralds?"

"Nah, the town, Emerald. North Queensland."

"Right ..." This is so interesting I could yawn.

"Anyway, they give us a new pair every year and Rosie's been onto me to toss these out. Lucky I didn't, huh?"

"Ah, so you're Rosie's husband? Our two-away neighbour?" Why did it sometimes take me so long to twig on? Must be losing my marbles.

"Mum, where's the sauce?" A voice from another planet - Planet Kitchen behind me.

"It's in the pantry. Look, Ricky is it?" He nodded enthusiastically. "Come in and ..."

"Yeah, ta ... aah, you're Kassey, aren't you? Taking notes last time I seen you," he said, his words stumbling together as if it was a race to get them all out. He took off his newer boots with a quick flick of each foot. One benefit of undone laces, I supposed.

"Mmm, yes," she said, reverting to her early-morning stupor, not wanting to engage. Like me.

"Tim's told me about you. He quite admires you, though I'm probably not meant to be telling you that."

"Oh hell," she said, the second word much quieter than the first as she blushed from the neck up.

"Look, it's really good to meet you but we've got a full day ..."

"Yeah, cool, I just wanted to tell you about defending yourself. Rosie told me, ya know. And you gotta find others. You can't be on your own. Safety in numbers."

It seemed like he had a whole bunch of sentences in his throat that he tossed out in the order they appeared.

"Yes, yes, Ricky, we've got support." I got three cups down from the cupboard and made a hot chocolate while we talked. "And I've got you guys here and some of the police."

"Really? Yeah, right, but we gotta make, like, a group that supports each other ..."

"We've got the grapevine number ..."

"The what? Yeah ... but, anyway, we've gotta, like, gang up like they do."

"Hey, hey, take a breath." I handed Kassey her hot chocolate as she'd almost demolished her pizza. I realised Ricky wasn't going far so grabbed teabags and poured water in the cups.

"But ..."

"Count to 10. Take a breath and listen. Please." He nodded, looked at me, a mite embarrassed. "I'm worried for Kassey and I and we're taking steps like you said." In fact, I'm way ahead of you, Ricky Boy, and what the heck am I doing telling you all this? "I agree with you but right now, Kassey and I need breakfast and then I'm off to the police station and then to the hospital ..."

"Hell, are you okay? Did you hurt yourself last night?" He now looked shocked.

"It's not for us. We're visiting a friend. Now, do you know about the Lucky Café?"

"Yeah, but they just sit around and do nothing. We need to be taking more action."

"One of them, a lawyer, is taking me to the police station. Actually, he was the one who tackled the two burglars, last night. Constable Markham is part of the café. And that Telstra guy." I gave him his cup of tea and pointed to the milk and sugar on the bench. He shook his head, as more words needed to tumble out.

"Yeah, yeah, but ... I don't know. There's lots of others on their own. There should be an organised group they can go to. I mean, Rosie's on her own with Tim half the time and a couple of buggers in the street get to do what they want cos the others won't do a bloody ... sorry, a thing. Not a thing."

"Look, Ricky, I agree with you." I said, leading him into the lounge room to give Kassey some space.

"Yeah?" His face lost all nervousness and fell into a sort-of peace. He smiled. Silently.

"Of course I do. I've discovered that there's a paedophile ring, rather than just individuals ."

"Hell, yeah. No one believes me. You do." He sat down with a whump, spilled some tea on the wooden floor, apologised, wiped it with a woolly sock, spilled some more and swiped it with his foot again.

"Hey, hey, Mr Enthusiastic, stop the wiping and apologising. It's okay. It really is. It's only tea on this 300-year-old floor and it'll drip through the cracks anyway."

"Yeah, yeah." He sat back and breathed out in relief. I sat, too.

"So, how about you and Rosie come for tea tonight, if that works? I'll see if James, Geoffrey and Sarah are free too so we can have a round-table chat."

"Hell, no one's ever agreed with me before." He looked close to tears. "Rosie's on night shift tonight but how about tomorrow night? Saturday?"

"Okay. It might be boring for the kids, so do you know anyone nearby who could babysit?"

"Child sit!" said Kassey loudly, from the kitchen. I think she chuckled quietly, too.

"Yeah, old Gloria next door might do it. They wouldn't be far away then."

"Okay, drink up, go and ask Gloria and Rosie and write down your ideas. Get them clear and on paper for us to discuss."

"Yeah, right." He looked a bit deflated, like a man striding out to save the world and finding it was already perfect.

As he left the house, Kassey and I breathed out.

"Wow, he's a ..."

"A whirlwind, love?"

"Yes." Kassey was shaking her head, wondering what it was all about.

"But he's very kind. Wants to help. I was thinking of asking him if he could take you to and from school when I'm running late. What do you think?"

"Mmm, Tim's really nice ..."

"Really?" I butted in cheekily.

"Yeah, for a boy. He's quiet, not like his dad. I suppose it'd be okay."

"We could try it once. Anyhow, I haven't had breakfast and my stomach's playing the Intestine Symphony."

"The what?"

I pointed to my tummy.

"You're weird, Mum."

"I know and that's why you love me." I hugged her and she squirmed away and took off for her room, leaving me in peace at last.

James at the Police Station

James insisted on being present when I pressed charges against the Wilber brothers, though Sergeant Thomlinson vigorously resisted, which made me more determined to have James as a witness. Like drawing a pistol, James drew a tiny machine - like a large matchbox - from his jacket pocket that he said was a tape recorder. Well, that got Thomlinson right up his tree and his three chins followed. He slammed his fist on the desk, yelled threats at us and then something occurred to me.

"Why are you defending those boys before you hear the evidence? Should we question your impartiality?" I felt oddly calm for a moment, amid his tantrum. Perhaps I'd become immune to them after my previous relationships. I was either immune or scared, depending on the day, it seemed.

Thomlinson suddenly went quiet. And still.

"My client asked you a question, Sergeant." James sounded quietly confident, a hundred times more confident than I felt as my calm disappeared, my heart crashed around in my chest and my hands shook. I feared I'd start giggling. It was the second time I'd been here with this man, and it had been the start of everything that had happened ever since.

"It is illegal to tape this interview," said Thomlinson, regaining some of his massive composure.

"You're taping it," I said.

"It's not illegal." James retained his confident composure.

"Yes it is," said Thomlinson and I expected them to start that schoolboy game of yes it is, no it isn't till the sun went down.

James stared at him, quietly and steadily. I tried to copy his stance. Thomlinson slumped back and scratched his head.

"I'll record the same as you're recording," said James.

"But it's illegal."

"No it's not and ours will have no editing."

"What you accusing me of?" Thomlinson sat forward, staring at James.

"Our similar recordings will prove no tampering on either part."

Thomlinson seemed to consider this with the speed of a sea cucumber ... and most likely with the same mental acuity.

"This is my client's written statement," said James, handing the cop the statement he'd got me to write before we left home.

Natalie Gallo had received us at the station and Thomlinson had quickly pushed her aside.

"But Markham I and attended the scene last night, sergeant," she'd said through gritted teeth.

"So, have you written up your report?"

"Yes."

"Well, give it to me and go and put signs around that oil spill in Brisbane Road, outside the school."

"That's the fire brigade's job." Her voice was respectful but her eyes were afire. Then she shrugged at me and walked off.

So, he thought he'd have me by himself and then he found he couldn't shake off my persistent terrier, James. And then he couldn't shake off James' terrier, his tape recorder. I could just see the cogs slowly whirring as he thought, Why didn't I leave that bloody Gallo to this smart-arse lot?

Karen's Home

James wanted to go with us to Karen's but I had to say no. I couldn't have him close by for too long, mucking up my hormones. I mean, I'd promised myself no more men, for Kassey's and my protection. The more he was around, the more I could feel my resolve dissolve. He would have been helpful to have along - another pair of hands to find and carry things - but it wasn't about a pair of hands at all.

A pair of smiling blue eyes and pairs of other things - tight butt cheeks, taut pecs ... hell, what am I going on about him for? God, why am I blushing? Okay, change the subject, get my mind onto other things ... more pressing matters than him pressed against me ... oh, hell, there I go again.

Right! Karen. I made all sorts of unlikely excuses that Karen's was a private job, pulled myself away from his presence, drove back to pick up Kassey from Ricky's and then drove to Karen's in Cascade Street, in Raceview, a bit further out of town than us. A brick unit, second in a line of six attached brick units that faced another six brick units across a rectangle of dried grass/dust and surrounded by a high chain-link fence on three sides. Very ordinary. Very unmemorable. And this was where Karen had lived for the last 20 years? It felt very lonely, somehow. An old chap was sitting on an upturned, blue plastic milk crate, smoking a roll-your-own cigarette, looking as sun-tanned and withered as a dead lizard. He humphed at us as he looked up and then dropped his vacant eyes to the dirt again, lost in some distant thought..

"It's not very nice, is it, Mum," said Kassey, looking around with that look as I unlocked the door. The one all girls have mastered by the age of nine, the one that comes over them when the world doesn't fit their paradigm, when we embarrass them, when they embarrass themselves and try to transfer the guilt to us. Yes, you know it well and it's impossible to ignore or not to feel deflated, no matter how many times you've seen it.

"Come on, love, we're not here to judge."

"Yeah, but, like, Karen ..."

"Yes, you're right. I thought she'd have something smarter. All her life working at the TAFE and she always looked so smart. So together, somehow."

"I suppose we shouldn't judge, though," she said. I nodded.

I suppose we shouldn't, I thought as I walked into the small but very modern kitchen. One of those newfangled microwaves, a coffee machine, a garbage disposal in the sink, a huge food processor or blender, whatever they were called, a pop-up toaster. I checked two cupboards and was surprised at the amount of Tupperware that all the in-people had now.

The colours weren't in fashion but the emerald-green walls were a welcome change from the standard browns and oranges of every other kitchen in Australia. This kind of creative spark was more of what I expected, rather than the outside of the building - an artist inside, hiding in a boring exterior.

"I feel like we should be doing something to make it nice for her when she comes back."

"Oh, Mum, she just wanted books and magazines and things."

"I know, love, and you can sit around looking pretty while I vacuum the place," I said, walking to the laundry where the vacuum cleaner was.

"You serious?" called Kassey from the kitchen, unwilling to move any more than she needed to, particularly in the direction of cleaning.

"Yes, it's only two bedrooms so I won't take long. Do you want to look for her books and magazines?"

"Right," she sighed.

I quickly vacuumed the laundry, lounge and kitchen and then felt a light tap on my shoulder which sent me shooting into next week.

"Kassey!" I shrieked, then crawled back down from the ceiling.

"Sorry I yelled but you didn't hear over your singing."

"Right." I clicked the machine off and prayed for my heartbeat to return to double digits. "God, you gave me a fright. I was miles away." Then I noticed she was giggling behind her hand. "It's not funny, you horrible girl!" I giggled too.

"Sorry Mum. You went lots of different colours then."

"I could be the colour of death if you're not careful." I couldn't stop giggling but was relieved that I could laugh at myself. "What did you want, anyway?"

"A duster."

"A duster? You want to help?" I tried to keep the surprise out of my voice but doubt that I succeeded.

"I may as well do something while you're busy."

"Right, how about you look in the laundry cupboard. If she hasn't got a duster, wet a sponge or rag and do what you can - benches, tabletops and so on. And you promise me no more heart attacks, huh?"

Her answer was more giggling as she disappeared around the corner.

Reminisce Two - Partners

There was a time I was certain about my life and how it'd work out. Despite the Miserable Minis that were my parents, I had a knowing about my future. I didn't know what it'd be but I knew it'd be alright. Even through the insanely early hours at the bakery, the shitty jobs cleaning pubs, being harassed by drunks and employers and the constant put-down by boys and men, a quiet fire remained inside, warming my heart.

Yes, there were times of anger, desperation, depression and bitterness but that fire stayed alive and warm. I forgot it many, many times but when I stilled myself, stilled my mind and let my current angst go for a moment, there was that cheery little fire, quietly telling me I was okay, that the world was okay. I always made better decisions when I stepped aside from my latest drama, put my hand to my chest and listened to its simple and, sometimes, illogical advice.

I forgot the fire when Deryk fluttered his manly biceps and wowed me with his brewery breath and high-octane bravado, the bravado that pretty soon alternated with low-octane depressions and abuse, of alcohol, drugs and, eventually, me. It was the possible abuse of Kassey that had me up and running, the day after I'd hit the cold, wet bottom of the possibilities I had left. I might have committed harikari if not for Kassey. She gave me the reason to go on and, with nowhere else to go - mentally or geographically - I went inside of myself where an overwhelming peace overcame me. I cried tears of relief, knowing beyond a silhouette of a doubt that everything was going to be okay, despite the evidence.

Anger and depression are the two faces of disappointment and the next day, Deryk displayed both of them in an ever-changing kaleidoscope of behaviours - kicking a cupboard door, cringing and apologising, yelling at Kassey, hugging me with 'please forgive me', grabbing my handbag and taking all the money from my purse, promising to pay it back with the voice of a frightened schoolboy, yelling at me, punching me on the arm and rushing out the door. Then rushing back to say he loved me. Then he called me a bitch for not responding immediately in kind and stormed out the door, never to be seen again. I got the call from the cops about 10 o'clock and I had to identify him the next day.

Mysterious Pursuers

You ever have the feeling that something isn't right, even though you have nothing to pin it on? I mean, beyond the obvious - the paedophiles in Ipswich, the police thuggery, your house being attacked with bricks and dog poo, the whining neighbour, the corrupt mayor and whatever else happens to be going on in your life? You know what I mean, I think - there's this nagging feeling that someone's following you or mucking with your life in some way. It can't be explained or justified, this icky feeling, but it won't go away. There I was, cautious about going around every corner, over-protective of my daughter, checking locks three times, constantly scanning the street. It was there in the shivers up my spine and a lump of cold, dead squishiness in my stomach, and it wouldn't go away.

I tried to remain calm and look relaxed in front of Kassey but she stared at me, now and then, and I wondered if she knew I was on edge. I was pretty sure that she knew and I wondered if she felt that same horrid, creeping uncertainty.

So, should I talk with her, get it out in the open? But what if it was just my imagination? I'd be worrying her for no reason.

I shut my mouth, pretended I was relaxed, her normal mum, and tried to keep my mind on what we needed to do that day. I'm a good secretary and one reason is that I am more organised than most. Though my mind was a bit foggy, my Miss Planner had remembered the visiting hours correctly.

We were lucky, sort of. The sign on the door said visiting hours were 10.00-12.00 but, before we could go in, the staunch bitch at the reception desk stopped us - five foot one, large bosom, straight blonde hair pulled back tightly to reveal her grim, plump face -.

"Your contact details," she said with a plastic smile, the smile of an assassin about to pull the trigger. She pushed a clipboard across the Formica counter at me.

"We didn't have to do this last night."

"Your name and contact details."

"Please?"

"Pardon?"

"Does please go with your request?"

"It's not a request."

"Why?"

"Why what?"

"Why do you need my phone number? How will it help you?"

"Just fill the form in before you enter."

"Why? What's the point of the form?"

"It's a requirement. Hospital policy."

"So you don't know?"

"Mum. Please." Kassey's pleading eyes stopped me in my tracks. I hate being told what to do when there's no reason. Morris always said I had a problem with authority but, as I always pointed out, a shortage of brain cells was the problem when people were abusing their authority or didn't know why they were enforcing the rules. It's one of my weaknesses, being unable to follow stupid orders. But another weakness was Kassey and I couldn't upset her any more than necessary.

I signed my name as Josephine Bjelke Petersen and made up a phone number and address. If these persistently worrying thoughts turned out to be real, I wasn't giving my pursuers any more evidence of my whereabouts than necessary. I pushed the clipboard back and she took it without comment.

"Can we go in, now?"

"Of course," she said, without looking up.

Visiting Karen Again

We approached the nurses' station, with Kassey correcting me at several turns. My Miss Planner was clearly on holiday and it worried me that I seemed to be shedding little grey cells and becoming dumber by the day. Maybe I needed to talk to someone. Someone professional.

"Do you think I'm normal, Kassey?" I asked, stopping mid-corridor.

"What? Normal?"

"Sorry. Do you think I'm acting normal, like I usually do?"

"Uh, I suppose so." She was now looking seriously worried.

"Look, I forgot the way here and we only did this last night."

"Mmm, you usually remember things, Mum."

"I'm sorry, love. I don't want to worry you but I've got to be honest. I have moments of total clarity and then I forget little things. I'm wondering if this is all getting to me. Perhaps I could talk with someone."

"That policeman said we could get a free psychologist ..." She smiled uncertainly as I interrupted her.

"Of course! I'd forgotten." I'd remembered DI Edwards' offer a millisecond before she said it.

"What do they do, Mum?"

"Just talk, I think."

"How does that help?"

"Look, I'm not sure, love. Maybe they're trained to ask the right questions. It could help and it's free.

"I thought only mad people had psychologists."

"Maybe I'm mad! Sorry, just joking. But I want you to have the best mum you can and maybe it'll get me settled.

"Mum, would it work for me?"

"You? Do you think ..."

"I don't know, Mum," she said, taking my hand in hers. "I feel like something's going to happen or someone's spying on me. Is that mad?"

"Honestly, love, I don't know. Maybe we should both get experts to help us. Would you like to try it?"

"I don't know ..."

"Look, I could come along to the first session and you could stop any time. Just give it a try."

"Okay," she said quietly, her other arm going around my waist. I noticed her eyes were damp.

"Look, love, neither of us has done anything wrong, but we're in this stupid pickle. So, we'll both do everything we can to get through it. And, in the end, we'll come out shinier and happier than ever."

She collapsed against me and I think she said, "Thanks Mum," a muffled sound into my t-shirt.

I held her while she held me and, after a minute that seemed like a lifetime, she let go, straightened up and wiped her eyes with her fist.

"Ready to smile and make Karen's day a better one for her?"

"Yeah, 'course!" She stalked off ahead of me and called back, "Hurry up, slow coach."

I gathered my scattered wits off the pale green and white linoleum and marched after her, smiling a real and easy smile.

The nurse's eyes lit up and she waved us through as if we were royalty when I said we were there to see Karen Massey. "She's expecting you," she said, smiling like she'd just won Lotto. Cor, such a difference from the reception down at Station Fraulein Hitler.

Karen was sitting up in bed like a kangaroo on springs. The three tubes were still attached to her arms but she'd done her hair and makeup and her smile couldn't be blown off by a volcano. I'd like to take credit for her change of mood but I was sure we'd caught her in a bad moment the night before.

"God, you're looking better than last night," I said, as Kassey shifted things around on Karen's small cabinet to put the magazines and books there.

"Thanks, dear. You're as tidy as your mother, aren't you?"

Kassey went bright red, shrugged and stepped back beside me, her previous confidence evaporating under a sincere compliment.

"Sorry love, I didn't mean to embarrass you," said Karen, looking as abashed as Kassey did.

"Come on, Kassey, she's just being nice to you."

"I know, Mum. I dunno."

"Actually, I was reading about a recent study," said Karen, ever the researcher, "where they had school students, boys and girls, walk around in particular poses or stances ... sit down you two ... and what they found was that of those who walked around confidently - upright, looking ahead, smiling, striding out, arms pumping - less than 10 percent were bullied or jeered at. However, of those who walked around looking to the ground, with hunched shoulders, hands in pockets, unsmiling ... well, over 83 percent were bullied in some way, verbally or physically."

"Just like wild animals that pick on the weaker ones," I said.

"Gosh, I'd never thought of that. It's almost like we invite abuse or admiration by how we view and present ourselves," Karen said and then lowered her voice, looking down at her hands on her lap. "Wish I'd known that before I was attacked."

"What? You were attacked?" I blurted out. Kassey's eyes flew open.

"Janice! Not so loud," Karen whispered.

"Sorry," I said in a whisper, wondering why we were whispering. Patience, and you'll find out soon, girl, I thought. "When were you attacked? I didn't know. No one said."

"No, of course they didn't. Men protecting men ..."

"Did a man attack you?" asked Kassey,.

"Yes he did, love." Karen's voice was still soft as if she was whispering state secrets to us.

"Was it that sleazy bugger at work? Jacob?"

"Yes, exactly, Janice."

"What did he do to you?" Then I wondered if I should be ploughing in on my supercharged bulldozer, asking everything.

"Mum, that's private," said Kassey, looking to rise from her seat on the opposite side of the bed.

"No, no, Kassey. That's what I thought but I later realised my silence was the worst thing I should have done," said

Karen, her voice rising in volume a bit. "So I'll tell you if you want to know."

Kassey nodded briefly and smiled awkwardly. I nodded more emphatically.

"Well, it started with Jason making rude and lewd comments that increased to become a daily ritual."

"Did you tell him to bugger off?" I asked.

"I said nothing. I felt ashamed he saw me like that, as if a spinster would be desperate for sex from anyone. Even him. I think, now, he took my silence as agreement. I should have told him to bugger off, like you said, but I was tongue-tied. I didn't know what to say. I didn't know anyone I could trust to talk about it. I tried to escape as quickly as I could, each time, till one day, he bailed me up in the stationery room. Yes, cliché of clichés, the stationery room. I know I should have screamed or something but I couldn't utter a word, I was so terrified. And I felt so alone, so utterly alone. That scared me more than anything."

"And you of all people, Karen. Never lost for words." I patted her hand.

"Exactly, Janice." Her mouth smiled but her eyes didn't. She shook her head. "I never realised how fear would clam me up."

"That's awful," said Kassey, flicking her gaze between Karen and me.

"Yes it was, love. He pushed me against the big safe, grabbed my dress, yanked it up. He stuck his hand on my ... well, where I'd never been touched. I'm not sure how, but something kicked in and I finally found my voice. And my legs. 'Go away,' I said and raised my knee into his groin.

He leapt back, called me a cock teaser and other vile insults while I just stood there, too shocked to move. Too scared to move, for I didn't know what revenge he'd inflict. Then he stalked out and told the security guy ..."

"Damo?"

"Yes, of course, him. He swung the door open, saw me with my dress still hooked up, panties down and fanny to the world and he immediately assumed the wrong thing."

"But you explained it all?"

"Nope. Didn't get the chance. Disciplinary meeting where I was soundly denounced as a Jezebel, and here I am."

"What?" I had so many questions about the disciplinary meeting, how it had led to Karen being in hospital, why she wasn't working. I knew she had glossed over the most painful parts of her experience, and I didn't know where to start.

"Call it stress. Call it what you like. Shell shock is my term. Like I've been through a war."

"Didn't you fight it?"

"I tried, but the Fair Work office was as useless as knees on a fish."

Kassey giggled and I frowned at her.

"But he attacked you ..."

"Well, did he? I might have made the whole thing up. The security guard saw him looking shocked with his pants up, so there was no proof of anything."

"But it did happen. That's so wrong, wrong, wrong."

"After 38 years at TAFE, I was suddenly found to be incompetent with no evidence. Fired. No, released from my contract, is how they phrased it. I went home and cried for a week. Yelled and ranted as well. Fell into a torpid stupor.

I couldn't function, couldn't make decisions. Didn't eat. Didn't wash. Just sat around. Then Reg, my neighbour ..."

"Not that smoking druggie ..."

"Yes, Janice, him. The most unlikely of angels. He'd served in Vietnam and knew the symptoms. He reckoned I had PTSD. He harassed me till I got out of bed and opened the door. Harassed me to eat. Harassed me to visit my doctor. Harassed me to take the tests."

"God, he looks like such a drip!"

"Yes, can't look after himself, but give him a mission, someone else to save, and he's a number one warrior."

"And the cancer?"

"I chose to put it down to stress. The liver is connected to anger. You know, a shitty liver, an angry mood. The funny thing was that I'd just had an annual check-up, three weeks before, and nothing. All clear. Doctor pronounced me in the best of health. He was confused and started throwing all sorts of labels at me, like spontaneous development, masked diagnosis and hereditary accumulation."

"What a load of codswallop!"

"Yes, they make these things up on the spot to cover their ignorance. Oh, God ..."

I realised her eyes were leaking and she swiped at them with her right hand, the one that wasn't impaled by a needle.

"Oh Karen," said Kassey, who'd sat in wide-eyed silence till then.

"You got any hugs for me, lass?"

"What? Ooh, yeah!" Kassey stood up beside the bed, looking uncertain.

"Up here. Give me a hug."

Kassey looked at me, I nodded and she climbed onto the bed beside Karen who shifted sideways a bit to give Kassey some space. They hugged and hugged and hugged while I sat there feeling like a porcupine in a condom factory. A nurse popped her head in, alerted by Karen's sobbing. She smiled at me and slipped out again. Eventually they both lay back, Karen's right arm under Kassey's neck.

"And the big lesson is, speak up, young Kassey. If something doesn't feel right, it isn't. Speak up immediately."

"Exactly, Karen," I said, thinking of my own failure to speak up immediately.

"I didn't speak up for over a month and, when I did, the fit hit the shan."

"But it was resolved, eventually?"

"Sort of. If I'd told him to weigh anchor the first time he propositioned me and if I'd told someone, then this wouldn't have happened."

Kassey and I nodded and smiled at each other - two guilty, not-speaking-up people.

"See, they observed that the incident came out of the blue, no previous drama. If there'd been previous complaints, it'd have been a very different story."

"Sorry Mum," said Kassey, looking at me with her basset hound eyes.

"What for?"

"I didn't say anything when that man talked to me in the playground. We should have all said something."

"But were you too scared to tell anyone?" asked Karen.

"Even to her mum," I said, reaching over to pat Kassey's hand. She grabbed my hand for a moment and I thought she was going to cry. But the moment passed and she didn't. "Yes, Kassey, you should have told someone earlier and I should have told someone earlier, at work. I'll never know how many children I might have saved."

"So, Janice, what have you been silent about?" asked Karen, looking much more composed. Perhaps it was a relief for her to focus on someone else.

I told her the shortened version and she aahed and gasped all through my story.

"I can tell you the longer version some other time but I have one question, Karen. And I'm not trying to be smart ..."

"Yes?" Karen sat back looking like I'd just unsheathed a knife.

"You sure?"

"Yes, hit me with it, as they say." She smiled grimly.

"Okay, you put your cancer down to anger. Well, if you can let your anger go, will the cancer go?"

The nurse popped her smiling face in again.

"Oops, am I in trouble again?" asked Karen, her hands to her mouth in mock fear.

"No, no," said the nurse, "but visiting time is now up and we need to check on your vitals."

"My vitals! Of course." We all chuckled, the nurse included. "Actually, nurse - Hetty isn't it?"

"Yes, Hetty."

"Right, Hetty, I know this sounds illogical but I feel so much better. I don't know if I should actually be here."

"But your operation is tomorrow, if your blood pressure comes down far enough."

"Yes, yes, but please hear me, dear. I know my blood pressure was up but it feels distinctly down. I just know it. I feel it. I don't feel queasy or headachy and my joints aren't hot, particularly my feet."

"That's great, Karen, so you'll feel a thousand percent better after your operation."

"That's not mathematically possible. How can I feel better after someone's cut my stomach open, sliced out part of it and sewn me up, and I've lost some blood and risked dying under the knife?"

"Oh, aah." Hetty looked embarrassed.

"Sorry, love, I'm not getting at you or the doctors. Not at all. I've been treated better in here than I have in all the 38 years I was at TAFE. I just ... I feel amazingly better and I don't know why." She looked quickly at me and smiled while Hetty turned away. I felt Hetty was wishing to escape this conversation altogether. "And I've just had a BFI."

"BFI?" asked Kassey, looking sideways at Karen with a questioning smile.

"Blinding flash of inspiration."

"That's BFOI ..."

"You pedantic rhetorician." She gave Kassey a quick hug around the shoulders. "Anyway, this BFOI, if you must, you little possum, is that the growth has been here for a long time. Perhaps 30 years or more?" Hetty nodded to Karen's upraised and questioning eyebrows. "And it's only become apparent when my body was weakened by stress. So, if it has taken so long to get to this stage, why the rush to rip it out? Why not stop and think about it. Would another week, another month, matter?"

"Well, I ..."

"And I don't expect an answer from you. Perhaps no one knows. But I just realised that I feel much calmer, less puffy, less achy and, with that, I have a clarity I didn't have before. What do you think, Janice?"

"Well, my non-medical opinion is that it's your body, your life and the only remedies the doctors have are both painful and unproven, with uncertain results. There's actually more logic on your side, Karen."

"What do you think, Hetty?"

"I'm here to ensure you're fit for the operation and I suppose you should stay. But I'm happy to talk about this away from here." She pointed her chin towards the nurses' station, as if to say that others could be listening. "You'd need to talk to the doctor, though, before you leave."

"When could we get him here?"

"Perhaps first thing in the morning."

"Too late. And that's just an insurance thing, not a medical one, having permission from the doctor. See, the more I think about it, the more convinced I am it's the right thing to do. I'm sure you have a form to sign, to exonerate the hospital from me suing. So, my dear, could you please get someone to slip the pipes out of my body and then get me the form?"

"I'll go and see the ward sister."

"Or the matron?"

"Yes, it could involve the matron too. I'll be back as soon as I can."

"Are you really sure about this, Karen?" I asked, patting her arm.

"Is she allowed to, Mum?" asked Kassey, looking worried.

"Is she the cat's whiskers, my dear?" Karen and I smiled while Kassey looked confused. "If you're asking me, Kassey, my answer is that this is not a prison. I can go anytime I like."

Nurse Hetty returned with an older nurse in a white uniform, not a pale-blue one like Hetty was wearing. "This is Sister Marian." And so ensued the same conversation ... I want to leave now ... you need to wait for the doctor ... I am leaving now ... The two nurses fled and returned 10 minutes later with another nurse, presumably a matron. Karen's bag was packed by then, largely with my help, and she had shimmied out of her pyjama bottoms and slid on slacks. However, she couldn't change her top until the tubes were removed.

The conversation repeated itself ... I want to leave now ... you need to wait for the doctor ... I am leaving now ...

"So, matron, do I just pull this syringe out of my hand like this?" asked Karen, dragging gently at the needle.

"Oh, no, let me do it!" exclaimed the matron. And she did so, while instructing the other nurses to remove the other two needles. "Now, we have a form ..."

"Yes, did you bring it?"

"Aah, no, I think it's at reception. And the doctors have them."

"Please get it before I change my top and leave. Janice told me about the armed border patrol at the front door and I do not relish any confrontations." The three nurses stopped their ministrations and stared at Karen and then at each other, as if the veil of confusion had been whipped away and they realised Karen was actually leaving. No excuses were going to stop her.

"Yes, yes. Sister, please get the exemption form." The sister rushed off.

"Look, I mean no disrespect to any of the medical or nursing staff, as you've all been so kind to me, but the beast, Hitler's sister at the entrance, is another kettle of fish."

"Yes, yes," said the matron, smiling at Nurse Hetty in some shared joke. "Sister shouldn't be long."

Suddenly a man stood before us, a bear of a man, overweight and puffing.

"Please close the curtain, sir, I'm getting dressed."

"I'm your surgeon." I think he expected us to fall to our knees in supplication, such was his pious expression. Serious and looking down his long nose and black-rimmed glasses.

"You're the one who's not available till tomorrow morning?"

"I happened to be passing the hospital when my beeper went off." He patted a thing on his belt but I couldn't see it for the massive hairy hand that covered it.

"Just happened, huh?" asked Karen, smiling sweetly at him. "Please turn around."

"Pardon?" He looked shocked as if no one had ever dared to give him an instruction before. "I am a surgeon."

"Please turn around. You are a man."

He huffed, hesitated and then turned while Karen took off the bottom-baring gown the hospital had foisted on her.

"You know you cannot leave ..." he said, still facing the curtain.

"I am leaving, young man."

"Doctor," he said sternly.

"What?"

"I am a doctor."

"Oh, I thought you were a surgeon. Anyway, call me teacher, if your status is so important to you. You can turn around now."

"Look, you cannot just up and walk out." He was scratching his sparsely attired scalp and his lips were quivering as if there were words desperate to get out of his mouth but he wasn't letting them.

"I can and I am."

"But you have your operation planned for tomorrow morning, if your vitals are suitable, and we'll have to reschedule ..."

"Yes, your golfing schedule. I'm sorry, doctor, and I mean no disrespect but I, in my myopia, see that my continued health is more important than your change of schedule." She buttoned the last button of her blouse. "There now, I'm ready to go if you have that form, please."

"No, and I cannot allow this. You do not have my permission to leave. You must ..."

"I must do what is right for me and you must do what is right for you. If my actions are illegal, handcuff me and drag me off to the police station." She held out her hands, holding her wrists together.

"But you need this operation and I forbid you from leaving. I absolutely ..."

"I will be the judge of that." She gave Kassey one bag, me the other and gathered a few remaining oddments into her hands. "Lead on, Macduff."

"What?" asked Kassey.

"You can lead us out and Mr Doctor, here, can mail me the blessed form if he can't find it in the next 20 seconds."

The surgeon's head and shoulders slumped. He hesitated, shook his head and disappeared, returning a moment later as we were saying goodbye to the nurses at their station.

"Great, where do I sign?"

"No, you must understand ..." said the surgeon, his big frame blocking Karen's path.

"Yes, I can read and understand English. Now, let me have one of those wheelchairs that I must be wheeled out in. Another insurance issue, huh?"

I was surprised at Karen's evident exhaustion when we got her back to her little home. Her flash of fire in the hospital had sputtered out. She flopped onto what was obviously her favourite chair, in front of the TV, and sat looking as if she was lost.

"Is she okay, Mum?" whispered Kassey to me, looking concerned.

"You ask her."

"What? Really?"

I nodded.

"Are you okay?"

"Not really, Kassey, and thanks for asking. A cup of oolong would help." Karen smiled at her weakly.

"Oo what?"

"Oolong, Chinese tea, love." Karen sighed deeply as if she was settling into her chair and about to fall asleep.

"We'll find it, Karen. Oolong coming up," I said, with more bravado than I felt.

"Come here, lass, and talk to me while your mum makes the tea."

Kassey looked at me uncertainly and I shooed her into the lounge room while I fished around for the oolong tea, which happened to be on the bench by her electric jug. Obviously her favourite tea. In such a small unit I could hear them chatting next door.

"Now, Kassey, do you think I've done the right thing? I'm not so sure now."

"Aren't you?"

"No, I was all fired up, surrounded by people telling me what I should and should not do. Now that I'm here on my own, I'm not sure. What are your thoughts?"

"My mum always says you should follow your intuition."

"Mmm, good advice, but what if your intuition keeps changing?"

"Well, she would say that's not your intuition."

I was surprised Kassey sounded so confident about things I'd told her over the years, things she'd often dismissed as silly.

"It's not?"

"Not if it's always changing. Mum says God's voice never changes."

"God's voice? I didn't realise she was religious."

"She's not. She says it's spiritual."

"So, what does your wise mother suggest I listen to when I'm confused?"

"The peace."

"The peace? There's not much of that in my brain at the moment. There's confusion. Exhaustion. I'm a bit afraid, I don't mind admitting."

"But peace is always there if you ask for it."

I was pouring hot water into the teapot and stopped, stunned at my amazing daughter sharing this information so capably and so matter-of-factly, as if she did it every day.

"You really are quite a remarkable girl, aren't you," said Karen, and Kassey mumbled something back. "So how do you find this elusive peace?"

"Um, well, just think of your decision."

"Which one?"

"The most important one you need to make."

"Right ... should I sue TAFE for wrongful dismissal?"

"Is that your most important decision?"

I'd found a tray and cups but delayed pouring tea so I could listen to this fascinating conversation between a 13-year-old and a 57-year-old. And the younger was instructing the elder.

"Actually, my most pressing decision is whether to have the cancer operation or not."

"So, close your eyes and put your hands out," said Kassey.

"Really?"

"Yes, hold your hands out, palms up."

"And?"

"Think of the decision to have the operation and you'll feel it in your left hand. Then think of not having it and the feeling will be in your right hand. Which one feels more peaceful?"

"What?"

"Which hand feels lighter?"

"The right hand, definitely."

"That's where your peace is. You can open your eyes now."

"Really?"

"Absolutely," I said, putting the tray of cups and teapot down on the coffee table. "Every time you ask that question, from now on, you'll get the same response, unless outer conditions change - your cancer gets worse, a different surgeon, a new medical breakthrough or whatever."

Karen stared at me, at Kassey and back at me, all signs of confusion and exhaustion gone. She suddenly started to glow, somehow, with a soft, relieved presence. She sat up straight and accepted the Limoges cup and saucer I handed her. Her eyes seemed to be misting over, as if she was about to cry, and she took a handkerchief from her sleeve and dabbed her eyes, nodding gently as if caressed by a gentle breeze. Kassey and I looked across Karen at each other and smiled. No words were necessary. It seemed like the birds went quiet, the chatting pedestrians went quiet, the passing traffic went quiet. The quiet's gentle shroud descended as we sat there, absorbing the moment.

"There is a peace in here. I never thought there was." Karen patted Kassey's hand.

"I think we all forget. Mum says that, anyway."

"You have an amazing mother, Kassey." Karen looked at Kassey, smiled and then looked at me. "And how did you learn all this?"

"Because of all the mistakes I've made to date. There had to be a better way to make more effective decisions and, after trying many ideas, I stumbled on A Course in Miracles."

"Miracles? That sounds a bit ... I don't know ... off with the fairies."

"It's the most practical thing I've ever come across and I use it as often as I can. Whenever I remember. I often forget, as Kassey says."

"So, this decision process is all there is to it?"

"No, it's a book of 1,333 pages, with a reading and a lesson for every day of the year."

"Right, I'll have to find out more but just now, I feel so bathed in peace and certainty over my decision not to have the operation, I'll make the most of it."

"And you have no need to explain or defend your decision?"

"Actually, no, I hadn't thought of that. No need to defend."

"Our defencelessness is our strength."

"You are an amazing woman, Janice Brown, with a remarkable daughter. I never knew this about you."

"I only started with A Course in Miracles after I left TAFE, after I left Morris, actually. Anyway, we don't preach. We don't need to - our defencelessness is our strength, the course says. We ask the Voice for God when it's needed, like you asked Kassey."

"Indeed I did. Indeed I did."

"Now, there's a rider to all of this. Many of the decisions chosen by peace will seem illogical, stupid or risky. But they always come out right. For example, I could beat myself up for taking that job at the school, given the grief we've had since then. However, that decision has led me back to you, it has led me to meet a fascinating group of individuals - one in particular - and to learn so much about myself, my daughter and about the world, things I didn't know or appreciate before."

Karen looked at me, long and hard, and then smiled.

"So, now that you're in a receptive mood, I'd like to ask the question I asked in the hospital and was interrupted," I said.

She looked at me with a smile and raised eyebrows, perhaps enjoying as much silence as she could.

"If you think your liver cancer is related to anger, do you think it might go if your anger did?"

She nodded and smiled serenely while Kassey looked at me, frowning, wondering why Karen wasn't talking. Anyway, I barrelled on.

"Do you know how to release your anger?"

Karen shook her head, frowning a little.

"Would you like to try something?"

She nodded and smiled beatifically.

"Now, anger comes from unmet expectations," I said. Karen frowned. "For example, if I promise to get you a bottle of milk but forget to, you become angry. We plan on having a happy life and it doesn't meet our expectations and so we become angry with life. We plan a successful career or joyous marriage and that doesn't happen so we get angry at ourselves. Okay?"

She nodded with pressed lips.

"So, we set up the anger by setting up the expectations. The world does what it does, but we try to interfere with our little plans. These little plans can be tiny, daily expectations or big, life-long expectations. The anger can be at the weather, at politicians, at God, at employers, at friends but, ultimately, it's at ourselves. You follow?"

She nodded slowly as if something was coming to her mind, as if she knew my next question before I asked it.

"So, like the decision process before, what is your most present regret or unmet expectation? Not the biggest or most important but the one that speaks to you right now."

"You," she said quietly.

"Me?" I looked into her eyes for her meaning.

"To be like you."

"Me?" I was obviously rationed to one-syllable words. She nodded, looking teary-eyed. "How?"

"I wish I'd taken more risks in life. Like you."

"Uh?" My words were becoming shorter, like my understanding.

"You left home when it became unbearable and lived with that gang. You risked love ..."

"And I was beaten and abused for it."

"You didn't give up. You loved again. You were kicked into the gutter to live in a caravan park, you kept fighting and working hard and now you have a nice house ..."

"It's rented."

"Shush, you annoying toad. And a job and a beautiful daughter and a whole host of amazing experiences I'll never have. But more than anything, you don't seem bitter."

"Well ..." Back to one syllable.

"I wish I'd taken more risks, experienced love, dared to dream big and crazy. Left my safe job when it became dangerous many years ago. Instead, I stayed home with my abusive father and alcoholic mother ..."

"I didn't ..."

"Shush! And so I got a safe job for life and settled for this little unit in rumbunctious Ipswich with a cat and a druggie neighbour - my only other friend - and all I've got to show for it is these things, few experiences and this dashed cancer ... I ..."

She seemed to peter out, run out of words and energy.

"You had all these plans for a bigger life and here you are."

She nodded and pulled the white handkerchief from her sleeve and dabbed at her eyes.

"I'm sorry, young lass, to be a blubbering mess."

"That's okay," said Kassey uncertainly.

"So, can you forgive yourself?" I asked.

"What?" Karen looked startled as if she'd forgotten I was there. Or hadn't expected such a question.

"Forgive yourself?"

"What? For being such a ... a failure?"

"No, for setting up expectations you couldn't meet."

"Oh!" That idea seemed to stun her and she looked at me with a crooked smile. "Forgive my expectations?"

"Mmm."

"My, my, I'd never thought of that."

"Should she hold her hands out again, Mum?" asked Kassey, bright-eyed and sitting up straighter.

"You can take over, love." Kassey frowned at me and I smiled and nodded.

"Um, just hold your hands ... oh, you've got them out already!" Kassey chuckled and Karen smiled. "Put them together and close your eyes when you are ready."

"Mmm," said Karen, nodding.

"Now, think of your expectation and see it in your hands."

"Mmm."

"What colour is it?"

"Green. Snot green." We all chuckled.

"What shape is it?"

"Mmm, sort of soft and gooey."

"Is it hot or cold?"

"Cold as a grave."

"Anything else?"

"It's sticky. Icky."

"So you can see it in your hands quite clearly?"

"Absolutely, horrible thing."

"Now, can you forgive it?"

"No!"

"You made it, remember?" I said.

"Forgive it?"

"Or just send it love. Can you do that?"

"How do I send ..."

"Just do it."

She exhaled heavily and screwed her eyes up as if steeling herself for something unpleasant.

"Stay with sending it."

"Hell, it's shrinking, turning yellow."

"Don't analyse. Just watch. Keep sending it love till you stop."

"Can I stop now?" Karen almost pleaded like a little girl.

"Stop anytime, Karen. Open your eyes when you're ready. Go back to it anytime you like."

There was a knock on the door.

"Okay, Reg, wait a moment," called Karen, rising and then collapsing back into her chair.

"How do you know who it is?" I asked.

"Can you smell him?" she asked, smiling but obviously in pain.

"Aah, a smoker. Your neighbour?"

She nodded.

"Are you alright?" asked Kassey, a second before I asked the question.

"Mmm, lass, a trifle out of oomph."

"You've been abused at work," I said, "fired, diagnosed with cancer, plugged with needles and filled with unpronounceable liquids. No wonder you're out of oomph. Take it easy and I'll get the door. Okay?"

She nodded wearily, still smiling unconvincingly through her grimace.

"Hey, Karen!" came a raspy, tobacco-strained voice from outside as he knocked louder and louder. I opened the door to a fist near my nose, ready to knock again.

"Sorry mate," he said as we shrank away from each other.

"Come in, Reg," called Karen.

"Youse here before, aye, with a girl. Your daughter?" he asked.

"Yes, we were just getting some things for Karen. I'm Janice and Kassey is my daughter. And you're Reg?"

"Yeah, I'm Reg. Why you home?" he asked Karen, walking to the lounge doorway.

"It sounds odd, Reg, but I had this moment and realised hospital isn't the place for me."

"Yeah, best idea. Not goin' with them doctors. Wouldn't know they arse from they bum ... sorry." He stopped short, seeing Kassey there. She had her hand over her mouth, stifling a laugh.

"Get in here, you old rogue. What do you want?" asked Karen.

"Aah, yeah ... jeez, you look like shit. Aah, sorry," he said, stepping into the room.

"Well, now you have dispensed with the customary greeting and compliments, how can we help?"

"Yeah, well, aah ... well, see, this might piss on your wedding cake, messin' with your day for nuttin', but there's a black car out there. Cruisin'. Stoppin'. Cruisin'."

"He's out there now?" I asked, my blood going cold and my face going hot. I opened the door a crack and looked out. I was sure it was him. "Kassey, this is broken tooth's car, isn't it?"

She looked out carefully, nodded and stepped back, staring at me.

"I don't know what it means, Kassey."

"So, he bin followin' youse?"

"Yes, he stopped me, smashed my window, tore my dress ..."

"Well, I just happen to know where the louse lives." He suddenly looked fired up and straighter.

"You know him?"

"Yup. Bastard ... oh, sorry. My bloody Sergeant Major in Vietnam. Bully Bastard Blowers is what we called 'im, s'cuse my language."

"Look, Reg, stop apologising for your language as you can't not swear, anyway," said Karen, smiling at him.

"Yeah, right." He scratched his sparsely covered head and smiled like an embarrassed schoolboy.

"So, who does he work for? What does he do?" I asked, mildly comforted that we might have something over this thug. The point of secrets was to keep people in the dark and hold more power over them. Thugs lose their power in the light of day.

"Think he hires hisself out to any joker who'll pay him to punch holes in others. I hear he moves around a bit. But I know he's in with the mayor and his mob."

"So what now?" I asked everyone, including God, sitting back down with a feeling I'd had before yet another beating from Deryk or a yelling match with Morris. Here we go, all over again, and I'm trapped in this forever, I thought. But I'm not alone this time. That counts for something, though a broken war veteran and a sick older woman might not count for much.

"You want me to put a hole in his car or his leg?" asked Reg mildly, as if he was asking for another biscuit.

"You've got a gun?" Karen suddenly sat upright, eyes wide and alert.

"Not so's I'd tell ya, Karen, but just in case you want holes in things, all you need to do is ask." He grinned cheekily.

"And do you have a licence for this gun you don't have?"

"Well, if I don't tell you I have it, there's no licence needed."

"You're a worrisome man, Reg." Karen shook her head, smiling at him.

"Yeah, well ..." He looked embarrassed, as if she'd just told him he was the most handsome man on the planet.

"But Mum," said Kassey, pulling on my sleeve, "what about that man with the black car?"

"The one outside?"

"No, the nice man. You know ..."

"James?"

"Yes."

"What about him?"

"Well, he said he'd help. You could ring him."

I smiled at her, recognising our connection and how she thought my thoughts. I'd thought of James as soon as Reg mentioned the black car outside. I knew James would help, if he could, but I didn't want to come across as a whining, helpless, demanding woman.

"I'm sure he's quite busy enough."

"How will you know if you don't ask?" she said, hands on hips, smiling that smug smile and shaking her head. I sometimes wish I hadn't repeated those Zen words and other pearls of wisdom over the years. She didn't forget a single one.

"You bossy bag." I smiled back and went to Karen's phone on the wall. "Do you mind if I ..."

"Of course not, Janice, if you have some lover boy who can help out." Karen smiled as smugly as Kassey did and I blushed and couldn't think of a suitable retort. I turned my back, rang him and breathed a huge sigh of relief when he answered.

"James, if you're free ..." I said, and he kept talking over me. Then I realised it was one of those recorded message things and felt a bit stupid. I stumbled over a reply at the end and put the phone down and hoped I'd left my name and Karen's phone number, which was on the dial. I never know what to say to those dippy things.

"Mum, you didn't say where we are."

"God, I suppose I should have."

"Can I do it?"

"What?"

"Call him back?"

"Uh, I suppose so. I'll dial and you can leave a message." Which is what she did, talking to the robot with more confidence than I'd managed.

"That bastard's still there," said Reg, right behind me, his voice sounding like sandpaper dragged over rocks, giving me a hell of a fright. I jumped and Karen laughed. Reg laughed too.

"Hell, man, warn me next time you're approaching. My mind was miles away," I said, hitting him on his bony shoulder.

I was still quivering when the phone sounded, a minute later. I lunged for it but Kassey beat me, her cheesy, triumphant smile beaming around the room.

"Yes. Yes. There's someone following us. Yes. Okay, I'll tell her." She stood there smiling at her frowning audience as if pleased she knew more than we did. "Yes, we're okay. He's sitting out there."

"Who is it? James?" I tried not to sound too desperate or pathetic but I don't think I succeeded. Kassey nodded and smiled indulgently, one of those it's okay, you'll be alright soon, Mum, and I've got this organised kind of looks.

"Ten minutes? Someone else? Okay." She put the phone down and stood there in silence, as if she was expecting an interrogation from me. And she got it.

"So, he's going to help?"

"Of course he is. He likes you, Mum."

"Did he say that?" And there went the blush, all over my face again.

"No, but he does."

"So, you do have a lover boy," said Karen, with a smirk to beat the sunshine.

"He's just a friend."

"Yeah, right, and the pope's just a Catholic."

"So he's not coming?" I asked tentatively, needing complete clarity with what was happening, and hoping I was wrong.

"No."

"Someone else is?"

"Yes, Mum."

"Who?"

"He didn't say but he said we'd know him."

"How'd he call back so quickly?"

"He didn't say. Might be one of those pager things."

"Yes, like Cummings had at the school." My stomach lurched queasily as I said his name and that brought it all back up. I felt immediately annoyed at myself for not doing anything for all those girls and boys in danger. But Karen was important too. Should I save the whole world or only a tiny part of it?

"So ya don't need holes in things?" asked Reg, quieter than before.

"What? Oh, that!" said Karen, heaving herself up as if she was lifting the moon. "I need to stretch. My back's killing me in this chair."

I stepped over, grabbed her hands and helped to ease her up.

"So, I'll just go, right?" He sounded deflated.

"No, no, please stay, Reg. I'm sure James will need your skills," I said, mainly to buoy him up. He was so thin I wasn't sure he could lift a gun. "Take a seat and I'll make us all a cup of tea."

"Yeah, right. I'll have a fag outside while you do that, okay?"

"A cup of tea would be lovely, Janice, but I think I need to lie down for a minute. I'm exhausted," said Karen.

"Kassey, can you please go with Karen? She might need some help," I called as I walked into the small kitchen. Kassey didn't reply and a dark thought popped in.

"Kassey?"

"Yes, Mum, I'm in here." I spun around and stalked over to Karen's bedroom. "Thank God!"

"Are you alright, Janice? You look like you've seen the Bogey Man." Karen looked very comfortable in her bed, snuggled under the covers. More relaxed than before.

"Yes, I just ... doesn't matter. I'll go and make that cup of tea." Which I did, my shaking hands rattling teacups, milk jug and sugar bowl. I loved and treasured my girl but now, it fully dawned on me how precious she was to me. Some mothers were ferocious lionesses for their children but I felt like a frightened mouse beside them. I really did need to dredge up some grit and courage.

"Tea's made, Reg," I called as I took the tray into the lounge room. The kitchen was too small for a table, with just a breakfast bar and two stools.

"Yeah, right, Missus."

"I'm Janice."

"Yeah, sorry. Forgot your name. Bloody memory," he said, dragging in a draft of tobacco-stained air with him as he entered.

"But you remembered the guy in the car."

"Yeah, long term seems good. Can't remember my last fart ..."

"Hey, did he see you?" I asked when a thought struck me in the back of the head. "Did he recognise you out there? You might have scared him off."

"No way, aah, Janice. Got me cloak of invisibility on."

"Your what?"

"Just summat learned from the Abos when I went bush," he said, sitting down and spooning sugar into his tea. I tried not to look surprised. "Yeah, six spoons of sugar but I don't stir it. Don't like it sweet!" He laughed like a rusty chainsaw and I laughed too, taking a cup of tea and a hot chocolate into Karen's bedroom.

"She's asleep, Mum," said Kassey, with her finger to her lips. I nodded sideways and she followed me back to the lounge room.

Then another knock on the front door.

The Telstra Man

God, no rest for the weary," said Reg.

Despite the huge gulp in my stomach, I was at the door before the other two, who trailed behind me.

"Who is it?" I called out.

"Just open it," said Reg.

"No." With pufferfish and other door-knockers, I wasn't taking chances. But the door swung open and I had to jump out of the way. I realised Reg had reached over and pulled it open, and there stood that scruffy chap from the Lucky Café. The one who'd worked at Telstra. That's right, Phil was his name. Slightly overweight, tall and unkempt, he was unlikely to take anyone on, especially not our thug of a sergeant major.

"Jeez, get all the riff-raff in here, don't we!" said Reg.

"You can damned well talk," said Phil, smiling and punching Reg's shoulder.

"I just made a cup of tea ..."

"Who did?" I asked indignantly, punching his other bony shoulder.

"Yeah, you did. Whatever." Reg chuckled, his face crinkling up like a crumpled road map. "Get in before he sees ya."

"Doesn't matter. I've set him up," Phil said, as we hustled into the lounge room and sat down.

"Set him up?" I asked.

"Put a tracker on his car." Phil brought out a little black box, not much bigger than a matchbox. "See," he said, showing me, "four lights. Left and right for direction and up and down for proximity."

"And you put something on his car without him seeing you? That's a risk."

"Yes, but the scruffier you are, the less people notice you. I stopped in his mirror's blind spot and the magnet sticks inside the wheel arch."

"Right, that's so brave. He could ..."

"That's so cool," said Kassey, eyes aflame, giving a huge smile.

"Yeah, well," said Phil, obviously embarrassed.

"Hey, have yer tea and stop the bloody gloating," said Reg, laughing uproariously for a second and then collapsing into a coughing fit.

As Reg's coughing fit died down, Kassey pulled on my sleeve.

"Can we follow him ... you know, with the thing in his car?" she whispered shyly, only her whisper wasn't quiet. I raised my eyebrows at Phil, passing Kassey's question on silently.

"Yeah, that's the idea," he said, pushing a mop of hair back from his forehead. It flopped straight back down. "But if we follow him now, he'll see us following him."

"But how far does it work?" asked Kassey, sounding as if she had a plan in her mind.

"We know it works for at least three miles but maybe further." He looked at Kassey, frowning, not understanding why she was asking it, like me.

"But, if we frighten him ..."

"Make him act irrationally?" I asked, hoping I'd stumbled on her reasoning.

"Yes, so he doesn't think properly. If we scare him, he might, I don't know, lead us the wrong way."

"To where he doesn't want us to go. To his masters?" I asked, nodding at her.

"Yes, Mum." She looked delighted that I was going along with her.

"Nah, you can't scare that prick," snarled Reg.

"So we just sit in here and he sits there and we do nothing?" I asked, looking at everyone in turn.

"Maybe he's told his team where we are and they're on the way," said Phil, raking his fingers through his untidy mop of wavy hair again.

"Yeah, maybe," said Reg. "So, yeah, we gotta do something. But what?"

"You're right, we've got to give something a try," said Phil, rubbing his hands together, his slouch transforming into alertness. "Whose are those bricks I saw at the back of the house, when I was scouting the joint before I came in?"

"Karen's, I suppose," I said, looking at Reg. Reg shrugged. "How many do you want?"

"Just two, I think," said Phil, a smile now on his face.

"You've got a bloody plan, haven't you?" asked Reg, frowning at Phil and then smiling. Two soldiers gearing up for action.

"I'll ask her," I said, peering into her bedroom, where I saw she was sitting up, looking as bright as a sparrow. "You're feeling better?"

"Yes, much better," she said. "The fatigue comes and goes and, weirdly, the pain in my stomach is much reduced."

"But you've had morphine and other painkillers that'll have reduced ..."

"Yes, I know that, Janice, but it's like something has got into me. A sort of power I haven't known before. I can't really explain it."

"Well, take it easy. You could collapse again, any time, like you did 20 minutes ago."

"I know, I know," she said, smiling at me when I stated the obvious. She flung the covers off and sat on the edge of the bed. "I should be feeling woozy but I'm not. Not at all."

"What's she say?" came Reg's gravelly yell from the lounge room.

"Apparently there are some bricks out the back. Can we take two of them? We assume they're yours," I said.

"Of course you can."

"Yes, take them, Reg."

"What for?" asked Karen, standing up and walking to her wardrobe, looking very stable.

"We're being stalked by a paid thug and we want him to move on. You can stay in here ..."

"Not likely! That sounds exciting. Give me a minute and I'll be with you."

"But Karen ..."

"Don't but me, Janice." She waved me out of her bedroom as she reached in for some clothes. Somehow, there was more power and certainty in her movements than I'd seen since we'd brought her home.

Concerted Attack

I shut the door and turned to see Reg with a brick in each hand. Phil was fiddling with his little console. His cheeky grin was so different from his normally dour face. They looked at each other with their silly grins and I knew they had something planned.

"So, what's your idea?" I asked.

They quickly explained the plan they'd hatched, in whispered tones, as if Karen shouldn't hear them. But whispering was the best way to alert her.

"What are you all planning? Something I should know about?" she demanded, coming out of her bedroom.

"No, aah, we's gonna scare the shit outta ... oops, sorry, scare the buggery out of that dork. Maybe he'll rush off."

"That's the plan?"

"Yeah," said Phil.

"And my part in it?"

"Yer, well, we just thought ..."

"That I'm too weak and pathetic, huh?"

"Well, yeah, put it like that," said Reg.

"So, spill the beans and I'll tell you what I'll be doing," said Karen, arms akimbo.

It was great - and surprising - to have Karen back to her school-mistress self. How long her burst of energy would last, I didn't know.

"Karen, are you sure ..." I started to ask.

"Look, all of you, as long as I'm walking this earth, I'm not giving up. I nearly did give up and Janice, here, showed me what a wimp I'd been."

"I did?"

"Your presence in the hospital reminded me how many times you'd been knocked down and still got up."

"Gosh," I said, and the two men looked at me awkwardly. Were they looks of confusion and admiration together? Whatever. I shrugged.

"So, right now, I'm up and I'm staying up till I fall down. Right?"

"Yeah, right," said Reg quietly. Then his face lit up. "Hey, she could be the diversion," he said to Phil.

"Of course, the decoy," said Phil.

"That sounds deliciously dangerous." Karen rubbed her hands together and grinned fiercely.

"What about me?" asked Kassey.

"No, Kassey, it's too dangerous," I said, patting her shoulder.

"Actually, Janice, she could be another diversion, hidden in here," said Phil.

"Hey, good one, mate, but Kassey could whistle from my place so Blowers doesn't think it's from Karen's place. I hope you're a good shot and don't go whacking them things on our heads," said Reg, handing the bricks to Phil.

"No problem, mate. I'm the Ipswich darts champion."

"Not the same thing, but come along, Kassey, and I'll show you your mission, should you choose to accept it."

Kassey went with Reg to his unit, three away, with a smile so big I thought her face would crack.

When he returned a few minutes later, he said, "Yep, she's got it good and proper."

Kassey's whistle sounded from inside Reg's unit while Karen strode out, all fiery five foot two of her, with a walking stick. She banged on Sergeant Major Blowers' car bonnet, stepped back and started yelling at him while waving her stick.

Blowers' head swung towards the invisible Kassey and her whistling and then to the mad woman screeching at the top of her contralto voice.

"Shut the hell up, ya stupid bitch! Get outta my way or I'll mow you down." He started his engine to prove his intention.

The invisible whistle blower blew again and his head spun towards the sound and back to the screaming harridan in front of him.

At the whistle's second sound, I popped up at Blowers' driver window and his head spun towards me. I could hear the cogs ticking over in his brain as I yelled at him to get the hell out of my life. On and on I went, wondering where the flow of invective came from. It felt so very good to let my anger out and I felt none of the fear I should have so close to the brute.

"Open your bloody door, Sergeant Major, and I'll open your fat neck up!" yelled Reg from outside the passenger door, waving a machete around.

The poor man's head spun left, right, front, and Kassey blew her whistle again. Then came a resounding crash on the car roof. One of Karen's bricks. The whistle went again and another brick crashed onto the roof.

Karen leapt up onto the footpath as Blowers slammed his door, pressed his accelerator to the floor and fled up the street in a squeal of tyres.

I was about to jump for joy when Phil yelled out.

"Quick, in my ute!" I hadn't realised it was his double-cab ute parked behind Blowers' vehicle. The others looked equally surprised and I called to Kassey.

"Here, I'll navigate and you drive, Phil," said Karen, quickly turning from wild woman to bossy woman.

"You know how to use it?"

"Can't be that difficult for a daft old harridan, can it?"

Phil mumbled something uncertain but handed it to her. Kassey sat between Reg and me in the back seat and the navigator started giving instructions immediately.

"The right-hand light is on. Turn right, Phil."

"Would if I could but there's houses in the way, you bossy bugger."

"Of course ..."

"Another way of doing it is to turn the box till the two side lights go out and then it's facing the direction he's in."

"Yes, but still turn right where you can."

"Yes, ma'am," said Phil, smiling broadly while he focused on the road and turned right into Raceview Street.

"Next turn left, driver." Karen was chuckling along with Phil.

"Absolutely, navigator. Hey, is that James behind us?"

The three of us in the back tried to look around but were too cramped to turn properly. Then Kassey squirmed around and knelt on the seat, looking backwards.

"Yes, it's him," she said, waving at James. Phil wound down his window and waved his arm out as he turned left into Warwick Street.

"Straight ahead through the roundabout, driver," called Karen with the biggest smile I'd ever seen on her face.

"Is James waving to us or is he asking us to stop?" I asked.

"Yes, hadn't thought of that with this navigator inside my ears." Phil and Karen smiled at each other. He looked in the rear vision mirror and held his hand palm upwards, as if asking James the question. "I think he means keep going."

"He wants us to stop, Mum," said Kassey, quietly to me.

"Speak up, love. Tell Phil."

"He's waving to the side," she said, louder. "I think he wants us to stop."

"Yeah, maybe you're right ..."

"Oops, turn left here, driver!" yelled Karen. "Sorry, I was distracted."

"Ugh," said Phil, spinning the wheel quickly, making Kassey and I slide into Reg.

"Jeez, girls, I never knew you cared!" said Reg as we pushed away from him, apologising. "Na worries. Best cuddle I had in a long time."

"Think I'll pull over," said Phil, and he swerved into a parking spot between two other utes, 100 metres from the hospital.

"Whew, that was a masterful piece of driving," said Karen, as James drove up beside us, leaned across and wound his window down.

"Are you following him?" asked James.

"Right on his tail," said Karen, waving Phil's navigation box in the air.

"Good, so can you wait up a bit while reinforcements arrive and the cavalry can lead you in?"

"Who's coming?" asked Phil.

"You might be surprised. I'll let you know."

"You secretive bugger, as always. How will we know who they are?"

"Oh, you'll know. And I'll tell you if you don't see it." James sat there looking ahead.

"Jeez, like the flipping army. All panic one minute and then sitting around for hours, doin' nothing. I need a fag." Reg jumped out.

"Hey, Reg, we might need to take off quickly!" yelled Phil.

"Yeah, and the pope might need a wife."

"Reginald!" commanded Karen and Reg jumped. "Get inside and wait."

"Jeez, give a man a bloody heart attack, woman." He stuck his middle finger up at Karen and started to walk off while continuing to roll his cigarette with the other hand.

Karen stuck her head out the window. "Reg, if we take off and leave you behind, you're easy pickings if Blowers sees you on the street by yourself. Or any of his bogey men do."

"Yeah, right, I'm the most likely prick to bring their gang down. Let me have a smoke and walk in peace."

"You are an infuriating man, Reginald." Karen sat back with a sigh. "I'm sure you like the danger and scaring the bejesus out of us."

"Stop yer nagging, woman," he said, reaching the corner 20 metres away. "It's a damned fine day to be out so let me have a bloody smoke." He disappeared around the corner to antagonise Karen some more.

"Bloody men!"

"All of them?" asked Phil quietly.

"No, not all of them, Phil." Karen looked at Phil with the softest eyes and smile I'd ever seen on her, as she patted his knee.

"Hey Mum, you should go after him," said Kassey, tugging my t-shirt sleeve. "He could get in trouble."

"Kassey, my first priority is you and I can't be in two places ... Kassey!" I grabbed at her as she leapt across and opened the door.

"But he ... Mum ..."

"Kassey, stay here."

"One person exposed is better than two or three," said Karen, turning towards us as much as her stout body would allow.

"But he's ..."

"Yes, he's very silly and possibly in danger. But Karen's right, love. One's quite enough," I said, my thumping heart quietening a little as she shut the door and sidled back beside me.

There was an awkward silence I wished I could fill but I had no words. The need for action and words was for my own sake to take away the fear of the moment. I'd had this feeling before, especially when I knew Morris, my ex-boyfriend, was in one of his moods and that I was going to be the release valve for his anger. I wasn't alone, this time,

but the unknown danger was easier to bear with action and/
or chat. No one moved and no one talked and my stomach
churned while my heart felt like a gorilla banging on the bars
of its cage, trying to get out. I clutched Kassey's hand too
hard, protection crossing the line to pain.

"Mum, you're hurting."

"Sorry, love," I said and let her go as Karen turned to
Phil, wanting to fill the uneasy void with noise. Perhaps
Karen wasn't as scared as I was but I wanted her to be so I
didn't feel so bad. Perhaps I should stop making up perhapses
and sink into acceptance of the moment, as my meditation
teacher had taught me. I tried, but it didn't work. It was so
much easier being peaceful in a room of quietly meditating
people than when I was facing the likelihood of some fracas
with an unknown number of thugs. What the hell was I
doing there? Why the hell was I dragging my daughter into
this? Just stupid!

"You're a brave man, Phil, taking these risks," said Karen,
to my great relief. "How long have you been doing this
surveillance work?"

"Aah, never," he said, shrugging and smiling shyly.

"Never?"

"I'm a Telstra technician. Well, I used to be. I've never
done this before."

"I thought you were trained in following culprits and
unarmed combat and all that stuff. But you're not?"

"No, I always win my fights by agreeing with everyone."
He sniggered and I wasn't sure if it was at his joke or at the
odd impression Karen had of him. Maybe it was a frisson of
fear for his unknown future.

"Gosh, so what are we all doing here?" Karen looked back at Kassey and me and then at Phil. "Are we all stupid?"

"Stupid, probably," said Phil, shrugging again. "It was a spur of the moment thing and here we are, all shaking in our boots."

"So, if you're scared but still here, that's being brave, Phil." She punched his shoulder lightly and they smiled at each other, while the gorilla in my rib cage thumped even harder. I was stuck in here with a bunch of amateurs. None of us knew what we were doing, I realised. God, I hoped James was gathering some experts to our cause.

"God, there he is, the stupid twit," said Phil, the only one looking forward. "Who's that with him?"

Behind Reg was a growing line of old codgers like Reg, rounding the corner towards us. They were all shapes and sizes, fat and slim, tall and short, bald and silver-haired.

"They're marching," said Karen, as I realised what was similar about them. Some had walking sticks, some had brooms and other long-handled things, and all were marching, as best they could, erect and smiling, soldiers from another war called to arms again. There were about 12 of them marching behind their leader, skinny, bent, alcoholic, tobacco-addicted Reg who looked quite a different man with his head up, chest out, smiling to beat the sun and calling out, "Left! Right! Left! Right! Left! Right!" and then, "Halt!" as he reached our ute.

"So, who's the daft bugger now, huh?" he demanded, cocky as a crow, as his followers slewed to a halt, slightly less efficiently than they would have in their years of war.

"What's with all these old buggers?" asked Phil, leaning over to ask through Karen's open window.

"You ever see a battalion of one soldier, mate? Gotta have the numbers and we got the numbers. Simple."

"But what are you all going to do?"

"We'll follow you and help you deal with these buggers."

"Deal? What the ... I mean, what are you planning on doing?"

"What if it's more than a short walk away?" asked Karen, looking at Phil and smiling.

"We know where you're going." Reg looked very sure of himself.

"How do you know ..."

"Some of us have inside knowledge and some of us have been silenced for too long. This is our chance to speak up."

"You know exactly where Blowers is going?" asked Karen.

The Old Soldiers

Oh my God," I said, feeling like I'd gone out for a bottle of milk and been abducted by aliens, "are all these older soldiers going to be in our way?"

"Too late to worry about that, Janice," said Karen matter-of-factly, "they're here now."

"Mmm."

"Oh hell, here he comes," exclaimed James from his car. We looked up and there was the mayor's red Ferrari - yes, Italian through and through - speeding towards us.

"Attention! Left turn!" bellowed Reg, and his raggle-taggle army suddenly fell into line and then marched as one coordinated caterpillar across the road. "Halt!" They stopped in a line, confronting the Ferrari as Reg bellowed, "Left turn! Present arms!" Brooms, shovels and assorted stick things were lowered and pointed at the car which slowed hesitantly and stopped.

"Platoon split! First six from right take command post behind enemy vehicle!" Six of them strode around and behind the vehicle as if they were men 50 years younger, the years peeling back like old wallpaper revealing something clean and unsullied after years of being hidden.

Reg was in his element - serious, upright, focused and apparently without fear. Then he winked back at us, totally in his element and having fun, as the Ferrari sat between the two lines of old soldiers. The mayor's fat head swivelled around at the broomstick soldiers, before and aft. He shrugged at his passenger, the gorgeous Philomena Doughty, who accompanied him on official engagements when his wife couldn't, which was most of the time. Philomena had removed her designer sunglasses, patted her blonde coiffure and looked panicked. As she opened her door, Reg stepped forward and shut it with force.

"So, what's the battle plan?" I asked, hoping someone knew what to do next.

"Looks like Reg has taken the plans out of our hands," said James, smiling gleefully from his car. He got out and told Reg to tell us what he needed from us, the young commander handing over to the old fighter. Reg nodded, smiled and shrugged. My pessimistic mind imagined he was standing there with no idea what to do next, while my optimistic mind hoped he knew exactly what he was doing and was enjoying taunting the mayor and his expensive mistress in the 34-degree midday summer heat.

James walked to the mayor's door and waved at him, indicating he should lower his window. Bruno Sparelli sat there as if they'd frozen his head. Philomena was talking at him rapidly and he kept waving her away. She kept up her petrified tirade and he slapped her with the back of his hand, a miraculous movement given that his arm moved swiftly while the rest of his body remained frozen in space. I didn't think he should have done that and she looked like she agreed with me. Bruno stared straight ahead while Philomena swivelled her head at him and then shrank into the red leather seat, frozen and silent.

Reg opened her door and hauled her out, jewellery, Versace bag, high heels and all.

"This is a citizen's arrest and you are charged with theft from the people of Ipswich," said Reg, raising his voice so we could all hear.

"Let me go, you stupid man!" she squealed. Undeterred by her insults and writhing body, he waved at his old army mates, held up two fingers and two of them strode over to take each of her arms and pin them behind her back.

"Your turn, James," said Reg, smiling and wiping his hands with the glee of years of revenge satisfied.

Phil leapt out of his car and I wondered if we should follow.

"He'll tell us if he needs help," said Karen, as if reading my thoughts.

My nerves were so jangled and itchy, I had to move, to do something, so I leapt out, stared around me and decided there were enough people in the melee. I'd only add confusion, I realised, and, pretending it was intentional, spun around and hopped into Phil's seat.

"Someone's got to be ready for a quick take-off," I said with a smug smile. "You never know what's going to happen next."

"Good idea," said Karen, leaping out and jumping in behind the wheel of James' car. I could just see the top of her head and then she sat upright, giggling, so I could see her eyes. Her head disappeared as she presumably looked around to find the seat adjustment levers.

Kassey giggled and eased herself over to the front seat, beside me. Then I realised Reg was in the passenger seat of Bruno's Ferrari. He'd reached across and seemed to be pinching Bruno under the arm, which accounted for the scream of pain from Bruno. Bruno quickly eased his chubby body out of his low-slung car while Reg slid across the console and into the driver's bucket seat with the agility of a yoga devotee.

And that was when Blowers' utility turned up and skidded to a halt behind the six men who were behind the Ferrari. The smoke from his brakes filled the air and the smell of burned rubber assaulted us. He obviously didn't expect the old soldiers to stay put.

Blowers leapt out of his vehicle and another crew-cut block of humanity leapt out of his passenger door. They all stood there, holding their open doors, assessing the scene. They would have known what to do when faced with young, fit, armed men, but a row of stony-faced geriatric guerillas with spades, brooms, rakes and shovels wouldn't be in their training manuals. Blower could see that Philomena wasn't in Bruno's passenger seat while the boss himself had his hands behind his back, courtesy of James.

"Get back in your vehicle or this man suffers!" yelled James, hoisting Bruno's hands higher. Bruno squealed and Blowers stepped back and looked at his sidekick across the SUV. An awkward shoulder hunch was his reply and Blowers scanned the scene again.

"You have 30 seconds to leave here, Billy Blowers of 23 Markers Street, Goodna," yelled James, squeezing another squeak from the mayor.

Blowers stepped forward and then back again. Having his address publicly announced wouldn't have been his favourite moment, especially being a secret agent for the mayor, in effect. Not so secret now. He looked quickly at his sidekick, shrugged, pointed his finger at James, mumbled something that sounded threatening and then they both slunk back into their seats and hesitated. Eventually, they shut their doors and Blowers backed away.

The Boys Club

James shoved Sparelli into the back of Phil's ute and sat beside him. Phil leapt in the other side of Sparelli. Meanwhile, Philomena was shoved into the back of James' car with an aged captor on either side of her.

"Drive on, chauffeur," said James and I realised he meant me.

"Oh, yes." I started the car and then realised I didn't know where to go. "Sorry, James, I'm not quite with it."

"Are you okay?" he asked kindly.

"Yes, just sensory overload. Right, I'm onto it now. Where to, m'lord?"

"Not to the police station with the dubious influences there. Hop out and I'll tell you and Karen out of earshot of Sparelli and Doughty."

I called to Karen and she got out.

"We're going to The Boys Club in Parrott Street, over the road from the cemetery," said James quietly. "You lead off, Karen, and you're okay to take my car?"

"Yes, I'm sure it's beautiful to drive." She looked like a kid with a new toy, balancing on her toes.

"Feel free to take a circuitous route, okay?"

Karen nodded, rubbed her hands together and skipped back to her driver's seat. As I got back in, I noticed someone had secured a blindfold over Sparelli's eyes. The same with Philomena in the other car. I realised, then, why a circuitous route was preferable, so the two captives didn't know where we were going.

"You can't ... by God you'll pay for this, sonny. Take me to the police station!" demanded Sparelli until Phil slapped his rough hand over Sparelli's mouth. Sparelli struggled but James made a small movement and the fat man screamed behind Phil's meaty hand. He then shrank into silence.

I glanced sideways at Kassey and she smiled broadly as if she was having a great time. She wasn't looking scared as I thought she might be. So, I determined to look calm and in control so she wouldn't be spooked.

Reg yelled from Sparelli's car to his men. One strode over to get in beside Karen, and then Reg did a U-turn while the rest of his soldiers assembled on the footpath to give us a saluting, smiling farewell. Karen led the way, me next and the Ferrari followed us to The Boys Club, which should have taken five minutes but took 15. We arrived on the outskirts of town and past the cemetery that I'd visited on occasions when I wanted some peace. It always bemused me that we work, play and love with people of different faiths, without knowing what those faiths are, but in death, in the cemetery, we are marshalled into religious sectors - Catholic, Anglican, Jewish and so on - as if to save St Peter from having to do the drafting and sifting when we pass through the pearly gates.

Across from the cemetery we cruised through an industrial estate that contained a wholesale carpet outlet, a panelbeater, a large charity shop, a car parts shop and numerous tradesmen's storage facilities. The place had the chemical smell of burnt rubber, oil, diesel and paint.

A young man was standing outside the bare concrete block industrial unit that had no signage on it. Young? Well, maybe 30, with a mop of uncombed hair and a cheeky smile.

"Jeez, mate, you bring the whole world and his wife, huh?" he said as he unlocked the steel door. "That newfangled bloody ... oh, sorry ladies. That CB radio you gave me is handy."

I had finally gathered my wits and quickly put two and two together. "Did you know we were coming here before we met the mayor?"

James replied. "It was the strongest possibility, so I had this scoundrel wait here, as he and just one other have the keys."

Who's that?" I asked.

"No names," said James, quickly.

I nodded, feeling like I was chastised.

"Look, let's get our cargo inside, safe from prying eyes, and we can talk of future action," said James, "and don't mention anyone's name, okay?"

This sounded very clandestine and I should have been shaking with fear but, instead, I was buzzed up with curiosity and excitement, a long way from my otherwise ordinary, boring life.

Bruno was led into the unit with no more sounds than tiny grunts, and Philomena said nothing, looking white and petrified. James pulled out two sets of handcuffs, clipped one to each of Philomena's and Bruno's wrists and then chained them to a swivel ring attached to an upright steel girder on the wall of the building. There was a massive rope attached to the ring and I suspected it was used for fitness, as several other more obvious fitness apparatuses were there, including a treadmill and barbells.

"Right, everyone this way," said James, "and say nothing till we're there." He pointed to the mezzanine room above the stairs. We wound our way between fitness equipment, three carpentry benches, two pool tables and assorted machinery and then up the open stairs. The 12 of us just fitted around the small table, and James introduced us all again. I noticed Billy had limped up the stairs and hoped no more injuries were impending today.

"Bloody hell ... sorry, but you're the Janice what's in the papers, huh?" he asked, shutting the door. "The one what spoke out for the kids?"

"Well ..." I started to say, embarrassment overcoming me. Again.

"Yes, that's my mum," said Kassey, putting a proprietorial arm around my waist. A proud, proprietorial arm, I realised.

"Jeez, you're a hero," said Billy and his right hand shot out. I shook it. "I never said this to anyone but I am really honoured to meet you."

"Oh, right." Words still evaded me and I felt really dumb. Surely I can think of something to say, I thought. "Thanks, Billy. No one's actually been so effusive about it before."

"Musta' been a hard decision to make, to speak up."

"It seems so long ago ..."

"It's only a week, Mum." Kassey was staring at me with undisguised admiration.

"But so much has happened and not all of it good. It's been a bumpy ride, good and bad."

"But it should be sweet, now, right?" asked Billy, looking concerned.

"Yes, there's all you lovely people, but there's also still my neighbour and Thomlinson."

"Yeah, tubby Tomlinson. A right shit. Sorry." He looked embarrassed.

"Yes, Billy, a right shit sums it up and he works for the mayor, here, I think."

"Not for much longer." He winked at me and nodded quickly back towards the mayor. I wondered what plan they had for this fat mayor and then I saw Phil, Reg and the three Dad's Army chaps bringing full coffee mugs to the table, along with two plates of biscuits.

"Coffee time!" yelled Phil and we squeezed ourselves around the small table. Everyone went silent.

"So, with the help of two council employees, including Sparelli's disgruntled secretary, two councillors have installed a mate of mine, Donald, an auditor from ShaverNelson, to go through the papers in Sparelli's office," James said.

"Is that legal?" I asked.

"Aah," said James, with a crooked smile, we will inform the Australian Securities and Investment Commission and the Local Government Association of Queensland today, but we wanted to pre-empt the process. There's the possibility that Sparelli's in league with senior government agencies and personnel."

"Right," I said with a similarly crooked smile.

"Crossing Ts and dotting Is."

"And photographing and photocopying documents that implicate certain parties that could so easily be removed," said Phil.

"So, you're in on all of this intrigue, Phil?" asked Karen, smiling weakly, obviously impressed by everything and especially by Phil, while her body seemed to be losing energy again.

"Well, mmm ..."

"None of us are admitting to instigating or participating in anything," said James, smiling around the packed table as we sipped our coffees.

"And I'm not even here," I said, chuckling.

"Oh, Mum," said Kassey, giving me a gentle backhander on the thigh.

"My legal advice would be not to lie but not to say anything," said James.

"Nothing?" asked Kassey, looking surprised.

"Exactly, young lady. Just because people, any people, ask you questions, it doesn't mean you have to reply."

"Silence is golden, huh?" said Reg.

"Just so."

"So, if a policeman stops me in the street ..." I started to ask.

"They can't unless they're arresting you. You're at liberty to keep walking as if he's not there," said James, sitting back and looking around at us as if expecting more questions. "Alternatively, you can stop and stare at the policeman, patiently waiting for him to finish his little pantomime. When he's run out of words, carry on walking. That's your legal right."

"And that's anyone, James?" I asked. "Police, council workers, teachers, neighbours, whoever?"

"Yes, we are sovereign beings and no one has a right to impede our passage or demand an answer if we haven't committed a crime."

"I'd love to try that sometime," said Karen, rubbing her pudgy hands together. Her tiredness or illness seemed to be coming and going.

"You are a very naughty girl, Karen Massey," I said, "always looking for trouble." Several of us chuckled, including Kassey. I was pleased she wasn't looking anxious or confronted by any of this.

"Yeah, wish I'd known this years ago," said Reg, "the times I put me big, flat foot in it."

"And Reg, dysfunctional neighbour that you are," said Karen. Reg's head snapped up as if readying for a fight. "You excelled yourself today. Amazing. I didn't know you had such leadership qualities in you."

"Yeah, nor did I." He wiped his eyes and nodded at Karen with a shy smile. "Happened in a moment, not planned, and I was suddenly 20 again, 50 years ago. This voice in me head said go into the RSL and it all just happened, really."

"Jeez, mate, it was a barrel of fun," said Bill, one of the soldiers.

"Yeah, bunch of back-flips," said Danny, another old soldier. "Most fun I had with me undies on."

"Better'n anything I done with me undies off, too," said Colin, the third soldier, while rolling a cigarette.

"There's no smoking in here," said Billy quietly.

"Sorry." He popped the rolled cigarette in his shirt pocket. "I hope the RSL don't mind the missing spades, brooms and whatnot. Bloody impressive firearms, aye?" Laughter rippled around the room.

"So, what next, James?" Billy asked the question that was on my mind. Probably on everyone else's mind, too.

"We need to give the auditors enough time to get what they need and then we'll let them go," said James, looking behind him through the window and down at the mayor and his fancy woman, both sitting on the concrete floor like two naughty children. "He's very obedient at the moment."

"Like all bullies, he's big and tough when surrounded by his thugs and goons," said Karen, her chuckle-face suddenly gloomy. "I lost my job because of cowardly bullies like that. Get them on their own and they crumble into the cowards they really are."

"Exactly, Karen, and we need to keep him as isolated as we can," said James.

"And we need to disable that Blowers," said Phil, with air quotes around disable. "Any ideas?"

"Can we have him arrested or detained?" asked Billy. "There's a couple of cops might enjoy the job - McLeod, Gallo and Marky."

"Can we disable his vehicle?" asked Karen, sitting forward, obviously enjoying the thought. "You seem quite handy with machines, Phil."

"Would you like to leave that to the Barmy Army?" asked Colin, looking at his elderly mates. "We know his address now."

"You got something in mind, Col?" asked Stan, a huge grin breaking out on his brown, wrinkled face.

"Yeah, maybe. Safety in numbers, so to speak, and we can talk about it at my place. Don't want to implicate the rest of youse buggers here."

"There's also his son, Nico, Kathryn's husband," said James.

"Ex-husband," said Billy, "since she kicked him off her farm and took away his drug storage unit. He's got lots of druggy mates."

"Yes, right, so you diggers deal with Blowers and we don't know anything," said James, "and we'll think about Nico and his mob."

"We better let the dumb pricks go before we get charged with something," said Reg.

"We're already up for abduction and I'm hoping the auditors have found enough to balance the books, so to speak." James stood up and we followed him out.

The blindfolded Bruno and Philomena were loaded into separate cars, driven in different directions and eventually dropped off at their residences, a clear signal that we knew where they lived. Bruno's blindfold was removed and he stood there like a starstruck starling, his wings flapping. Reg parked the Ferrari, tossed the keys to Sparelli and hopped in the back of our car. I drove off, Kassey in the passenger seat and Phil, James and Reg in the back.

Lucky Café and the Farm

Back at Karen's to pick up my car, I was ready to go home and put my feet up and my heart down for a rest. However, Karen was still buzzing.

"Can you take me to that café of yours?" she asked after James had dropped her off. Phil had driven off and Reg had sauntered back to his unit looking less than the marauding soldier he'd been an hour earlier, although his great big, cheesy grin never left his face.

"Yes!" chirped Kassey, her imploring look still impossible to ignore.

"Are you sure, Karen?" I asked. "Two hours ago you were bedridden."

"Don't you see, Janice? I've got something to live for." She stared at me, shaking her head with a dopey smile plastered all over her face. Her mouth, her teeth, her eyes, her wrinkles and even her ears seemed to have joined in the smile.

"But maybe take it easy ..."

"Janice Brady, you have given me life!" Then she gripped me in the fiercest hug her stout body was capable of. And it was fierce, I can tell you. Her head went against my chest and I think she was crying.

"Uh-oh, let me breathe. I'm turning blue."

"Sorry." She released her stranglehold a little so I could inhale and I noticed Kassey looking decidedly awkward. Embarrassed, even. I put my arm out and she joined us in our thrug, a hug of three.

Eventually, we let each other go and wiped our eyes.

"Plus there's all those hunky blokes stepping up for us and against the abuse. I just wish someone had stood up for me. Like that Phil ..."

"You like him, don't you," said Kassey.

"Well, maybe ..."

"I saw you looking." Kassey chuckled as I winked at her.

"Hush child and let's find this café." Karen chuckled too, as she marched outside. "Come on, you two. We've got life to live."

I was disappointed Constable Markham wasn't there, as his presence lent an air of authority and safety.

"Good afternoon, fine ladies," said Samuel, standing up from the outside table. "I hear tell there has been a measure of kerfuffle emanating from you people."

"Kerfuffle?" I asked, smiling at his cheerful, hair-tangled face.

"Ruffling of feathers, let us say."

"You know about that already ..."

"First, let me introduce my esteemed self to your confused friend. I am Samuel, madam." He held out his hand and Karen shook it uncertainly while looking around as if to escape somewhere. "Yes, I'm not your customary company and you are most welcome to take a seat and avail me of your delightful company." I realised Kassey was already sitting and giggling. I was pleased she felt so comfortable with a man, after her upbringing by a dysfunctional and sometimes violent father and stepfather.

Karen looked at me, shrugged and sat.

"You might rather sit inside, madam," said Samuel. "I think our Phil's in there."

Karen looked startled and she sat back, staring at Samuel as if he'd grown antlers.

"My apologies, madam. Just knowing things is one of the gifts of loss. Mayhap that Phil will come to us." He smiled cheekily at Karen, who still looked stunned, as if she'd discovered her dress was tucked into her pantihose.

"Who wants coffee?" I asked, hoping to dispel the awkwardness. "Samuel, this is Karen." I was grateful he said no more, just nodded pleasantly to her while I went inside to order.

Phil stood back to let me pass and then he walked outside to the table. I stood there, transfixed, much like Karen earlier. That bloody Samuel, I thought, what doesn't he know?

"Hi Janice," said Geoffrey. He was wearing a black café top with the buttons off-centre like a chef's jacket. I turned to him. "You were in the paper and we've met before, in here."

"Yes, of course, Geoffrey. Sorry, it's been a dislocating day," I said as my misty brain cleared and reality slowly came back into view.

"As if you've slipped through a hole in the trampoline of your life?"

I chuckled and nodded. "Yes, something like that but my description's not as poetic as yours. I went around to see a lovely teacher of mine, found she was bedridden and suddenly, I'm driving shotgun on an adventure I couldn't have imagined. Oh, hell, sorry, we're not supposed ..." My words died as I decided that less was better.

"Not supposed to say anything about anything. However, Janice, we know everything about everything and then we become remarkably deaf and our memories are dreadful." He winked at me. "Three coffees and a lemonade?" I stared at him, the words stuck in my throat. "Three adults and one child. Nothing psychic there, Janice."

"Right, three cappuccinos, please. All large."

"Did you know Samuel used to have contracts with the military in Britain and Australia?" asked Karen as I sat down, still trying to bring my brain back from the brink and onto solid, level land again.

"Right. Hi Billy," I said.

"Hi Janice. I hoped you'd be here. I gotta get back to work, but Kathryn and Christine said you're welcome to pop out to their farm at Gatton, if you like."

"Kathryn?" I'd heard that name recently.

"Yeah, her ex is Nico Sparelli, Bruno's son."

"The druggie one?"

"Yep, that's the one."

"Is it safe there?"

"Yep, safe as draught horses."

"But, well, it might be nice but we can't just turn up can we?"

"Mum!" exclaimed Kassey, her eyes imploring again.

"It's okay, we've all had a chat and you're very welcome." Billy winked and marched out.

"Look, I'm going out to fix their TV aerial," said Phil. "I can take you all if you like."

Karen's eyes grew wide and glistened. "Maybe Karen can come with me and you and Kassey can go in your car to give us flexibility."

"Mmm, looks like I'm outnumbered," I said, feeling like something was going on without my knowledge. That made me feel a little edgy. But Phil and Karen would be there.

The Farm

An hour later I drove down the long, sweeping gravel drive behind Phil and Karen, noticing that their heads hadn't stopped nodding and turning during the whole 20-minute drive from the city.

"They must have a lot to talk about," said Kassey, echoing my thoughts.

"Just what I was thinking, Kassey. I hope Karen's not overdoing it, running on adrenalin."

"Do you think she might hurt herself?"

"Well, she's been bedridden for days. Maybe weeks. She should be taking her recovery more slowly. She's as determined as someone else I know."

"Who's that?"

"You!"

"Oh, Mum!"

The tyres stopped crunching on the gravel when we reached the large Queenslander with the wraparound balcony. It looked like it had been a grand old house, now looking fatigued with peeling paint. The farm did too, with weeds in the driveway and long grass under the fences. There was a tractor lumbering around, cutting long, brown grass. Thankfully, the dust from it was blowing away from us. 20 metres away the large, red, corrugated iron implement shed also had faded and peeling paint, with grass and weeds growing in and around it.

"So you're Janice?" came a strong Aussie twang by my right window.

I wound my window down. "I was looking around, in another world."

"No worries," said the ample-breasted, freckled redheaded woman in shorts and riding boots. "I'm Christine." She stood back as I got out and we shook hands.

"This is Kassey."

"Hi love." They shook hands too. "Now, let's get you lot inside, out of the heat," she said, leading Phil, Karen, Kassey and me up the four steps, two of which seemed a bit wonky. "Yeah, the whole place needs a love-up and it's getting it, bit by bit, starting with the bit that makes money - the crops." She waved her hand in the direction of the circling tractor.

A long passage led from the front door and first left was a large farmyard kitchen. A black-haired woman pushed herself up from the huge dining table and smiled at us.

"This my sister, Kathryn," said Christine, striding across the kitchen and setting to making tea and getting scones and plates out. "She's not in the best of health ..."

"Chris, I can speak for myself," said Kathryn and I wondered if she could. She was the same height as Christine but an emaciated version of her. "I'm recovering and better by the day."

"Sorry, Kat," said Christine and Kathryn waved her away.

"Take a seat, you lot," said Kathryn and even her voice sounded thin.

We all introduced ourselves and it was obvious they knew Phil well.

"So," said Christine, once we were all seated with cups of tea, hot chocolate for Kassey and scones, "Phil tells us you're not safe where you are."

"Has he now?" I asked, glaring at him. The heat rose in my head. I hadn't been warned about this.

"Well, yeah, that neighbour and his wife and all that ..." Phil dropped his head as if he was a tortoise, backing into his shell.

"How'd you know about that?"

"Ricky, your neighbour, told us."

"God, is nothing confidential?"

"Mum, I think they want to help," said Kassey quietly.

"And this danger you told Christine about, were you going to mention it to me?" I felt a bit sorry for ignoring Kassey but my dander was up and as the words came out, I knew I was overacting but my mouth wouldn't stop. The fury had erupted from somewhere inside me and I couldn't contain it. I really, really don't like people interfering in my life, especially without my say-so. Just like my two exes ordering my life around without my having a say in it. Then I realised everyone was still and silent, staring at me. "Hell, I'm sorry, Phil ..."

"No, Janice, if Phil organised this with everyone else without asking you, it's not on," said Christine, staring at me fiercely. "I thought I'd seen the last of bossy men thinking they know better!"

"Yes, me too, Christine," I said, nodding at her.

"Um, Janice," said Phil softly, "I'm really sorry. I'd meant to tell you but we got busy ..."

"Hey, hey, you two," said Karen, joining us in the boxing ring, her hand on Phil's shoulder, "he's just looking out for you, Janice. Keeping you safe. How about some gratitude, huh?"

"I'm sorry, Karen, but I can't be grateful when I don't know what's been done or organised. So, Phil, what have you been up to?"

"I thought you'd be safer away from your place," he said, his head only half coming out of his shell.

"What have you done? Not what have you thought!" I said, sharper than I meant to.

"Gee, well, I, like ..." he stammered.

"He organised for you two to stay with us for a couple of days," Christine explained succinctly.

"On a farm?" asked Kassey, her eyes wide with delight.

"Yes, on a farm, love," said Christine.

"But I haven't got any clothes," I murmured.

"We've got plenty here," said Christine. "You're about my size, Janice." I looked at her bust size and thought, yeah, right!

"But why couldn't you have asked me first, Phil? Or told me," I asked, realising I was becoming more whiny by the word.

"I'm really sorry, Janice, I really am," said Phil, leaning forward and looking me in the eye, his fluffy face fully out of its shell and full of concern. "There's been, y'know, a lot going on. And ..."

"Hey, Phil, I'm sorry, too," I said, trying to retrace my whining steps. "I'm really grateful. And embarrassed. God, can someone give me lessons?"

"Lessons in what?" asked Phil.

"Lessons in how to stuff my fist down my throat when my mouth won't shut itself." There was a momentary silence while they all looked at me and then their relieved smiles broke out. "Look, despite everything going on, you thought of me and did something about it. I'm really grateful to all of you, Christine, Kathryn ..."

"And Edward," said Christine, "my partner on the tractor."

"I'm just ... I don't know ..."

"Yes, we know what it's ..." said Karen, before I interrupted her.

"Enough, Karen!" I'd never spoken to her like that and partly regretted my words. But only partly. "Look, I've said sentences before so I don't need others to say them for me. Now, let me gather the shattered remnants of my brain together." Christine touched my arm and smiled and nodded to me again. "So we're here for a couple of days?"

"Mum! Yes!" said Kassey, with that imploring look again.

"So, everybody gets a cup of tea while I'm slaving away out there," said a slim, six-foot bloke with blond hair and a shy smile. His thin, pale hands looked more like an office worker's than a farmer's.

"Oh, Edward love," said Christine, standing up. "Your cuppa's coming up. Can everyone introduce yourselves to my partner?"

"You're Janice?" he asked and I nodded. "You were in the paper."

"Dang, spotted again." I smiled on the outside but my insides churned over, thinking I'd become a celebrity without my permission.

Christine put his cup of tea in front of him and grasped his shoulders from behind, massaging them.

"Aah, that's so good, love," he said, closing his eyes as if falling into a trance.

"Yes, my post office boy isn't used to farm work. But you're doing such a great job." She bent over, slipped her arms around his chest and gave him a good hug. He smiled and kissed her on the cheek.

"Get a room, you two," said Kathryn with a little more strength than before.

"I'm not used to any of this but I'm learning to drive the tractor and the truck and finding out about farm things. It's hard but I'm getting there."

"And you're making such a difference, helping to get this property cleaned up," said Christine, standing up and sitting next to Edward.

"Yeah, right, get at me, why don't you," said Kathryn with a straight face.

"Kat, I wasn't getting at you. I'm just thrilled my clerical man is willing to put in all this work. You should be grateful too."

"You think I didn't do any work here?" demanded Kathryn.

"Sorry Kat, but it's not always about you."

"Yeah, whatever." An awkward silence crept in and filled the room.

"So, anyway, I'm told two or three of you are staying here," said Edward.

"Three?" I asked. "Are you staying too, Karen?"

"Phil suggested it as we could all be targeted," said Karen, looking at Phil with a sweet smile.

"My God, this love match fired up quickly," I said and immediately wished I'd said nothing. "Oh, sorry."

"You and your big mouth, Janice," said Karen. I felt like shrinking under the table with embarrassment. This was my friend. "But it's okay. We can't hide it, can we Phil?"

"Suppose not." He looked more embarrassed than I felt.

"Suppose not?" demanded Karen, glaring at him.

"Well, we just met this morning." He scratched his woolly beard and ran his fingers through his unkempt hair, looking at everyone but Karen.

"Yes, we met and we clicked, I thought." She didn't take her fierce eyes off him.

"But, Karen, I didn't know, like, we were going to tell everyone. I mean ..."

"Phil, you can't hide it," I said. "Kassey even commented on it."

"Yeah, but we haven't even talked about it," Phil said, blowing out air through his pursed lips, looking exasperated. Or embarrassed. Or cornered. Or all three.

"I'm sorry, Phil," said Karen softly, touching him on the arm. "This isn't how I wanted it to go either. But the cat's out of the bag."

"Should he kiss her?" asked Kassey.

"Kassey!" I exclaimed.

"But that's what people do, isn't it?" The voice of innocence.

Christine started sniggering and I couldn't help but join her. So did everyone else, one by one, until we were all belly laughing for no good reason. The need to let off steam after the morning's adventures, adding to Karen's and Phil's embarrassment.

"Come here, you big juicy lump," said Karen, grabbing Phil's head and kissing him long and hard. "That wasn't so bad, was it?"

"Mmm, no," he murmured, obviously shocked. Then he grabbed her head and kissed her long and hard.

"So, it's consummated," I said. "They're officially a couple." We all laughed, including Phil and Karen.

"Look, are you staying or going?" I asked her.

She looked at me, at Phil, and then around the large farm kitchen and sighed heavily, her shoulders rising and slumping. A big decision.

"I suppose I've got to get back home," she said with another sigh. "I've got all my medications there."

"That's the only reason, Karen?" asked Christine, smiling. "Looks like you don't need them, unless Phil's second name is Medication."

Karen slapped Christine on the arm, harder than intended.

"Sorry, Chris!"

"Ya violent sod." Christine punched Karen lightly on the shoulder.

"I'm gonna let you women fight over me while I get this TV aerial fixed. It'll be dark in a couple of hours."

"Do you need some help?" asked Karen, standing up and walking to the door. Phil smiled and shrugged. Probably realising Karen wasn't to be refused.

"Do you need a ladder or any tools?" asked Edward, standing up.

"Na, mate, got everything I want, thanks."

"Good, I'll get the horse paddock finished today then." Edward followed Phil and Karen out the door.

"Edward, wait a minute. Janice, do you think Kassey might like a ride on the tractor?" asked Christine.

"I'm not sure. Is it dangerous?" I started to say.

"Mum!" said Kassey, leaping up.

"Kassey, I'm talking with Edward and Christine." She sat, looking embarrassed. I hated curbing her enthusiasm but she did need to learn respect.

"I'll show her what to do and keep her safe," said Edward. "She'll be fine if she listens."

"Did you hear that, Kassey? You listen to Edward, okay?"

"Yes, Mum." She smiled awkwardly, slid off her chair as if I wouldn't notice her moving and followed Edward out. I nodded when her slinking turned into a bounce. "Thanks Mum," she said, smiling at me as she disappeared. I was so pleased that Edward had asked me. I wasn't being overruled, thankfully. And they were gone, leaving us four women around the scarred, wooden dining table. Gosh, what memories this table and this kitchen must hold, I thought.

"Look, Janice, I'm a terrible host," said Christine after Phil, Edward and Kassey had left, "but there's things I need to do round here."

"Great, how can I help?" I asked, having sat and chatted for long enough.

"You want to help? Great."

She kitted me out in slightly-too-big jeans, a floppy t-shirt and short gumboots and we headed out the door.

"You think I can't do something outdoors?" demanded Kathryn, her arm up the door jamb.

Christine turned, obviously surprised and said nothing for at least half a minute. She took some breaths and seemed to be considering which speech to make. She eventually chose a kind reply.

"Of course you can come, Kathryn. I just thought you might like a rest after having all these people here."

"I'm fine." Kathryn pulled on her boots and we all went out to the implement shed.

"This might seem like a cosmetic job but we've got to look after the machinery. After we've removed the grass and weeds, we can see what sheets of iron need to be replaced to make the shed weather-tight again."

We dug and grubbed and weeded for an hour, with Kathryn not doing much. She looked so tired all the time but seemed determined to put in her appearance. I was afraid to talk with her in case she bit my head off. But I eventually had to say something as she wasn't talking.

"I'm not used to such hard work but it's good to look back and see the difference we're making," I said while Kathryn was next to me and Christine had disappeared around the corner.

Kathryn took a deep breath. "Look, Janice, I'm sorry." Her forlorn face really did look sorry.

"Sorry?"

"Yeah, I know I can be a bitch and I know when I'm doing it." She stopped for a breath and I said nothing. "I just can't stop myself and then I always feel worse."

"Right. Somebody said you'd been on drugs."

"Yeah, lots of them. That bloody husband of mine."

"Nico Sparelli?"

"Mmm, the mayor's son and the second worst criminal after his father."

"And he gave you the drugs?"

"Yeah, and I didn't know."

"You didn't ..."

"Snuck them in my food. I spent the last four years high and not very dry." She smiled wryly at her little joke.

"But now you've cut the drugs out?"

"Yes, I did the cold turkey a few weeks ago at Stephen and Flora Daniels' place."

"Stephen? Does he run the flour mill here?"

"Yeah, with his wife. Lovely people. So caring. So ..." She started to cry and I let her. Soon she stopped. "I can't say enough about them and they probably saved my life."

"And Christine?"

"Yeah, I suppose she started it all by turning up here after 11 years away. I never thought she'd come back. Thank God she did. She and Edward kicked my stupid husband out. She got badly injured in the process. They got the cops involved, Christine's stupid ex-husband turned up - dumb as mine, really." She smiled, took a breath and breathed out heavily as if trying to regain some energy. "Billy helped out as well."

"I met Billy today, if it's the same bloke."

"Yeah, salt of the earth. Funny as a fight and he'd sell his good leg to help a friend out. And Emma ..."

"Gosh, lots of people stepped in to help you out. You must be worth it."

"Mmm, dunno." She looked at me with a shy smile, seeming on the verge of tears.

"You obviously are."

"Maybe." She waved my words away. "Oh, yeah, Sergeant McLeod and Constable Markham ..."

"Marky?"

"Mmm. God, I'd forgotten most of them till you brought it up."

"They say drugs can damage your memory."

"Suppose so."

"Now, just a thought. Not telling you what to do, but have you thanked any of these people for saving your life?"

"What?" She stood up straight, looking shocked. "Hell no. I never thought of that. Especially Chris ..."

"Who gets the most of your abuse?"

"Yeah, you're dead right," she said, her hand on my shoulder. I thought she needed to sit down. "Thanks Janice. I feel so embarrassed but cleaner, if you know what I mean."

"I know exactly."

"Hey, you two hags haven't done much, have you!" shouted Christine cheerily from behind me.

"We've been sorting out all the problems in the world," I said, smiling back at her.

"You haven't sorted out much of the weeding."

"Aww, get off my back, will ya," said Kathryn, leaning on her spade as if she was about to swing it at Christine.

"Kathryn, just thank her," I said quietly.

Kathryn looked at me and then visibly relaxed and nodded sadly to me.

"I need to go to the loo," I said, loud enough for both women to hear. Then I whispered, "Thank her."

Kathryn nodded and smiled at me again, and I walked back to the house with no need to go to the toilet. I didn't look back till I got up onto the verandah and saw them facing each other, talking quietly and then hugging.

"Thank God for that," said Edward, right behind me. I jumped and squeaked. "Sorry I surprised you."

"You sure as hell did, you scary man! Where's Kassey?" I suddenly felt that sucking hole in my stomach when I knew something was wrong. Particularly with Kassey.

"She's okay. I needed to go to the toilet and I usually go behind the tractor but I couldn't with her there. She's doing another circuit and I'll catch her ..."

"She's driving the tractor? On her own?" That sucking hole sucked harder and deeper.

"Yes." I could see a strange glint in his eyes and his lips were quivering. "She's fine. She's playing with Brutus the dog."

I slapped him on the shoulder. "You bloody shit, you really had me going." He chuckled, patted my shoulder and walked off. "Hey, hey, back here, you horrible little man." He stopped on the step and turned, his smirk replaced by a frown. "What'd you say 'thank God' for before?"

He faced me squarely, hands deep in his blue overalls. "Let's just say that Christine's homecoming hasn't been one of dreams."

"With Kathryn?"

"With her. With her husband ..."

"Ex-husband."

"No, they're still married. She ... well, we shunted him off the farm, burnt his clothes, police confiscated the sacks of heroin he kept in the cottage. He's gone for now but we don't know where to or when he'll return, if he ever does."

"Oh, hell."

"The worst for me as an only child is that I was looking forward to a lovely sisterly love story, but it's everything but."

"Right, Kathryn seems very brittle, moods up and down."

"Exactly. Mainly down with Christine who's done so much for her."

"I was afraid to talk to her and when I did, she was so sweet and nice."

"Yes, with their father gone - a tough old bastard, apparently - I hoped peace would reign."

"And now they're hugging."

"It might not last. Those damned drugs do awful things to people. I'd better go and make sure Brutus hasn't mauled Kassey." With a straight face, he turned. I grabbed him by the shoulder as that sucking hole started up again. He smiled shyly. "Sorry, just joking. Hey, you're really upset. I'm really, really sorry."

"That's my daughter."

"Oh, right."

"God, we've had so many scary moments and they catch up with me at times." He grabbed me as sobs choked me up and I had to lean on his shoulder a step below, shaking. My legs might have given way if he hadn't held me up.

"You want to sit down?"

"Shut up and hold me, you horrible man." We both chuckled - me through my tears - and I basked in the arms of a safe man.

"Do you want to come out and see what Kassey's up to?" he asked as we eventually separated.

"Hey, you two lovers, what're you up to?" shouted Christine when we passed the implement shed, which was now looking much tidier than when we'd arrived.

"I made a joke and it wasn't very funny, it seems," he said.

"Two not-funny jokes, actually. Hey, your eyes are red, Christine. Same with yours, Kathryn."

"Yeah, this bloody dust gets everywhere," said Christine, putting her hand on Kathryn's shoulder as both women wiped their eyes.

We found Kassey running in circles and Brutus, a lumbering pug dog, following her around. Brutus looked like he was laughing as much as Kassey was.

"Look, Mum, he does what I do." She stopped and jumped up and down and so did the dog, in its arthritic way. Then we all turned towards the scrunching gravel on the driveway to see an old ute rattling down to park in front of the implement shed.

"Hiya Edward!" shouted Billy. He leapt out in a cloud of dust.

Edward waved back and spoke to us. "Look, I've only two more circuits to do to finish this paddock so you go down and meet Emma and Jeanie."

"Can we take Brutus?" asked Kassey, her priorities worn on her sleeve.

"Of course, Kassey," said Edward, climbing back on the tractor.

Brutus had been sitting and staring up at Kassey the whole time and now, he followed right behind us when we walked back to the house. A woman and a girl got out of the other side of the rusty ute.

"So, what're you here for, Billy? You're too late to be doing any work," said Christine, chuckling as she walked around the ute to hug the elfin-like woman.

"Nah, not too late. Just insufficiently early." He chuckled, smiling shyly, running his fingers through his unruly off-blond hair, a haystack in spring. "You're a suspicious woman, aren't you, Christine Colquhoun."

"Well, it's right on dinner time." She grabbed him and hugged him as he sauntered by.

"Yeah, well, funny you should mention that," he said, squirming out of her arms, diving into the ute and hauling out a huge newspaper-wrapped package. "But I know youse don't like fish and chips, right?"

"You bugger, you didn't have to do that." Christine looked suddenly embarrassed. Almost tearful. Kathryn went up to the younger woman and gave her a tentative hug, smiling more than she had since I'd arrived. The woman hugged her back tenderly.

"And you must be Janice. I'm Emma," said the woman, letting go of Kathryn, stepping forward and holding her hand out. "Unless you do hugs."

"Absolutely!" I said and we fell into each other's arms. She smelt faintly of washing powder and cologne, a housewife dabbing her cheeks before coming out. It's funny how some people you just like. They even feel like old friends though you've just met them. That's how I felt with Emma. I didn't want to let her go, to lose the contact, but I felt Kassey standing there.

"This is my daughter, Kassey." Kassey was enveloped in a hug and her eyes went wide in surprise and then she smiled as she melted into Emma.

"And this is my daughter, Jeanie," said Emma, straightening up.

"And you do hugs, Jeanie?" I asked and the dark-skinned girl, a bit older than Kassey, turned her head to the side and shrugged shyly but didn't step back. I enclosed her gently and she tentatively hugged back. "Are you okay, Jeanie?" I asked, holding her shoulders at arm's length. She looked down at her flip-flops as if she couldn't look straight at me.

"Yeah, I'm good."

"She's not used to all this huggery," said Billy, limping up the steps. Actually, it was the first time I'd noticed his limp since he got out of the ute. Then I remembered him limping at The Boys Club. He hid it well. "Grub's up, ya buggers. Dig in." We all followed him in, his smiling harem. "Where's Edo?"

"Edward," said Christine, correcting him.

"Yeah, sorry, Edward. Where is he?"

"He's on the tractor," said Kassey. "He said he wouldn't be long." I was surprised at Kassey volunteering that information as she'd normally be too shy to say anything. "Mum, can I feed Brutus?"

I looked at Christine.

"Of course, love, go down the hall and out to the left, on the verandah, there's a fridge. Grab a plastic bag of meat for him."

"Do you want to come, Jeanie?" asked Emma.

Jeanie nodded shyly.

"Okay, come on," said Kassey and the dog followed the girls out, wagging his tail.

"So, how old's Jeanie?" I asked Emma.

"We think she's 15."

"You think?"

"Mmm." Emma pursed her lips.

"You can tell her," said Christine. "There's no shame on anyone here."

"Yeah, so we adopted her," said Billy, ripping open the fish and chips wrapping.

"Let your wife have a say, will you." Christine smiled and wagged her finger at him.

"Oops," he said, chuckling.

"So, Edward found her," said Emma, smiling awkwardly and shrugging. Perhaps a family secret she was still getting used to.

"I'm being mentioned in despatches, am I?" asked Edward, in his overalls and thick, grass-covered socks.

"Do you want a shower, Edward?" asked Christine. "I can heat your dinner up. The girls are feeding Brutus."

"Yes, I just checked on them. Maybe I'll clean up and then I'll feel more sociable."

"I'll see if the girls haven't been eaten," said Billy, leaping up like an overwound spring while I gasped. "Na, he wouldn't hurt a fly," he said, smiling at me, "but he did have a go at Christine's ex-bloody-husband. Brutus nearly got hisself killed for it." Then he was limping and gone and us four women sat in silence, looking at one another, the calm after the storm.

"You don't have to protect me from Billy, Chris," said Emma kindly. "I get to say what I need to."

"Sorry, Emma, it just came out," said Christine.

"Were you abused before?" I asked, looking at Christine, and wished I'd plugged my mouth up. None of my business.

"Well, since you ask, yes I was." Christine's eyes went all glassy, clouded over by a memory.

"A normal reaction," I said. "We know what it's like to be knocked around so we're damned if we'll let anyone else be treated like that." I didn't know I knew that till I said it and I smiled. Yes, I had learned something from it after all.

"Billy wouldn't hurt a fly," said Emma.

"I know he wouldn't," said Christine, patting Emma's arm. "I ... I don't know, just reacting from my own abuse, I guess."

"Exactly," said Kathryn. We all looked at her as if we hadn't noticed the mouse in the corner. She breathed out heavily, possibly selecting from a huge range of things she could say. "I hadn't thought about it till you said that, Janice. I'm always frightened but I think it's more for others than for myself."

"You're right, Kathryn," I said, as a few more pieces of my emotional jigsaw fitted into the puzzle. "If it was my own terror I might have less. Half of what I worry about is Kassey. If I didn't have her to worry about, I'd be calmer. Maybe."

"And I worry about Edward on the tractor as he's an office worker," said Christine. "I worry about you, Kathryn. And you, Emma. And Billy and Stephen and Flora. And if Nico and his gang will ever come back. The whole bloody world, really."

"But we're fine, Chris," said Emma. "No need to worry at all."

"I suppose so. My logic knows you're right but I can't seem to help myself. I mean, I never had a care 11 years ago when I left here. I thought about you, Kathryn, on the farm with Dad, I suppose, but I just got on with life."

"Then you met your husband?" I suggested.

"Yeah, it was fine for a while but he became more creepy and sinister and then abusive."

"And he opened you up to worry about everyone else?" I patted her arm "That's how it's gone for me, I realise."

Christine nodded at me dumbly, her pursed lips holding back a cry. Holding back a lot more besides. "Abuse is like ink on a blotter; it spreads to every other area of our lives."

"God, I've never been through any of that stuff," said Emma, looking at each of us in turn. "My parents were lovely and Billy was a smoker, drinker and twisted sod when I met him. Stayed out drinking a lot and struggled like hell when he lost his leg in Vietnam, but he was only abusive to himself."

"He could have taken it all out on you," said Kathryn, shaking her head. "I mean, losing his leg - that's more than we've gone through. More than our men have gone through."

I said, "At a course I did after Morris, my ex-partner, was taken away they said that anger and abuse is because there's something about ourselves we don't like."

"And everyone has a choice of whether to project it onto others or not," said Kathryn, completing my sentence. I realised she was sitting straighter and her voice was firmer, as if she had stepped into a more powerful part of herself.

"So, we choose men who choose to infect us with their stupid self-hatred, rather than sort it out for themselves," said Christine.

"Hey, it hasn't all been a sweet ride for Billy and me," said Emma. "We've certainly had our stupid moments."

"Yes, I'm sure you have, Emma. We're all walking in shit. The only thing that changes is the depth."

"That sounds depressing, Christine," I said, unable to get the ghastly image out of my head.

"Maybe, but we've all got our demons, haven't we."

"Oh God, I've just realised," said Kathryn, sitting up with a start. "I mean, I know the theory but I've just realised I've been abusing you, Christine, because I feel so bad." Kathryn stared at her sister as if looking for absolution.

"You have, Kat, but I knew there was a good person in there. I was just waiting for her to come out."

Jeanie had stayed at the farm before and was happy to stay overnight with us. Karen decided to stay at Christine's so Billy, Emma and Phil left and the rest of us collapsed into bed. I slept like a dictionary and then had a weird dream that the world had become kind and compassionate place but all sounds had gone from the planet. When I woke up, I worried that I'd gone deaf and finally realised it was morning and the traffic sounds of the town were absent. The only sounds were cicadas and geckos making their chirps, and then I heard the crunch of gravel and knew someone was up.

I wandered out to the kitchen in my borrowed pyjamas and it smelt like heaven - fried eggs, bacon, potatoes, baked beans and toast, along with the aroma of coffee. The two girls were setting the table and Kathryn was supervising them while flipping something in the large frying pans.

"Breakfast is ready, Mum," said Kassey rubbing her hands together and smiling hugely.

"Well done you three girls. Is Karen up?"

"Not yet," said Kathryn.

"Okay, I'll check on her." Karen was awake, lying back on the pillow looking pale but happy. "Ready for breakfast? I'll bring some in."

"My God, I've never been served in bed!" She suddenly looked much brighter. "Why not, if you're offering."

Karen got up at midday and looked much better. No great bursts of energy but at least she had a sweet look of contentment. The rest of us helped around the house, in the implement shed and on the tractor. The girls came in at the end of the day covered in dust and looking deliriously happy. While they were in the shower, Billy and Emma turned up again and Phil followed 10 minutes later. We all tucked into Kathryn's cooking.

Then there was the rumble of tyres on the gravel driveway.

The Invasion

Bugger, here they come," said Billy, standing up and grabbing the girls by the shoulders. "Get yer boots on, Edward." I turned to see Edward with wet hair and bare feet, wearing a t-shirt and shorts. He stared at Billy, nailed to the spot. "The cavalry's coming, mate, so get your boots on. Now!' He waved Edward away and Edward shook his head and sauntered out to put his boots on, I presumed.

"Hell," said Phil, stalking in with Karen on his heels. He dumped his tradesman's bag on the floor. "I think it's Nico and co. And that damned Blowers."

The crunch of gravel indicated there was more than one vehicle.

"Oh, gosh," said Edward, hopping into the room on one foot while he pulled his second boot on.

"Right," said Billy, "can someone take the girls somewhere safe? Maybe all you women too."

"I'm not going," said Christine, standing up and grabbing a knife from the knife block on the bench.

I don't know who entered my body but I found myself saying and doing the same thing ... and then wondering what the heck I was doing there with no idea what to do with a knife. Or why I was not running. Strangely, the knife in my hand was rock-solid steady.

"I'll take the girls," said Kathryn. "I know places even Nico doesn't." She leapt up, grabbed the girls' hands and marched out. It was good to see that stronger person was still inside her, as the girls were swept up in her grim force and neither spoke nor resisted.

"I'll come with you, Kathryn," said Karen, who quickly followed.

The dog started to follow them and Edward grabbed it. "I think we'll need you here, mate," he said to Brutus. The arthritic old fellow stopped and stared at Edward. Then stared at the doorway through which the girls had gone. He opted for the lesser effort and sat at Edward's feet, panting.

"Look, they might have guns and stuff," said Billy. "Don't know what they've got so we've got to play clever, not tough."

"I've got some gear in my van," said Phil. "I can immobilise their vehicles. Or track them."

"But you've got to get close enough to do that," I said.

"I know. Just letting you all know." Phil smiled and nodded to me.

"So, there's five of us and we could separate out, confuse them," said Edward, his palms open as if proposing a motion.

"Well, I'm calling the police," I said, as the idea hit me. I leapt up, dialled and got Constable Natalie Gallo. As I was talking to her, Christine slipped a piece of paper into my hand. Call Stephen on 28741 or, if he's not there, Flora his wife on 28624. "How many cars are there?" I yelled, trying to answer Gallo's question.

"Two!" yelled Edward.

"Two," I told Gallo.

"Can you identify anyone?" asked Gallo. "I've alerted Sergeant McLeod, who's on his way as we speak."

"Who's there?" I yelled again.

"I seen them," said Billy, next to me.

"Here's Billy who can give you more information," I said to her. "McLeod's on his way," I told Billy, handing him the receiver. He said the visitors were Nico Sparelli, Bully Blowers and five others I didn't know.

"Hell, seven against five!" I said.

"Seven against six," said Edward, patting the dog.

"I need string, hammer and nails," said Phil, and Christine towed him over to the kitchen cupboard beside the back door. He nailed a rope across the front door, about ankle height. And then some fishing line across it at eye level.

"That might delay the buggers. I'll do the same at the kitchen door and the one at the end of the hallway. So don't you all forget, okay?"

His initiative got us all thinking and soon, there were upturned chairs near the three doorways and other obstacles scattered around.

Brutus caught the excitement and leapt up, following each of us around, his arthritis magically healed.

"So, they fall over. What next?" asked Billy.

"You have any of those plastic tie things?" asked Phil.

"Yes," said Christine, rushing back to the kitchen and rifling through the drawers. "Woo hoo!" she yelled, pulling out a packet of cable ties. "Stick some in your pockets."

Beyond the exciting adrenalin fog I realised we were in a lot of danger. We could be injured or even killed, and I felt like my excited and weirdly peaceful self was floating a millimetre above my frightened self. Both existed, somehow, and I could choose which one to inhabit. It was surreal as I watched the others rushing around in a practical and excited frenzy.

"Ring Stephen," I said to myself, as if coming out of a daze.

"Just did that, Janice, from my office," said Emma.

"I'll ring James."

"Stephen said he'd do that."

"Phil, you've got one of those portable phone things connected to the Lucky Café. Can you tell them?" asked Billy.

"Oh, of course. How could I forget." Phil rummaged in his bag of electrical stuff and brought out a grey, brick-sized thing with buttons on it.

"Shit, they're coming up the steps," said Billy. "Edward, go and call out the hall door. Might divert them."

"Call out what?" Edward seemed to have lost his genial cool for a moment.

"Any bloody thing, mate. Call them wankers. Whatever. Chris, you go with him."

"Right," they both said and rushed up the hallway, opened the door, stepped between the rope and nylon and both yelled obscenities at the invaders.

"You and Phil yell out the kitchen door," he said to me, and we did. All that swearing felt so, so good. Meanwhile, Brutus rushed up the hall after Edward and Christine and then back to Phil and me.

"Hey, come here, mate," said Billy, crouching down and patting the now excited dog. "We're together on this. Oh, Emma, you okay?"

"Not really, but I'll stay here and help where I can."

"Get the hell outta here, ya pricks!" yelled Nico from outside the front door.

"Get the hell in here, ya dork," yelled Billy, crouching against the kitchen door frame, holding Brutus by the scruff of the neck. "Door's not locked, ya bloody coward."

The front door swung open and Nico flew in horizontally and crashed to the polished wooden floor, his gun skittering along it.

"Get him," whispered Billy to Brutus, loud enough for Phil and me to hear. Nico grunted, screamed in pain and then went silent. I later found out that Brutus had leapt on Nico's legs and savaged them, while Billy yanked his arms behind him and immobilised him with cable ties. That was why they had to carry Nico out later. "Hey, hey, Brutus, enough!" Billy yelled.

"You won't be tripping me up, you clever buggers!" yelled Blowers from the verandah.

Apparently, he looked down, stepped over the rope and then grunted as his legs kept going while his head didn't. Billy leapt upon him as he toppled about, and Phil rushed to help fell the corpulent giant.

"Hey, hey, Brutus, enough!" yelled Billy again, as Blowers swore and yelled.

Without warning, there was a hand at my throat, and I screamed and tried to run to Phil and Billy. The hand let go and a body crashed beside me.

"Leap on his bum and I'll tie his hands," said Phil. I complied in the moment and later, realised what a stupid, suicidal thing I'd just done. But the arms were quickly tied as the man screamed in pain before we dragged Brutus off. Then he went quiet and still.

"Don't fucken move!" ordered the normally placid Phil.

He and I looked up and into the wrong end of a rifle. We froze. Then there was a loud crash at the far end of the house and the barrel swivelled away. Phil grabbed a hanging broom and speared the gunner's head at the same time as Brutus dealt with the bottom end of the attacker. He fell and I leapt after him for no logical reason, my inner warrior taking over. I forgot about the rope in the doorway and fell headlong over the body, now laid out backwards down the steps.

"Good move," said Phil, who grabbed the rifle and smashed the butt into the man's face, thankfully missing mine by a few millimetrs. I rolled out of the way and Phil flipped the man over and tied the hands as he groaned and looked bewildered. Phil then stood and pointed the rifle at someone I couldn't see outside.

"Hell, hey mate!" that someone said, his voice rising as Phil approached him.

"Drop it," commanded Phil and something clattered on the gravel pathway. "On ya knees. Now on ya face. Don't move." I followed and he handed me the rifle and tied the man up. Thankfully, Brutus seemed to have tired of his game and sat at my feet, panting.

"I've got two rifles!" yelled Phil.

"We've got one!" Edward yelled back. "And one tied up, one loose."

"Three tied up here!" yelled Phil. "I'm out to my car."

"Two tied up here!" yelled Billy. "One's still loose." Then I realised Billy was next to me, on the step. I stood up, shaking like a guitar string. "Shall I take the rifle?" he asked quietly. I was relieved to get rid of it.

"Loose one gone to his car!" yelled Edward.

"Jeez, Phil," whispered Billy. He leapt down the steps and raced around the corner as fast as an ungainly, bung-legged man can. I wanted to sit and cry but instead, forced my resistant body to move. I looked around and Brutus wasn't there. I walked in through the door more carefully than I had walked out of it and collapsed onto a chair, shaking, my head on the kitchen table.

"He's taking his car!" yelled Edward, rushing down the hallway, past the kitchen door and out onto the verandah, thankfully missing the booby traps.

I heard a car start and then the spin of wheels on gravel, stones hitting the iron of the implement shed. Then the car stopped.

"Well done, Phil!" yelled Billy. "Oh no, here come more of them! No, it's James!"

My shaking turned to sobbing and relief flowed through my body like rivulets of grief.

The Shaking Therapy

I'mm not sure how long I lay bent over that table, sobbing and shaking, but it seemed a split second later that a hand landed gently on my shoulder. It gave me a fright and I sat straight up, like a dingo sitting on a hedgehog. My head felt woozy from the sudden movement.

"Sorry to startle you, Janice," came a soothing male voice I recognised.

"James, I probably startled you." I remained still and let the vertigo drain away and then had a sudden thought. "Kassey. Is Kassey alright? Where is she?"

"It's okay. Both girls are okay. Kathryn took them somewhere and then just reappeared. She won't say where they went but they're all good. Well, they're a bit shook up but all good." He pulled a chair out and sat facing me. I've got to say that daughter of yours is a resilient girl, isn't she."

"Is she?" I wasn't sure what he meant.

"Yes, she seems back to her bouncy self, helping put all the chairs back and chatting to everyone. She's a great pick-up for Jeanie who's been through absolute hell. Although she's a bouncing personality when she feels safe, she retreats into shyness with strangers."

"Well, Kassey's seen me beaten up a few times and she's been molested by my ex. I don't mean that as any sort of competition. I get a bit defensive for her."

"I understand." His eyes pierced my heart with their kindness.

"You do? From your own experience?"

"Not directly." He looked around as if to check for listening ears. "Look, I've only told two other people this so please keep it under your hat."

"Of course." My brain had finally returned to its default setting so I turned my chair to face him, knees to knees.

"Okay, to the nub of it." He took a huge breath as if sucking in courage and steadiness. He looked down and then up into my eyes. "I think I told you my sister was brutally raped by a group of them. I found her."

"You said she was raped but not who did it."

"They were the Sparelli gang."

"You know who they are? Your sister's recovering?" I had so many questions about how it had happened and when, how he'd found out who did it, why he was telling me, if that was why he became a lawyer, whether they had been prosecuted or were still free men, but I kept my mouth shut.

"Yes and no." He looked down, possibly deciding how far to go with this.

"Pardon? No, hang on, it's not my business. You don't have to say anything at all."

He smiled, blew his cheeks out and exhaled. "Maybe we talk about this another time but, in short, Jessica didn't know who they were but I tracked them down. And, no, she's still not coping well, after seven years."

"Oh." I put my hand on his knee and he put his hand on mine. He looked at me and I thought he was about to cry, but he wiped his eyes with the other hand and smiled.

"You've had your own tough experiences as well," he said quietly.

"Yes, another time, huh. Let's join the others, wherever they are."

He nodded and stood up, our hands still touching. He pulled me up.

"They're outside with the cops and ambulance."

"Ambulance?" I immediately feared for Christine, Emma, Billy, Phil and Edward.

"Yes, for Nico and Blowers. That dog did a thorough job on them and they need stretchers to get them to hospital where they'll be under police supervision."

"Whew. And my girl?"

"She's in the office with Kathryn and Karen while the police process the intruders, get witness statements and fingerprint the guns."

"Where's the office?"

"Left up the hallway and second on the right. As a lawyer, I'd better attend your friends while they give their witness statements." We unclasped our fingers and I felt an immediate emptiness in the chest.

"Hey, Mum, that was scary, huh!" said Kassey, running up to me with her arms wide. We hugged and my uncertain world righted itself as I felt her whole and hearty against me.

"How about you, Jeanie?" I asked over Kassey's head. "You've had a tough time lately, huh?" She nodded and looked me in the eye for the first time. "Join us if you like." I put my arm out and she looked at me uncertainly, smiled and joined us in a grug, a group hug. "Where did you all go?"

"Went up, Mum. It was cool," said Kassey.

"Please don't say any more," said Kathryn, rising from an office chair, her previous energy evaporated.

"Sorry, James said it was a secret," I said. "I'll say no more."

"I don't like being locked in but these ladies were nice. Scary, though," said Kassey, smiling up at me as she released her arms from me.

"Look, if you shut the door, Jeanie, I'll show you," said Kathryn, finally smiling.

"Keep it between us girls," said Karen, standing up from a stuffed leather chair.

"Karen, I didn't see you there in the shadow!" I said as I walked across the long rug on the timbered floor. Kathryn walked to the back of the room, between a big, old roll-top desk and about 12 shelves of books that covered the whole of the side wall. I couldn't quite see what Kathryn was fiddling with but she then stepped back, pulling the wall with her to reveal a well disguised door.

"A secret door!" I exclaimed. She put her finger to her lips and frowned. "Sorry," I whispered. She waved me over. Behind the door was a flight of steps leading up.

"Uh huh, so you were safe." I breathed out in relief.

"But we heard all the noises and yelling and thumps," said Kassey, her eyes bright. Almost unnaturally bright.

"And the dog," said Jeanie, "we heard the dog." She seemed animated but a bit jumpy. I smiled at her.

"Hey, Karen, are you alright? This morning you were bedridden," I said.

"I think it's caught up with me, actually." She sat back down, looking pale.

"Do you want to lie down?" asked Kathryn. "Yes, you do. I know. Come here." They both left and I took the girls out on the verandah as two prone people were being loaded into the ambulance. The other invaders were sitting on the ground against Blowers' huge black car, their hands behind their backs, an ambulance officer attending to the legs of one of them.

"I don't think this is a good sight for young girls," said Constable Markham, coming over to us.

"Yes, you're absolutely right," I said, sorry I'd let them see those evil men. What was I thinking? I took their hands and led them back inside and they didn't speak or resist. "You're shaking, Jeanie. Let's go back to the office to sit down. You're shaking too, Kassey."

"Yes, Mum, I was alright before but I don't know. I feel giddy."

I towed them into the office and shut the door. It seemed such a safe place with its mahogany walls, its wall of books, imposing desk and green leather seats, the coolness an escape from the harsh sun outside.

"Give me a hug, both of you."

"Yes, missus," said Jeanie quietly.

"And how about you both stay here in my arms till the shaking stops." The girls' silence assured me they'd stay. "So, let me explain," I said. "They found that when animals are harmed, like being attacked by another animal and escaping or after being shot with a tranquilizer and waking up again, they all do the same thing. They all shake. Dogs, cats, buffalos, zebras and all other animals shake after being really upset. It's as if they shake to get rid of their bad feelings. Maybe they shake the fear or scaredness out of themselves. Then, when they stop shaking, and this is really interesting, they always take three deep breaths. Not two breaths. Not four breaths. They take three deep breaths and then leap up and run away."

"I always try and stop my shaking when I'm scared," said Jeanie.

"And you've been scared a lot?"

"Yes missus."

"So, from now on, don't stop it. Let it keep going till it stops by itself. Okay?" She nodded yes into my tummy.

I noticed Kassey had become still. I released her and she took three deep breaths, as I'd previously taught her. She smiled and then hugged Jeanie until she stopped shaking.

"Now, three deep breaths," said Kassey. Jeanie looked at us with apparent cynicism, her brows furrowed. Then she inhaled and exhaled three times and then stood there staring at us as a smile spread across her face.

"I never knew how to feel good after," she said.

"After a bad moment?" I asked.

"Yes. I feel, like, calm." She hugged me again and then skipped to the door. "Can we go out again now?"

"Just a moment. I didn't notice you there, Karen. I thought you'd gone with Kathryn."

"She took off and I ... I needed to sit down. So I'm sitting here shaking as per your lesson. I'm letting myself shake and I do feel better. I don't know why we try to stop it."

"We're too busy trying to look good," said Kathryn, from behind me.

"Look good?" asked Karen.

"Shaking and breathing heavily and crying don't look good. They don't look cool. They look silly, apparently. Animals don't think like that."

"Exactly, Kathryn," I said. "And you're okay?"

"I really need to lie down, actually."

"Me too," said Karen. "I'd better get home before I crash."

"No, stay here. I've made a bed up for you." Kathryn sounded strangely assertive and I wondered if she enjoyed looking after someone else, after so many others had looked after her over the last month or so. "Come with me."

"And you girls can come with me and make cups of tea for everyone out there, okay?" I led them down to the kitchen.

"Can we do that? For all those people?" asked Jeanie, sounding amazed.

"I'm sure you can. You helped with breakfast."

"Mum showed me how to make tea." Jeanie's bright eyes showed her eagerness to show off her skills.

"She's a quick learner," said Emma, right behind me. "Thanks for looking after her while I helped Billy with his prosthetic leg. It got a bit damaged before."

"He's okay?"

"He's always okay, even when he isn't. Men!" We both laughed. "You can show Kassey how to do it."

"But I know how to make tea," said Kassey, a little annoyed. I put my finger to my lip and winked as Jeanie marched across the kitchen to her mission. "Help her out, whatever she needs."

"She's only been with us for three months and I'm amazed at what she hasn't been taught," said Emma, shaking her head, "and what a quick learner she is."

"How did she come to you?"

"She escaped from a child trafficking ring in Alice Springs. Edward found her on the road. He was trying to find Christine, his lost love, and he brought Jeanie here. Then we adopted her. She's pretty tough in a lot of ways when she needs to be. And then has these moments of, like, frailty."

"A bit like Kathryn?"

"Mmm, I suppose so. The stupid things we do to others to hurt them. We really are a stupid species. Anyhow, let's see how the girls are going. Wow, look at that - all done, I think."

"Kassey, have a look in those cupboards to see if there are any biscuit tins," I said. The girls giggled to each other and I didn't know why. I didn't care, either, as it was good to see them happy. Jeanie was pouring hot water into the huge teapot and I nearly rushed over to help her when I realised she was coping rather well.

"We haven't had the fish and chips yet," said Emma. "Christine put them in the oven just before those idiots broke in. I'll turn it on now."

Someone came into the kitchen. "Hello, I'm Constable Natalie Gallo."

"Natalie? Aah, yes, I talked with you on the phone."

"Yes you did. Janice?" I nodded. She was built like a gymnast, strong but with not an ounce of fat, bouncing like a youngster. Her black hair was tied back neatly. With swarthy skin but definitely not Aboriginal, she was all energy and business.

"We've finished with the invaders and have taken witness statements from your friends. You can do the same now, or come to the station tomorrow if you prefer. We have enough corroborating evidence to keep them locked up until tomorrow."

"Yes, tomorrow, please. I'd like to stay with my daughter right now, if that's okay."

"Good. I'll be on duty from midday if you'd like to pop in then?"

"Yes, and should I bring Kathryn and Karen in as well?"

"Yes, that'd be good. Good night." Then she was gone as fast as she had appeared.

"The girls have made tea and the fish and chips might be another 10 minutes," I said as Christine came in. I looked around and Emma was gone.

"She's checking on Billy," Christine said. "He always says he's fine but he'd say that if he had a fence post through his head."

We both chuckled and I noticed the table had been laid out with cups, saucers and plates.

"Wow, you've worked your magic, girls," I said, waving my hand over the table. They giggled together again.

Then Billy, Emma, Phil, James and Edward came in, stared at the pristine table and sat down. Not a word was said and, now that the panic was over, I was not surprised. Time to absorb the stupidity of the surreal attack.

"Hey, Mum," said Jeanie, looking bright-eyed and cheerful, "do you know about shaking and breathing?"

"Shaking and breathing?" asked Emma, looking confused.

"Well, the lady ..."

"Call me Janice," I said.

"Janice?" asked Jeanie. I nodded. "Well, um, Janice told us all about it."

"Mmm, you'd better tell us all." Emma sipped her tea, unable to hide the obvious surprise on her face. She winked at Billy who remained uncharacteristically quiet with a curious smile.

Jeanie told them everything I had, with occasional interruptions from Kassey. After their five-minute speech, in which they left nothing out, there was complete silence.

"Damn, the fish and chips!" exclaimed Christine, who leapt up and dragged the large baking tray out of the oven. She plonked it on the wooden breadboard in the middle of the table. Tomato sauce was squirted on plates and everyone tucked in.

"You know, Janice," said Emma quietly, as I gingerly held a piece of hot fish aloft, "that's the longest speech I've ever heard from Jeanie in these three months."

I shrugged. "Maybe it's a subject close to her heart."

"Mmm, maybe Billy and I have been shielding her from it. Perhaps we don't have to."

"There's no fixed rules with parenting and much of it is learned by getting things wrong. However, the shaking might give her a technique for releasing the terror she might have trapped inside her."

"That'd be great."

"Look, it's not the whole solution, but it certainly helps. They've had success with getting Vietnam vets with PTSD to assume stressful poses that induce shaking. It seems to release past trauma and fear."

"Poses?" asked Billy suddenly, turning to me, his mouth full of chips. "I was in Nam."

"Things like holding the plank for 100 breaths. Sitting cross-legged on the floor. Lying on your back with your legs in the air. Leaning against a wall, standing at a right angle. Any stance that's slightly uncomfortable so that you'll eventually start shaking as tiny, little-used muscles kick in."

"How come I didn't know about this?" he asked, having swallowed his chips and now looking indignant. "I was a vet."

"Do you fix animals?" asked Kassey innocently. We all laughed.

"Animals? Nah, I was a veteran soldier. I been to war. They call us vets. Veteran, vet."

"Can I remind you, Billy," said Emma, staring right at him, "there was this particular vet who refused all the counselling and the therapy offered. I think his words went something like, 'Nah, not having any of that namby-pamby shit.' You remember him, Billy?"

Edward chuckled and Billy hit him on the shoulder and then smiled sheepishly.

"Yeah, okay, mighta been someone I know," he said, pursing his lips in embarrassment.

"Dad, try it now!" said Jeanie, leaping up and looking wildly enthusiastic, her arms waving like a windmill on steroids.

"Let me finish my grub first, love."

"But Dad." Jeanie's features dropped like a dead fly.

"Okay." He hauled himself up and soon, everyone was doing planks and other poses under my supervision, as I'd learned at the Woman's Refuge three years before. Along with the shaking were all sorts of emotional reactions - crying, laughter, mumbling and so on. I counselled them to keep crying, laughing, swearing or whatever they were doing and eventually, everyone collapsed, exhausted and chuckling.

"They say that each time we do it, we release another trauma ..." I started to say.

"You mean the trauma's in our bodies, like," said Phil, obviously stumbling over his words, "like a solid, physical thing?"

"Yes, that's what some people say. It's not the only way to get rid of trauma, anger and so on and I'm not sure it clears everything, but done regularly, they say it helps to replace fear and anger with peace and clarity."

"Rotary hoe, it's time to go," said Billy, rubbing his hands as he stood up. "Time to get our daughter to bed."

"But Dad, can I stay here?" asked Jeanie, much more confident than when I'd met her.

"Aw, hell, are there enough beds?"

"Janice," said Emma, "would Kassey like to stay overnight with us?"

"Ooh, yes, Mum," exclaimed Kassey before my brain could process the question. "Can I?"

"Um, I, well ..."

"We've got spare pyjamas, toothbrushes and stuff," said Emma, standing up.

"And tomorrow's Saturday," said Jeanie, sharing her excited look with Kassey.

This would be the first time Kassey had stayed overnight with anyone but me. I faltered, even though there was no earthly reason to hold her back.

"You'll be alright with it, Kassey?" I knew her answer but needed another moment to let the idea sink in. Kassey put her hands on her hips and frowned, as if she was about to tell me off. That was all the answer I needed. "Right, if it's okay with Emma and Billy." They both nodded. "You make sure you behave yourself."

"Oh, we'll do that. I got me stockwhip," said Billy, grinning like a little boy.

"Billy, don't scare the girl!" said Emma, slapping his arm.

Kassey giggled and Jeanie's eyebrows shot up and she groaned. She knew Billy's humour well.

"Just joking," he said. "I'll only use it on Emma tonight." He dodged another slap and hobbled out of the kitchen.

"Oh, that man's mouth's going to get him in trouble one day." Emma shook her head and smiled.

"It already has," he said, looking around the doorway from the hallway. "It asked you to marry me."

"And you've regretted that?" Emma walked right up to him, challenging.

"Nah, the only regret is I didn't do it sooner." He grabbed her in a hug.

"Aah, Billy Mullins, you big softie." Emma shook her head, smiled and tried to push him away. He grabbed her head and kissed her on the lips. She didn't resist.

"An' I never regret that." He marched off out the door, down the steps, calling, "Come on you lot. It'll be morning in a minute."

"Oh, that man," said Emma, her elfin face turning red, right up to her very short fringe. "Come on, girls, let's get us all to bed. It's been a tough day."

I whimpered as my girl followed the other three out the door. She looked back, smiling, triumphant. "You're sure you'll be alright?" I asked, feeling like a screwdriver in a box of nails. "At least give me a hug." She dashed back, gave me a quick hug and was gone. My girl, off with strangers, staying overnight for the first time. But they didn't feel like strangers at all, more like old friends I'd known all my life. Phil broke my sad reverie.

"I'd better get home. I'll come back for Karen in the morning." He had walked past me by the time my brain returned to normal thinking mode.

"I can bring her into town with Kathryn. We've got to make statements at the police station at midday so you can meet us there, if you like."

"Right, if it's not too much trouble," I said. He turned and hugged me, this fuzzy, clever tower of kindness. "Thanks so much for everything, Janice."

I nodded, not knowing what 'everything' he was referring to, but I was happy to let it go. It was nice to make another person a little happier. Then I thought of everything that the big, hairy bugger had done for all of us and turned to thank him but he was gone, thumping down the steps and across the gravel.

"Right, Janice, Kathryn's room is a mess so you might as well use the second bed where Karen is," said Christine. "There's other bedrooms but the beds aren't made up."

"Whatever's easiest," I said. "I want to crash out and not wake up. I've realised how exhausted I am. Mentally as well as physically."

"I'll just clean up here ..."

"Oh, I'll help." I suddenly felt guilty.

"No, get to bed. It's only fish and chips so I'll be quicker than a goat's fart."

I smiled and followed Edward down the hallway.

"How did you find Jeanie?" I asked him, just before we got to the door.

"I'm happy to tell you this long story, Janice, but how about in the morning?"

"Sorry, I'm not thinking. Or thinking too much. My brain's too tired to be tired."

He smiled politely. "I'll get you a towel, flannel and toothbrush." He walked off.

"And that pink tracksuit in my second drawer!" yelled Christine from the kitchen doorway.

I lay down for a moment till Edward returned and was woken by someone shining a torch in my face. It was the sun and someone was letting the blind up. I groaned. God, morning already?

The Lucky Café - Saying Yes

We arrived at the police station five minutes late and Phil was waiting on the front steps.

"He's already waiting," said Karen, cooing gently.

"God, Karen, you're going soft," I said as I indicated and turned up Roderick Street to park in the small carpark at the back of the station.

"What I don't get is you're five foot two," said Kathryn from the back seat.

"Five foot two and a half, thank you," said Karen defiantly.

"Okay, five foot two point four eight seven nine inches. And he's six foot two. And you look so neat and tidy and he's as scruffy as a furball in a food mixer."

"They say opposites attract, don't they." Karen's voice had softened a bit.

"On the outside with you two, obviously. But he's a very clever man and I'm guessing you're up there with intelligence, too."

"Look, do you mind, Kathryn," said Karen, turning around as far as she could go to look at Kathryn, "but we don't need to be analysed and prodded like scientific specimens."

"Okay, Karen, I'm so sorry it sounded like that."

I stopped the car and pulled on the handbrake but stayed sitting while Kathryn finished. "I'm trying to work out relationships. How did I choose Nico and get it so wrong? I can't for the life of me see what I was attracted to."

I chuckled. "I ask myself that question every single day. I've had two failed relationships - one killed himself with drugs and the other one's in gaol for molesting Kassey and for beating me. How could I get it so wrong?"

"Oh, here he is," said Karen, in answer to a tap on her window.

"Are you girls getting out?" asked Phil, holding Karen's door open. He'd actually brushed his unruly mop of hair.

"We're talking about relationships."

"Shall I get sun loungers and martinis?"

"Ya cheeky bugger. Now, give us a hug and we'll get this stuff down for the police," Karen said.

"Yes, that Natalie Gallo was here right on midday; as efficient as she looks."

"So you were here before that, Phil?" I asked. "You must be keen."

"Yeah, well." He blushed right down to the roots of his hair and looked down at his thongs.

"Come here, you big lump." Karen grabbed him and hugged him. She had to stand on tiptoe and he remained bent towards her, looking happy and relieved.

"Sorry, constable, we're coming," I said, noticing Constable Gallo on the back step. I felt like a naughty little girl under her impassive stare.

"Just one of you at a time," she said, waving us inside. "You're welcome to wait in our reception area to stay out of the heat."

"Yes, what is it today?" asked Kathryn, getting out of the back seat.

"Thirty-five degrees," said Phil, looking at his monstrous watch. "That's 95 Fahrenheit."

"What's that you're looking at?" Kathryn went over to look at his watch.

"Who's coming first?" asked Gallo, her impassive look more menacing than any furious look.

"It's just something I made," said Phil, still absorbed in his technology.

"Right, I'll go first," I said, tossing the keys to Phil. "Lock up if you don't want to stay in the car."

"We'll come inside." He tossed them back to me.

"Oh, will we?" asked an indignant Karen.

"Get ye inside to yon hovel." He laughed, picked her up and trotted inside after me.

"Oh, you beast," she said as he put her down.

"Are you okay, madam?" asked Gallo, stopping suddenly and turning around to us.

"Sorry, ma'am, we're just being silly," said Phil.

"I asked the lady."

"Oh." He looked embarrassed again.

"And the lady is perfectly fine, thank you. Like he said, just being silly," said Karen.

"Right. Please sit down and do not alarm the staff here with anything unnecessary. We get too many women covering for their abusive partners and so we're sensitive to such behaviour. Okay Janice." She walked off and I followed her with a suitably serious face.

After giving my statement, I needed to get out of the station. I knew the police were helping us and we couldn't do without them, but we can't do without dentists either. I'd had to resort to police help way more than was good for me, whenever Kassey or I had been in danger. I don't understand why people have to be shits to each other. Why can't the stupid people all go and live on an island and be horrid to each other while leaving us normal ones to get on with our ordinary, boring, peaceful lives?

I stepped out of the air-conditioned station and came up slam bang against a wall of heat. With all the concrete, bricks, tar seal and glass to reflect heat, town was always hotter than places with trees, dirt and grass. As I was reconsidering my escape, I happened to look up and, past my car, was another car in the park right next to the road, facing out as if ready for a quick getaway. Call me weird but I think cars are like houses in that they exude personalities - sad, happy, abandoned, loved and so on. This was an ordinary green Holden Premier, anonymous amongst thousands of other green Holdens in this country, but it exuded something icky. I stepped back inside involuntarily, my primitive flight response. The glass double doors shut and I peered out and sucked in a big breath. Sunlight was on the windscreen so I couldn't see clearly, but I could have sworn it was my grumpy neighbour, pufferfish George Barbieri.

"Are you alright, ma'am?" asked Constable Markham, his white teeth lighting up his dark face.

"Holy macaroni, where did you come from?" My heart skipped to Malloo.

"Sorry ma'am, you look frightened."

"And you just added to it. You've got to warn a girl you're approaching. And we've met so you can call me Janice."

"We're in the station," he said, shrugging and smiling awkwardly. He patted my arm and my heart returned to a manageable beat. "Is everything alright?"

"Yes ... no." I tried to collect my scattered thoughts. "There's a green Holden in the carpark and I'm sure it's my neighbour, George, who came to my house yelling at me and insulting me for speaking up. He's hasn't committed a crime but he's sitting there staring at me. He's been there all the time we've been talking."

Markham looked through the door. "I see what you mean. Can you stand in the doorway and hold the door ajar so he focuses on you? I'll take a short walk."

"Right," I said uncertainly, the prospect of putting myself in the firing line - even if it was only the firing line of his horrid stare - wasn't an enticing prospect. I don't know how my Creeping Jesus managed it, but it seemed like only seconds later he was standing beside the driver's door of the green Holden. The window went down and it was definitely George. Suddenly, the car started up and Markham leapt around to the front of it. After a protracted exchange, the car went quiet and Pufferfish George squeezed himself out and walked with Markham around to the front door of the station. Markham arrived at the door just ahead of his reluctant visitor and waved me away. I stumbled down the concrete steps and hopped into my car.

Even through my jeans the seat burnt my legs. With my fingertips on the hot steering wheel, all aflutter, I nearly collided with a passing van. It tooted at me and I slammed on the brakes and sat there, getting my body and brain back together, my heart pounding. I drove out with no idea where to go - apart from away - and suddenly remembered. The Lucky Café! I could have walked there from the police station but I wasn't going back. I parked in the library carpark, across Roderick Street from the station and under the only tree for 3,000 kilometres.

As I walked into the Lucky Café I felt anything but lucky. I felt like I'd just escaped from prison.

"Janice, how are you?" asked Sarah, Geoffrey's wife.

"Um, okay."

"You don't look okay. Would you like to sit down?"

"Could I please borrow your phone first? I need to ring the police station to tell Kathryn I'm here. I have to take her home." I smiled with relief when I realised that part of my mind was working logically, strategically.

"I'll do that," she said. "And a cappuccino for you?"

I nodded dumbly and stared at the high ceiling. Then Kassey came to mind. I'd spoken to Emma from Christine's that morning, and Kassey was happy to spend the day with Jeanie. That had given me the mental and physical space to ferry Kathryn and Karen around.

That was when the shaking started. This time it was infinitesimal vibrations inside my body that no one would see from the outside. It was as if my organs were on a kind of electrical circuit, all vibrating at different rates. My fingers were shaking too so I put them on my knees, under the table. I sat with the vibrations and the uncertainty of their cause. Anal-ysing is shitty thinking, I'd heard, and I tried to stay empty as the vibrations slowly died down.

"There you are, dream boat," said Christine in her riding boots, jean shorts, polo shirt and akubra hat. The very model of a modern madam farmer. With her flaming red hair, fair freckled skin and the way she filled out her polo shirt, she made a statement just being who she was. Her assertive personality outshone but comforted, in equal parts.

"Get back on the farm, woman! Don't you know your place?" I said, deciding to risk a little humour. By God I needed it.

"Yes, ma'am, and I suppose you want me to butter your scones for you." She curtseyed low, trying to suppress a smile.

"Scones? What scones?"

"These ones," said Sarah, popping down a plate of two scones, jam, cream and a cup of coffee.

"I didn't order that."

"Too damned bad," said Christine, sitting down, her suppressed smile finally breaking out. "If ma'am will permit me to sit at her table?"

"Okay, just this time." I waved my finger at her. Sarah came up to the table and I asked her, "How do you make a living, here, giving away your profits to dream boats like me?"

"We don't. This is thanks to an anonymous benefactor, ma'am," said Sarah, curtseying as low as Christine had.

"Not you too!" We all giggled. "So, what are you here for, Christine? You had a whole list of things to do at home."

"I did, but Edward dislodged a rusted pipe when he was mowing. It's not leaking yet, but we need to fix it and bury it deeper before ploughing the paddock."

"Or reroute the whole pipeline around the edge of the paddock," said Edward, coming in. "Besides, I'm really struggling with the heat. I said to Christine that I needed a day off and then I discovered the pipe."

"How fortuitous," said Christine, smiling at him and putting her hand on the back of his neck. I almost cried at the tenderness of that small gesture and realised how much I missed a man's caring touch. Perhaps I'd never had it. "I'll get you a cup of tea, Edward, and anyone for any more?" I wiped my eyes quickly and Christine asked, "You alright, Janice?" Her hand brushed my shoulder and the tears welled up again as my chest felt that familiar, unwelcome hollowness.

"Just having a moment," I said, not wanting to make a scene.

"You're not having a moment, Janice. You're crying." She sat sideways on a chair, facing me squarely. "Edward would say that crying is the body's poetry and that's how it sings its need and pain to you."

"Gosh, that's beautiful. I know not to ignore it, but not here. Not in public."

"Janice, listen to me. The more tears we shed, the more we understand others' tears. And I've had enough for a dozen lifetimes. Get it?"

"I'll get your coffee," said Edward, patting her shoulder. "Anyone else?" No one answered and he walked to the counter.

"Get what?" I knew what she meant but was too embarrassed and uncomfortable talking about it.

"That I bloody care. That we all bloody care. We know what it's like for the world to be against us and to feel alone with it."

"Exactly," said Geoffrey, patting my shoulder as he passed with a tray of coffees and cakes for another table. "Sorry to interrupt." He turned to move on and I stopped him.

"So, you've been through the wringer, Geoffrey?" I found it hard to imagine a successful, white businessman having problems.

He smiled but continued to the next door table.

"Wait till I tell you Geoffrey's story and you'll be glad you were never in his shoes," said Christine.

"Or anyone else's shoes," said Edward, arriving back and sitting down on the other side of me. "We've all had a taste of it and none of us wish our own brand of misery on anyone."

"You too, Edward?" A man, a white man with a loving partner? I thought.

"Yes, I've been threatened at the end of a pistol, petrified, beaten and I shot a man. Christine's been beaten by her father and her husband. Geoffrey's been homeless and in gaol, Samuel's been ..."

"Old chap, save your chops, for this fine lady knows the outline of my decrepit story," said Samuel, pulling out a chair right on cue as if in a well-rehearsed play.

"Oh," was all I could think of to say.

"And here we are, all normally functioning members of this bizarre apparition we call society." Samuel sat back with a contented smile beneath his tangled beard. He waved at Geoffrey as he passed and no words were necessary for whatever communication passed between them.

"So, the question you want me to ask is, 'what got you through it?'" I looked around and they all nodded and smiled as if I'd won the lottery.

"Community," said Edward.

"Friends," said Christine.

"The mottled assortment of souls encased in skin that we happen to come across," said Samuel.

"That we happen to come across sounds so random," I said. "But how do we find these people to reach out to? I mean, I'm really lucky I found you ..."

"Oh, no, no, luck has nothing to do with it, my dear."

"But surely ..."

"Let me propose to you a practical philosophy, Janice, my dear." Samuel scratched his beard and pulled his chair closer to the table while fixing me with his clear blue eyes. "See, I'm not cognisant with the meaning of life. No one is. But, on this rock I stand, the way to live life is to say yes. In business, in relationships, in everything, just say yes."

"Say yes?" I asked, sitting back, a willing pupil.

"Allow me to take a daring risk and suggest that you have been alone. Or, more importantly, you've felt alone."

"Hell yes."

"That's what all abusers do - partners, governments, police, parents - they keep people apart to make them feel vulnerable. Powerless."

"Oh, right."

"Then one fine day you said yes."

"Mmm, not sure."

"Oh, you did, young lady. The universe wants us to say yes so it initially waits. It bides its time, for it has an abundance of minutes, days and years. It waits for you to say yes. If you don't, it will eventually intervene with a reason to cajole you into saying yes - a small accident, injury or something that commands your attention. If you ignore that, it will deliver you a larger inducement. The inducements reach a crescendo until you eventually have to emerge from your cocoon and say yes. Or maybe you say, 'I've had enough of this,' which is an alternative to saying yes."

"Mmm, maybe," I said, knowing the truth of his words.

"Only maybe?" asked Christine, smiling.

"Okay, I didn't take action with my ex-husband but he eventually died from the drugs he was taking. After that I knew I should have left him long before that. Then I took action after my ex-boyfriend started molesting Kassey. But I left it longer than I should have. And this child trafficking at the school? Yes, I spoke up, asked for help but I should have done it much sooner."

"You are a very bad person, Janice," said Geoffrey seriously, as he brought Samuel his coffee and a muffin. "You should have acted sooner." He chuckled and the others joined in his rising laughter. "I'm sorry, Janice, but that's what we all say - 'I should have acted sooner'. Everybody says that and we all feel guilty."

My confusion cleared and I started to feel less embarrassed.

"Don't forget your scones," said Christine, "or the flies will get them." I looked down and realised I hadn't touched my food or drink.

"Your coffee will be cold. Let me get you another ..." said Geoffrey, until I interrupted him.

"No, it's fine. I don't mind it cold."

"You're just being nice."

"No, I'm not. My coffee at home usually ends up cold and I don't mind it. Really."

He nodded and trotted off to the counter as a young couple came in.

"And, my dear, you have now been apprised of the fact that we all feel guilty for not acting sooner." Samuel wiped coffee foam off his beard.

"I suppose I should feel better knowing that, but I'm not sure I do."

"I like your honesty, lass. So, the final question for the day. Then the examination will be over." He clasped his hands and stretched his arms out as if preparing for exercise. "The question, your honour, is why do we all delay speaking up and asking for help? We all do it."

"We're frightened of consequences?"

"But if we're being beaten or abused in some way, the consequences of speaking up must be better than our current state, right?"

"Well, that's logical but ..."

"But logic doesn't work, particularly when we're enduring trauma."

"Don't I know that!"

"So, logic is impotent. What, then, induces action? Or inaction?"

"Fear of the unknown?"

"A valiant attempt, madam, but you failed that examination."

"Oh."

"The reason we don't act when we should is because we feel guilty."

"Because of what?"

"I didn't say we are guilty. I said we feel guilty. An important distinction."

"When Samuel told me this," said Christine, leaning forward and looking into my eyes, "I didn't believe it. I thought the idea was rubbish. But then, I eventually got it and everything fell into place."

"So I should expect to reject this practical philosophy of yours, Samuel?"

"That is an option, but truth doesn't care if you believe it or not."

"Okay, hit me with your absurdity."

"I love your cynicism, madam. You're a discerning thinker. So, allow me to propose that the reason we do not act in our own best interests is because of guilt."

"Guilt. Right."

"Indubitably, my dear. It's called our existential guilt. We are all born with it and it dogs our ragged existence till we die."

"Every minute?" I tried desperately to suspend disbelief but it was hard.

"Let us assume you are strolling along Brisbane Road, here, without a care in the world. Suddenly, a car beeps its horn. What's your first thought?"

"That I've done something wrong," said Christine, stealing my words.

"Yes, you spin around, wondering what you've done wrong. They were probably tooting at someone else, but you assume it's all about you. Now, if your boss says, 'can you see me in my office?' what do you think?"

"I assume I've done something wrong, I suppose," I said as the light began to dawn.

"Why do we never assume a tooting horn has nothing to do with us or our boss wants to congratulate or promote us?"

"Mmm, we don't, do we? It's silly, really," I said, musing on my weirdness. "But why do we have this existential guilt in the first place?"

"That, my dear, is a conversation for another day but, reeling back to our original thesis, we don't take action until the last minute because, quite unconsciously, we assume we are the offenders. We are the guilty ones, the ones always in the wrong. This ever-present, illogical guilt interferes with and short-circuits logic. And so we don't serve our own best interests ..." He stopped speaking, then said, "Here comes Kathryn and a friend."

I turned to see the very slim, almost anorexic, Kathryn and the quite dumpy Karen walking arm in arm. Opposites attracting again. It was nice to see them both happy.

"I've just realised," said Geoffrey, coming back to our table as Karen and Kathryn sat down, "I wasn't thinking about anything in particular and then it hit me. You're in Bundara Street, aren't you, Janice?"

"Yes." Something uncomfortable was squishing around in my chest.

"And you're opposite George Barbieri? The removalist for the gang, as they call him."

"Removalist?" I started, wondering if this was all real and if Geoffrey was pulling my leg.

"Let's say he's their transport manager." Geoffrey stopped talking, looked around and then back at me. "He organises the transport of drugs, people, guns, money, whatever."

"Money?" This was getting weirder and weirder.

"Yes, they're involved in everything unsavoury, including money laundering. The cash transfers are to avoid tax and to avoid detection. The police probably thought they got you a nice safe house but you're right under George's prying eyes. The worst place you could be, now that the mayor's been silenced for now."

"Oh hell." I felt hot and cold all over my body, even down to my toes. And paralysed, in brain and body.

"I don't want to alarm you, Janice."

"Too late for that, Geoffrey."

"No, this could be an advantage because if he can see you, you can see him. Or, more correctly, we can see him."

"What in tarnation are you cooking up, you old charlatan?" asked Samuel, smiling and scratching his beard.

"It's only a half-formed idea and needs some fleshing out, but with Janice's permission, we could arrange it so that Janice and Kassey aren't the only ones going in and out of that house."

"And you have concocted a good reason for this ... what? This subterfuge?"

"Did I overhear another of Geoffrey's manic schemes?" asked Sarah, coming up to the table and putting a proprietorial hand on his shoulder. "Although I do have to say that most of his hare-brained schemes work better than they sound."

"Thanks love," he said, smiling at her. "Okay, one reason is that a woman and child could be seen as vulnerable. They might want to attack you in revenge for speaking up and to warn off others who are thinking of doing the same."

"Oh hell!" I said again, and the waves of hot and cold were joined by nausea.

"Geoffrey! That's ..." said Sarah.

"Yes, it's awful to say but let's get it out in the open. Then we know what we're dealing with and what we can do about it," he said.

"I suppose so," I said, not sure if he was right or not. Not sure if my world would ever feel the same again.

"The second reason is, with other people coming and going from that house, we might confuse George and be able to set up some sort of surveillance on him."

"So, Janice would have the whole world and his wife in and out of her house. And with a young daughter," said Sarah, turning Geoffrey to look at her.

"Look, everyone, I said this plan isn't etched in stone and your ideas are welcome," he said, bright-eyed and undaunted by Sarah's stolid stare. "I think Janice and Kassey need to be protected and we could turn the tables by helping them while thwarting or confusing George and, thereby, his devious colleagues. Come on, put your thinking caps on."

"Hiyup, everyone," said Phil, stomping in, the brightest he'd looked since I'd met him. Then he stopped when he saw our silent, granite faces.

"I believe he needs to know there's not just a woman and a girl living there," continued Geoffrey.

"I've got a pair of men's work boots at my front door," I said, hoping to add a little humour to a humourless subject. But the humour didn't register.

"I'd hit the bloody prick with them!" said Kathryn, suddenly rising from her stupor. "Bloody men."

"Well, if anything's to work, we've got to scare him off permanently," said Karen. "I mean you ... aah ..." She looked at Geoffrey.

"I'm Geoffrey and this is my much better half, Sarah, and we own this prestigious establishment," said Geoffrey, bowing with a flourish.

"Oh you silly man," said Sarah, shaking her head, unable to stifle a smile. She shook Karen's hand.

"Geoffrey? I've heard of you and finally get to meet you. I'm Karen." They shook hands across the table.

"I sign autographs at 2 o'clock."

"Oh, Geoffrey," said Sarah, giving him a soft backhander on the shoulder.

"Anyway, as I was saying," said Karen, sighing heavily, "Geoffrey said they might send us all a message to discourage us from speaking up, like Janice did. Could we send them a message too?"

"Wouldn't that start reprisals and a gang war or whatever?" asked Sarah. "Sorry to be dramatic but we've got to think it through."

"So murdering him won't do?" asked Karen, laughing.

"For God's sake, this is my life and Kassey's life!" Part of me wished I hadn't gone to the café.

"Sorry Janice."

"Just exploring options," said Geoffrey, finally sitting down. "So murder's out. Could we influence him through his wife?"

"She's a terrified little woman," I said.

"Who wants out of her whole situation, I'll bet," said Kathryn. "Been there, done that."

No one spoke for a moment, almost like a one-minute acknowledgement of Kathryn's pain and experience.

"So if she's got nowhere to go other than to other terrified women in her circle," said Sarah slowly, "what if we present her with an alternative, a truly safe place to go?"

"She wouldn't come here, I know that," I said. "She's been manipulated to believe that what the headmaster and her husband are doing is nothing bad."

"The harder you pull back the bow, the faster will the arrow go," said Edward quietly. I remembered that phrase from my Zen classes.

"Why did you say that, Edward?" I looked at him, wondering if he'd studied Zen Buddhism.

"I'm not sure. But I do know that when people are really keen on one thing, they can switch to being really keen on the opposite when they realise they're wrong."

"The greatest opponents to a cause will become the greatest adherents when they're converted." I wondered if I was quoting someone or making it up. "Like Nicolas Chauvin who switched sides and became Napoleon's greatest champion."

"Nicolas Chauvin?" asked Karen.

"Yes, after whom we get the word 'chauvinist'. Someone who is dedicated to a cause, any cause."

"So it doesn't mean woman hater?"

"No, the women's libbers bastardised the meaning."

"You are a deep and profound woman, Janice Brady," said Samuel, smiling and nodding at me.

"Why, thank you, sire." I went hot all over and knew I had flushed red everywhere possible.

"I mean it sincerely, Janice. We must honour and acknowledge the best in all of us. And, if I may say something without embarrassing anyone, our cause of peace and forgiveness can only be furthered by knowing the best in each other. In so doing, we can take the true talents in our group and apply them for a gently powerful conclusion. Apologies for my diversion, but I feel the imperative to know each other as well as we can."

"A Course in Miracles talks about there being no secrets," I said.

"Oh God, this is getting too spooky for me," said Kathryn, looking like she'd just chewed on a lemon.

"Thank you, Samuel, and I agree," said Sarah. "Oh, more customers." She promptly left and another silence descended.

"Mmm," said Kathryn, the awkward look still hovering on her face, "If I can't kill the bastard ... Sorry, Janice. What if I talk with George's wife, Maureen? I can relate to her."

"But would you relate with peace or killing on your mind?" asked Geoffrey softly, his hand landing gently on her bony forearm.

"With her, I'd cry and hug. Him, I'd yell at and stab." Her grim face convinced me she'd actually do those things.

"But what if she tells you you're evil or stupid and everything you're saying is rubbish?" I asked. "That's what she said to me."

"She wouldn't ... that'd be stupid."

"But think about how you've been with me," said Christine. I'd almost forgotten she was there and her words were timorous, as if she was afraid of confronting Kathryn.

"Shit Chris, I apologised for all that!" said Kathryn, her voice rising as much as Christine's had dropped. "Jesus, you think I'd yell at her?" She was close to yelling now. There was a momentary silence and then Kathryn sank back into her chair. "Oh hell, sorry. I ... I don't know." Her palm went to her forehead. She looked down, shaking her head. Geoffrey didn't touch her this time. No one did. She looked up at everyone in turn. "This is so frustrating. I know I can help others. I really want to but ..."

"Not yet," said Christine, still softly and with a beautiful smile.

Kathryn looked up defiantly and I thought she was going to yell at her sister for interrupting her. "Yeah, you're right, Chris. Not yet, huh." She blew her cheeks out and exhaled loudly.

"You'll have your time, Kat." Christine patted her arm.

"So, how do we get Maureen into conversation and in a receptive mood?" I asked. "She's been to my place and I doubt she'll ever talk to me again."

"A woman would be best," said Edward.

"Yes, how about you, Karen?" asked Phil. "You could lure her away while I booby-trap the house."

"By booby-trap, you don't mean blow it up or anything destructive?" Edward frowned as he looked at Phil.

"Hell no!"

"I'd need a pretext," said Karen. She ran her fingers through her short hair. "Like Edward said, what exactly do you mean by booby trap, Phil?"

"I've got some ideas. No one will die. They might have to vacate and ask others for help. Set up smoke bombs to go off at odd times, maybe?"

"But how would you get in?" asked Geoffrey. "Oh, my nearest and dearest needs me." He stood and walked off.

"Maybe I could be a fire warden from the council or something."

"I could give you the required beard-trim, my man," said Karen.

"Yes, your bushy outgrowth would not pass for a council inspector," said Samuel.

"I suppose I could make a sacrifice for the cause," said Phil, smiling awkwardly as he scratched his beard and mussed his previously brushed hair.

Operation Bundara Street

I have an idea," said Edward, as if it had jumped into his brain that second. But it hadn't. He'd been quiet all this time - peacefully quiet, it seemed. He looked like the kind of man able to hold his thoughts unless they were relevant, quite the opposite from so many people who can't stop themselves from voicing every thought that crosses the threshold of their brains, no matter how stupid.

They say that stupidity is like death. Apparently, some people die and don't know they're dead. Similarly, some people are so stupid they don't know they're stupid and no amount of telling them will get through their thick carapace.

Anyway, Edward seemed to be the opposite. A deep thinker, who monitored every word for usefulness, logic and sanity - a good foil for his effervescent partner, Christine.

We all turned to him as he explained his plan, which seemed fully evolved and detailed before it left his lips. Our confusion turned to smiles and glee as it unravelled.

He explained that, in 1968, the pope, St John Paul II, flew into New York for the first time and, as popes usually do, descended the steps, bent and kissed the ground. As he was standing up, a reporter rushed between his bodyguards and asked him, "What do you think of the brothels in New York?" Understandably, the pope was astounded by the question and mumbled a reply before he had time to think properly. Consequently, the headline in the next day's newspaper was, "The first question the pope asks on arrival is, 'What about the brothels in New York?'"

"Anything," Edward said, "can be taken out of context, whether it's contrived or not."

The next thing he explained was that newspapers were happy to accept topical articles if they were well written and accompanied by corroborating photos. These articles and photos helped fill up column inches and the newspaper didn't have to pay reporters to write them.

It turned out that Kathryn had a lifelong fascination with photography and possessed a rather smart SLR camera, a few years old but perfect for our job. When Christine confirmed Kathryn's love and expertise with photography, Kathryn visibly shone and seemed to grow taller in her seat.

It was Saturday and our operation was to kick off on Sunday morning. Karen had sat through Edward's speech with a frown but right at the end, she burst out laughing, as if she had just got it. We all joined in.

Constable Markham chose that moment to pop his head in, but then he quickly stepped back. He later told me he'd thought we were laughing at him.

"Hello, my esteemed colleague," said Samuel, rising as the laughter died. "It might be propitious for you not to hear this conversation, but we will need your services tomorrow. Might you and I have a private chat in a few minutes?"

Markham shrugged, smiled and went outside to his usual seat where he rolled a smoke. Meanwhile, Edward explained some of the finer details and who should do what and when. Not a second of the operation was omitted and not a person was left out or in doubt as to their tasks.

"So, Karen, we have much to do, huh," I said, remembering I was driving her home. She nodded and stood up, more ready than I to go, it seemed. Her move started the rush and we all waved goodbye to Sarah and Geoffrey and then went our separate ways.

I dropped Karen off, said hello to Reg, to make sure he knew Karen was home, and drove to Emma's to pick Kassey up. I explained the operation to Emma in brief and apologised to her for picking Kassey up so early.

"You must be exhausted with everything you're up to," Emma said, "so would you like a cup of tea and a sit?"

"My mind needs more of a rest than my body but thanks, a cuppa would be nice."

"You causin' more trouble, woman?" asked Billy, stomping into the kitchen.

"Billy? Your boots," said Emma.

"Yeah, nice boots." His boyish grin was disarming.

"Billy ..."

"Yeah, okay, I'll take 'em off." He chuckled while I went over the plan in detail, he and Emma maintaining their silence and nodding regularly.

"Yeah, that Edward's a deep bugger, isn't he? Great plan," said Billy. "I'll give Phil a ring now and coordinate our part in it."

I bid them goodbye, with Kassey reluctantly in tow. Once home, I phoned James to give him his instructions, if he wanted to participate. He listened intently as I explained the plan. When I'd finished his only questions were about me.

"Do you really want to do this, Janice?"

"Yes, of course."

"Do you understand the risks?" In two short sentences I'd fallen off the plateau of elation to the valley of concern.

"I think so, but I also understand the risks of not doing this tomorrow."

"This could blow up in any number of ways, you understand, right?"

"Because I don't know what I don't know?"

"I suppose so. You're talking about the criminal puppet masters of the mayor, his son, your neighbour and everyone else on the ground. Some people even say these invisible string-pullers control the newspapers."

"Oh, really?" My stomach was sucked into that dark hole and I gasped. Thankfully, there was a chair behind me and I sank onto it. I felt lightheaded.

"Are you okay, Mum?" asked Kassey. I nodded and smiled unconvincingly.

"But, as you say, doing nothing has risks as well," said James, trying to console me. "I'm not trying to talk you into or out of anything. I just want to have an open discussion so you know all the alternatives. One positive is that you're not resorting to force, the one thing these criminals understand and have mastered. Resort to that and you're lost."

"Right." My mind was empty.

"Janice, are you okay?"

"Actually, not really." It felt easy to be honest with him.

"Would you like me to pop over? Talk about this face to face?"

"But it's getting late."

"It's 3 o'clock and I can be there within the hour."

"Oh, James, you must be a long way away."

"No, I'm in Brisbane. It's not far."

"If that's alright with you, it would be lovely." Then someone else inside me blurted out, "Would you like to come for dinner?" The idea terrified me, as I was a terrible cook ... well, I was an okay cook but I didn't like cooking, as I had no real interest in food. Stick it on a plate and put it under my nose and I'd eat it. Then I saw Kassey across the lounge room smiling and trying not to giggle behind her hand. She obviously approved of my appalling plan.

"Yes, that'd be lovely. I'll see you soon."

"By the way, I'm going to have a chat with my neighbours, Rosie and Ricky."

"Yes, I know them."

"Right. So, if I'm not here when you arrive, I'll be two doors down."

"You like him, Mum," said Kassey, her giggling fit dying down.

"He's a good friend to have." I plumped down on the couch as my wild and woolly thoughts cantered around in my brain.

'Be still,' my Zen teacher had taught. 'Allow the thoughts to rush or saunter as fast or as slowly as they like. They are not your thoughts; they are just the thoughts floating by. There is no need to claim them. Simply be in that still, quiet centre that you are while everything else rushes past.'

I tried to obey those wise words from three years before and, eventually, the panic in my stomach and uncertainty in my brain settled a little.

I'd arrived home so sure of myself in our fun and simple solution to the violence and abuse in this town. Then James' cautionary mood had flipped my thoughts 360 degrees and it took some mental effort to return to centre. I was getting there, but slowly and with mental effort.

"Come on, madam," I said, leaping up, "let's go and see Timothy and his parents." Movement sometimes helps to shake the brain back to normal. Sometimes, not always.

"Hang on, Ricky," I said as he let us into his house. "I thought you were back at work today." He didn't look at all like the happy chappy I'd seen the day before.

"Yeah, well, supposed to be there but a cave-in at the mine. Happened three days ago and they only just told us yesterday."

"Hell, they just told you?"

"Mum, can we go in?" asked Kassey, pushing me into the house.

"Oh, sorry."

"Hey, come in, take a seat. You wanna beer?" The kitchen was painted a bright yellow and the lounge room was a deep blue on two walls and white on the other two. Strong colours everywhere, a relief from the standard brown, orange and white in most houses.

"No thanks." After my drunken ex-boyfriend, I couldn't touch alcohol again.

"Ricky, maybe they'd like tea or coffee," called Rosie from up the hallway. "Sorry, I'll be there in a minute."

"She's on the phone to the hospital. They want to kick one of her patients out an' she has nowhere to go," said Ricky, waving us into the lounge room.

"Oh, hell."

"Yeah, long story. Hey, Kassey, is it?" She nodded. "Come down here. Tim's in his room with his Meccano. Adult company's probably boring for you." He walked back to the lounge room. "Right, now, what are we doing? Aah, yeah, tea or coffee? Rosie will have a tea."

Five minutes later, Rosie joined us, looking serious and distracted.

"You okay, love?" Ricky asked her, putting his arms around her shoulders. She leaned into him and was silent for a moment.

"Sorry," she said, straightening up.

"Do you want to talk about it?" I asked, noticing her eyes were red-rimmed.

"Not right now, Janice, thanks." Her worry was a stark contrast to her bright green and yellow dress. "A change of subject would be good." She sat on the blue floral couch and sipped the tea Ricky had put on the coffee table. "Thanks Ricky, love."

"So, Ricky's been telling me about the accident at the mine," I said.

"Yes, did you see anything about it on TV or in the papers?"

"No."

"Exactly. They kept it out of the news, as they usually do."

"How?"

"We think the mine owners, living it up somewhere overseas, control the papers. And the TV. Too coincidental," said Ricky.

"You think they own the media, whoever they are?" I asked, the sinking-stomach feeling taking hold. Maybe James was right, I thought.

"James?" asked Rosie.

"Oh, I must have been thinking louder than I realised." We all chuckled. "James was just telling me about who most likely owns or controls the media."

"Most likely owns and controls," said Ricky.

"Anyway, I have some good news. Could be scary, could be fun, and we have no way of knowing which way it will go," I said, not sure how to start.

"So we're gonna get back at them?" he asked, sitting forward, trying to read my thoughts.

"Yes, we've decided that doing nothing only encourages them, while violence and force enrages them. So Edward has come up with this idea for tomorrow. Starting tomorrow, anyway." I paused, not sure how to go on or if I should go on. I thought they'd be on board with the operation but I didn't know them that well.

"Okay, sister, spit it out," said Rosie, easing back on their floral couch, beaming widely. The first time I'd seen her smile. So I told them.

"Too bloody right!" said Ricky when I'd finished.

"So you'll be ready at 9.30, with a table and stuff out on your front lawn, having a barbeque?" I wanted to check they'd understood their particular tasks.

"With bloody bells and whistles on, mate!"

"Are you okay, Rosie?" I asked. She was smiling but quiet as she played with her wedding ring. Something was going on in her big brain, probably scanning the universe for all the ins and outs.

"What about the children if it turns bad, somehow?" She looked at Ricky and me, in turn.

"Na, they'll be alright."

"Ricky, we don't know that." All the exuberance I'd seen in her the day before was gone. "Look, sorry, there's been a lot going on. I've had a battle with the hospital over my patients, and the mine was going to send Ricky and his team back in before it was properly inspected and secured. The union did nothing and I shudder to think what would have happened if some of the men hadn't threatened to go to the newspapers and TV."

"Yeah, well ..."

"It's not yeah well, Ricky. Some things don't fix themselves. I'm not getting at you, love. You knew nothing about the cave-in till yesterday. So, the yeah well is that you could have been killed, along with your mates." She put her hand on his leg and he put his hand on hers as they looked at each other, him in his faded, patched shorts and singlet and her in her colourful dress, necklace and bangles. Two peas from very different pods and yet bonded by something truly beautiful. I could see that.

I wasn't sure what to say and took longer sipping my tea than needed.

"You okay, Rosie?" asked Ricky, softly.

"Yes, I suppose so," she said slowly, as if coming out of a stupor. "Look, I agree we need to do something. We've had enough racial abuse from that thug over the road and his cronies, and we've both got kids."

"Yes," I said.

"God knows what could happen to them if it all goes wrong but at the same time, God knows what could happen if we do nothing."

"We could make them stay on our property and if things go stupid, we could get them out the back and over to Damien's place," said Ricky, his apparent bravado turning strategic and practical. "I'll go and see him now. He'll be good with it. He doesn't need to know all the details, huh."

"That's good, Ricky. I feel better now," she said.

"And I'll talk to Janice's back neighbours, Jack and Doris."

"You sure?" I asked. He nodded.

"God, it feels like I've been fighting all my life," Rosie said, sitting back and wiping her forehead. "Just one day off would be good. I mean, why can't people get along, be nice and accepting of each other. How hard is that?"

"My thoughts entirely," I said. "I've been asking that all my life."

"And you're a white woman," said Ricky.

"Ricky!" said Rosie, slapping his thigh.

"I mean ..."

"It's okay, Rosie, Ricky. I am white and some people think we get a better deal of it but I'm not sure. I've been beaten, Kassey's been molested ..."

"Yeah, we had none of that," said Ricky. "I just meant, like, well, like she said, people think it's worse for us black fellas and maybe it is and maybe it isn't. That's what I was saying."

"It depends on each individual," said Rosie, smiling at Ricky and me again. Not the jubilant smile of the day before, more of a resigned smile. "Anyway, enough philosophy. "Let's do this thing, my lover." She patted his thigh gently this time.

"Right, I'll go and see Damien now, and you have Kassey here by 9.30 tomorrow."

There was a knock at the door so Ricky leapt up, answered it and let James into the room.

I had a restless night's sleep - or non-sleep, really - because James was on the couch, probably uncomfortable, and my guilt had him sharing my comfortable, queen-sized bed. My desire had him doing the same thing with a different outcome. It seemed extraordinary that I could have a man in my house, especially overnight, but it had seemed silly for him to drive the hour back to Brisbane and an hour back here in the morning. It was a huge relief that he agreed to join our little project; he seemed to bring an aura of order and reliability to a group of people who I didn't really know and included Ricky, Samuel, Phil and Kathryn. I'm sure that they could all be relied on but none of them were cut from an ordinary mould. James, however, could be totally relied on. I just knew that.

I got up half an hour earlier than I needed to and spent that extra time on my appearance. Apart from the occasional muted lipstick, makeup was a stranger to me. Today, however, I applied mascara, blusher and eyebrow pencil - not necessarily in that order - with the expertise of someone unused to such rituals, and the finesse of someone nervously doing it before a date, which this wasn't. So, yes, I did have to rub off crooked and misplaced lines and do them again and the 30 minutes were well and truly exceeded.

I wasn't suspicious - well, not really - about James happening to have brought a change of clothes, toothbrush and razor. He returned from the bathroom as I was making coffee and he looked the very model of every other lawyer in Brisbane on a Sunday - shiny black shoes, grey suit trousers, black polo shirt, clean-shaven face and tidily cropped hair. Not a button or piece of lint out of place. I checked myself in the glass of the oven door, self-consciously, to ensure my amateur paint job hadn't slipped.

"Oh, Mum, are you going out, like ..." Kassey asked, still in pyjamas and bare feet.

"Your usual breakfast, love?" I said, butting in to divert her conversation. She giggled and nodded and I feared another deliberately inappropriate outburst.

"Good morning, James, and would you like a coffee to start with?" I asked.

"Actually, can I have a drink of water, please?" he said, standing uncertainly in the kitchen doorway as Kassey helped herself to cereal and milk. "I like coffee but not till I've had food first."

"Oh, right." I hadn't heard of that before. "Look, I've done bacon and scrambled eggs, if that's okay. You can have cereal if you like ..."

"No, no, bacon and eggs sounds perfect." His beautiful smile flashed as I handed him a glass of water and my nervous heart settled a little. But just a little.

"Take a seat and I'll bring it out."

"Can I take something; cutlery, salt and pepper ..."

"Thanks." I dived into the drawers and then thrust knives, forks and bread plates at him, unintentionally stabbing him with a knife. He was gracious enough not to say anything. I noticed the red mark was still across his wrist as I finally sat down, forced myself to breathe evenly and tried to smile normally at him.

Man In My House

We were polite, passing salt, pepper and butter to each other and our stilted activity disguised our awkward silence, but not very well. As host, I should have provided conversation, but my dry brain and dry mouth wouldn't obey. I should have been thinking about the day's plans that could go in any of several ways, but I kept feeling like a shy teenager on a first date, which I'd never really had.

Though awkward, this felt like a sweetly sacred moment and I didn't want to desecrate it with my bumbling babble.

Despite the eerie silence, there was a rightness about having James there. It felt like I was with two people - a stranger and an old friend - in one body.

He gave a little cough and I looked at his face, which seemed to be turning red. "I'm afraid I'm not very good with small talk, Janice." He looked at me and then quickly down at his nearly-empty plate.

I smiled and sighed in relief. "I'm usually an expert at this, James. I can talk the legs off a table for hours about nothing at all. I'm the hostess and I should be much more entertaining, but my gabble mouth seems to be having a holiday today. It can't think of a single thing to say right now and it's as confusing as it's embarrassing."

"Well, it seems to be working perfectly right now," he said. Kassey giggled as he smiled at me.

"Mmm, I suppose so." I put my hand over my mouth to stifle a titter.

"Don't apologise. It's nice to be here, whether you're talking or not."

"Really?" I shouldn't have said anything but my mouth shot open and betrayed my appreciation of his comment.

"See, I told you, Mum," said Kassey, between slurps of milk.

"Told her what?" asked James, looking at her, a huge smile on his face. It felt like his eyes were twinkling and I knew I was ambushed and in trouble.

"Nothing. Here, let me take your plate," I said.

"It's okay. I'll take it, and I'd love to know what Kassey has to say." He looked at her and she shrugged and smiled, preparing her body for an incriminating speech. I gave up and prepared to take what was coming.

"I said you like her," Kassey said, straight-faced.

"Oh," he said.

"And I know she likes you but she won't say it." Oh, hell, I'm done now, I thought, going hot all over. I decided to say nothing. When you're in a hole, Janice, stop digging.

"Does she now?" he asked Kassey, with the biggest, cheesiest grin.

"Yeah, and you like her, don't you." That was a statement, not a question.

"You are dead right, Kassey. I do like your mum." He looked at me, smiling bashfully. I looked back and my smile would have looked twisted or a grimace or something cringey. He raised his eyebrows as if expecting a reply. I kept my big gob well and truly shut - no hole-digging going on here now. "And you like me?"

I nodded, my lips firmly stuck together as my eyes were drawn into his deep, blue ones.

"You do? How much?"

"She likes you lots," said Kassey. Thank you, my annoying, loyal daughter.

He looked around the room as if searching for hidden cameras or an audience, wiped his now-glistening brow, stood up, walked around to me, put one hand on my shoulder and kissed me on the cheek. Then he backed away.

"Hey!" I leapt up, grabbed him and kissed him on his surprised mouth.

"Oh, yuk!" said Kassey, as he leant into me and returned my kiss. God, I was enveloped in it and nothing else existed as his arms went around my shoulders. Then he was gone and sitting down again while I stood there in a daze. I quickly sat and grabbed my coffee cup to cover my embarrassment, confusion or delight. Or all three.

"So, do we still like each other?" he asked with a cheeky grin.

I choked and coughed and the cold coffee flew up my nose and across the table. My two adversaries laughed their heads off while I tried to wipe the mess from my face, clothes and table. Oh, and the floor.

"Well, that was awkward," I said as I returned from the kitchen with a mop and dishcloth. They were still tittering together, so I ignored them and wiped up.

"Would it be awkward if we did it again?" James asked when he'd regained his composure.

"If we did what - coffee, coughing or kissing?" I knew which one he meant but I wanted to hear him say it.

"The kissing," he said, with more confidence than he'd displayed when we first sat down to breakfast.

"You want to do the kissing again?" I felt very unromantic, standing there with a dirty, wet mop and dishcloth and my mascara likely transformed into a work of modern art.

"Ooh, yuk," said Kassey, looking yukked out as she took her plate into the kitchen.

"Yes I do, Janice. In your arms I feel very, aah ..."

"Horny?" I squeezed my eyes shut and looked down, thoroughly embarrassed by Janice Brody. Why do I have to blurt out stupid things at the most tender moments? "Sorry." I forced myself to look up at him.

"No, not that." He stood up, walked over to me and put his hands on my waist, looking directly, softly, into my eyes. "I'm not sure how to explain it, so please be patient. I feel at home with you."

"Oh." I hoped my disappointment didn't show but I'm sure it did.

"Sshhh."

"Sorry."

"I feel at home with you, in your arms. In your company. In your house. I feel like I belong. That we belong. It's something so natural I don't have to try. I can be myself."

"Shy? Cheeky? Serious?"

"Yes, all of it. And even when I'm embarrassed, I don't feel stupid about it. Like, you're not judging."

"Oh." I looked right into his earnest eyes, almost into his soul. This self-contained man was becoming transparent before my eyes and that lifted my spirits.

"And the other thing ..."

"Other thing?"

"Yes, you know." He looked embarrassed again.

"Oh, the horny?"

"Yes, that. It could happen quite quickly, but that's not the overwhelming thing. I just feel that I want to be with you."

"But I'm a solo mother with a young daughter, an ordinary car, a rented house, and you're a qualified lawyer with a fancy car and most likely a mansion in Brisbane."

"Home is a place to hang my clothes."

"Your suits, you mean." Oh, shut up, Janice!

"Yes, to hang my suits and store my food and it's remarkably modest for a wildly successful, big-shot lawyer with a madly prestigious car. But none of that matters, Janice. I could lose my home and car tomorrow and you could win the Lotto tomorrow. All these things can pass."

"Jeez, this is sounding like a ..."

"No, it's not a marriage proposal," he said, reading my thoughts. How does everyone do that? He took a deep breath and then breathed out and I realised his hands were still on my waist and mine were still on the cleaning equipment. "We hardly know each other and I would like to see you again and again and really get to know you."

"Well, you could start by kissing me, then." He pulled me to him and the mop hit him on the head and the dishcloth dabbed at his crotch as I tried to keep my balance. Laughing, he pushed me back by the shoulders, grabbed the cleaning stuff, placed it on the floor and then took me in his arms and kissed me beautifully.

"Ooh, yuk," came Kassey's voice behind me, and then she screamed and I heard a bump as she hit the floor. I spun around to see the mop tangled in her legs while she kicked out at it and pulled the wet dishcloth off her face. "Oh, Mum, this is stupid." Then she stopped struggling, lay back on the floor and laughed deliriously. Meanwhile, James grunted and ummed and aahed as he tried to get the mop off her.

"James, leave it," I said. "You're making it worse."

"But," said my man of action, Tae Kwon Do expert and all that, looking flustered and uncool. I hauled him up by his collar.

"Let it be for a moment. You can't fix everything."

"Mmm, suppose not."

"Kassey will sort herself out when she's over her hysterics so let's try that kissing thing again," I said, as Kassey groaned. I dragged him away to a safer, non-thrashing, non-laughing part of the dining room. So we kissed and hugged and kissed and hugged and stood there as I finally realised what he meant - it felt homely, like coming home, like I belonged in him, with him, and he with me. Even thoughts of jobs, ages, houses, cars and other transient things dissolved away and all that was left was an essence - not even his body, really - that merged with me. I allowed myself to soak into it as my head rested on his shoulder and his arms held me firmly. Then the spell was broken as I recalled my promise.

"You know, James," I said into his shirt that smelled of laundry powder and aftershave, "I just broke a promise." He grunted. "I told myself no more men. In my house."

"You broke that one."

"Mmm. In this house. In my life. In my bed. I was done with them."

"You might have broken the second one as well."

"I might have." I leaned back and smiled into his tranquil face that showed the trace of a smile. The third promise I wasn't talking about right now.

"This is so nice," he said, "but ..."

"But we have a mission today."

"You stole my words. The outside world awaits our battle cry."

There was a knock on the door.

"Would you like me to answer it?" asked James. "This is your home."

"Oh, yes, that's fine," I said, not expecting that question; such respect for me and mine. "Oh, do we say you stayed here?"

"My car's outside."

"Of course." I let go of his hand and stood there feeling slightly weird, as if I'd landed on planet Earth and didn't know what to do or where to turn.

"Are you alright, Mum?" asked Kassey, another Creeping Jesus suddenly by my side. I put my arm around her shoulders and felt slightly more grounded. I realised James was talking with Ricky, Mr Strongly Peaceful with Mr Jumpy Chatty. The contrast tickled my funny bone and I tittered. Kassey looked at me, frowning.

"Yes, love, a lot seems to have happened in a short time. Things I didn't want to happen that have happened and I'm glad they've happened."

"You're weird, Mum." She was still frowning at me.

"Mmm, probably."

"But he's nice, isn't he?"

"You like him?" That was one of the shortest questions I'd ever asked her but one of the most critical.

"Yeah, he's good." I felt a huge relief to hear her say what I'd suspected. The relief washed over me like a cleansing shower. "And he does Tae Kwon Do. He said he could teach us."

"Yes, maybe he could. But let's get through today first, huh." We walked to the front door, arms around each other's waists.

"Hi Janice and, er ..." said Ricky.

"Kassey," said Kassey.

"Sorry, yeah, Kassey. Are you ready to come down to our place? Tim's ready, aren't you, mate?" Ricky stepped sideways to reveal a shy looking Tim, his white teeth a gleaming contrast to his brown skin and black, curly hair.

"I thought we were meeting at 9.30," I said. "You're a bit keen."

"Yeah, well, we were ready, so we got on our horses. Big day."

"Look, Kassey's not ready so does Tim want to come in?"

"Mum!"

"Wait in the lounge while Kassey gets ready and they can go back to your place together?" I smiled at her as she bumped me with her shoulder. "That alright?"

"Yeah," she said with an audible outbreath.

"Dad?" asked Tim, looking up at his father.

"Yeah, of course, if it's okay with you, Janice. You wanna help set up the barbeque, mate?"

"I've just got to clean my teeth and make a phone call and I'll be down soon," said James, looking at me as if there was a hidden message in his speech. It was too well hidden for me to see.

"Do you want to watch the TV while Kassey gets ready?" I asked Tim.

"Uh," he said, looking at me shyly. "Can I read a book?"

"You don't watch TV?"

"A bit. Not really. I like reading, though. And my Meccano."

"Well, help yourself," I said, pointing to a bookshelf in the lounge corner, filled mainly with Kassey's books. And a few of mine. I noticed James nodding at me as is if wanting me to come into the dining room.

"I could have gone with Ricky, but it seemed rude to walk off without saying a proper goodbye."

"What, you want a brass band and speeches?" Oh, Jeeeesus, Janice, that crass mouth of yours. "Sorry, that was stupid."

"I'm usually the embarrassed one, but do you find intimate talk awkward?"

"What? Why?" I wasn't expecting that question.

"You seem to say funny things in these nice moments."

"Stupid things, you mean. I'm sorry," I said as I hugged him. "Maybe I do get embarrassed."

"A defence mechanism, maybe."

"God, James, there are no secrets with you, are there?"

"Look, we hardly know each other and I'm already analysing you. Sorry."

"No, it's okay. It really is. I suppose ... well, maybe I've become a bit uppity around men."

"You've been hurt." That was a statement, not a question.

"Yes, a bit." I was glad I had my eyes shut and my head close to his shoulder, not his eyes.

"A lot?"

"Yes, a lot, actually."

"And you don't know when they'll strike next. You're maybe waiting for me to suddenly turn from nice to nasty, huh?"

"Hell, James, that's deep." I felt tears come to my eyes and a cold spark rise up my spine as I pushed myself away from him a little. I remembered my Zen teacher saying there was always a bodily reaction when we were touched by Truth and my reaction, I found, was a cold spark or ice cube up my spine. "Deep and true. Maybe."

"Maybe?"

"Oh, shut up, Mr Wise Arse. Just hug me for a moment. No talking." So we did, and I felt a transcendent peace flow over me. I turned my ear to his heart and could feel it beating strong and full of care. I realised I'd never felt this safe before and wasn't sure I was ready to trust in that safety. God, what a twisted brain I have, I thought, I've found gold and now I want to squander it.

"So," we both said together.

"You first," he said, the perfect gentleman.

"Okay, you called me over here for something."

"Yes, I wanted to hug you goodbye, connect before I go."

He smiled, we hugged and he got ready to leave for the outside world and whatever it was going to throw at us that day. I felt strangely complete when he pulled away and stopped at the front door, turning to me as Kassey appeared with wet, brushed hair and a huge smile.

"Come on, you guys, come with me," called James and they followed the Pied Piper to Rosie's and Ricky's place.

I stood there, smiled, shook my head a little and felt strangely grounded, as if I finally knew my place on this earth. I didn't know what that place was, but I knew I'd found it, if you know what I mean.

I washed the dishes and tidied the dining and lounge rooms, doing all these practical tasks while existing in a sweet, parallel universe at the same time.

I knew James didn't complete me - that was my job. I must have completed myself, and he'd have done the same, so that two completed humans - as completed as incomplete humans can be - came together to confirm that they'd done the work of stitching up their own hearts and would help each other's stitches dissolve. I don't know how or why these thoughts came to me, but it felt like a warmth creeping up my spine and I smiled and stepped out into my front doorway and into the Queensland sunshine in a clear, blue sky.

Sunday Project

Edward knocked on my back door at 9.30. Ricky had arranged with my backyard neighbours, the Yarrans and his good friends, that Edward could come through their place. This was so that when Edward, the Yarrans and their friends emerged from my front door, George Pufferfish would have less inclination to confront me. We knew Pufferfish would be out on the street, as his driveway would accidentally be blocked by Phil's ute that had just broken down. He couldn't go to golf and the ruckus around Ricky's barbeque would suck him out, like a bloodhound drawn to a colony of rabbits.

Edward had his reporter's pad and pen, and Kathryn followed soon after, her smart camera slung around her neck. Her energy was up, going by her bright eyes, although I thought she should pace herself. It was hot outside, and we didn't know how things would go - energetic, calm, frantic, happy or dangerous.

"Would you like a seat?" I asked her.

"You think I can't stand?" She stopped suddenly and stared at me, challenging.

"Uh ... no ..." My embarrassment quickly turned to indignation. How could this woman? In my house?

"I noticed you didn't ask Edward," she said, her voice still sharp.

"I'll respond when you learn some manners, Kathryn." I turned my back to her. "Would you like a cup of tea, Edward? Or coffee?"

"Uh, oh, tea please," he said hesitantly, looking behind me at Kathryn and then at me.

"Milk and sugar?" I walked past him and into the kitchen.

"Neither, thanks." He'd followed me. "Do you think you should, like, antagonise her, Janice?" he said as I filled the jug with water and turned it on.

"Edward, this is my house and no one, but no one, has my permission to speak like that."

"Oh, right." He'd pocketed his pad and pen and stood there, twisting his fingers.

"I gave permission to two men to disrespect me and my home," I said, turning to him. "And disrespect my daughter. I later realised I didn't have to give anyone that permission."

"Well, that's very ... admirable, Janice. I understand that, totally. Christine and I have both given others permission to disrespect and abuse us too."

"And Christine still gives Kathryn permission."

"Yes, she does." He looked embarrassed as he ran his fingers through his short, blond hair. "But it's harder with family."

"The hardest things are often the ones most worth doing."

"Maybe you're right." He nodded and looked sad.

"Um," came a small, distant voice. Behind Edward, Kathryn was standing in the doorway, clutching the architrave as if it was about to fall down.

"Yes, Kathryn?" I asked.

"Could I have a cup of tea, please?" A little girl voice, pleading.

"No."

"Oh."

"Apology needs to come first, Kathryn. We can't pretend nothing happened." She straightened up and took a tentative step towards me. She looked down, pressed her lips together and then looked me in the eye.

"I'm sorry, Janice."

"For what?" I felt like a schoolmistress, but I wasn't having her think she could throw her tantrums around me.

"For ... for speaking to you sharply. Rudely."

"Apology accepted." I strode over and she looked shocked as I hugged her. "And I'm sorry I presumed you didn't know what you needed. Do handstands if you like." I smiled and she laughed nervously and then freely.

"Perhaps I should sit down. Never know what's in store today ... oh, you've already got three cups out!" she exclaimed, shaking her head and smiling at me.

"Yes, I knew we'd both come round in the end. Here, Edward, take these biscuits into the dining room please, and I'll bring the tea in soon. And, Kathryn, take this milk jug and sugar bowl and no bloody arguing." Her eyes popped out in shock and quickly crinkled into a smile.

"Yes, ma'am," she said, walking away, chuckling.

As I sat down with Edward and Kathryn, there was a knock on the back door. Edward leapt up.

"Oh, do you mind if I let them in?" Another gentleman respecting my house.

"Thanks for asking, Edward, and yes, please do."

"God, can't a girl enjoy a cup of tea in peace?" I asked as Doris and Jack Yarrans came in.

"Cheeky bloody white fellas," said Jack, shaking my hand as I stood up. "An' where's our cup of tea?"

"In the bucking kitchen, Jack. Are you going to introduce me to your friends?" I asked, hugging Dora.

"Friends? What friends? We don't have any ... Who're these fellas?" He turned in feigned surprise. I hoped it was feigned.

An older, grey-haired Aboriginal man stepped forward. "I am Stan, madam, and this cheeky bugger, Jack, is my son-in-law."

"So, no friends, Jack? Just relations?" I shook the old man's steady hand and looked into his deep, grey eyes. I wish this man was my grandfather, I immediately thought. Or even my father. There was such a depth of knowing and grace about him. And pain, I guessed, which precedes such love and compassion.

"Are you okay, aah ..." he asked, his gaze soaking into mine.

"Janice."

"Janice, are you okay?" I wanted to hug him. He put his arms out as if reading my thoughts.

"This sounds pretty stupid, but I feel like I've finally met my real family." I wished my blabby mouth would shut itself up, but it wouldn't. "Like, well, this is ... I don't know, I'd love you to be my grandfather. Now I really do feel silly." I fell into his arms, partly to hide my embarrassment and partly as it felt so damned good.

"I was," he said quietly. I stood back, my hands on his shoulders.

"What? What did you say?"

"I was your grandfather. And you have a daughter?"

"Yes." This was getting creepy. Was he psychic?

"She was my daughter. Your mother."

I peered at him through my confusion, but he looked serenely serious. I looked at Edward and Kathryn to try to root myself in reality. They both looked perfectly calm and unperturbed. I had so many questions.

"When?"

"When the white fellas came here. Maybe 200 years ago."

"Where?"

"At Kippa Ring, west of Humpybong, now called Redcliffe." He explained to me that Humpybong meant 'leaving home'.

He seemed so sure of himself that it was impossible to argue. "It's a long story ..."

"And a sad one?" I asked.

"Yes. I can tell you more later, dear." He turned away for a moment. "This is my wife, Ruby."

Ruby waddled two steps forward and enveloped me in the folds of her short, ample body.

"You weren't my grandmother, were you?" I asked, partly joking.

"Not yet, dear, but maybe next time we meet." She smiled as we separated, and she pulled out a chair and sat.

"I need a smoke," said Stan, patting his pocket.

"Yeah, me too," said Jack.

"Not in here," I said. "Out the back or the front door."

"We'll go out the front. Start up the silly bugger over the road, huh?"

I looked at Edward, as that wasn't part of his plan, but he shrugged and smiled.

"Take two chairs out," I said.

"Nah, Janice, we got grass bums," said Jack. "Ground's the best chair ever invented."

"Shut the door," called Ruby as the men left.

It shut behind them and the five of us sat and stared at one another.

"Once more into the breach, dear friends," I said, guessing the men had finished their smokes and opening the door. Kathryn, Edward, Doris and Ruby followed me out and the two men joined us as we gathered at my mailbox, chattering and telling jokes, making a noise. Phil arrived across the road and his ute spluttered to a stop across George's driveway. Steam rose from the front of the bonnet in a brilliant display of a dead vehicle.

Maureen's front door opened and her head appeared around it, disappearing quickly when George strode out and marched down his driveway, red, round and ready to burst. Maureen's head reappeared, as if she was ready to retreat at any moment. A woman on the sharp edge of life.

"Get off my driveway! You can't park there!" yelled George, puffing himself up, his breath coming in indignant gasps, audible from across the street.

"Can you give us a push?" asked the hairy and extra-untidy Phil with a ripped, checked shirt, ripped and greasy shorts and unlaced, worn-out boots with the metal toecaps showing through. Not the sort of person normally seen on Denmark Hill. Phil sniffed and wiped his nose with his arm and gave a great impression of a bogan's bogan. It even looked like he'd painted tattoos on his legs and arms and something on his forehead.

"Get this heap off my property," said George, waving his hands like a broken windmill.

"Yeah, think me reverse gear's gone. Need to push it forward."

"Up the hill?"

"Yeah, few blokes'll get it going fast enough to crash-start it."

"But the steam out of the bonnet?"

"Yeah, it does that, mate."

"I. Am. Not. Your. Mate."

"Yeah, right. Hey, can I get some water off ya? Top up the radiator." Phil stood up from looking under his bonnet and started to walk up George's driveway.

"Hey! Hey! Get back!" George spluttered and wobbled after Phil, who strode out in his seven-league boots.

"Just gettin' some water, mate. Use your hose, okay?" Phil's great performance of being unperturbed by the florid, prickly George on his heels was impressive.

Around me were people telling silly jokes and laughing louder than necessary. As George was berating and chasing Phil, he was flicking quick glances across at us, perhaps wondering how he could deal with both problems at once.

Phil marched, seemingly oblivious to the yappy dog at his heels. He turned the hose on and started unravelling it towards his ute.

"You can't do that! This is private property! You ... you ..."

"Look, mate," said Phil, stopping and turning on George who looked up at the looming hairy man and nearly toppled over. "You want my ute off your driveway? I need water to get it going, right?"

"Yes, but ..." George suddenly turned for some reason and yelled at Maureen. "Back inside, you! Call the men." Maureen's head disappeared and the door shut slowly. Softly. As if the door really didn't want to be shut.

George spun back to Phil. "Oh, you still here?" he asked as if Phil and his ute were supposed to have dissolved with a click of his fingers.

"Actually, George."

"You know my name?" George froze, almost lurching forward.

"Yeah, every prick knows you. You can help me. Come here." Phil continued unravelling the hose, got to his ute and waved George over. George looked around as if God might smite Phil and his kind from the earth. But God did no smiting, and George shook his head and followed Phil.

"What about the rabble across the road? They could help," said George as he caught up to Phil, all puff and sweat.

"Oh, yeah, hey you guys!" yelled Phil. "Can someone give us a push?"

"Yeah, course," said Jack. Along with Edward, Kathryn and Stan, Jack sauntered across the road.

"Hey," said Phil sharply, "hold that, will ya?" He handed George the radiator cap and George obeyed without question, juggling the hot cap. Kathryn was taking photos of George helping Phil while the two Aboriginal men walked around behind George. Stan put his hand on George's shoulder, which George didn't seem to notice while juggling the hot radiator cap, and Kathryn snapped away.

I noticed three other men walking down their driveways and peering into their mailboxes, although mail wasn't delivered on Sundays. They were furtively looking down the street towards the kerfuffle at George's. They looked at one another, shook their heads and shrugged. None of them moved. They all looked a generation younger than George, and I wondered if what Ricky had said was right; that they were employed in George's nefarious enterprises.

One of the men eventually stepped out onto the footpath and the other two followed suit. They walked towards George, a small phalanx to protect their leader, but stopped 10 metres away.

Edward had his pad and pen out, per the plan, and said to George, "It's admirable that you're helping a stranger in trouble. How often do you do this? How do you know the two elders of the Aboriginal community?"

George's mouth opened and shut without a sound emerging, while Kathryn swivelled and took pictures of the car, George, Phil and the two Aboriginal men in the foreground, along with the three stooges uphill and in the background.

Edward then marched away from the car and up to the stooges. "I'm from the Ipswich Times. Can you please tell me your names? It's great that so many people in this community step out and help others in trouble."

They stood there open-mouthed and rooted to the spot.

Street Battle

We hadn't known how many - if any - of George's bodyguards would come out, so the fact that all three of them had was a bonus. None were left undercover. It amazed me, as an afterthought, that DI Edwards, from the Child Trauma and Sexual Crime Unit, had installed me in a street infested by these vipers. Perhaps he hadn't known, but he soon would. That'd be my first phone call the following day.

I hadn't realised Billy was part of this. He turned up in his ute, which was covered with the usual panelbeater-red patchwork, and parked right behind Phil's ute. Karen, Jeanie and Emma got out of the car as Billy rushed over to give Phil and George some sage advice.

Karen and Emma waved to us and the three of them walked down to Ricky's barbeque.

"Get that heap of crap out of there and off my street!" George yelled at Billy, loud enough for us to hear, and almost loud enough for DI Edwards to hear in Coolangatta.

"All good, I'll get his ute going," said Billy, as Phil screwed the radiator cap back on and slammed the bonnet shut.

"But who's taking your heap away?" demanded George of Billy with unerring logic. And fear.

"No worries, mate." Billy leapt into Phil's driver's seat.

Phil waved at us while George had his head stuck in the window, trying to convert Billy to some logic.

Doris, Ruby and I scooted over the road as fast as Ruby's little legs would carry her. Maureen's head disappeared and she shut the door as we trotted up her driveway. Doris knocked on the door. No answer.

"Maureen, we know you're being abused and ..." said Doris.

"No, I am not," said Maureen behind her door. "How dare ..."

"And it's only getting worse."

A moment's silence, then, "How do you know?"

"We know and we can help you out of this."

"You're not safe and we can make you safe," said Ruby, something I wish a kindly grandmother had said to me a few years ago. Even a few weeks ago.

The door opened slowly and we stood back to give Maureen space. She looked out at the two utes where the shouting match was getting louder, while George seemed to be frantically looking for back-up between berating Billy and Phil. Maureen opened the door wide enough for her full body to show, and Ruby took two quick steps and enfolded her in a motherly embrace.

Maureen struggled half-heartedly for three seconds and then collapsed into Ruby. I was sure I could hear sobs, and it looked like Maureen did not want to let go. Doris and I kept looking back at the arguing men, hoping George wouldn't turn around. If he did, we'd have to go to Plan B, and I didn't want any violence at all.

"Can we come inside, love?" asked Ruby, stroking Maureen's hair with one hand and holding her shoulders with the other. Maureen nodded and backed into her foyer, with Ruby still attached. Doris and I followed and I shut the door slowly and quietly. Once inside, Maureen looked up and released her hold on Ruby.

"How did you know?" asked Maureen.

"Everyone knows. Everyone," I said.

Maureen stared at each of us, all the arrogance she had showed in my house melting into a puddle of fragility.

"You are not safe here, love," said Doris, as we all followed Maureen into her lounge that was filled with Queen Anne furniture, nice paintings and a chandelier, something of a rarity in Ipswich, I'd imagine.

"And you?" Maureen said as if just registering my presence as I entered the lounge, looking around. "You told on Cummings?" I nodded silently, giving her space to come to her own conclusions. "But you did it for the children, didn't you?"

"Yes," I said, "to keep them safe."

"I always thought George and Cummings and Bruno and the others would stop sometime."

"Like George has stopped abusing you?"

"Mmm." Her crooked smile told me her thoughts were racing in every direction. "He's getting worse."

"And you're afraid?"

"Yes."

"You're afraid to tell anyone? Afraid to ask for help?"

"Yes." Maureen sat down and waved to the scattering of upholstered chairs, indicating we could sit. Then she bent over, her head in her hands.

"This is no time to hide from the truth, love," said Ruby, her hand on Maureen's back.

"Oh, dear." Maureen sat up. Then a lightbulb seemed to go on in her head as her red-rimmed eyes lit up. "I might not have another chance, right?"

We all nodded.

"But ... but ... where can I go?"

"Come with us," said Ruby softly.

"But ... how?"

"Pack a bag and follow us."

That sounded incredibly simple but I knew it wouldn't be. I was sure Maureen knew that, too.

"Pack? Leave here?"

"One minute at a time, love. One minute at a time," said Doris. "And we don't have many."

"One minute. Right." Maureen breathed out heavily, put her palms on her knees and pushed herself up with a new force. "This is stupid, but ..." She stormed off down the hallway, her head shaking as if disagreeing with her body.

Ruby and Doris followed to help her pack while I called out, "Where are your car keys?"

"Car keys?" Maureen stopped, turned and frowned as if my voice had come from a different galaxy and she had trouble interpreting my question. Then she shook her head and smiled as if she knew our plan, although she didn't. "In the kitchen, hanging above the microwave."

"Come on, love, let's get you packed," said Doris. "I'll do the bathroom and Ruby will help you with your clothing."

"Yes, yes." Maureen complied with her new First Nations friends while I grabbed both sets of keys, went out the back door quietly and tried the side door of the double garage. It was locked, so I experimented with several keys before it opened, dreading that Furious George might see. Thankfully, there was a wooden screen between the garage and house. There were switches inside, by the door, and the first one turned the lights on. The second started the automatic door rising and I quickly turned it off, dropping the door while I fervently prayed it wouldn't thump to a stop.

I chose the larger of the cars, George's green Holden Premiere. The Ford Anglia had to be Maureen's. I worked out which key fitted the Holden, tossed the other set into the glove box and waited. And waited. And waited. It was probably only two minutes, but any second George could turn up with his thugs and do whatever to us four women.

Finally, I heard the side door slam shut. Then open and slam shut again. This was the sign for Billy to scream off in Phil's ute. Maureen's bags were thrown into the boot that I'd kept open and they all scrambled into the car. I rushed over, pushed the door switch to open, leapt back in and heard Phil slamming Billy's driver's door, to my immense relief.

The plan's working so far, but for how long? I asked myself as I backed out, turned around on the concrete pad beside the garage and hoofed it down the driveway. I saw George flailing about and Phil waving to me from Billy's ute, but then I lost peripheral vision and focused on the 10 yards ahead of me. I belted onto the road without giving way and turned right, thankful there was no other traffic. We turned left into Warwick Road, into Carr Street and then left into Cemetery Road where Christine was waiting for us. As the other three women transferred themselves and Maureen's two suitcases to Christine's car, I took both bunches of keys and followed them.

Christine drove us into Rosie's and Ricky's driveway and we bundled Maureen in through the back of their house. Maureen's mouth kept protesting but her body followed our instructions.

We persuaded her to put on one of Ruby's dresses; plain black, the right length and a bit wide in all places. Ruby tied a red scarf around her head and Doris applied bright-red lipstick and thick mascara and slapped a straw sunhat on her head. They stood her in front of Rosie's mirror and she laughed and then cried a little, smudging the mascara.

Maureen took three deep breaths while we stood silently, fearing she was going to change her mind and escape. "This has been the most stupid morning of my life."

"But ..." Doris started to say while Maureen waved her words away.

"The most stupid, scary, insane and fun. The most fun I've had with my pants on. With my pants off, if I'm honest. I'm just ..." Then she ran out of words.

"Are you okay?" Christine asked.

Maureen waved her away and wiped her wet eyes. "Sorry, please give me a minute." She took two deep breaths while looking at each of us, in turn, in the mirror. Then at herself. "I'm blumfurcated."

"You're what?" I asked.

"Blumfurcated. I just made it up. There's no other word for it. So many things and, yes, I know I'm not free yet. I know it's going to be a choppy ride ahead, but what I really want to say to all you people is I don't know you at all and you, Janice, I was so rude to you in your own home. I felt justified at the time but, now ..."

"It's alright, Maureen, it really is," I said. And I meant it.

"See, I don't deserve this and you're all risking so much. Why me?"

"You needed help, love," said Ruby, her hand on Maureen's shoulder.

"But, well, I hate to say it but you're black. I'm white. Why?"

"Because you're human," said Doris. "You needed help and we can give it."

"And you, Janice, you're, well ..." Maureen looked decidedly embarrassed but kept her eyes on mine. Like a kind of confessional.

"I'm poorer than you. I'm a solo mum, I rent my house?"

"Yes, we have nothing in common, nothing at all, but you ... oh, you." She leant sideways into my shoulder.

"Look, Maureen, if this helps," said Christine, "I'm half Irish, Edward is Lithuanian and Ricky is quarter Chinese, quarter white and half Aboriginal."

"And I'm part Spanish and part Iranian, and Kassey is part Italian," I said.

"We're all just people, Maureen, love," said Ruby.

"Oh God, I must sound so dreadful," said Maureen, straightening up, leaving mascara stains on my white t-shirt. "Oh, I wish there was a bigger word than thank you."

"Blumfurcated will do," said Christine, and we all had a group exhale and a laugh.

"We need to be practical now, Maureen," I said. "George and his thugs might wonder where Ruby, Doris and I got to, if they're not still distracted by our photographer and reporter. They could force their way into my house. So we're going to join the barbeque on Ricky's front lawn to draw them down. We'll bring you food in here. You probably won't be recognised but why take the risk?"

"No, but I never wear black. Or a scarf on my head."

"Or sunglasses," said Rosie, coming into the room and handing Maureen her mirror shades.

"You're right, Janice. I won't risk all your good work so I'll stay here if that's okay."

"Okay," said Rosie, "the back door's locked and we have sentries at the front. Kassey, Tim and Jeanie are on the step."

"Thank you, everyone," said Maureen as everyone except Ruby filed out. We stepped between the three kids and there was teacher Karen seated on a folding chair, before the kids, getting instructions on the latest fashions from her pupils. She looked very much at home.

And George had walked over to harangue Ricky about who had stolen his car, his henchmen standing behind him, looking unsure about what to do for their boss from behind their sunglasses.

"Call the cops," said James, as he turned sausages over.

"Yeah, I just might," said George, not looking like he was going anywhere to phone anyone.

"So, your boss, the mayor, is isolated and can't help. Thomlinson is under suspension for some misdemeanour," James continued.

"Oh hell, is he? Why wasn't I told?"

"And there might be charges brought against you for abuse of several people."

"Oh yeah? Who? Tell me, sonny!" The three stooges moved closer as if to engage.

"Time will tell," said James evenly, as he put four cooked sausages onto a plate.

George leapt at James, James ducked and George sprawled under the barbeque. As George quickly rose, he burnt his bald head and screamed and flopped back down. Stooge Number One grabbed James around the neck from behind. James dropped to a squat, escaped the circling arms and bucked up into the man's chin. The man yelled in pain and fell back. Number Two grabbed James' collar. James' left arm went under the man's arm, his right arm reached across and he turned so quickly I hardly saw it. Then there was a sickening sound of wrenching tissue. The man fell to his knees, groaning and holding his arm.

"Your turn," said James to Number Three as he picked up a barbeque fork. Number Three held his hands up and backed away. "The three of you have two weeks to get out of Ipswich."

"But we live here," complained Number Three.

James ignored that. "We'll be checking on you and anytime we see any of you in this city after the two-week deadline, there will be broken bones."

"But ..."

"But get packing. Now!" James advanced on the man, brandishing the long fork, and the man fled. "Call an ambulance when you get home." James turned and gave George a good hard kick in the crotch as he got up to kneeling. George fell prone again with a grunt and silence. "That's for bothering my woman." James looked pleased with himself as he looked over at me and I wished it was me who had given the kick. Yes, me who hates violence. I'd loved to have kicked the sod. I smiled back and took in to Maureen and Ruby the plate of sausages and buttered bread that he handed me.

After the Battle

After the ambulances had taken the three men away and they'd confirmed with Sergeant Gordon McLeod that they didn't want to press charges, we stood around the barbeque looking happy and relieved.

"That was an anticlimax," said Edward, stepping forward to pick up a sausage in buttered bread.

"Yeah, totally, mate," said Ricky, looking like he had ants in his pants, wanting to do something but not knowing what. He fiddled with the sausages unnecessarily and kept looking around as if he was being spied on.

"Ricky, just breathe," I said.

"What?" He stared at me as if I'd asked him to chew his nose off.

"Take a breath. Let it out. Take another."

"Okay, okay, I got it. Feel like an itchy bum now it's all over. What's next? Nothing?"

"Not for those three," said Phil, looking at James who kept a straight face.

"And Maur ..." Kathryn started to say.

"Sshhh," I said and she looked at me, obviously embarrassed.

"Okay, you lot," said McLeod, stepping off the footpath and up to the barbeque to take a sausage. He flicked it back on the barbeque. "Hell, that's hot!"

"Barbeques do that," said James, laughing.

"But Edward picked one up."

"He's superman, tough as old boots."

"He used the bread, mate," said Ricky. "An old trick." He handed the sergeant a sausage wrapped in buttered bread.

"Yes, I know that. Not thinking.," said McLeod. "Now, since most of you are here, can I have your assurance that you don't have any more plans for violence?"

"Edward's the master planner," said Christine, putting her arm proudly around his shoulders.

"Geoffrey had the original idea and I just added some details." Edward looked decidedly embarrassed. "But no more plans, sergeant."

"So I can safely leave you all in peace, can I?"

"No guarantees, mate, but we'll try to behave," said Ricky, handing McLeod another sausage.

"I've had one sausage, thanks."

"Nah, you can't fly on one wing."

"Okay, thanks." The sergeant could probably have done with fewer sausages, given his portly stature, but there was no point in judging a song by the singer. He seemed to be a straight shooter, honest as the day is long, so he could have as many sausages as he liked.

About to get into his car, he suddenly stopped. With his driver's door open, he looked back at the house.

"Are you okay?" asked Rosie, her eyes following his eye-line.

"Yes ... no ... not sure. I swore I saw George's wife in the window. Am I dreaming?"

"Ya must be. Dunno," said Ricky.

I looked back and saw Maureen looking out the window, her sunglasses and headscarf removed. Bugger. I turned and walked back inside as nonchalantly as I could.

"Maureen, get away from the window," I whispered to her from the bedroom door. These weatherboard Queenslanders weren't insulated for sound or heat.

"Oh, sorry," she said, trotting out from the bedroom, nervously patting down her dress and looking flustered. "I thought ... I thought it was over. Sorry."

"I think Sergeant McLeod has seen you."

"Oh," she squeaked.

"Yes, he has," said Sergeant McLeod, from right behind me.

"Oh hell." I backed against the wall.

"So, what are you all hiding?"

"Well, Maureen," I said, and then wondered why I thought it was a secret or a crime.

"Sergeant," she said plaintively.

"Hang on. Hang on. I'm surprised to see you here with these people," he said, looking around at the crowd gathering at each end of the corridor. "Are you here voluntarily, Mrs Barbieri?"

"Yes."

"No one has forced you to be here?"

"No one. They helped me escape."

"From where? From your own home?" He was frowning and looking more confused by the minute.

"Yes, sergeant, it was a prison."

"Let me get this straight. You are leaving your husband and these people are helping you?"

"Yes, it was becoming dangerous." She was still smoothing her dress and looking like a naughty little girl.

"So you are here under your own free will?" She nodded yes like that naughty little girl. "So why the secrecy, now that the men have been taken away?"

"Existential guilt," I said.

"Exis what?"

"The innocent protecting the innocent from the guilty and still feeling guilty," I explained, but not clearly enough for him, obviously. He smiled awkwardly, shook his head and put his hand on my shoulder.

"Let us leave philosophy class till later, ma'am. I want to make sure that Mrs Barbieri is here of her own free will and that everyone is safe."

"I've never felt safer, sergeant," Maureen said, sounding like a little girl asking permission to go to the toilet, her eyes beseeching his.

"That's good. My next question is, do you want to press charges against your husband?"

"Oh, I hadn't thought of that. I don't know."

"Yes, it's probably too soon, with everything that's happened, but please consider it. Without putting too fine a point on it, your pressing charges would help in protecting your neighbours. I understand that Janice here had an unpleasant encounter with him." He looked directly at me. "The more charges are presented, the greater chance we have of incarcerating him. Would you agree, James?"

"Absolutely, Gordon. The more people who come forward, the greater chance of having him and his, aah, his associates brought to justice."

"So speaks the lawyer," said Gordon.

"And so speaks the policeman," said James.

"Okay, I am satisfied, as an officer of the peace, that no one is breaking the peace. So I'll leave you all to consume those disgustingly awful sausages." He smiled, turned and left. I followed him to the front door.

"Hey, one more disgustingly awful sausage, sarg?" said Ricky, handing him one.

"Alright, just one more to save you all from having to eat it." And he was gone, leaving us standing there, staring at one another.

"So, there's no after-plan plan, Edward?" asked Rosie. Edward looked a mite embarrassed and I didn't know if it was for not having a plan or for being singled out. I suspect it was the latter for this humble man.

"What I can tell you is it's not over," said James, looking around at us all.

"Whaddya mean?" asked Billy, coming out of the house with Phil. They'd just parked their utes up the driveway and Billy had gone straight inside to see how Emma and Jeanie were. "Ya wopped them, didn't you?"

Phil had changed out of his ripped and baggy checked shirt and had borrowed one of Billy's t-shirts. The length was alright but it was skin-tight. I'd assumed the man was a bit flabby under his usual oversized, green bush shirts but I had to look twice - quite a firm body, there. From floppy to tight clothes, the man needed to find a middle ground though. However, he did seem in grave danger of tidying himself up. I'd better warn him.

"James is absolutely right, I suspect," said Edward, holding hands with Christine in such a natural way that they could have been together for years, not just in the last month they'd got to know each other. "Today's a victory and we should honour that. But they're like hydra - cut off each head and two more appear."

"Yes," said James, smiling at Edward. "I can't tell you the extent of this organisation but I know it expands far beyond little old Ipswich. Maybe beyond little old Brisbane or, even, Australia."

"Struth," said Ricky. "I know the unions aren't run by the workers and that they have their greasy little mitts into the newspapers and politicians and everywhere you don't want them to be."

"Well, that's sucked the wind out of my sails," I said. "I was starting to feel really good and free for the first time in forever, if I'm honest, with you lot around me and seeing we can actually do something about these people. We're not totally helpless."

"I did say we should honour the victory, pat ourselves on the back. But still stay alert," Edward said.

"Yep, we gotta be alert," said Ricky. "Australia needs more lerts. Shit, I'm funny!" He burst out laughing and some of us joined in.

I noticed Maureen looking out from the bedroom window, without a smile on her face. She might be safe, but I realised she was now in former enemy territory, with people she'd never associated with. People that the people she normally associated with wouldn't approve of her associating with. I guessed she might be feeling pulled apart. She had tossed aside her frightening but familiar life in a panicked moment of a rash decision. She probably couldn't go back to her old life without serious consequences. But how would she go forward to an unknown future? I wouldn't be smiling either.

I hadn't smiled either when my two relationships ended. There's something comfortable about a familiar life, even if it's dominated by abuse. An unknown future seemed scarier than the abusive past but, eventually, the abuse grows - it never becomes less - until we have no choice but to set out on that terrifying new road with no road signs.

Not much smiling happens during a metamorphosis. The caterpillar doesn't just transform into a butterfly. Its body first dissolves into a pulp and the butterfly then develops from that liquid soup. We need to give up everything we once were and everything we had - assets, friends, interests, jobs, locations, beliefs. Not everything has to change but most things do. It's terrifying to give up our familiar careers, neighbourhoods, habits, accommodations and religions but it's always, always, always better on the other side. On this rock I stand.

However, the better doesn't happen immediately and I'm sure it's God's cheeky ruse to test our determination to stick with the change. When he/she/they know we won't back down, then people and circumstances arrive to support our scary step out into space. Road signs turn up. That's my opinion, anyway.

I wished I could tell Maureen all that but I knew that, when you were standing on the edge of the cliff, you couldn't be consoled by someone's theory about a safe landing. All you could think of was the terrifying fall.

I smiled up at Maureen and she looked at me, a faint smile flickering at the edges of her mouth. It felt like a look of recognition, somehow.

"Look, we've got this lovely community of people here, we've got the telephone tree, we've got a meeting place in the Lucky Café," said Edward, as if checking items off a list.

"We've probably scared the hell out of the thugs for a couple of days," said James.

"And hopefully we'll have the story in tomorrow's Ipswich Times," said Kathryn.

"Yes, I hope they don't mess too much with the story I send in," said Edward, "and it probably won't appear for a few days."

"Well, I could install cameras and alarms at each end of the street," said Phil. He must have washed his tattoos off and quickly brushed his hair.

"That's good, but what about James and Edward and Christine?" asked Ricky.

"And me," said Kathryn, arms akimbo, her ferociously fragile expression still in place.

"And the kids at the school?" asked Rosie.

"Aah, hell, they're probably the most vulnerable," I said, as that familiar terror sucked at my stomach. I looked around for Kassey and she wasn't there.

"It's okay, Janice. Karen's filled the paddling pool at the back." Rosie smiled at me with a fierce look that said something like, Mothers in arms. I felt a huge relief to know it wasn't just me looking out for Kassey.

"I start back at the school tomorrow so I can't keep an eye on the kids," I said, feeling a bit helpless.

"I'm told the new principal, Carol Dougherty, was chosen for her tough and fair attitude towards behaviour," said Rosie. "I've met her and she appears to be making changes already and making her views known to parents and staff."

"Look, while we're here, can we get Maureen's car and a few other things for her?" I said, realising we had a window of opportunity.

"Good idea, Janice," said Emma, from the front door. I admired her unobtrusive diligence, quietly in the background being with Maureen, getting plates, cutlery and food for the chefs and, I found out later, helping Karen with the paddling pool and supervising the kids. "I'll get Maureen."

I waited for at least a minute and no Maureen. I looked around and everyone else was silently watching the front door. I couldn't wait any longer.

Ruby was sitting on Rosie's bed, beside a weeping Maureen.

"I can't do it." Maureen spoke between sobs. "He's not such a bad man. We've been together for 43 years. Forty-three years."

"It's a long time," said Ruby."

"And he's only got silly recently. It's just a phase."

"When did he first hit you?"

"Oh, he never ... well, the odd slap. Pushed me into the bedroom wall. Kicked me once. Only once."

"When did all that happen?"

"Oh, not sure. Not long ago. He's not that bad really." Her crying had stopped while answering Ruby's questions.

"How often?"

"How often what?"

"Did he physically harm you?"

"Oh, not much. I don't know. Maybe ... like, once a week."

"He hurts you once a week. He slaps you. He kicks you. He punches you. He pushes you into a wall."

"Well, it's not that bad. It's not, really ..."

"When did he start yelling at you?"

"Oh, that's alright. He gets angry with the stupid people he works with."

"And takes it out on you."

Maureen looked around at Ruby, Rosie, Doris and me, all pouring our sympathy into her.

"I'm sorry, Maureen," said Rosie, "but good men do not abuse or hit women. Good women do not abuse or hit men. We just don't do that to others."

"But he's been under stress lately. It'll get better soon," said Maureen, looking around, imploring us to understand.

"Maureen," I said, "abuse never gets less. It never improves unless the abuser does the work."

"The work?"

"The inner work. Takes responsibility. Admits to their bad behaviour. Promises not to abuse again and never does. Gets help from others. He hasn't done any of that, has he?"

"No, but ..."

"So I will tell you what I know. It will only get worse. I've lived through it. Twice. So have Christine and Kathryn." I noticed Christine in the doorway, nodding.

"She's right, Maureen," said Christine, "it's only going to get worse. You are in real mortal danger. Time to wake up, girl."

"But ... but, oh hell."

"Yes, it's hard, Maureen." Christine came up to the bed, on the other side of Ruby, and put her hand on Maureen's back. "But it isn't harder than another 20 years of living in fear, of being trapped in your house, of being isolated from others, of being regularly hurt, of living every fucken day as if it's your last ... sorry."

"Oh." Maureen put her hand to her mouth as Christine spoke louder and more stridently.

"You're going to hear the truth - to live every fucken day as if it's your last. That's how it's been, hasn't it?"

Maureen looked up at Christine's fierce stare and eventually nodded.

"So, this is hard, girl. I get it. When I left my ex, he smashed me to the floor and I didn't know if I'd walk again. And he forced Edward, at the point of a shotgun, to walk out and dig his own grave. Leaving is shit." Maureen gasped again. "It's the truth. Never walking again was going to be better than not living. And I am not going to let you go back to a daily hell. You're a good person and you don't deserve this." As Christine was speaking in stronger and stronger tones, I could feel my anger rising.

"I totally agree with Christine," I said, grabbing Christine's arm tighter than I meant to. "Sorry, Chris." She shrugged and I kept hold of her arm. "Abusers never fade or get tired of abusing - they only ever get worse."

"But it was just stress at his work," said Maureen, with less conviction this time.

"Then he needs to take it out on those at work, not on you," I said, my tone becoming stronger, like Christine's. I didn't care. "It's not your fault. You're a good woman."

"No, I am not. I was nasty to you, Janice," she said, almost pleading.

"You did a bad thing but you're not a bad person. You've apologised and you meant it." I bent over and grabbed her shoulders. "You're a good person." That started her crying again.

"I was bad to you," said Maureen, through her tears. "I'm a bad person and I probably deserved ..."

"Oh no, I tried that one and I was dead wrong. Nobody, but nobody, deserves to be yelled at, punched, slammed against walls, ostracised from their friends. I bet he's done that, huh?"

"Uh, well, might have." Her voice had dropped to a whisper.

"He kept you from your friends?" asked Rosie, gasping.

"They're a bad influence, he said."

"Bad influence be damned," said Christine, her words as fiery as her hair. "No one gets to imprison anyone in their own home. God!"

"It's not a prison, really."

"Can you go out anytime you like?"

"Uh, aah, not really ..."

"Then it's a prison. So, how many more years will you sentence yourself to prison, my friend?"

"Friend?" Maureen asked so softly I could hardly hear her. "I'm your friend?" She looked shocked and sad at the same time as tears ran down her face.

"Too right, mate." Christine grabbed her tighter around the shoulders.

"And my friend, too," I said.

"And my friend, Maureen," said Rosie.

"And mine, too," said Doris.

"And mine," said Ruby, her eyes sparkling as she looked around at all of us.

I've never seen a face with so many emotions coursing through it. Maureen started with shock then disbelief and then dismissal. Then she softened at Doris' declaration and collapsed when Ruby confirmed her friendship.

"Oh you ... you can't," she tried to say as the panoply of emotions converged and tears cascaded down her face. Her arms remained at her sides as if all her energy had been drained away.

"No, Rosie," said Christine as Rosie put her arm around Maureen and went to pull her into a hug. "Let her cry and let's not stifle it."

Rosie let go and frowned at Christine, more in confusion than in anger.

"It's a lovely gesture, Rosie, but we often hug crying people because we feel uncomfortable and we want it to stop. It's usually best to let it run."

"Gosh, I'd never thought of it like that," said Doris, looking at Christine. "We do it to our kids, too."

Maureen's tears had stopped and she seemed disinterested in wiping them away. Her hands remained on the bed. She looked around at the coven of care and gently shook her head as if trying to take in the idea of friendship.

"Why do you all say I'm your friend?" she asked quietly. "I haven't done anything for you. For any of you."

"Because you're a human and a good person," said Doris.

"Someone said that before." Maureen kept staring at us, in turn, seeming not to notice as another bank of tears spilled down her pain-etched cheeks. I had no idea how old she was but was sure her cropped, curly hair wouldn't have been so grey if not for the abuse. Who knew?

"You're all such lovely people ..."

"Despite our colour," said Rosie, straight-faced, and Maureen looked at her in horror. Then Rosie burst out laughing. Maureen had the tiniest smirk that quickly transformed into a laugh, which gave us permission to do the same.

I happened to look out the window to see five men standing around the barbeque, two in boots, shorts and akubras, two in thongs and James looking impeccable as usual, not at all like a man who had used his fists to send three other men off to hospital. An interesting man.

It then occurred to me that, without design on anyone's part, the men had gathered outside as if guarding the women inside who were tending to the inner work. In the same way as men can endure immense outer pain, women endure immense inner pain. Thank God for the two genders. We complement each other so well, when we're emotionally mature.

When we are immature is when wars, fights and abuse happen. Maybe, as a species, we'll never grow up. I hope I'm wrong.

As I turned my eyes back to Maureen and the other women, an almighty scream erupted from outside. More than one voice, I was sure, and one was Kassey's.

I dashed out, followed by the rest of the women, to see Kassey and Jeanie standing there screaming while Karen sat silently, as if carved in stone.

I rushed over to Kassey while other women converged in the back yard and men appeared from around the corner to join us.

"Oh Mum!" she said as she quietened down but continued shaking, her eyes bulging. "Tim." She pointed to the end of the house where the two utes were parked. "Tim," she repeated between gasping breaths.

Jeanie stopped screaming when Emma hugged her. "They took Tim," she said between gasps.

"Who?" asked Emma, holding her at arm's length.

"Don't know. Two men."

"Black or white? Tall or short? Young or old?"

"White."

"Young," said Kassey breathlessly, her eyes red and staring. "Twenty-ish, I think."

"In a car or ute?" asked Emma.

"White ute," said Jeanie. Emma stood beside her, her arm around the girl's shoulders, while Kassey buried her face in my chest.

"Right," said Billy, "what direction?"

Jeanie pointed down the road. "They went left."

"Out of town?" Jeanie nodded to Billy and he was gone, quickly followed by Phil and Ricky. The two utes roared off and I wondered why James hadn't joined them and then noticed he'd disappeared. Then I heard his voice inside the house. I took Kassey inside and saw him on the phone. To the police.

"Right, Jack and Stan, can you guys stay out the front and make sure they don't mount a second attack?" asked James. "I'll stay out the back."

"Yes, yes," said Jack, brightening up from his look of confusion and paralysis. Both men went out the front.

"And can I have, say, two women inside, dedicated to relaying messages between us men, please? We shouldn't leave our posts."

"You got it, James," said Christine. "I'll be at the front door."

"And I'll take the back door," said Kathryn seriously.

"Sisters in charge," said Christine, and fist-bumped Kathryn on the shoulder. Kathryn nodded and smiled grimly.

"I'll stay out the back with you, James," said Edward. "I'm no fighter but another male presence may help."

"Perfect, mate," said James, grabbing Edward's shoulder. As close to as a hug as they'll ever get, I thought. I followed them out the back and there was Karen, still sitting there, cold and silent as a rock.

A white ute suddenly roared around the corner and up Ricky's driveway. We all rushed to see that Ricky was driving while Billy and Phil were on the back, with two young men between them. Then Tim's head appeared above the dashboard, looking like he'd conquered the world. Rosie rushed over, yanked open the door and hauled Tim out, hugging him tightly.

James rushed to Phil's side and grabbed the nearest young man who was wearing a singlet, baggy jeans and thongs.

"Don't let the other one out, Billy and Phil," commanded James, as Ricky came around to his wife and son. "We'll deal with them one at a time. Now, Ricky, Rosie, do you have any spray paint?"

"Spray paint? Oh, yeah," said Ricky, frowning.

"Then get it." The young man yelped and I saw that James had his hand at a very unnatural angle. "Get your clothes off." The youth stared at James as if he didn't understand English. "Clothes off or you're a goner. Now!" The youth took his singlet off, one-handed, and James changed hands to let it fall to the ground. "All of them!" The youth took his gold necklace off and kicked his thongs off. Pants."

"What?"

James gave a twist of the youth's wrist and he yelped. The boy fumbled with his jeans, one-handed, and they eventually dropped to the ground.

"Off with the rest!" The youth looked terrified and complied clumsily. "Lie on your stomach, on the grass." James led him to the grass beside the driveway and the youth lay down, looking around, his eyes wild. "Edward, put your foot on his back so he doesn't move." Edward rushed over and Stan followed, a bit slower. Each of them put a foot on the youth's back, one on each side.

"Whatcha doin'?" the youth cried out.

"Shut up." James pushed the youth's face into the lawn with his foot. "Don't move. Now, get the other one out." James dealt with the second one the same way. "Is there any string or rope here?"

"Yes, in the garage, Ricky," said Rosie, obviously not prepared to let her son go. Ricky handed a can of yellow spray paint to James and rushed off again. "Now, does anyone have any paper and a pen?"

"Of course, in my handbag." I was surprised to see Maureen out of the house and actively involved.

"So, take notes, Miss Jones," said James, smiling broadly at her. He demanded their names and addresses, along with the names and addresses of their parents, which they reluctantly gave while Maureen took notes.

"Who paid you?"

"Paid what?"

"Who paid you to abduct this young boy?"

"They wanted a girl, but the girls were screaming so we took the boy."

"Cowards. So who wanted a girl?"

The youths went quiet.

"Ricky, go and get your sharpest carving knife," said James, quietly and firmly. Ricky's eyes went wide and James winked at him and smiled. Ricky smiled, dropped two ropes at James' feet and turned to go.

"I know just the knife," said Ricky.

"Thomlinson," said one of the youths.

"Aah, shit, we're in trouble now, ya prick!" growled the other youth.

"How much did he pay you?"

"Two hundred up front. Three hundred on delivery."

"Thank you. That's in front of, what, 12 witnesses," said James, looking around at us all. Everyone nodded back. "Now, Ricky, can you tie their left ankles together, please?" Ricky looked uncertain and then smiled and complied. "Good. Now, Billy, can you tie their right wrists together please." All this entailed rolling them back and forth and, eventually, they were tied together, facing each other.

"Now, any artists here? Young man, would you like to spray these two criminals all over?" asked James, addressing Tim without using his name. Tim looked uncertain and then burst out in a huge smile as he broke away from Rosie. Soon they were covered in indelible yellow, from head to foot. Billy and Phil helped roll them over so no part of their anatomy was missed.

"Now, help them up and set them on their way," said James to Phil and Billy.

"Hey, our ute!" yelled youth one, trying to twist away from his mate.

"That's ours and we'll hand it over to the police to hold till the trial is over and you're in gaol." James smiled and shrugged.

"Gaol! No way!" cried youth two.

"Get on your way before that carving knife arrives."

"Okay, okay, we'll go," said youth one.

"We can't," said youth two.

"No choice." Youth one pulled on his mate and the yellow-painted youths stumbled out onto the street in the most ungainly fashion imaginable, falling twice in the driveway.

"Can someone please phone the police to tell them it was a false alarm. They're not needed now," said James.

"Right boss," said Christine from the top of the back step and she disappeared into the house.

"Thank you so much, you three," said James, looking at Ricky, Phil and Billy. "That was a huge risk you took, chasing those boys. They could have had an ambush waiting for you."

"Aah," said Billy, "never thought of that. We just needed to get Tim back." Billy patted Tim on the back and Tim leant into him for a moment, smiling.

"You all probably saved his life." Ricky, Phil and Billy shrugged and looked embarrassed.

"Cup of tea, anyone?" asked Ruby from the back step. I turned and saw Karen, still standing there. An anger rose in my chest from nowhere.

"What the hell were you doing, Karen?" I demanded. "You said you'd look after Kassey, after all the kids."

Karen looked up at me, frightened. "I ... I ... well ..."

"You did nothing."

"I didn't know what to do."

"Christ! You could have yelled. You could have grabbed the kids, taken them inside. You could have run inside and told us." My voice was rising with every word, like my anger.

"I didn't know what to do. Sorry." She started sobbing.

"You're sorry? You damned well should be! You lost a child, woman." I was yelling and I didn't care.

"Janice, Janice, please," said Rosie, her hand on my shoulder.

"But she ..." I yelled, shrugging her hand off me.

"She was terrified, Janice."

"She could have done something!" I know my voice was embarrassing everyone but I couldn't help it and I still didn't care. I could have lost Kassey. Her friend, Tim, had been taken.

"She was absolutely terrified, Janice. Please, please."

"She could have yelled out."

Rosie enclosed me in a fierce hug that I tried to struggle out of. She wouldn't let me go so I burst into tears on her shoulder.

"Oh Mum," said Kassey and I felt her arms around my waist.

"I'm so sorry, love." I stared down at her searching eyes. "I could have lost you." My tears welled up again. I stared at Karen, standing there staring at me as if too frightened to speak. I broke away from Rosie and Kassey and hugged Karen. She didn't hug me back, her arms stiffly at her sides.

"I'm so sorry, Karen. I just ... I don't know. I lost it."

"It's okay, Janice," she said quietly and her arms began to move. "I lost it too."

"Is this what happened when you were attacked at work?"

"Whew." She exhaled. "I suppose so. I ... froze."

"And that's how they got away with it? And the sacking?"

"That's harsh, Janice," said Emma, frowning.

"I'm sorry, I didn't mean to be judging you, Karen. I just meant they took advantage of your silence, of your panic."

"Oh, yes, I see." Emma smiled shyly at me.

"Our silence gives abusers permission to abuse more. I know from experience."

"I've never been in that position."

"You are absolutely right, Janice," said Karen, an arm going around my waist as she smiled up at me. "A lesson I have to learn."

"Okay, let's learn it now."

"What?"

"Scream. Do it now."

"Now? Scream?" Karen looked around as if petrified of everyone there.

"Mum, should I go and tell everyone inside what's happening?" asked Kassey, understanding my intentions.

"Of course. Tell Kathryn to pass the message on that we're going to be screaming and not to worry." Kassey trotted off inside while I turned to Jeanie, next to Emma. "Give us a yell. Show Karen how to do it." Jeanie looked at me, puzzled, and then she let a beautiful, big smile break out on her nut-brown face. She stood back from Emma and screamed to bring the sun down. Everyone else laughed.

"Your turn, Janice," I said.

"What? Me?"

"Yes. Go again, Jeanie. And Karen can join you. One, two, three, go!" Jeanie screamed again and Karen gave a short timid yell.

"Come on, you can do better than that."

Karen looked at me with an awkward smile, shrugged and let out the loudest, scariest yell I'd ever heard. People across the road came out of their houses and pedestrians stopped on the footpath.

"Anyone else?" I asked, and then Rosie, Karen and Jeanie all screamed loudly and stood there panting and chuckling.

"God, I never felt so good," said Karen, looking bright-eyed and ecstatic. "Next time, Roger Brown, I'm screaming."

"Gosh, Janice, you released a demon in her," said Rosie, chuckling.

"Yes, you all watch out." Karen screamed again. "That feels so, so good."

"And next time something like this happens?" I asked.

"I'll damned well scream and shout. It's the least I can do." Karen waved at the spectators over the road. "God, I do wish I had done this at work. Damn it! Now, where's that boy?" She trotted into the house, maybe to apologise.

Kassey had come outside and I asked her, "Do you know where Tim is?"

"I think he's inside, Mum."

"Shall we go inside and see how he is?"

"Okay." Not a lot of enthusiasm from Kassey.

"Hey, what's wrong, love?" She shrugged. "Come on, tell me." I led her away from the other people to a corner of the section that was shaded by the house.

"Well, you told Karen off and then you helped her." Her plaintive voice definitely wasn't her usually determined one.

"Yes?"

"And you want to see how Tim is ..."

"What's wrong with that. Come on, love, what's going on?"

"You haven't asked me, like, how I am." Oh, God, an arrow to my heart. My fault. Caught up in everyone else's stuff, I've been blind to my daughter.

"Oh, hell, Kassey, I am so very sorry." I grabbed her for a hug but she squirmed away.

"You were inside all that time. You didn't come out to see me."

"But I was ..." I realised I was making excuses and sounded like I was whining.

"Jeanie's mum was there."

"And I wasn't. I'm sorry. I'm really sorry, Kassey. Now, can you tell me what's really going on. Are you scared?" She nodded. "Do you feel vulnerable? Unsafe? Not protected?" She nodded each time. "With all these people around, you still feel like you're in danger?"

"Well, those boys got Tim." There's nothing more powerful than a simple fact.

"You're absolutely right, love. With all these people, they still got through."

"If you'd been there ..." She shrugged and looked away. It took me a moment to realise what she was saying.

"Are you saying it wouldn't have happened if I'd been outside with you?" She wobbled her head left to right. "Is that what you think?"

"Well, maybe." She looked up at me as if searching my face for the answer she needed.

"Look, love, I wasn't there and I am very sorry for that. You've been scared out of your wits and I know it could take some time till you're not scared. I appreciate that." She let me put my hand on her shoulder this time. "What would help right now? Go home? Drive out of Ipswich for a couple of days? Help Tim? I don't know, any ideas?"

My usually decisive girl shrugged, the poor thing.

"Okay, let's start where we are and go in and see if Tim or anyone needs any help, okay?" She nodded. "Then if another idea comes up, you tell me, huh?" She nodded again and looked up at me.

"Mum, I'm sorry," she said quietly.

"For what?"

"For telling you off."

"Hey, I told Karen off and I shouldn't have. Panic and stress and horrible people can make us do silly things." She smiled for the first time in an hour and I hugged her. "Okay, let's see if we can get through the next hour without doing something silly, huh?" She even giggled but I knew the fear and vulnerability still simmered under the surface.

"Are you alright, you two?" I turned to see Stan there.

"Yes thanks, Stan. We just needed a space for a private chat."

"I'm sorry to interrupt ..."

"We've just finished, and I've realised how hot it is, despite being in the shade. With everything going on, we forget our basic needs."

"Come inside then," he said. "The air con's on."

I turned to go inside the house and noticed a ute in the driveway.

"Yes, the three men got the utes back and the abductors' is on the lawn at the front," said Stan, as if answering my silent question.

❖ ❖

Tim was sitting at the oval pine dining table beside Rosie. She had a cup of tea and he had a glass of cordial. He was shaking a little,.

"Sit beside him," I said to Kassey, quietly nudging her. She looked up at me, frowning. "Just be there. You don't have to say anything." She nodded and walked over, and he smiled at her as she took the empty chair beside him. Ricky was sitting across the table from them, a cup of tea at his elbow untouched. He looked extremely uncomfortable and kept tapping his fingers while looking at Rosie, at Tim, around the room and out the window behind him. His eyes couldn't settle on anything.

"Hey, Ricky, it's okay." Rosie reached across and laid her hand on his folded arms on the table. "You don't have to say or do anything. Just be here."

"I'm no good at these emotional things, love. I want to go and smash their bloody brains in. I know that won't help you, Tim, but that's what I keep thinking. It won't help at all, will it, Tim?" Tim shrugged. "I feel so helpless. I just want to do something."

"Why don't you dismantle the barbeque and bring all the stuff in. I'm sure Billy would be happy to help you."

"You sure? You okay, Tim?"

Tim nodded and smiled weakly.

"Go, Ricky. You're making us all nervous with your jiggling knee and table tapping." Rosie smiled and waved him away. Ricky hesitated, maybe wondering if he was deserting his post.

"Dad, go, you're making this house look untidy." Tim smiled and looked at Kassey, who smiled back uncertainly.

Ricky laughed, got up, ruffled Tim's hair and went out to the barbeque, calling for Phil and Billy, his confidence restored now that he had something to do. Rosie sat back with a relieved smile and finished her cup of tea.

The Police Intervene

Oh, no, the cops are here," said Billy, turning back to us from the doorway.

"But I phoned them. Told Natalie Gallo we didn't need them," said Christine.

"Hang on, they're not Queensland police," said Billy, shaking his head. "They're New South Wales cars. Jeez, didn't know we were so famous." Of course, everyone crowded to the door or the window by the table.

"It's him," I said, as a tall, middle-aged policeman got out of his car and a younger policewoman emerged from the other side. Then I wished I hadn't said anything.

"You know them, Janice?" asked Ruby.

"No, I thought it was someone else." Kassey looked up at me, frowning, and I shook my head. She shrugged and turned back to watch DI Damon Edwards and Constable Trudy Perkins come through the small wooden gate. Something made me turn quickly to James who'd made his way to my side, and he looked like a naughty little boy, biting his lip and shrugging at me. Then he put his finger to his lips. I nodded. I guess he has his reasons for being a devious sod, I thought.

"Let's meet them outside so the neighbours aren't in any doubt we have police support," said James, loud enough for everyone to hear.

"Right, but just a mo," I said and turned to Kassey. "Are you okay if we go outside and talk with the police?"

"Yeah, we know them, Mum," she whispered, smiling.

Most of us stood around the DI and the constable on the lawn, while a few remained on the front steps. I was sure James knew them but they didn't acknowledge him, nor he them.

"Good morning, everyone," said DI Damon Edwards, introducing himself and his constable, who stood at his side with her arms behind her back. "We received an anonymous tip-off." He looked directly at James for a flicker of a second but I was sure no one noticed. "A tip-off that there could be an incident here. Has anyone been hurt? Is everyone alright?"

Some answered the first question and some the second one and nos and yeses were shouted out and he held up his hand and smiled.

"So, is everyone okay?"

Lots of yeses while Rosie and I said no. Everyone looked at us.

"No physical damage, sir," she said, "but my son, Tim, was abducted, although he was quickly recovered by my husband and his friends."

"I understand." Edwards walked over and squatted his six-foot two frame in front of Tim. "So, Tim, would you and your mum like to talk with Constable Perkins?"

Tim nodded silently and Trudy took him by the hand, with Rosie beside him.

"Now, madam," he said to me, giving no indication he knew me. "You said no."

"Yes, two other children were with Tim when he was taken," I said. "My daughter, Kassey, and Jeanie."

"Would you two like to talk with the constable as well, with your mothers?" Kassey and I nodded and followed Tim and Rosie into the house. I stopped at the top of the step and, like a delayed reaction, wondered why I hadn't thought of Jeanie.

"Now, young lady, how are you?" he asked as Emma brought Jeanie forward. She looked petrified, unwilling to approach the policeman. He took off his hat and crouched down again. "No one's in trouble. We just want to make sure you're okay, after what's happened. If I was you, I'd have been terrified. Were you?"

Jeanie looked up at Emma and Emma nodded.

"Yes sir."

"You were terrified?" Jeanie nodded. "And now, are you still feeling shaky?"

"Yes sir."

"I bet you are."

Jeanie nodded and a sneaky smile began to form, her confidence growing a little.

Constable Perkins welcomed the last two to our group and waved us all to chairs around the kitchen table.

"Now, I can't fix how you feel right now, Tim, Kassey and Jeanie. If you're feeling wobbly and scared and fragile, I understand. I was attacked several times when I was a young girl and that's why I do what I do now - try to help others like me and you. Anyway, I wanted you and your mums to know how we can help, okay?" Everyone nodded as she handed us her business card. She explained that safe houses were available and then gave us pamphlets with contact details of counselling and police services.

"All of these services are free for as long as you need them. See, soldiers who have been in a war can get PTSD. That means they can feel happy and good one day and then, suddenly, have what we call a flashback. Their brains try to keep out all of the terrible things they heard, saw and experienced, but sometimes, their brains get tired and can't keep the bad stuff out all the time. You understand?" Everyone nodded. "So, the same could happen to you."

Emma said, "Billy, my husband, said Tim was paralysed when they recovered him but by the time they got back here, he was jubilant. Then that faded and he's gone quiet again."

"So, Tim, are you feeling very up and down at the moment?"

"Yes, mmm ..." Tim said uncertainly.

"You can call me Trudy."

"Yes, Trudy." His small smile grew a little.

"And you two girls are the same?"

Kassey nodded.

"I still have them," said Jeanie, sounding like a pricked balloon, flat and lifeless.

I didn't know what she meant, but clearly Trudy did. "Okay, Jeanie, so are you saying you've had another trauma before today? A shocking thing that happened?"

"Yes." Jeanie took a big breath and looked at Emma who nodded to her. There was a momentary silence while the girl seemed to be deciding what, if anything, to say. Then she nodded and exhaled. "I was stolen in Alice ..."

"In Alice Springs?" asked Trudy.

"Yes, Alice Springs. And I ran away and a man saved me and then my mum and dad took me. Adopted me."

"The man was Edward, out there," said Emma, clarifying.

"Hell," I said, and immediately wished I could have kept those words in my mouth.

"Yes, hell," said Trudy, smiling kindly at me and then at Jeanie. "You probably feel like you've gone through hell, Jeanie?"

Jeanie smiled, nodded and wiped her leaking eyes.

"Okay, I hate to push you on but I can leave the six of you to have a chat. You can go to one of our safe houses today, for as long as you like. You might prefer to stay at home. Up to you. I'll come back in a few minutes." We all nodded and looked at one another for a moment as Constable Perkins strode out the door.

"Alright, Tim," said Rosie, breaking the silence, "would you like to go to a safe house, away from here for a few days?"

He screwed up his nose as if deciding. "I, like, don't want to be here but I don't want to go by myself," he said.

"Me too," said Kassey.

"Yes, me too," said Jeanie.

"There'll be an adult with you," said Emma.

"But like ..." Kassey started to say.

"But you'd want your friends with you," I said. She frowned at me. "Sorry, Kassey, I interrupted." She nodded and snorted her dissatisfaction at my interference. Under stress, some people clam up and I blurt stuff out, unfortunately.

"Yeah, be good to have, like, friends," said Jeanie, slowly becoming more open, like a lizard waking up in the sun.

"Right," said Rosie, "so the three of you want to go away to feel safer. I can't blame you. But I'm not sure if I can ..."

"I'll go with them," said Emma fiercely. No negotiating, there, I thought. The two women looked at me and my stomach churned. "Look, I feel really awful because I'd love to be with the kids, with Kassey, but I feel it's important I start work tomorrow. My first day back. I suspect there will be a focus on the school, where this all started, and it seems important to show we're not backing down, that we won't be intimidated. Does that sound awful?"

Kassey looked at me, smiling, as if she understood this adult world and its reasoning. "Mum," she said, "that's really good." She seemed to be proud of me. "We'll be okay with Jeanie's mum." Jeanie and Tim nodded and smiled along with her.

Constable Perkins brought Karen into the kitchen and pointed to a chair. Karen sat quietly. She seemed peaceful and at ease.

"Now, Karen was at the abduction," said Trudy," and is happy to be with you three children, if you want to go to a safe house."

"Do you have one that takes five people?" asked Emma.

"Okay, so you've already decided?" Trudy looked surprised. "And you're all sure?" We all nodded and murmured our yeses. "Gosh, what a decisive lot. Okay, how about you all go home with your mums and dads and pack a bag for, say, three nights, and we'll organise your transport."

"I can take everyone," said Emma.

"I can help, too," said Karen, brightening up.

"Good, so we won't tell you where they're going, Janice and Rosie. Tim and Kassey will ring you when they arrive. If you want to call your children, I'll give you each a password.

You'll use it to ring me and then I'll then put you through to them."

"Sounds like James Bond!" Rosie chuckled, looking more relaxed.

"You have my card and we don't write anything down. Parents, you'll call your children's schools, say they're sick, and don't mention the police. We want everything to appear as normal as possible, okay?"

"Everyone'll probably ring me as I take the calls at the school," I said. We all laughed and Karen stood up and ordered me to stand. I obeyed and she grabbed me in a bear cub hug. It would have been a bear hug if she'd been taller.

"Thank you so much for trusting me with Kassey," she said, leaning back with leaking eyes.

"Oh, you silly fart!" I said. "I'm so sorry I bawled at you before. I'm sure Kassey will give you plenty of guidance if you go wrong again."

"What about Maureen?" asked Edward, appearing in the doorway. Maureen followed him into the kitchen looking like a scared little girl, not as if she belonged with the adults. "She needs a safe space as much as anyone. Maybe more."

"No, I should be alright ..." she started to say.

"No you will not." Edward put his kind hand on Maureen's shoulder. "Could she go to the safe house as well?"

"Oh gosh," said Trudy, "I'm not sure if there's space."

"You're absolutely right, Edward," said Karen, stepping over to Maureen. "You go with Emma and the kids. I have an alternative." She turned back to wink at me and I smiled back. I didn't care what she got up to with Phil, or didn't get up to. I was relieved she wasn't alone. I was sure she was in for her share of flashbacks, nightmares and a rocky road of emotions. I was also sure today's experience would bring up the trauma she'd experienced at work. She'd found some inner strength and techniques but someone else there with care and love would be essential.

DI Edwards and Constable Perkins helped Maureen get her car and a few other things from her house while I helped Kassey pack for another 'holiday', similar to the Coolangatta one she and I had had just a week before. Kassey and Maureen followed Emma, Jeanie and Tim to their destination unknown, while the police followed at a discreet distance to spot pursuers, if any appeared.

I invited Ruby and Stan along to meet Geoffrey, Sarah, Sean and Samuel. It would be a comfort to them to know there were people and a place to go if needed.

"Honoured to meet some young people," said Samuel, chuckling as he shook hands with the two elders of our growing tribe. "I'm afraid I couldn't attend your, aah, street festivities, as I have a hereditary affliction of FOB, fear of brutality, sometimes called cowardice."

"I'm sure you're not a coward in everything," said Stan. "I'm sure you have confronted your demons face on."

Samuel was silent for a moment for a change, while he started at Stan.

"My good man, you have me at a loss for words." Samuel frowned. "Did you, by chance, clamber up my psyche and peer into my brain, into my thoughts?"

"You found that you gained everything when you lost everything." Stan's face was impassive and unreadable.

"My gosh, you know my whole sordid story. That should be unnerving but it's strangely comforting, my friend."

The two men smiled at each other and sat together in companiable silence. Edward, Christine and Kathryn turned up and then Phil and Karen joined us. Billy followed Ricky and Rosie in.

Ricky stopped, turned and looked down at Billy's untied work boots. "Jeez, you're a larrikin, aren't you? Coming in here in those flash clodhoppers." Then he looked down at his own worn, untied work boots.

"Yeah, and you've got the same designer holes in your singlet as me." Billy punched Ricky's shoulder and then jumped sideways to avoid Ricky's return punch. They sat down together, chuckling like a couple of schoolboys, and it amused me to think what brought people together. I wondered where James was. I wasn't worried and had a feeling I would see him soon.

Though Samuel, Geoffrey, Sarah and Sean hadn't attended the street festivities, as Samuel called it, we all chatted easily for we were drawn together by a higher aspiration, that of a world of kindness and respect. We all knew that evil never sleeps but good always triumphs ... but only if good stays alert and doesn't mind having to stir up the money-changers in the temple from time to time.

We all knew we wouldn't be free of abuse and insanity but we now had a group of slightly odd friends who would be there if we ever needed them.

An hour later before we dispersed to our respective homes, some for a much-needed siesta, James turned up at the café. He stopped at our table and looked around the café to see if anyone was listening. There was no one near us. He ducked his head and spoke quietly.

"Just to let you all know, Donald, my auditor friend, told me not to tell anyone else but his firm, ShaverNelson, has been asked by Queensland's premier to manage the administration of the Ipswich council."

"Administration?" asked Edward.

"Yes, it's an investigation that's been going for some time - longer than I was aware of. The mayor and all the councillors will be stood down and the council will be run by Donald's accounting firm. It's a bit like putting a company into receivership, where the receivers take over from the owners and managers and run the business until the problems are sorted out. We didn't make this happen but we certainly accelerated the process."

We looked at one another and smiled awkwardly.

"Please, please, please, don't say anything to anyone. The public announcement is due out on Tuesday, in two days' time."

There was lots of hand-shaking, back-patting and hugs, along with oohs, aahs and a few swear words. Quite a few swear words. Then everyone dispersed and many left with their heads still shaking.

James, Ruby, Stan and I stood outside the café and I wished James and I were alone. There seemed so much to talk about. He stood there looking decidedly awkward, shrugging while twisting his hands and a foot, and I wished I could have thought of something to say but no words arrived.

"Right," he said, "so, I'll see you soon."

I nodded.

"Very soon?"

"Yes, that sounds good." Why am I so embarrassed in front of Ruby and Stan? "Very soon sounds good, James."

Ruby looked at me and smiled. She knew something was brewing. James turned and walked off for 10 paces and then turned back around.

"My car's this way." His face was very red as he passed us and walked on.

I took Ruby and Stan back to their home and there was silence in the car the whole five minutes it took to get them there. Two minutes later I found James was parked outside my house with a large smile. My smile matched his.

In the Door

Realising I'd never be safe - not really - I took his manicured hand and led him into the house. His uncertain smile didn't deter me as I unlocked the door. In fact, nothing would deter me anymore. I'd held myself back from too much of life for too long. I'd acted small for longer than anyone should. I'd been scarred and refused to love. Now I chose love, despite the scars that might never leave.

I'd lashed out and taken risks at unexpected moments but had always retreated afterwards, expecting reprisals, from my father, husband and partner. I had always got what I expected and it had taken way too long to realise I could change my expectations and, therefore, my life. My change of mind had created a change of circumstances.

Kassey and I were still surrounded by vicious and stupid neighbours and their thuggy friends, but my change of mind had seen them, somehow, ease out of our lives.

When I'd needed help in the past, I'd felt alone and hadn't expected anyone to turn up ... and they hadn't. However, since changing my mind, help had turned up in unexpected moments from a motley crew of people I wouldn't have chosen as friends but who had turned out to be the best friends I'd ever had.

"Are you sure?" asked James, seeing me faltering at my front door, unaware of the thoughts floating through my quietly contented mind.

"Huh? Oh, yes, just thinking of how my life has changed since we came to this bogan town."

"You don't like it here?"

"Lots of people don't like this down-at-heel place but I'm realising peace can be found anywhere."

"It's easier to find it here than anywhere." He placed his right hand over his heart.

Another reason to get all hot and tingly about this man of steel - sweet as a Tim Tam and as deep as Buddha.

"Maybe we'll find what eluded us in the places we call home," he said.

I grabbed his other hand, towed him in and shut the door.

"By the way, my answer to your question is yes," I said.

"Which question?" He frowned at me as I smelled his breath of mint.

"All your questions, James. You deserve yes for every question."

"My kind of woman," he said, smiling broadly as he took charge and towed me into my bedroom, the bedroom I'd expected no man to enter and, now, I expected no other man to enter.

The next in the Scars series

Chapter One of Scars Don't Sweat

The spanner smashed against the machine, a shower of sparks. The men jumped back and I realised it was my own hand holding the spanner. My hand slamming the machine. My voice invading the mill, as unwelcome as the rat shit they'd just found in the flour.

I keep a cap on this anger. A tight cap that conceals a silent rage and no one sees it. But it slipped off today, for the first time.

I stop and the spanner pulls my arm down, dangling impotently in shame. I should hang my head in shame but we have flour to mill, jobs to do. I smile a brave and stupid smile and the men smile along with me, awkwardly, none daring to move.

I have spent these last thirty years gathering their willing trust and now I've broken it, I guess. This trust was built up by caring and sharing with them, cajoling and encouraging them every single day, and they think me such a saint – the boss who keeps them safe from anger and its sharp fangs. Despite the daily stupidities, the constant and unnecessary stuff-ups, I glide round the mill with my indulgent smile sewn on. I imagine throttling this chap, firing that man, throwing that other one into the Bremer River. But he might float and his relatives might recognise him. Yes, I attempt some humour to soften the moment in my own mind. So I keep my palms open, my head up and my darned smile in full view.

But the rage is ever close to the surface, ready to burst at a moment's inattention. Ready to burst the frayed thread holding my smile in place. It finally burst today and I have no words or actions to undo it.

"Sorry guys, just a bit of a hard week," I say, forcing myself to eye-ball each one of them. Their shoulders relax a little and their smiles become more genuine. "Tony and Giles, can you go through this batch, please, to make sure there's no more rat shit in here and Mike and Justin, we need to discuss how we can stop it happening again."

I move away and there's a silent murmur of relief, like a ripple across a pond that you feel when you're not really looking.

Mike, Justin and I walked between the fence of men and Mike stopped to give some instructions, pat some shoulders, before following us across the wooden floor to my office.

Justin stopped to let me into my office first. The new accountant, he'd only been here a week and he seemed to be a wet fish, a bit soft. But he had glowing references and they account for more than a pile of degrees from a gaggle of twerps who've never done what they taught.

But I wished Billy was here – gritty, annoying Billy with a swear word for every problem (though he's much better on that score, now) and a smart-arse answer for all of them. A damned good smart-arse answer, usually.

"Where's Billy this morning, Justin?" I asked as I pushed paper away from the centre of my desk and waved him to sit. He did so, hesitatingly, as if there might be a snake in the chair.

"I'm not sure, sir."

"Stephen."

"Pardon?"

"I'm Stephen, not sir," I said, forcing a smile through my grimace.

"Oh, okay, sir ... Stephen," he said, looking sheepish.

"Hard to say it, huh?"

"Not used to it, sir ... uh, Stephen."

"You'll get used to it. I might be the boss, the owner, but we're all experts here, in different ways, so no need for titles." He frowned at this as if I was explaining hieroglyphics, so I cut the banter, the niceties. "Perfect ruddy timing, huh?"

"Pardon s...?"

"Health inspectors due today and rat shit in the flour. Perfect timing, wouldn't you say?"

"Oh, gosh, I forgot they were coming," he said, pushing back his small, round glasses. "You're not suspicious, are you?" I wished people wouldn't say the things I'm thinking and don't want to speak about.

"Not sure ... yeah, can't help feeling ... yeah, suspicious, as you say." I leaned forward over my desk and he sat forward. "You don't get any vibes, do you?"

"Vibes?" he asked, looking confused.

"I know haven't been here long but you haven't heard anything ... muttering in corners, discontent, suspicious looks? Anything?"

"I'm afraid I haven't noticed ..."

"Bloody inspectors'll be here soon! Shit!" said Mike, bursting through the door, plumping himself in the chair as flour puffed off his white coat and floated in the air as if asking permission to settle. He sat there running his big hands through his thick, curly hair, muttering away as if no one else was in the room. He always seemed out of place in my leather, padded chairs, the hair of his barrel chest curling over the zipped-up overalls, but he still acted like he owned the chair. The whole mill, really, sometimes.

"So, we don't have time to find out how or who, right now, Mike," I said.

"Yeah, suppose so. Cover the crime, shoot the bastards later," he said, chuckling grimly as he slapped Justin's knee and sat back shaking his head. Justin looked uncertainly at the white patch on his knee, not moving.

"But if we know the source we can keep us clean," said Justin, after a pause, pushing his glasses back up his nose, looking flushed.

"What?" demanded Mike.

"Well, if the rats are getting in somewhere, what's to stop them getting in while the inspectors are here?" Justin asked plaintively.

"Look, sonny, we're busy enough cleaning up the problem and still keeping the mill going ..."

"We can't run the mill while there's still ... aah, um, impurities in the process," said Justin.

Hmm, not such a wet fish after all, I thought.

"Right, so we close the mill the day the inspectors arrive? They won't suspect a thing!" said Mike, his sarcasm ever to the fore.

"Oh dear ..."

"Look, guys, we need to keep the mill running but Justin's right," I said. "So, we just shut down number three, run the other two hoppers, clean out the droppings ... no, clean out all the flour, dump it, say we're having a total overhaul."

"Jesus, Stephen, the inspectors will love that," stammered Mike, his hands on the chair arms as if he was about to leap up ... or rip them off.

"Mike, steady, huh," I said quietly. "We're being cautious, more cautious than we ever need to be. Sacrifice more flour and production time than is necessary and they'll be impressed at our conservatism."

"Confuckingservatism? Christ, Stephen, they'll be all over us with that!"

"But we have to show sincerity," said Justin, quietly; quietly as an eagle diving on its squeaky prey.

"Sincerity? What's that bloody mean?" demanded Mike.

"It means, Mike, that we can run but we can't hide. Ever," I said. I let the silence envelop us, bringing stillness to the moment. The men eased back into their chairs. "Whatever we do, they'll know something and the more we cover up, the more they'll chase us and the more they'll find. So, I'm making a decision. We are totally honest, we go to extreme lengths to show we're concerned and we let the cards fall where they will."

"That's one hell of a risk, mate," said Mike, dropping his shoulders and looking away. "They could close us down."

"They could but let's have honesty run the day and, if we have to close down, we do." It was then that the chills hit me. Sharp, cold and vicious. *Close the mill? My god, that was unthinkable.*

"Close the mill? Close the bloody mill, Stephen? Do you know what you're saying?" demanded Mike, his fist hitting the chair arm, bouncing off with the force. "Christ, Queensland's first mill, opened in 1902 and it's been going, what, eighty-one years! That's not going to happen. It's not bloody happening, mate!"

"Mike, I don't want it any more than you do ..."

"Excuse me, Stephen," said Flora, popping her head in the door, "you have visitors."

"Okay, love, I'll be there soon," I said, concerned about the black look on her usually sunny face. "Give them a cup of tea and I'll ..."

"Stephen, you need to come out now. Right now." She could be persuasive but never demanding. Not till now.

As I looked up, I saw the rotten sods approaching. Sometimes I wish I didn't have glass walls – open door policy and all that – and, instead, just had solid panels between the carved timber mullions. Shut myself away from the world at times. Many times. But there it was, the transparent glass and three blustering cops, all smirking and trying to look serious and officious, adjusting their perfectly starched uniforms. Rat shit in the flour and, now, rats in the hallway, like stormtroopers on a mission. The mission was me. I just knew it.

"Thank you, ma'am," said the eldest and fattest, as Flora stepped back to let him in. "Stephen Daniels?"

"Yes, you know it is, Gordon," I said, not rising. We'd both been in this town longer than most and bumped into each other at odd times and different functions. Never by my choice, though. Bloody cops!

"We need to talk to you down at the station," he said, fiddling with his bottom button, as if he was trying to shine the shine off it.

"You can talk here, Gordon. What's your question?"

"It's a personal matter, sir ..."

"Personal? You barge into my factory, telling everybody you're here without waiting in the foyer, stomping through the factory in your big, flat feet and say it's a personal matter," I said, my hands open in despair, my head shaking.

"We can't help that, sir. We ..."

"Oh yes you *can* help that. So, you've made a public spectacle of yourselves, jack boots and all, turned a personal matter into a circus, what's your question? I've nothing to hide."

"We'll go, Stephen," said Mike and Justin together.

"Oh, sorry guys. Yeah, look, let's just shut down number three for now ..."

"Sir!" shouted the policeman. "We need you to come to ..."

"Ah, belt up will you Gordon! You can wait two minutes while we sort out the mill and the lives of the twenty people working here, can't you? Unless there's someone lying, dying in the street," I said, bleeding sarcasm.

"Actually, sir," he said, looking more flushed than his beer-reddened face usually was.

"What, someone's dying?" I asked, my hatred of authority stifling sensitivity.

"They have, sir."

The room went quiet. Mike and Justin stopped and no one moved. The dust seemed to stop in the air. Clouds blocked the sun and the room darkened.

"Jesus!" someone said. Probably Mike. Maybe it was me. The only thought was that I wished Billy was here. He always had an answer, a way out.

"Where's Billy?" I asked as if it was the most logical thing to say, which it wasn't.

"Billy is at the station, sir," said Gordon the Goof, as I'd always called him.

"Is he dying?" my big mouth said as I wished not to know the answer.

"No but, look sir, we need you to come to the station," said Gordon, trying to puff out his chest, which was no match for his swollen belly.

"Aah, shut up for a minute, will you! Let me get my senses," I said, not caring one hoot for his senses or his authority. "Now, Mike, can you sort out the mill and see to the inspectors. I'll be there as soon as I can. Justin, can you get Flora back in here and these gentlemen will tell us what's going on." Mike and Justin left while three cops stood there looking down as if I'd piddled on their boots.

"But sir, we need to get him to the station," said a younger one who I recognised from Harrison's, my son's, tennis team.

"Yes, Brian, I'll go to your station when you tell me what's going on. Sit down ... aah, Flora, take a seat, you other two argue over who's got the third chair and, Gordon, do some talking."

"Sir," said Gordon, hovering over the chair as if it might bite him.

"Oh, Flora, have you seen Harrison this morning?" I asked.

"No, I ..." she started to say when Gordon cut her off.

"That's ... Harrison is one of the matters we need to talk to you about."

"Billy? Harrison? And someone's dying? What the hell's going on?" I demanded. I needed to hear the bad news in my own home, in my mill, not in some snake pit of a cop station.

"Sir, we need ..."

"You need to cut the crap right now! What's happened?"

"Stephen, dear, perhaps you should go with them. Do as they ask," suggested Flora. A still, quiet part of me agreed with her but my rage – the rage of ages, the rage of a broken past, the rage of a hundred bent coppers – was having none of it.

"Okay, cuff me up and carry me out, kicking and screaming if you must," I said, my voice rising as I held my hands out over my desk to them. "Or sit here quietly and, in words of one syllable, tell Flora and I what happened. Can you manage that?"

The three cops looked at each other as if deciding which one of them had the brain that day. Another South Pole iceberg melted and a crow screeched outside. Gordon licked his lips.

"Right, so this is how you want it, Stephen and, since Flora's here as well, you need to know something," said Gordon, solemnly.

"But, inspector, he needs to go to the station," protested Brian, looking alarmed.

"I know he does, constable, but there's several pieces to this puzzle so let's just ride the horse in the direction it's going, shall we!"

Both constables nodded and smiled uncertainly.

"Stephen. Flora. We have to inform you that Harrison, your son, was found at six thirty this morning."

"Found?" asked Flora, a squeak more than a word coming out. I looked at her as my brain slipped off a cliff. My stomach churned over and I thought I'd vomit. Her eyes were fixed on the inspector's as if her body was frozen in place. I couldn't move and neither did she.

"Yes, found," said Gordon as a rising tide of emotion escaped beneath his formality. I thought he was about to cry when he wiped his eye and carried on, his voice quieter now. "He was found dead, Flora. Stephen."

"Dead?" asked Flora. "Harrison?"

"Yes, Harrison. I'm so sorry for you both. So sorry."

Words wouldn't come. Thoughts wouldn't come. Movement wouldn't happen. I lost everything of what I was in that moment. Every bit of hurt and happiness I'd ever known just slunk away. I was empty. Then I realised Flora had come round my desk and her hand was on my arm. I stood and fell into her arms like she was the last piece of flotsam from the Titanic and I wasn't letting her go. Yes, I cried for the loss of Harrison. I cried deeply and bitterly for him. And, too, came the bucket-loads, the ship-loads, of tears I'd bottled up for the past fifty three years. Tears I couldn't show my father when he lashed me. Tears I couldn't show my mum when I was scared and she was vulnerable. Tears of shame. Tears of pain. Tears of loss. Tears of betrayal. Tears of anger. The brittle, the soft, the painful and the anguished tears poured onto my desk.

I couldn't stop and I didn't care who was watching. I looked up for a moment and saw some of the men in the corridor, looking on with concern. If I'd wanted to stop the tears I couldn't have. I didn't need to, didn't care to, for the first time ever. I'd shown the men the anger I'd kept so well hidden and, now, the blubbering. I couldn't have shown them any worse and gave up worrying as Flora held me in her warm embrace. Yes, she had tears too but must have put many aside to enable mine.

I knew I should stop but wondered how as another wave washed over me. Perhaps movement would help. I sat down and pulled Flora onto my lap. Nothing helped with the empty pain that was clutching at my gut but the sobbing became controllable. Well, slightly more so.

I looked up and wondered what the three cops were doing in the room and then remembered as a broken sob burst forth and I was away again – Flora and I in tearful unison – while the two constables looked away and Gordon inspected his boots.

"Inspector, we have orders," said one of the constables, his acne-patched face the picture of confusion.

"Yes we have, constable," said Gordon quickly, wiping his brow. "But, right now, no one's going anywhere. No one."

That could have been taken as a threat or command to me – and I suspected it was both – but I couldn't care less what they wanted. I would have gone along with anything.

"You okay, lass?" I asked Flora as she wiped her eyes again and sat back a little, looking at me.

"No I'm not, love, but let's keep moving. Get this over, shall we?"

"Okay, give us the details you need to give us, Gordon."

"You sure?" he asked, looking at Flora and me. We both nodded. "Right, he was found at six thirty this morning by a cyclist. In Queens Park, Ipswich. Near the playground."

"How?" was all I could say.

"Looks like a gunshot. May be a pistol. We're still scouting the area."

"A pistol?" asked Flora. "Who has a pistol round here?"

"You do," said Gordon.

"Me?" she asked, shaking her head.

"Stephen. Stephen has a pistol," Gordon said quietly.

"I do?" I asked and then my memory kicked in. "Oh, yes, I do, I suppose."

"You suppose?" asked Flora, her eyes widening.

"Oh hell," I said, wishing I'd never kept *that* secret. "Always meant to hand it in. Gave comfort, somehow, seeing it kept Mum and I safe so many times."

"And you never told me?" she asked.

"No. Sorry." What else can a man say?

"And Harrison knew about this pistol?" asked Gordon.

"Don't know. Shouldn't have but maybe he did," I said, trying to put together a jigsaw with pieces that didn't fit.

"Inspector," Flora said and waited till the earth turned another two degrees while her mouth quivered. Eventually, her mouth steadied. "Are you saying he shot himself?"

"No, Flora, it doesn't look like it at this stage. We're treating this as a homicide, other person or persons involved."

"Who?" she asked.

"Okay," said Gordon, taking a big breath. "We have to start with the owner of the gun."

"Me?" I asked as the clawing in my stomach started up again. Logic and emotion clashed and neither won the fight. My mind went empty again.

"We need to talk with you at the station, Stephen," said Gordon. "Ascertain your whereabouts. An alibi."

About the Author

In New Zealand I experienced life as an accountant, credit manager, company director, business trainer, lecturer, shepherd, scrub-cutter, tree pruner, freezing worker, plastics factory worker, saxophonist, army driver, tour bus driver, stage and television actor and singer, busker, builder, lecturer, facilitator for men's groups, grief counsellor, reporter, columnist, magazine editor, publisher, writer.

In South Africa as an AIDS workshop co-facilitator.

In the Australian bush as a barman, horse and camel trekker and stock-whip teacher.

In England as a contract accountant, corporate trainer, estate manager, lecturer, singer/songwriter, website editor/writer and freelance writer.

Now that I'm back in Australia, house renovating, teaching, corporate training and writing, I'm wondering what's next!

The constant for me is *A Course in Miracles*, a psychological life-style course in forgiveness. Through it I have found the peace I had always been searching for - the journey to where I have always been.

Philip J Bradbury in social media

Website: www.philipjbradbury.com[1]

Website: www.writethatbooknow.com[2]

Buy me a Coffee: https://www.buymeacoffee.com/philipjbradbury

WordPress blogs: https://pjbradbury.wordpress.com/

Facebook: https://www.facebook.com/AuthorPhilipJBradbury/

Linked In - http://bit.ly/2aTzZMS

Smashwords: http://bit.ly/2aNjkic

Twitter: https://twitter.com/PhilipJBradbury

---

1.   http://www.philipjbradbury.com

2.   http://www.writethatbooknow.com

Other books by Philip J Bradbury

Non-Fiction

Whose Life Is It Anyway? – personal/spiritual development

Life Rejuvenated – personal/spiritual development

Write That Book Now – a takeaway course on writing

Change Your Life, Change Your World – personal/spiritual development

The Twelve Week Miracle (with Anna Bradbury) – personal/spiritual development

Some-Fiction

53 SMILES – 53 53-word stories

97 SMILES – 97 97-word stories

Glass Soul - poetry

Dactionary - a dictionary with attitude

Fiction

Scars Can't Tell – Australian thriller/romance (book 1 of the *Scars* series)

The Last Stand Down – a thriller in London

My Whispering Teachers – short stories

Circles of Gold – a fable

Gerald the Great of Gorokoland – a silly fable

The Meaning of Larf - humour

For more information on these books, see www.philipjbradbury.com